Books by BARBARA MICHAELS

❖❖❖❖❖❖

SHATTERED SILK
BE BURIED IN THE RAIN
THE GREY BEGINNING
HERE I STAY
BLACK RAINBOW
SOMEONE IN THE HOUSE
THE WIZARD'S DAUGHTER
THE WALKER IN SHADOWS
WAIT FOR WHAT WILL COME
WINGS OF THE FALCON
PATRIOT'S DREAM
THE SEA KING'S DAUGHTER
HOUSE OF MANY SHADOWS
WITCH
GREYGALLOWS
THE CRYING CHILD
THE DARK ON THE OTHER SIDE
PRINCE OF DARKNESS
AMMIE, COME HOME
SONS OF THE WOLF
THE MASTER OF BLACKTOWER

SHATTERED SILK

SHATTERED SILK

BARBARA MICHAELS

Atheneum

NEW YORK   1986

Library of Congress Cataloging in Publication Data

Michaels, Barbara, ———
   Shattered silk.

   I. Title.
PS3563.E747S46   1986   813'.54   86-47658
ISBN 0-689-11620-9

Copyright © 1986 by Barbara Michaels
All rights reserved
Published simultaneously in Canada by Collier Macmillan Canada, Inc.
Composition by Westchester Book Composition, Inc., Yorktown Heights, New York
Manufactured by Fairfield Graphics, Fairfield, Pennsylvania
Designed by Cathryn S. Aison
FIRST EDITION

TO *T*RISH

❖❖❖❖❖❖

a great editor and a good friend

ACKNOWLEDGMENTS
❖❖❖❖❖❖

I am indebted to many people and many publications for information on the subject of vintage clothing, but I would especially like to thank two friends here in my home town of Frederick. Carol Canty of Collage and Sharon Meachum of Lady on Skates encouraged and assisted me in every way. If I have made mistakes, it isn't their fault but my own.

SHATTERED SILK

C HAPTER O NE

*T*HEY refused to let her drive them to the airport. National was one of the busiest airports in the country, traffic was terrible; even native Washingtonians avoided it when they could.

"Except for the damned members of Congress," her uncle Pat had bellowed, pounding on the table to emphasize his opinion. "They've got their chauffeurs and their air-conditioned limos, so it's no skin off their butts if the rest of us get high blood pressure and dented fenders trying to reach the damned terminal!"

Which, as her aunt Ruth pointed out, was not only unfair and exaggerated, but irrelevant.

Karen didn't argue. The last she saw of them was her aunt's fixed smile and anxious eyes, framed by the window of the taxi.

The taxi hesitated at the corner and, with an air of squaring its metaphorical shoulders, plunged into the maelstrom of traffic on Wisconsin Avenue. Then at last Karen let her own fixed smile crack and crumble and drop off her face. She rubbed her jaw, wondering if Ruth's face ached too, after all those weeks of determined cheerfulness.

It was a relief to let everything droop—lips, shoulders, spirits. Her feet dragging, she turned back into the house. Though it was only midmorning, the streets of Georgetown shimmered with the heat and humidity that are hallmarks of a Washington summer.

Like the other older homes in this fashionable section of the capital, which had been a flourishing town in its own right before the founders of the new nation moved in across the creek, Ruth's house dated from the early nineteenth century. It was built of red brick, in the formal Federal style, with a classic balance of windows and exterior ornament. Every brick of the facade and every stick of furniture within was familiar to Karen. She had lived with her aunt and uncle for a year while attending college, and had visited often since. But as she stood in the hall facing the famous floating staircase, she had a sensation of utter strangeness.

The change was not in the house but in herself. Only a month ago she had been a suburban housewife, settled in a routine as a fly is embedded in amber, with every reason to suppose her position was as permanent as the fly's. Jack's schedule was as fixed as her own. When he wasn't at the university he was at a meeting or a conference, or closeted in his office working on one of the endless stream of books and articles designed to ensure his rise up the ladder of academic success. When she wasn't doing housework she was typing his manuscripts or checking his footnotes or doing research for him. Everything she did was predictable, even the food she cooked. Jack

4

was a meat-and-potatoes man, with no tolerance for ethnic- and health-food fads.

He had ordered steak the night he told her. He had suggested they go out to dinner, just the two of them—a rare occurrence in recent months. Afterward Karen realized she should have known something was wrong. But she didn't even suspect. His announcement, carefully timed to follow the cocktails, hit her with the stunning shock of a blow in the pit of her stomach.

Jack had mistaken her silence and her empty stare for calm acquiescence. He was relieved, he said, that she hadn't become hysterical. (Actually, he was rather disappointed; and he was visibly annoyed because she didn't eat the expensive meal he had ordered.) After dropping her at home, he had gone on to a meeting—Karen had a pretty good idea who would be at the meeting. The same person who had attended all the other meetings that had kept Jack so busy lately.

She went straight upstairs, packed a single suitcase, and called a cab. There was just enough money in their joint checking account to pay for a ticket to Washington, and she thanked God for modern banking methods as she withdrew cash in the light of the automatic teller.

It never occurred to her to "go home to Mother." When, several days later, she summoned courage enough to break the news to the woman who happened to occupy that role, she received, not an invitation to come home, but a shrill lecture. She must have done something. She must have failed in some way. She should not have left the house. She should have fought for her rights, and for her man. . . .

The diatribe didn't help Karen's morale, even though she sensed the fear behind her mother's anger. *It must be your fault. Because if it isn't—if you were in no way to blame—then this could happen to anyone. It could happen to me.*

Not all the wives Karen knew harbored that hidden fear. Her sister Sara, for instance. Sara, who had also lived with Ruth and Pat while she attended Georgetown University, now lived on the West Coast and had her hands full with four exuberant young children and an exuberant, adoring husband. That was one of the reasons why Karen had not sought refuge with her sister, but it wasn't the only reason. Sara's shining happiness would have hurt like salt in a fresh wound.

Ruth, her own mother's sister, was another of the lucky ones. But Ruth and Pat were older, childless, their joy in each other more muted in expression if not in intensity.

On the face of it, Ruth's marriage should not have worked. After a brief and disastrous first marriage, of which she never spoke, she had waited till she was over forty before she married again, to a man who appeared to be her exact antithesis. Pat MacDougal's anthropological studies had taken him into many of the wilder parts of the planet and had invested him with a loud contempt for the hypocritical conventions of civilization, a contempt he was not at all inhibited about expressing. Pat was big and loud-mouthed and clumsy; Ruth was petite and prim. Pat had a shock of flaming-red hair and a face that verified the theory of mankind's descent from a simian ancestor; Ruth's delicate features and fine bones were as dainty as those of a porcelain doll. Pat's language echoed with expletives; in moments of dire extremity Ruth had sometimes been heard to murmur a faint damn.

If Karen had wanted to find a scapegoat—and there were times when she definitely did want to—she could have blamed Ruth, not for the failure of her own marriage but for the marriage itself. She had met Jack while she was living with Ruth and Pat. Like Pat, Jack taught at the university. In some ways Jack reminded her of her uncle, the man who had made Ruth so happy she was a menace to single people.

And now Ruth was going with him to Borneo, to keep house in a jungle hut while Pat finished gathering the material for his book on magic and folklore. Ruth with her dainty pastel suits and her immaculate coiffures, Ruth who was now in her fifties. Her face had glowed like that of a bride when she told Karen of their plans.

It was amazing how their needs had happened to coincide, Ruth said. She wasn't worried about snakes or poisonous insects or the lack of sanitation, but she had been concerned about leaving her lovely house unoccupied for three months. She could have rented it—there were always visiting diplomats, politicians, and lobbyists looking for quarters in Washington, and many of them seemed to have more money than they ought to have had—but Ruth had a fastidious dislike of allowing strangers in her home.

"So you see, you're really doing me a favor," she had assured Karen. "An empty house is an invitation to burglars. I only hope..." The little puckers between her brows deepened, and she fell silent.

"You hope what?"

"That you don't mind being alone."

"Not at all. It's just what I need."

Ruth continued to look doubtful. "I'm not so sure. You do need time alone—time to think, plan, and," she added with a slight smile, "swear and scream and kick the furniture. Get your anger out of your system."

"I'm not angry."

"Then you should be." Ruth's voice rose slightly

7

and the delicate pink in her cheeks deepened—for Ruth, unmistakable signs of extreme annoyance.

"Why?" Karen asked reasonably. "Anger doesn't solve anything. I don't blame Jack; it would be dishonest of him to pretend an emotion he no longer feels, and . . . Well, just look at me! I've rather let myself go the last few years."

Ruth's lips tightened; but for once her self-control failed and the words she had tried to repress burst out. "I'm not going to criticize Jack, but I wish to goodness you'd stop criticizing yourself! There's nothing wrong with being angry. It's much more constructive than resignation and—and self-pity."

Karen was so surprised at this uncharacteristic outburst she didn't notice the insult, but Ruth was immediately repentant. "Darling, I do apologize. I shouldn't have said that."

"Don't worry about me, Ruth. I'll be all right. We all have different ways of handling emotional problems."

"Hmmm. Well, I won't lecture you. But as I was about to say, although solitude serves a useful purpose, you're going to be alone here for an awfully long time. You need someone to talk to. I wish I hadn't agreed to go on this field trip."

"Don't even think of canceling!"

"I'm not. I won't. But I wish . . ."

"I had someone to talk to? You're forgetting Julie. The problem will be to get her to stop talking."

"Julie doesn't carry on conversations, she delivers monologues. But I am glad you found an old friend who is still in town, and it was thoughtful of her to offer you a job. You need something to occupy your mind."

They had been interrupted at that point by Pat, yelling from the top of the stairs: "Where the hell did I put my damned shoes?" Ruth had gone trotting off to find the missing objects. It was a routine they went through several times a day, and both of them obviously delighted in it.

Now they were gone, and the house felt very empty without them—especially without Pat, whose very passage through a room made small objects rattle and tinkle. Despite her many visits, this was the first time Karen had been alone in the house for more than a few hours—and never at night.

Karen went to the door of the parlor. It was a lovely room, achieving beauty without sacrificing comfort. The big overstuffed sofas in front of the fireplace invited people to relax, at their ease; the bookcases flanking the French windows held not elegant matched sets but a motley collection of books that had obviously been read and reread. The only thing that had changed within Karen's memory was the color scheme, which had once been Wedgwood blue, to match the tiles around the fireplace. The draperies were now soft rose, and the couches had been reupholstered in shades of pink and lilac.

Karen entered the room and stood by the front windows. The parlor ran the entire length of the house. The back windows opened onto the garden; through the translucent glass curtains she saw a pastoral vista of green leaves and bright flowers, highlighted by patches of sunlight and softened by cool gray shade. It was hard to believe that the garden was in the heart of a large city. Birds swung and sang in the branches, and Ruth's favorite roses were in full bloom. High walls, part brick and part wood, enclosed the entire back yard, which could only be entered through the house or by way of a narrow walled passage along the north side.

It was very quiet. When the satin draperies shifted

slightly, Karen started and then let out a breath of laughter. The air-conditioning had just come on; there was a vent practically at her elbow, and the stream of cool air had moved the fabric.

She couldn't understand Ruth's oft-repeated concern about leaving her alone in the house. She was used to being alone. Jack was always going off to attend conferences and symposia—and "meetings." Their house was a prosaic, modern split-level in a subdivision of identical houses, and she had never been at all nervous. Was that why Ruth was worried—because this house was so old, with a history that went back a century and a half? The sort of house that might inspire an emotionally disturbed, unhappy person to start imagining the wrong things when a breath of wind shook the draperies or a board creaked in the night?

If that was Ruth's fear, it was groundless. Karen's eyes lovingly surveyed the room, from the gently moving draperies at the front to the sunlit garden beyond the back windows. The room had a feeling of peace. It was welcoming. The whole house had welcomed her back. It was like coming home.

She left the parlor and went along the hall to the kitchen. It was the only part of the house Ruth had changed after she inherited it from an elderly, childless relative. The appliances and cabinets were completely modern, but the brown tile of the floor and a corner cupboard containing Ruth's collection of teapots gave it a comfortable country look.

"Be sure you eat a good, healthy lunch," Ruth had ordered.

Karen made herself a cup of coffee—her fourth that morning—and sat down. She sat without moving for a long time, trying not to think or feel, letting the quiet sink into her bones. Every muscle in her body ached dully, after weeks of tension, of pretending a strength and calm she had not really possessed.

She knew what unspoken suggestion lay behind Ruth's remarks about needing someone to talk to. Ruth didn't mean Julie or even herself. She meant what she delicately termed "professional help"—a counselor or psychologist. Karen had tried—once. The woman was nice enough, but she was no help. She didn't answer questions, she asked them. "Why did you marry him?" "You say you let yourself become slovenly and unattractive—why did you do that?" "Did you resent the time you spent on his work?" "Why not?"

Why, why not? If Karen had known the answers, she wouldn't have had to go to a psychologist. Once was enough. She had canceled the second appointment.

Alone at last. She was half-dozing, head propped on her hand, when the telephone rang, and she started, spilling cold coffee across the surface of the table.

As she had expected, it was Julie. The latter's gravelly voice was unmistakable, as was her conversational style. Julie never said hi, or hello, or announced her own identity, but plunged right into the subject at hand with the air of a person who has no time to waste.

"Have they gone?" she demanded breathlessly.

"Yes, just a while ago. Why—"

"Are you coming to the shop?"

"I hadn't planned to. You said I could—"

"You have to learn the routine if you're going to take charge."

"I've been there every day for a month, and there's another week to go before you leave. Plenty of time. I really don't feel like it today. Besides, I promised Ruth—"

"Excuses, excuses. Don't think I'm going to let you

sit there moping and feeling sorry for yourself, and not eating properly."

"It wouldn't hurt me to skip a few meals," Karen said.

"That's true."

"Thanks!"

"You said it first." Julie sighed gustily. "You used to have the most gorgeous figure. Of course you're tall. When a person is five foot nothing like me, every damn ounce shows. I've just discovered a great new diet. You go on that for a couple of weeks—"

"Don't you have any customers?" Karen asked pointedly.

Hints were wasted on Julie. "Only a few wandering tourists. My regulars don't come out when it's this hot. As I was saying, this is a super diet. I'll come for supper and tell you about it."

"I don't want to cook tonight, Julie."

"I'll bring a couple of Big Macs."

"If that's the new diet, I'm all for it."

"Silly girl. We'll start the diet tomorrow. Oops, here comes a live one. See you later."

Karen gave herself the childish satisfaction of slamming the telephone into its cradle. Once she had found Julie's blunt speech and malicious remarks entertaining. Once she had been much more self-confident than she was now.

She wondered what Julie wanted. She had accepted Julie's old-buddy routine with humble gratitude at first, but it had not taken her long to learn that Julie never did anything without expecting something in return.

Now Julie had ruined her first day alone. She had kept her upper lip stiff and her smile nailed in place because she had too much pride to break down in public and

too much consideration for Ruth to subject her to a spec-
tacle of blubbering defeat. She had bathed and clothed her
disgusting body and brushed her nasty hair and tried to
eat, and pretended that these wearisome and meaningless
acts really mattered to her. She couldn't even sob and cry
at night, for fear Ruth might hear. But she had looked
forward to the moment when she could stop pretending,
if only for a few hours, and wallow in self-pity. Get out of
her bra and girdle, which were too tight—like every other
stitch of clothing she had brought—put on a sloppy old
housecoat, lie in bed, reading something banal and mindless, eat everything in the refrigerator that didn't require
preparation, go to bed early.

And cry herself to sleep.

With a martyred sigh Karen climbed the stairs and
entered her room—a guest room now, but once truly her
own, when she had lived with Ruth. It looked much as it
had then, except that now it was neat; the desk cleared of
books and papers and chewed pencils, the floor and chairs
uncluttered by clothing, shoes, and other debris. A big
mahogany wardrobe served as a closet; houses of the early
nineteenth century seldom had built-in closets. "Not that
you need them," Ruth had once remarked in a rare moment of sarcasm. "You never hang up your clothes anyway."

A reluctant, affectionate smile curved Karen's lips
as she remembered. What a carefree slob she had been in
those days! She had come full circle—still a slob, but no
longer carefree. She had intended to go back to school
after she married, get her degree. It had seemed easy then;
after all, Jack was on the faculty. But somehow there never
was time. She had taken a course or two over the years,
but there was always a manuscript that needed typing or
a list of references to be checked; and of course Jack's work

was so much more important than anything she could hope to accomplish.

She had learned to type. Jack had encouraged her in that—it was such a useful skill. It had certainly been useful to him, but she supposed she should be grateful that he had insisted, for now it was her only marketable skill. (What a hateful word—marketable—as if she were a piece of lifeless merchandise.) She had acted as Jack's research assistant for ten years, but without the formal title, or the salary. That was going to look great on a résumé. Perhaps Jack would write a reference for her.

Karen reminded herself, not for the first time, that she was in a better position than many women whose marriages have failed. Her marriage had only lasted ten years, not twenty-five or thirty. It wasn't too late for her to acquire new skills.

But which ones? There was nothing she wanted to do. Absolutely nothing.

Sunlight sifted through the curtains, warming the soft blue print of the ruffled pillow shams and matching spread, awakening golden shimmers in the polished surfaces of the furniture. The tall pier glass reflected the four-poster bed, with its knotted-lace canopy.

It also reflected Karen. Depression deepened into despair as she studied the pale defeated face and slumped body of the woman in the mirror. What made matters worse—if they could be worse—was that for an instant she had a memory-vision of the girl who had once smiled back at her from that same mirror. A tall, slim girl with long legs and bright dark eyes, and a mane of black hair that shone with a life of its own.

There was no gray in her hair, but it no longer swung free around her shoulders. Lifeless as charcoal, it lay on her head like a wig that might have been plucked at random from a shelf in a department store. Lifeless like her hopes and her ambition and her self-esteem.

The eyes of the memory-girl in the mirror seemed to sparkle, as if in mockery. Don't laugh at me, shadow girl. You, of all people, ought to sympathize. . . .

Karen fumbled with the fastening of her skirt. Her breath came out in an unpremeditated gasp as the zipper parted. She stepped out of the skirt and kicked it across the room, tore off her blouse, and wadded it into a ball. Shoes, pantyhose, and girdle followed. Her spirits improved slightly as her physical comfort increased, but she didn't look in the mirror again.

For once the trite complaint of having nothing to wear was the literal truth. She had packed one suitcase before she fled, throwing things into it without looking at them. She ought to call Jack and ask him to send her clothes. They were of no use to him; he would probably be glad to get the last reminders of her out of the house. But he wouldn't pack them himself, not Jack. He would ask Sandra to do it. Sandy, his super-efficient secretary, soon to be his second wife. Even if Karen could have forced herself to talk to Jack, she couldn't endure the idea of Sandy touching her personal possessions. Sandy would do the job neatly and competently, as she did everything; and she would smile with the intolerable pity of the young as she folded the size fourteens and the shabby, practical lingerie. Sandy was nineteen—the same age Karen had been when she married Jack.

My God, Karen thought despondently, I'm thinking like an old woman. I look like an old woman. When did this happen? How did it happen? I'm only twenty-seven . . . well, almost twenty-nine. Ten years ago I wore a size 6, played tennis, jogged, watched what I ate. Why did I let this happen?

She slammed the door of the wardrobe and crossed the room, giving the crumpled blouse a kick as she passed it. There must be some garment in the house she could wear without cutting off her circulation. No use looking in Ruth's wardrobe; her aunt was several inches shorter, petite, and small-boned.

Perhaps, she thought hopefully, Ruth had kept some of the clothes she and her sister had discarded or left behind—big shirts or big dresses—floats, or tents, or sacks, or whatever they called them then. Ruth laughed at Pat for being a pack rat, but she was almost as bad, she never threw anything away. Karen remembered once having helped Ruth carry some clothes to the attic to be stored. She had never seen an attic so neat, almost dust-free, smelling of cedar and mothballs.

It was worth looking, at any rate. She had nothing better to do. Slipping her feet into scuffed sandals and her arms into a faded cotton wrapper, she started for the stairs.

JULIE was late. Business must have improved, Karen thought, as she spun lettuce and chopped vegetables. It was almost six before she heard the doorbell chime and go on chiming, as Julie leaned on the button.

Karen opened the door and stepped out of the way. Julie came through like a bull charging into the ring. She headed straight for the kitchen, hurling words over her shoulder.

"What took you so long? It's hot as the hinges of hell out there; I thought I'd die. I had to go clear to M Street to get hamburgers—"

"Two blocks," Karen jeered, following Julie.

"The discomfort index is ninety-nine. I need a drink. Where's the gin? Where are the ice cubes?"

"Sit down, I'll fix it. Gin and tonic?"

"Right." Julie dropped her packages onto the table and collapsed into a chair. Her red hair, cut in the erratic style made popular by female rock stars, stuck out in stiff spikes, glued by perspiration and hair spray. She wore an off-the-shoulder blouse and a cotton skirt; rows of plastic beads formed a breastplate around her neck, and when she raised her hand to wipe her streaming brow, a matching row of bracelets jangled and clicked. The outfit would have looked ridiculous on most women, particularly the jewelry, which was of the type Karen categorized as "Woolworth's." But it was oddly becoming to Julie's sharp, vulpine features and stocky frame. "I look like a fat fox," she had once remarked, and although Karen had made polite protestations, there was a great deal of truth in the appraisal.

Karen offered a glass tinkling with ice cubes. Julie took it; then her eyes narrowed and she studied Karen as if seeing her for the first time.

"Well, well. I didn't know vintage chic had reached the far-off Midwest."

Karen smoothed the skirt of her dress self-consciously. It was yellow batiste faded to a soft cream and sprinkled with orange flowers. The deep ruffle framing the neck was echoed by short ruffled sleeves.

"I found it in the attic. It must have belonged to Cousin Hattie. She was a stout woman, though much shorter than I am."

"I thought I detected an aura of eau de mothballs." Julie's eyes moved down the loose, unbelted folds of the dress to the hemline, which reached just below Karen's

17

knees. "They wore dresses long in the early thirties. In the attic, did you say?"

Karen sat down with her own drink, plain tonic and ice. She had never been much of a drinker, and wasn't about to start now.

"Don't be subtle, Julie, you aren't good at it. I know you've been dying to get into Ruth's attic."

"I'd kill for the chance," Julie said coolly. "Acquiring stock is one of the biggest problems in the antique business these days. The good stuff has been bought up, and there aren't any bargains; every little old lady in the backwoods knows her junk is worth money."

"You've told me that a dozen times." Karen sipped her drink. "That's really why you hired me, isn't it? You had your eye on Ruth's attic."

"Hers and a few others."

"Such as Mrs. MacDougal's?"

" She's sort of an adopted grandmother, isn't she?"

"There is no relationship. She's Pat's mother, and he is only my uncle by marriage—"

"But he hasn't any children. I'm sure he thinks of you and your sister as his own."

Julie tried to look sentimental, without success. Her green eyes were as hard and calculating as a huckster's. Karen did not reply; without appearing to notice her distaste, Julie went on, "The old lady is a legend in this town. Her family was old Georgetown, crème de la crème, and she married big money. It was considered something of a mésalliance back then; Jackson MacDougal was one of those robber-baron types, a self-made millionaire with no culture and no class. I suppose his millions made up for his lack of table manners."

"Mrs. MacDougal wouldn't marry for money," Karen said stiffly. "She loved her husband very much."

"I'd have loved him too. Passionately. She was the most influential hostess in Washington for over forty years. And she knew how to spend old Jackson's money. That house is like a museum! I was in it once, on a charity tour. How old is she, a hundred?"

"In her nineties. Julie, you are not only a gossip, you are a ghoul. Do you sit around and pray for people to die so you can buy their antiques?"

"Well, sweetie, they can't take it with them, can they? I've heard rumors that she is going to sell the house and move to a nursing home, and dispose of most of her things. The important antiques will go to Christie's or Sotheby's, of course. I haven't the capital to deal with a collection like that, even if I had the entrée. But her odds and ends would make my fortune! In her day she was one of the snappiest dressers in town. I'll bet she's got designer gowns, hats, accessories—"

"I thought you didn't deal in vintage clothes." Karen added waspishly, "We aren't that out of it in the dreary Midwest. I know old clothes are fashionable—collectible is the word, I believe. Not that I would wear things like that—"

"That's exactly what you are wearing," Julie pointed out. "It looks fairly decent on you. And it's comfortable, isn't it?"

"Yes, but—"

"But nothing. I don't specialize in vintage, but I'd market shit if people would buy it." She leaned across the table and fingered the ruffle. "This is in super condition. I could get ... oh, say, seventy-five for it."

"Seventy-five *dollars?*"

"What do you think, yen? Maybe more. It's a good size, too. A lot of older clothes were made for those Scarlett

19

O'Hara twenty-inch waists. How much more of this sort of thing does your aunt have?"

"Boxes and boxes and bags and bags."

Julie sprang to her feet, her eyes gleaming with avarice. "Show, show."

"I will, just to frustrate you. Ruth isn't going to sell her things."

"You could ask her."

Karen tried to change the subject. "Why don't we sit in the parlor like ladies? I'll fix you another drink—"

"I hate that room," Julie said.

"Why?" Karen asked curiously.

"It's too damned formal. I can't put my feet on the coffee table."

"Oh. Well, you certainly can't. I swore to return Ruth's property in pristine condition, as I received it."

"Don't worry, I've too much respect for antiques to treat them carelessly. Which is why I prefer to sit in the kitchen." Julie gulped down her drink. "Let's go to the attic."

It was not long before Karen was regretting her careless offer. Her hope, that friendship had been at least part of Julie's motive for cultivating her acquaintance, looked more and more forlorn when she saw the look of pure acquisitiveness on Julie's face.

One end of the long room was filled with furniture, much of it Pat's. He had had his own house before he moved in with Ruth after their marriage, and—Karen now realized—much of his furniture had originally belonged to his mother. She had literally to drag Julie away from a set of dining room chairs with needlepoint seats.

The linens, clothing, and rugs had been arranged along one wall, separated from the bulkier objects. Some of the clothing was packed in trunks and cartons; others

20

hung from rods laid across the exposed beams. The latter were enclosed in garment bags, and a strong smell of mothballs wafted out as Julie began opening them.

"Let's take them downstairs," she said breathlessly. "It's too dark up here to see properly."

"Julie, I told you—"

"You said I could look. You know, linens and clothing ought to be aired and cleaned from time to time. You'd be doing your aunt a favor, really. If she ever does decide to sell them—"

"She'll never sell them. She doesn't need the money."

"But you do. I knew your dear husband when he was teaching at Georgetown; unless he's changed a lot, you'll have to fight him for every penny."

Karen's expression warned Julie that this time she had gone too far. "At least you can wear some of them, can't you? Surely Ruth wouldn't object to that."

"Of course not. She's the most generous—"

"Then let's take them downstairs and see what we— I mean, you—have. We'll play dress-up. Come on, it'll be fun."

Fun was not the word Karen would have chosen; Julie's open, unconcealed greediness cast a pall over the whole business. But she found the clothing unexpectedly fascinating. Thanks to Ruth's housewifely instincts and Cousin Hattie's lavish use of camphor, the dresses and coats were in excellent condition. Karen had done enough sewing to appreciate fine tailoring and beautiful fabrics, and only a woman totally devoid of imagination could fail to appreciate the charm of the ultra-feminine flowing frocks that dated back to Hattie's distant girlhood.

Karen wondered if fond nostalgia for a lost figure had inspired Hattie to preserve some of the dresses. Certainly they had been made for a willowy-slim woman which, to judge from the wardrobe of her middle age, Hattie had no longer been. Her favorites, packed in oiled paper and the inevitable camphor, ranged from a black-and-white calico day dress, every stitch sewn by hand, to a white batiste creation dripping with lace and eyelet insertion. Perhaps, Karen thought, they commemorated events in Hattie's life, happy times or sentimental moments. Parties and picnics, strolls by the river with a mustachioed gallant who looked into her eyes and told her how pretty she looked in white lace and ruffles....

Ruth's castoffs dated from the fifties and sixties, and Julie assured Karen they were also worth money. Money was the operative word for Julie, not sentiment. "It's a pity you can't wear your aunt's size," she said tactlessly, stroking a blue wool suit. "This is a Chanel copy, and a good one. Here, try this dress on. It looks like it belonged to the old lady after she got fat. Real silk chiffon."

"It makes me look like the old lady," Karen grumbled, as she slipped the dress on. "Where would I wear silk chiffon?"

"To work. Vintage adds a nice touch. Actually, it's a little big for you. How amazing."

Karen bit her lip. There was no sense in sparring with Julie; she was as subtle as an elephant, and her hide was as thick. "I could fix it," she said. "Take the skirt off, put in a few tucks and pleats..."

"I didn't know you could sew. That could be useful," Julie added thoughtfully.

Karen didn't ask her to elucidate. "I used to make all my own clothes. Academic salaries aren't that high, and Jack didn't want me to work, so..."

So she went to faculty dinners and receptions in homemade clothes while Jack ran up big bills at the best men's shops in the city. She didn't mind. Jack was such a good-looking man, and of course men couldn't make their own clothes. Her skill improved with practice, and she was naively proud of her work—until the night of the President's reception. It was the first formal gathering they had attended after Jack accepted the job in Dubuque. He was wearing the dinner jacket he had got at Brooks Brothers before they left Washington. She had slaved over her dress—raw silk, on sale for only eight dollars a yard.... Jack said it looked homemade. Very nice, my dear, but why didn't you buy something a little more sophisticated?

Suddenly Karen realized she was shaking and dry-mouthed with anger. Strange. She hadn't been angry at the time, only embarrassed.

The memory came and went so quickly that Julie, never the most sensitive of women, was unaware of her distraction. Julie had opened a box filled with time-yellowed lingerie and was emitting little moans of delight. "Victorian and Edwardian. Look at the handmade lace, the embroidery.... I could get a hundred and fifty for this petticoat!"

It was then that the idea was born, sparked by Julie's greed and founded in long-suppressed resentment. Why you? Karen thought. Why not me?

THE hamburgers Julie had brought were reduced to grease and sogginess by the time they sat down to supper. Karen nibbled on salad; Julie absently devoured the disgusting sandwich, too intent on her own thoughts to notice what she was eating. Karen knew she was planning a new assault, but had not yet determined the right strategy. They parted with mutually insincere expressions of affection. Karen locked up, turned off the lights, and dragged her weary body up to bed.

Of course it wouldn't have occurred to Julie to help clean up the mess, Karen thought crossly. Her bedroom was as littered as it had been during her college days. She couldn't even get into bed; it was piled high with "whites," as Julie called them—petticoats frothy with lace, night-gowns trimmed with crochet and tatting, camisoles and corset covers and funny, voluminous bloomers. Karen was tempted to push the whole lot onto the floor—they all needed washing anyway—but habit prevailed over ex-haustion, and she began folding the garments and return-ing them to the cartons from which Julie had taken them. They were in poorer condition than the carefully packed dresses, but Julie had assured her the dust and dirt would wash out.

When she came upon the petticoat Julie had priced with such extravagance, she examined it curiously. It was beautifully made; eight inches of narrow tucks circled the lower part of the skirt, and the wide double flounces were trimmed with yards of knitted lace, fine as cobwebs. Karen held it against her and looked in the mirror. Crumpled and stained as it was, it conjured up images of romantic femininity, like the scent of ghostly, faded perfume; as she turned from side to side, the wide flounce swung out in a coquettish flare.

The lace had pulled away from the fabric in several places and there was one rent in its web. She could fix that. Julie had insisted the stains would bleach out. Dark brownish stains, like dried blood . . . Surely no one would pack a bloodstained garment, though. The stains must be those of rust.

A hundred and fifty dollars?

Karen was almost ready for bed when the telephone rang. She wondered irritably who could be calling so late, and then realized it wasn't quite ten o'clock. She was tempted not to answer. If the caller was Julie, primed with new excuses for plundering Ruth...

However, the caller was not Julie. Ruth's soft voice was blurred by background noises of laughter and conversation. She and Pat were spending the night with friends in New York before flying out the following morning.

"You weren't asleep, were you?" Ruth asked.

"Good heavens, no." Karen laughed lightly. "It's only ten o'clock."

"I forgot to ask you to please call the repairman to come look at the dryer. You'll find his number in the file."

"What's wrong with the dryer? It was working fine yesterday."

"Sometimes it makes a funny noise when it spins."

"I didn't hear any funny noise."

"It's intermittent," Ruth said.

Karen couldn't help smiling. There was nothing wrong with the dryer; that was only Ruth's excuse for calling. Now she could ask the questions she really wanted to ask. Did you eat something? Are you nervous alone? Are you sad, afraid, lonely?

"Okay," she said. "Don't worry, I'll look after things."

"And yourself."

"And myself."

"I hope you had a nice quiet day."

"Julie came for supper."

"Good."

"Not so good," Karen said perversely. "She's had her eye on your attic for a long time. She barely waited till you were out of the house before she pounced."

25

"Oh, Karen, I'm sure she came because she's so fond of you—"

"Ruth, darling, you needn't stroke my ego. Julie is as fond of me as she is of anyone, but she is primarily a merchant. She drooled over those chairs of Pat's."

"Well, she can't have them. Honestly," Ruth said indignantly. "Of all the nerve, making use of your friendship to pry around in my house—"

The sentence ended in a gasp and a burst of smothered laughter, and Ruth's voice was replaced by that of her husband. Karen moved the receiver a few inches from her ear.

"What did you say to infuriate my wife?" Pat demanded. "You know I can't allow her to be upset, she's a holy terror when she's angry."

Karen heard Ruth's voice in the background. "Give me that phone, Patrick MacDougal!"

"Only if you let me listen in."

Sounds of a scuffle ensued; Karen waited resignedly until the MacDougals had arrived at a consensus. Then Ruth said somewhat breathlessly, "Don't let that pushy female have a thing!"

"I will defend your property with my last drop of blood," Karen assured her. "You don't mind if I wear some of the clothes, do you?"

"Clothes? What clothes?"

"There are piles of them. Some of yours, some that must have belonged to Cousin Hattie, and even older things. Vintage clothing is in style, and I thought—"

"Oh, those old things. I was going to give them to Goodwill, but I never got around to it."

Pat interrupted with a comment Karen didn't catch; it was obviously a rude remark about Ruth's refusal to throw anything away. Suspecting that another prolonged

26

bout of affectionate horseplay was about to take place, Karen said loudly, "Would you give them to me?"

That stopped the argument. After a blank silence, Ruth said, "Darling girl, you can have anything in the house. It will all be yours and Sara's one day—"

"But not for a helluva long time," said Pat.

"Stop it, Pat. Darling, you'd be doing me a favor if you cleaned that whole lot out. Take what you can use and call Salvation Army or someone to pick up the rest. And while they are at it, they can clean out Pat's study. Just tell them to take everything—"

"If one scrap of paper is missing," Pat shouted, "I'll put the grandfather of all curses on ye!"

"Are you sure you meant to throw them away?" Karen persisted.

"Absolutely. What do you have in mind?"

Karen explained. "I suppose it's presumptuous of me to think I could open my own shop," she ended. "But I've learned a lot from Julie, and with your things to get me started . . . Julie says acquiring stock is one of the major problems."

"Darling, I think it's a marvelous idea. Of course you can do it."

"Just don't set up shop in the parlor," Pat said. "It isn't zoned commercial."

"You know I wouldn't do that."

"You have no sense of humor, damn it. Go ahead, become a seller of rags and bones; judging from what I see in shop windows, some people will buy anything. Go see my mother. Maybe you can talk her into cleaning out *her* attic."

"I intend to call her, of course—but not for that."

"Why not for that? I've been trying to get her to move out of that mausoleum on R Street for years. She says she can't because none of the retirement homes will let her take that damned dog. . . . Hey," Pat said brightly.

"Oh, no," Karen exclaimed. "Oh no, you don't, Pat."

"Why not? It's a great idea. A dog would be protection for you."

"Not that dog. It bites everybody who walks in the house."

"That's what a guard dog is supposed to do."

"It bit *me* last time I visited your mother."

"You can train it not to do that."

"How?"

"Club, cattle prod? God, that is really a terrific idea. I can't imagine why I didn't think of it before. I'll call the old girl right now. Come on, Ruth, you've been on the phone long enough, everything is fine, right? Good night, Karen."

The phone went dead, cutting off Ruth's halfhearted protest.

If she had had the telephone number of the friends with whom Pat and Ruth were staying, Karen would have called back. Ordinarily her uncle's antics filled her with a blend of amusement and outrage. Tonight she was not amused. If she knew Pat—and she did—he would be carrying out his threat this very moment, explaining his brilliant scheme to his mother in an enthusiastic bellow. Karen could have killed him. She didn't want a dog. She particularly didn't want Mrs. MacDougal's dog.

She got into bed and turned out the light, still fuming, but after a time she realized she was probably getting upset about nothing. Mrs. MacDougal would yell right back at Pat. She wouldn't give up her home, filled with a seventy-year accumulation of memories and bric-a-brac, for the sterile safety of a nursing home. Not Mrs. Mac. At ninety-three she had more zest for living in her little finger than some people of twenty-seven going on twenty-nine had in their whole bodies.

A board creaked in the hall. The wind was rising; a leafy branch brushed the windowpane with an eerie rustle. A white lingerie dress flung over the back of a chair shimmered dimly in the darkness, limp as a swooning Victorian maiden.

A hundred and fifty. There were at least six petticoats in the box, the same number of nightgowns. Say a hundred dollars average on the petticoats. . . . A hundred times six, plus six times fifty—perhaps seventy-five. . . .

Karen had fully intended to indulge in the long-awaited fit of weeping, but she was so busy adding and multiplying she fell asleep before she had shed a single tear.

CHAPTER TWO

❖❖❖❖❖❖❖❖❖❖❖❖❖❖❖❖❖❖❖❖❖❖❖❖❖❖❖❖❖❖❖❖❖❖❖

*T*HE ringing of the telephone was a vulgar intrusion into the blissful vacuum of sleep. Karen opened her eyes. Rain whispered at the window, and the room was gray with shadows. The illuminated dial of the clock read six-thirty.

The phone went on ringing. Karen squinted unbelievingly at the clock and pulled the sheet over her head. The thin fabric did nothing to mute the sound; putting her fingers in her ears didn't help much either. Who on earth would have the nerve to call at this hour? Pat? He was on his way to Borneo by now. Julie? She never got up at six-thirty. In fact, there was only one person she knew who rose at that unearthly hour.

"Damn," Karen said. She took her fingers out of her ears and reached for the phone. She knew it would go on ringing until she answered.

"Hello?" she croaked.

Julie and Mrs. MacDougal had only one thing in common: their reluctance to waste time on meaningless amenities. "I hear you're going into business," Mrs. Mac said brightly.

"Not right this minute," Karen muttered.

"What? Well, you ought to be thinking about it right this minute. Time is money. Come for breakfast and we'll talk about it."

Karen had been taught to be courteous to her elders, and Mrs. MacDougal was as much her elder as any living person could be. Besides, she adored Mrs. Mac-Dougal. At least she adored her most of the time. The gloomy skies outside, the corresponding gloom that enveloped her spirits, and a hideous fear that she was about to be bullied by not one, but two, MacDougals made it necessary for her to summon up every ounce of good will and good manners in order to refrain from screaming at her old (in every sense of the word) friend.

"I was planning to call you later," she began.

"No time like the present. Just slip on a raincoat and come on over here."

Mrs. MacDougal's bland assumption that she was already up and dressed would have amused her under far different circumstances. While she was trying to decide whether to admit to slothfulness or find some other excuse for delay, Mrs. MacDougal went on, "I was about to suggest some such scheme myself. Delighted that you thought of it too. Now I happen to own a little place that would be perfect for your shop—it's on Thirty-first, just off M Street—and I've been thinking of names. Something evocative but not cutesy. Dreams of Yesterday, or—"

"Mrs. Mac," Karen said desperately. "You're very kind, but I . . . It was just an idea. I wasn't serious. You know Pat, he always jumps on careless remarks and blows them up into big dramas. I can't . . . I don't know anything about . . ."

"Nonsense. What you mean is that you've developed cold feet."

"No, I mean I've come to my senses. It was a crazy idea, and now that I've had time to think about it—"

"Crazy ideas are the best ideas," said Mrs. MacDougal. "Child, I know exactly what you are going through. Your pride has been mashed flatter than a pancake; there is nothing more humiliating to a woman than to have a man tell her he doesn't want her—especially a worthless, low-down creature like Jack. The next few months are going to be hell. You'll be up one minute, and way down the next. But take my word for it—if you decide on a course of action and stick to it, through hell and high water, something will always happen to shake you out of the depths. Now put on your clothes and get over here before I come and fetch you."

The MacDougal house on R Street was almost invisible from the sidewalk; only the massive chimneys showed above the trees that surrounded it, and a high wall enclosed the grounds, which filled an entire city block. It was one of the few remaining mansions of George Town, half a century older than the capital city of which it had become an appendage (a word Georgetowners past and present would have indignantly repudiated).

The gates were closed, but a smaller entrance stood invitingly ajar. Karen shook her head at such carelessness, but as she approached, a voice made robotlike by electrical circuits squeaked, "Good morning, Miss Karen. Please close the gate after you have entered. It locks automatically."

Karen returned the greeting. The closed-circuit television was a new addition, but she recognized the voice of Joseph, Mrs. MacDougal's butler. He must be almost as old as she; the other servants were equally superannuated. Pat was right, it was high time his mother gave up the house, for security reasons if no other. Its museum-quality collections of furniture, fine art, and silver were an irresistible lure to professional thieves, and the aged staff would present no obstacles to a team of burglars.

Like the gate, the front door stood wide open and Joseph waited on the steps, beaming from ear to ear. Ignoring his formal bow, she threw her arms around him and hugged him, and felt a pang at the frailty of the body she clasped. She knew she was the darling of the household and accepted the fact with humility; it was not her own graces that endeared her, but the fact that she and her sister were as close to grandchildren as Mrs. MacDougal would ever have. Pat was an only child, and he had married late in life.

She suspected that Joseph was as shocked by the change in her as she was by his aging, but he was far too well-bred to let his feelings show. He bowed her into the house and helped her off with her coat, tsk-tsking over how wet she was. "You should not have walked in such weather, Miss Karen. Had Mrs. Mac informed me earlier of your coming, I would have sent the car around."

"Sent?" Karen repeated, with an affectionate smile. "I thought you refused to let anyone else drive for Mrs. Mac."

A shadow of vexation crossed Joseph's dark, patrician features. "I regret to inform you, Miss Karen, that the absurd laws of this municipality have forbidden me that activity. However, there is a young person—"

Before he could go on, a parrotlike shriek proclaimed the arrival of Mrs. MacDougal. She wore one of the fantastic garments for which she had long been famous in Washington society. Karen was accustomed to her hostess's eccentricities in dress—Mrs. MacDougal had once received her in a Cossack uniform, complete with slung pelisse and furry hat—but this ensemble reached new heights of bizarreness. It appeared to be a wedding gown of ivory satin, the low-cut bodice encrusted with pearls and brilliants, the skirt overlaid with panels of lace. The effect was marred not only by Mrs. MacDougal's face—which, as her son had once remarked, resembled that of one of the handsomer Egyptian mummies—but by the patter of pearls falling from the bodice and the fact that the dress had been made for a taller, more full-bodied woman.

As Mrs. MacDougal clasped Karen in an affectionate embrace, a perfect hail of pearls splattered onto the floor. Karen gave a cry of distress. "Your beautiful gown!"

Mrs. MacDougal grinned broadly. "My wedding dress. Never think it, would you? I seem to have shrunk. Did you ever read *She?*"

"No," Karen said, bewildered.

"Immortal woman," Mrs. Mac explained. "Bathed in the fire of Life—two thousand years old—superbly beautiful. Went back into the fire, reversed the process—aged two thousand years in five minutes. Nasty. Felt like that myself when I tried on this dress."

"You look wonderful."

Mrs. MacDougal guffawed. "Age cannot wither nor custom stale my magnificent variety. Or something like that. Let me get out of this antique before it collapses completely. I just put it on to give you a sample of my wares."

She yanked at the dress, and a shower of tiny satin-covered buttons joined the pearls littering the floor. Karen caught at the crumpling folds with careful hands, and Mrs.

34

MacDougal stepped out of the dress. Under it she wore purple jogging pants and a sleeveless, low-cut T-shirt emblazoned in multicolored sequins with a motto so extremely vulgar that Karen's eyes literally popped. Joseph was well accustomed to his mistress's habits; he took the wedding dress from Karen's palsied grasp, and as Mrs. MacDougal escorted her out of the room she saw him advancing on the scattered ornaments with a whisk broom and dustpan, his countenance bland as cream.

Mrs. MacDougal led Karen along a corridor. "Decided to close most of the house last year," she explained. "Too much for Joseph and the others. Moved my bedroom downstairs. Easier for everybody."

The room they entered had been one of the small parlors. It had French doors opening onto a terrace and the famous Japanese garden. Mist blurred the outlines of the bridge and the pagoda and turned the miniature waterfall into a swaying phantom form, but the room was bright and cheerful with its red satin draperies and rose-spattered wallpaper and every light blazing. A small table was set for breakfast. Every other piece of furniture in the room, including the grand piano, was strewn with clothing.

"Show and tell," shouted Mrs. MacDougal, as Karen stared. "Got it out this morning. Lots more where that came from."

The collection resembled Ruth's only in the variety of styles represented, from the beautiful hand-worked lingerie of the Edwardian period to the notorious silver caftan and turban Mrs. MacDougal had worn on her first meeting with her future daughter-in-law. Ruth still hadn't gotten over the shock of that caftan; she talked about it to this day.

But these were no designer copies—they were the

originals. One glance would have made that plain to any woman with the slightest sense of fashion. Karen touched a flapper dance dress whose crystal beads shimmered like fragments of ice, and bent over to read the label. "Balenciaga," she said.

Mrs. MacDougal nodded. "There are a couple of Worths around somewhere. He made my trousseau. I gave some things to the cleaning woman—"

Karen let out an involuntary but heartfelt groan. "You gave Worth gowns to the cleaning woman? But he was—he designed for all the royal houses of Europe and England."

"There's still a lot left. I was quite a clotheshorse in my day." Mrs. Mac indicated a white net dress over-embroidered and banded with lace. "I had dozens of those—proper wear for innocent young maidens back then. And this..." She lifted a coat of gold-and-silver brocade whose collar and wide sleeves dripped sable. "I wore this to *The Girl from Utah* at the Knickerbocker Theater in 1914." She began to croon in a loud tuneless voice. "La-da-de-da-dah, da-da-da-da—"

"Jerome Kern?" Karen said, grinning.

"Right. See, you have a feeling for the antique. What's the term—vintage?"

"These aren't vintage, these are classics—museum pieces." Karen spread her hands in a gesture of denial and appreciation. "I can't accept—"

"Who said I was giving them to you?" Mrs. MacDougal's deep-set black eyes sparkled wickedly. "The markup is about two hundred percent, isn't it? I'll collect my third, never fear."

Karen laughed helplessly. "You're impossible."

"Thank you. Let's eat, shall we? I'm starved." She

lifted a silver cover and steam rose from a yellow foam of scrambled eggs framed by sausages.

"I certainly don't need to eat," Karen said. "I'm overweight."

"I'll bet you've started to lose it. Your appetite isn't too hot these days, is it? A little queasy all the time? I had a friend," said Mrs. MacDougal reminiscently, "who lived for a year after her divorce on gin, smoked oysters, and artichoke hearts."

"You're making that up."

"Child, I don't have to make up bizarre stories. People do stranger things than any writer can invent, and after ninety-odd years I've seen it all. She lost twenty pounds," Mrs. MacDougal added. "Not that I recommend her method, mind you. Have a sausage. After breakfast we'll go around and look at the shop I have in mind."

"Mrs. Mac, it's out of the question for me to open in Georgetown. Rents and taxes are sky-high. I'll have to look around in the suburbs—Gaithersburg, Rockville, Falls Church. That's what Julie did; she only moved to George-town a few years ago, and I think she's regretting it."

"I agree," Mrs. MacDougal said calmly.

"You do? But you said—"

"Oh, I just threw that out to see whether you had forgotten to use your brains. I'm glad to find that you haven't. What are your plans?"

Karen wasn't aware that she had made any plans. However, prompted by encouraging grunts and nods of approval, she heard herself glibly propounding schemes that must have developed while she slept; she certainly hadn't consciously considered them during her waking moments. Trips to museums to study costume and find materials on textile treatment and preservation, weekend visits to outlying towns looking for a suitable location and checking out future sources such as local auctions and yard sales. . . . By the time she finished breakfast she realized she had a campaign mapped out, at least in broad outline, and she looked incredulously at Mrs. MacDougal, who was licking her fingers after eating six sausages.

She's a witch, Karen thought—a genuine, eighteen-carat witch. How did she know what I was thinking when I didn't even know myself? Or did she put the ideas into my head? No wonder Pat became interested in the history of magic and superstition. He had been inspired by watching his mother in action.

"It sounds as if you have everything under control," Mrs. MacDougal announced. "As for sources, I can help there; I have several friends who adore picking up an extra buck or two on the side."

"I'll have to pay you a commission."

"How much?" Mrs. MacDougal asked hopefully.

Karen started to laugh and then thought better of it. Mrs. MacDougal wasn't kidding. "Are you sure?" she ventured, indicating the finery littering the room.

"Quite sure. I wouldn't give my bossy son the satisfaction of admitting it, but he's right; this house is too much for me and my servants. Joseph would rather die than omit a single one of the rituals he considers essential, and one of these days he will—die, I mean. The rest of them are as old as Joseph—Rachel, my maid—you remember Rachel?—and the cook, and the others. I've tried to get them to retire, but they won't; and to be honest, I couldn't imagine life without them. They're my friends. So I'm going to sell, probably at the end of the summer."

"Pat doesn't want the house?"

"What would he do with it?"

"But it's a shame to have this lovely place pass out of the family after so many years—"

Mrs. MacDougal sniffed. "Sloppy sentimentality, my girl. The place is a damned white elephant; it ruined my father, trying to live up to an income he didn't have, and it was falling down around our ears until I married Jackson. Besides, things don't matter. People matter. There isn't a thing in the house, up to and including the house itself, that I wouldn't give up to add a year to Joseph's life."

"Well, of course. But—"

"But nothing. That's it. Have you finished?" Without waiting for an answer, Mrs. MacDougal rang the buzzer that summoned the maid. Rachel opened the door so promptly that Karen knew she had been hovering outside. Before the elderly servant could enter, a shaggy form squirmed through the opening and made a beeline for Karen. The latter hastily hoisted her feet, and the dog, missing its intended goal, snapped viciously at the leg of the chair.

"Bad dog! Bad dog!" Scolding in chorus, Rachel and Mrs. MacDougal converged on the animal. Mrs. Mac-Dougal reached it first and lifted it in her arms.

Rachel gave Karen a hug. "I hope that nasty creature didn't hurt you, honey," she exclaimed. "I tried to keep him out, but he got by me somehow. I guess I'm not as light on my feet as I used to be."

"He missed." Karen returned to her chair, keeping a wary eye on Alexander.

Alexander's chief claim to fame was that he had won an "Ugliest Dog in Washington" contest. Mrs. MacDougal had been one of the patrons of the affair, held in aid of a worthy charity. It had been love at first sight, and she had persuaded the owner to sell him.

Alexander looked like . . . Karen's imagination always failed her when she tried to find a comparison. Alexander resembled no other creature, extinct or extant. He was about the size of a miniature poodle, but his legs were no longer than those of a dachshund. He was as fuzzy as a sheepdog from snout to rump, but his tail and rear end were obscenely bald. His coloring resembled that of a calico cat, patches of orange, black, and white on a gray background. But it was his head that had won the title. His ears reached almost to the floor. His canines stuck out at right angles to his jaw, which provided a useful guide to the location of his mouth, otherwise totally hidden by hair. Hair covered both his eyes. From time to time he would give his head an irritable shake, baring one optic for a brief period—mercifully brief, for Alexander's eyes were the most malevolent Karen had ever seen on a living creature. Compared to Alexander, buzzards and crocodiles looked kind. Mrs. MacDougal claimed that he located objects by a kind of radar rather than by sight, and he certainly could home in on an intended victim with diabolical speed and accuracy. His bite was worse than his bark, but not by much, for the acute angle of the canines prevented him from sinking them in, and the rest of his teeth, though sharp as needles, were not very long. He was only interested in two things—eating and biting people. His adoring owner insisted that the two were related, and that Alexander's attempts to take chunks out of visitors were the result of his poor sight. To give Alexander his due, it must be said that usually he only bit people once. Usually.

"Bad, bad doggie," Mrs. MacDougal crooned. "You remember Karen. You mustn't bite Karen. You love Karen. Karen loves you. Karen won't let you come and live with her if you bite her."

"Rrrr," said Alexander disagreeably.

Karen looked helplessly at Rachel, who was clearing the table and watching the proceedings at the same time. Rachel's plump shoulders lifted in a shrug. Rachel sympathized, but Rachel was not going to protest. She hated Alexander and had from the start.

"You mean you're going to give Alexander up?" Karen asked, trying to keep her voice from quivering.

"Of course I'm not going to give up my darling." Mrs. MacDougal squeezed Alexander. He burped in a vulgar fashion. "I'm not going to move into one of those nasty sterile nursing homes where the nurses call you honey. I'll buy a nice boring condo surrounded by barbed wire and security guards. Rachel will come with me, of course, and so will Alexander—was he his mother's darling, wassums? I just want you to keep him for me this summer while I travel."

"Where are you going?" Karen asked.

"Borneo." Mrs. MacDougal's sagging jowls split in a malignant grin. "Can't you see Pat's face when I come riding into the clearing on a donkey, or a gnu, or whatever they ride in those parts?"

"But," Karen gasped. "But—but—you can't—"

"Yes, I can." Alexander began squirming and Mrs. MacDougal put him down. "It will be my last fling. If I survive, I'll settle down at Golden Acres or Bide-a-Wee and behave myself. If I don't—well, hell's bells, Karen, I've had a good run. No complaints. I thought of going some time ago, but I couldn't leave Alexander. He doesn't get on well with Joseph, and Rachel is terrified of him— silly old fool. You are a silly old fool, Rachel, to be afraid of a poor little dog."

"Poor little dog nothing," Rachel exclaimed. "That's no dog, that's part alligator and part devil. Don't you take him, Miss Karen, honey. You won't have a spare inch of flesh on those pretty ankles."

41

"Nonsense. Once he gets used to Karen, he won't touch her. He never bites me."

"He don't like the way you taste," said Rachel.

"That's no way to talk to your employer," said Mrs. MacDougal, grinning. "Get on out of here or I'll make you go to Borneo with me."

"That's no threat, that's a promise," Rachel said grimly. "I am going to Borneo with you. You think you gonna go traipsing off into them jungles without somebody to take care of you, you got another think coming. You're the one that's a silly old fool. Never heard such a wild idea in my life."

She stamped out with the tray, her heavy tread shaking the table.

"I can't let her go with me," Mrs. MacDougal said. "She's too old."

Karen guessed that Rachel must be in her mid-seventies, which made her almost twenty years younger than Mrs. Mac. She tried desperately to think of an argument that might dissuade the old lady, or a way of preventing her, and realized she didn't have a leg to stand on. Even if she had had the legal right and the moral smugness to take such a step, Mrs. MacDougal could not be declared incompetent; she was quite sane—or, to put it another way, she was no crazier than she had ever been. Moreover, Karen sympathized with her point of view. When one's time approached, how much better to go out in a blaze of glorious lunacy, on a gnu, than to dribble one's life away in a rocking chair.

Alexander, smelling the ghosts of the sausages, was cruising the room. He tossed his head. One large brown, evil eye emerged from the brush. It focused squarely on Karen. She shuddered.

The rain had almost stopped by the time she started along Wisconsin Avenue on her way to work, but the steep slope of the sidewalk was slick with greasy water, and a fine drizzle dampened the shoulders of her raincoat. In the gray summer heat the street looked like any grubby business district instead of the fashionable shopping area it actually was. Traffic snarled the street, exhaust fumes blending with the fog to form a dirty substance that looked, and was, inimical to human health. Throwaway plastic containers and paper napkins from the fast-food stores littered the sidewalk. At least the bad weather had driven the street vendors and the vacant-faced, stumbling alcoholics indoors. Ten years ago she had loved Georgetown, had been stimulated and excited by its eclectic liveliness— bars and fortunetellers rubbing shoulders with chic boutiques, vendors selling cheap gold chains outside a fashionable jewelry store, elegant antique shops sandwiched between People's Drugs and McDonald's. It must be another sign of premature aging that made her find the area tawdry and unappealing.

Julie's shop was not on Wisconsin, but on one of the side streets. Climbing vines rooted in antique iron buckets framed the doorway, and the single window held an eye-catching arrangement of odds and ends, their very incongruity demanding the attention of the passerby. The name of the establishment was lettered in gold: old things. No capital letters, just the two simple words. Smart of Julie. Not only was the name chichi clever, but it made no claim. "Antiques" implied, at least, that the dealer knew what the word meant and was willing to stand behind its implication.

Karen was sardonically amused to see that Julie had a new window arrangement. A rusty well pump stood next to a dainty Louis Quatorze–type sofa covered in delicate brocade. Across the sofa had been flung, with seeming carelessness, the best of Julie's few antique gowns, an Edwardian tea dress of pale-blue muslin. The ensemble was completed by a pair of heavy work boots.

Karen had felt a certain letdown after leaving Mrs. MacDougal. The old lady was like a strong wind; one had to brace oneself to stand upright against it, and when the wind stopped blowing, the victim had a tendency to sag. But the sight of Julie's window stiffened Karen's drooping spine. The Edwardian dress was a promise to customers of things to come—a promise Julie had no right to make.

The bells over the door chimed as Karen entered the shop. Julie was on the phone. Though she noted Karen's entrance immediately, she talked with such machine-gun rapidity she finished the sentence she had begun before she was able to stop herself.

". . . just your size, Friday at the latest." After a glance at Karen, her half of the conversation turned monosyllabic. "Yes. Right. Yes. Okay. By."

"Hello," said Karen.

"Hi. Don't just stand there, you're dripping all over my antique Kerman."

Karen opened the door at the back of the shop and went into the office. Rob, the only other employee, was seated at the desk, his yellow curls bent over a pile of invoices. "Hi there, sweetie," he crooned, glancing up. "Want some coffee? Fresh brewed by my own white hands."

"No, thanks."

"But, sweetie, you're drenched, poor baby. Here, let me take your coat."

A gold earring glinted as he rose to his full height—well over six feet—and reached for Karen's coat. He was a pretty thing, with delicate, epicene features, and many of the older women customers assumed he was gay. They were very sweet to him, and Rob cooed and gurgled and giggled at them like one of the girls. The customers could not have been more wrong. Rob's effect on younger women was devastating and was callously exploited.

Despite his air of camaraderie, Karen suspected Rob didn't like her much. He had made a halfhearted pass at her shortly after she began working, and she had complained to Julie. Julie had responded with contemptuous hilarity and had promised to speak to Rob, who had sulked for several days. Dumb, dumb, Karen thought disgustedly. I should have handled it myself, not made a big deal of it. That was one of her problems—she had gotten out of the habit of acting independently, without consulting someone else first.

And to make matters worse, she had realized too late that Rob's motive had been kindness rather than lust. She wasn't his type. He liked his women young, or rich, or both.

Like Jack.

Karen muttered under her breath and Rob turned his head. "What did you say, ducks?"

"Nothing. Thanks, Rob."

She went back into the shop and surveyed the cluttered interior of the small room with a newly critical eye. Julie had a style of her own. The shop was absolutely crammed with objects; one had to sidle sideways through the clutter. Yet the clutter was rather charming, suggesting an old-fashioned general store where customers willing to burrow through stacks of Levi's and yard goods might discover treasures the owner had forgotten and underpriced.

Karen admired the effect, but she knew she could not imitate Julie. She would have to develop her own individual style. A picture formed in her mind—a big, high-ceilinged room with crown moldings and chair rails, the white walls warmed by sunlight from tall windows; ornate, gold-framed mirrors, green plants in Victorian cachepots; some of the more striking garments, like the Chinese ceremonial skirt of Mrs. Mac's, hanging like banners against the walls. . . .

"What?" she said, starting.

"I said you look like Dracula. Didn't you sleep?"

"I slept very well, thank you—until six-thirty, when the damned telephone woke me up."

"Well, for God's sake put on some make-up and try to look pleasant. A customer would take one look at you and run screaming into the street. That skirt is too tight. Why didn't you wear the blue silk? Who called at that ungodly hour?"

"Mrs. MacDougal." Karen glanced into a nearby mirror. It was eighteenth-century Chippendale, with a curved frame and a gilt eagle on top. The wavy, time-worn glass made her face look bloodless and distorted. She fished in her purse for her lipstick.

"Mrs. MacDougal," Julie repeated.

"Uh-huh."

"How is she?"

"Fine." Karen returned the lipstick to her purse. "I had breakfast with her."

"I don't suppose you talked to your aunt."

"Yes, I did. She called last night."

"She said you couldn't wear the dress?"

"What . . . Oh, that damned blue silk. You have the most incredibly one-track mind, Julie. She said I could have anything I wanted and do anything I wanted with it."

"Marvelous." Julie's eyes glistened. "I'll come over this evening and we'll go through the clothes. You're a friend, so I'll give you a square deal. Half the retail price.

I'm really cheating myself, because the usual markup is three hundred percent—"

"Two hundred," Karen said.

"Not in Georgetown. Do you know what my overhead is?"

"Yes, I do know. You told me at least twice a day every day last week. You can have a few of the clothes to sell on consignment for me. I believe twenty percent is the usual charge. The rest I'll keep. I'm going to start my own business in the fall."

"Son of a bitch!" screamed Julie.

The argument raged for a good ten minutes. Rob came out to see what the ruckus was about and lingered, his eyes moving from one combatant to the other as he emitted impartial cries of encouragement. "That was a good one, Karen. Right on, Julie darling, you tell her."

After accusing Karen of gross ingratitude and predicting instant bankruptcy for her proposed business, Julie suddenly gave in.

"Oh, well," she said coolly. "It was worth a try. You never had much gumption, and I figured you were so down in the dumps you wouldn't have the guts to strike out on your own."

"My pal," Karen said.

"I offered you a job—"

"Because you wanted to get away for a few weeks and you didn't dare leave Rob in charge. Oh, Rob, I'm sorry—"

"No sweat, sweetie," Rob chirped. "I'm a frightful cheat and no one knows it better than Julie. Not vicious, you know, just weak. Now Julie is just the opposite—not weak, just vicious."

"Shut up, Rob," Julie said. "Okay, Karen, what about your aunt's furniture and ornaments?"

"I don't think she plans to get rid of anything," Karen said. "If she does, I'll make sure you get your chance."

"Mrs. MacDougal's too?"

"Oh, for . . . All right."

"Fair enough. Rob, I want those bills out by closing time. What are you standing around for?"

Her voice was placid, almost cheerful, though she had been screaming like a harpy only a few minutes earlier. Rob retreated, with a grin and a wink at Karen. She was grateful for his silent encouragement; her palms were wet with perspiration and she felt slightly sick. Confrontations always affected her that way. Yet Julie's casual contemptuous words still rankled. "You never had much gumption." Was that really true? Karen had always thought of herself as quiet and well-bred rather than weak, and aggressive self-confidence is not a characteristic possessed by many eighteen-year-olds—especially eighteen-year-old women. Jack had caught her at that most vulnerable of times, and certainly he had done nothing to reinforce her self-esteem. . . . With an effort Karen shook off painful memories.

"What do you want me to do?" she asked.

"Straighten the place up. You can start with that table by the door, the one with the books and pamphlets. People make such damn messes. . . ."

The pamphlets, devoted to Georgetown shops and sights, had been disarranged, but not to the extent Julie's comment implied. As she sorted and stacked them, Karen's eye was caught by an item that had not been on the table the day before. Like most of the other local guidebooks, it was paper-bound and appeared to have been published by a small vanity press. The cover bore the title *Legends of Georgetown* in blazing scarlet letters above a hand holding a dagger dripping with the same lurid shade.

Karen picked up a copy. Julie, who had been watching her, said casually, "Eye-catching, isn't it? I just got it this morning."

"There's no author's name."

Julie chuckled. "Take a look at the table of contents and you'll understand why."

The innocuous title of the book certainly did not suit the contents. "The Sinister Specter of the Murdered Madam" was one chapter title; others included such provocative gems as "The Georgetown Strangler," "Lizzie Borden or Jack the Ripper?" and "Murder in High Places."

"All the standard Georgetown ghost stories are included," Julie said. "But there are some nice gruesome modern scandals too. That's why the author prefers to remain anonymous. A lot of people are going to be howling for his blood when they read about their family skeletons."

"His? Do you know who it is?"

Julie hesitated. Karen could see she was dying to boast of inside information, but discretion won out. "I used the masculine pronoun for the sake of convenience, darling. Yes, I know who *it* is, that's one of the reasons why I said I'd stock the book. I always like to give a helping hand to old friends who are down on their luck. Have a copy on me—go ahead, take it. You need something to amuse you during those long, dull evenings alone. Who knows, you may recognize some of the subjects. Wasn't there some funny story about that house of your aunt's?"

"Not that I know of."

"Well, of course she wouldn't want to tell you— being all alone and defenseless in the house as you

49

are. You know this area has the highest rate of violent crime—"

The door opened and Julie went to greet the entering customer. A smile of satisfaction curved her wide mouth.

Karen retreated into the office with the book. She had won the battle, but Julie intended to make sure she didn't enjoy her victory. Julie knew a lot of ways to needle people.

Karen was sufficiently disturbed by her hints to examine the grisly little volume in more detail while she ate a late lunch at the café next door. There was nothing about Ruth's house. One chapter—the one entitled "Lizzie Borden or Jack the Ripper?"—mentioned a "certain red brick Federal house not far from Wisconsin Avenue," but the case turned out to be a horrible double knife murder that had occurred several years before Karen came to Georgetown.

She was obscurely relieved. Not that it should have disturbed her unduly to learn that the house had been the scene of a past crime; few houses that age had histories unstained by tragedy of one sort or another. All the same...

She was leafing idly through the book when a name jumped out of the page at her with the impact of a poisoned dart. Mrs. Jackson MacDougal—"the former Bess Beall, spoiled debutante darling of that luxurious era when even adultery had a glittering glamour." The sentence was only too typical of the author's style—bad syntax combined with innuendo that never quite toppled over into actual libel. Karen's eyes widened as she read on, about the ambassador "from a noble family of impeccable lineage," who had cut his throat in the MacDougal billiard room, leaving a note accusing the mistress of the mansion of toying with

50

his affections and then casting him aside. The billiard table had to be cast aside too.

A thin sheaf of grainy black-and-white photographs in the center of the book showed some of the author's victims. Karen would not have recognized Mrs. MacDougal; but she recognized the dress. She had seen it only that morning—a flowing gown of white crepe and satin, dripping with swaths of white fox. The wearer's figure was as fashionably slim as that of a young boy, and even the poor quality of the photographic reproduction could not impair her gamin prettiness. Soft dark hair cupped the beautifully shaped little head, and the wide eyes were framed by extravagant lashes. But the grin was unmistakably that of Mrs. MacDougal.

"Age cannot wither..." Karen's eyes were wet as she gently closed the book. Perhaps that gallant laughter was the only thing time could not destroy.

Business was slow, and by four o'clock Julie's mood was as gray as the weather. "I don't know why I don't just close up for two weeks while I'm in New England," she grumbled.

"Why don't you?" Karen asked.

"I have to pay rent and utilities and insurance anyhow. You never know—some sucker might wander in and fall in love with one of the white elephants I've been trying to sell for months." Julie sighed noisily. "You're out of your mind to think of opening your own place, Karen. If you knew half the headaches..."

Karen ignored this not-too-subtle hint and retired to the office. Rob was out making a delivery. He would probably not return that day; the customer lived in Virginia, and traffic on the bridges during rush hour was horrendous, especially in bad weather, for all of Washington seems to go mad when the roads are wet. Karen sat down at the desk and opened the file containing Julie's purchase orders for the past six months. She was curious about Julie's sources and profit margins. It behooved her to learn as much as she could, before Julie decided there was no sense in running free classes in merchandising for a potential competitor.

It was all she could do to force her tired eyes to read Julie's writing. The interview with Mrs. MacDougal had been exhausting; she felt as if the old lady had turned her inside out, hosed her down to clear out the cobwebs, and hung her up to dry. Then the strident argument with Julie . . . Julie was right. She couldn't start her own business. She didn't have the guts, or the know-how, or the strength.

She was drooping over the papers—having noted, with a faint surge of malicious interest, that the so-called Pennsylvania highboy had been part of a shipment from Glasgow, Scotland—when she heard the door chimes. Reluctantly she pushed the papers aside and got to her feet. Shoplifting was an everpresent problem, and it was hard for one person to keep an unobtrusive eye on several customers at once without spoiling the air of gracious ease antique dealers liked to create.

As she started to open the door, she heard Julie's shrill voice. "Karen! Karen, come on out; here's an old friend who's dying to see you."

Karen was tempted to close the door and pretend she had not heard. Several "old friends" had visited the shop since she started working, and when she was feeling particularly low she suspected Julie of calling all her former acquaintances and inviting them to come and gloat over her. Morbid and absurd, of course—but she still winced when she thought of Miriam Montgomery, née Spaulding, and Shreve Danforth. Shreve was now Mrs. Assistant Secretary of State Givens; she was as slim and sleekly muscled as she had been ten years ago, when she and Karen had competed for top seed on the university women's tennis team. They had competed in another arena as well. . . . Shreve had not forgotten; she had ordered Karen about like a servant, her eyes bright with malice. Just like Shreve; but Karen had rather liked Miriam Montgomery. The latter's cool indifference had really hurt.

Julie hallooed again, more emphatically. Karen knew she was in for it. She eased the door open a little more and looked out.

Even on a sunny day the interior of the shop was not brightly lighted. According to Julie, the dusky illumination created an atmosphere of relaxation and peace. (It also made it difficult for customers to spot stains, scratches, and other minor imperfections in the merchandise.) However, the newcomers were standing directly under a Delft chandelier, and such light as its sixty watts produced shone directly on the face of the taller of the pair.

For a moment Karen felt as if a pair of giant hands had seized her body and squeezed. Hearing, vision, sensation, even breathing were suspended. Then her battered senses rallied, though her hands, fallen nervelessly to her sides, were sticky with sudden perspiration. She had not seen Mark for ten years. Yet recognition had been instantaneous and overwhelming.

He hadn't changed—and yet he had, in a number of small ways. Numbly her mind listed them. The chestnut-brown hair was sleekly, expertly styled, whereas once it had been tousled and unruly. He had tugged at his hair whenever he was excited or intensely interested in something, and he almost always was excited about a theory, an idea, a vision. His expression was intent and slightly frowning, but the parallel lines between his dark brows were deeper now. That was how she remembered him, grave and intent, not smiling. He didn't smile often. He was too serious, too committed to the causes he cared about—more than he cared about individuals. . . . Of medium height and rather slightly built, he seemed taller now. It must be the way he carried himself, straight and erect instead of casually slouching, with a new air of authority.

The greatest change was in his clothes. She couldn't remember ever having seen him in anything but jeans and a faded shirt. She had teased him about that shirt, accusing him of owning only one, which he washed every night and never pressed. Sometimes, when the weather was freezing, he condescended to wear an old navy windbreaker, worn through at both elbows.

He was now wearing a tan trenchcoat that looked as if it had just come off the rack in one of the more expensive men's stores. It was open in front, exposing a shiny-white shirt and a dignified dark-blue tie—the conventional Washington bureaucrat's uniform, predating the Yuppie era by several decades.

The woman with him was blond and petite and very pretty.

The ringing in Karen's ears subsided and she heard Julie say, "Yes, she's back. Poor dear, I was glad to help her out. You know how it is, she's pretty low. I'm afraid she's changed a great deal. I'll go get her, I know she'd love to see you."

Julie started toward the office. Mark raised his hand as if to detain her, but then shrugged and let her go.

Karen fled, hoping the obstacle course in the shop would slow Julie long enough to let her make her escape. She snatched her coat as she headed for the back door, not because she gave a damn about getting wet, but because if the coat was on the hook Julie would know she had not gone far. She closed one door just as Julie burst through the other, and darted into an adjoining doorway, where she huddled ankle-deep in soggy trash.

Hearing the back door open, she pressed herself back into the alcove. Julie's voice echoed hollowly. "Karen? Where the hell are you?"

Karen put her hands in her pockets and hunched her shoulders. Her heel had crushed a plastic trash bag. The stench of rotting fruit was so strong it made her stomach twist.

She went to the end of the alley and around the block, and stood under an awning across the street until she saw Mark leave. He didn't look in her direction. His eyes were fixed on the face of the woman, who was smiling up at him from under a very becoming rain hat. After they had turned the corner, Karen crossed the street and entered the shop.

"Where did you go?" Julie demanded.

Karen had had time to invent an excuse—not a very convincing excuse, but it was better than none. "I thought I heard a cat crying outside."

"So you chased it all the way down the alley and around the block?" Julie's eyes narrowed. "By a strange coincidence you just missed an old friend of yours."

"Oh, really? Who?"

"Mark Brinckley."

"Mark . . . Oh, of course. What shame I wasn't here."

"He'll be back," Julie said, not one whit deceived by Karen's pretense that she had forgotten Mark's name. "His girlfriend is interested in that armoire. She pretended to be interested in the lowboy, but it was really the armoire.

55

If she comes in while I'm gone, you can give her the usual ten percent, but only if she asks; make it look like a special favor to the dear friend of an old friend. You know the procedure."

"I ought to. It was the first thing you taught me." Karen started to unbutton her coat.

"Don't bother to take off your coat, I'm closing," Julie said. "Mark said to tell you he was looking forward to seeing you again."

Karen doubted that he had said it, or, if he had, that it was anything more than conventional politeness. She did not reply, so Julie abandoned indirection and went straight for the jugular.

"Weren't you engaged to him once?"

"People didn't get engaged in those days, remember?"

"I've forgotten what we used to call it, but I know what I mean—and so do you. He's not married."

Karen shrugged. "The lady may not have been his wife, but that doesn't mean he doesn't have one."

"Oh, my, what a little cynic you are. I happen to know he's not married because the *Post* ran an interview with him. You heard he was elected to Congress last year, didn't you?"

"Oh, was he?" Karen turned to the mirror and stared blindly and intently at its clouded surface. She had heard of Mark's victory. It had not been one of the big, exciting races, but she had heard about it. Mostly from Jack. He had been very interested in that particular House seat.

"So," she said, "he's living in Washington now?"

"Well, darling, he has to when Congress is in session, now doesn't he? He's as gorgeous as ever, don't you think? Oh, I forgot—you didn't see him. Well, take my word; just standing next to him made me break out all over. You two had quite a thing going for a while, as I recall. When you and Jack ran off and got married, we were all surprised. Especially Mark. He couldn't have been too desperately crushed, though; he certainly consoled himself fast enough. Of course Shreve had been throwing herself at him all year. All he had to do was turn around, and there she was, ready and willing. From what I hear, she still is. Of course her husband is a lot older than she. You know how that is, don't you, sweetie? I wonder if Shreve knows about this new little lady. Mark didn't introduce her to me. I can't imagine why...."

Karen stood unmoving, feeling as if she were under attack by a whole horde of wasps; one sting followed the other so rapidly that numbness finally overcame pain and she felt nothing at all.

She turned blindly toward the door and Julie said gaily, "I hope you aren't brooding about the nasty things I said today. You know how I am, I just get mad and let everything hang out. My shrink says it's the only way to cope with stress. I didn't mean anything by it. You do forgive me, don't you?"

A deprecating smile curved her lips and her eyes were wide and candid. She really meant what she said, or at least she thought she did, which came to the same thing. Do forgive me for cutting you into little aching pieces, it's just my cute, harmless habit. No reasonable person would hold it against me.

Karen murmured something noncommittal. It satisfied Julie; with a practiced smile she put up her umbrella and darted into the pedestrian traffic.

Karen stood staring after her for a moment. Then she shook her head and turned toward home.

What a day. What a horrible, tiring, unbelievable day! Only a few more miserable blocks, a few more terrible

minutes, and she could collapse. A glass of wine, a chocolate bar, and thou, oh, muscular hero of television—not
singing in the wilderness, but wrecking cars, making love
to lissome ladies, fighting villains, and always winning.
Just what she needed. Someone who always won.

Head bowed against the rain, hands in her pockets,
she trudged northward, wondering whether to stop at a
carry-out restaurant for something to eat or forage in Ruth's
freezer. To hell with the diet she had started. Tonight she
needed all the comfort she could get, and a Hershey bar
was cheaper than a psychiatrist.

At least she wouldn't have to worry about seeing
Mark again. He must be as anxious to avoid her as she
was him. It must have come as a nasty shock to him to
learn that she was back in Georgetown, a lone, lorn
divorcee-to-be. He would assume she would try to renew
their old acquaintance. Karen was not the first of her circle
to face divorce. She had seen it happen before, and she
knew the signs of desperate pursuit—the forced, bright
smile, the too-youthful wardrobe, the telephone calls to
married friends. "I do hate to ask, darling, but if Jim (or
Joe or Bob) has a few minutes, could he come over and
fix my stopped-up sink (or check my snow tires or change
the lightbulb). . . ."

Too bad Mark couldn't know he was safe from that
sort of thing. Just as she was safe from him. He would
stay as far away from the shop as he could. He wouldn't
seek her out there.

She was right. He didn't go to the shop. He was
waiting for her on the corner of P Street and Wisconsin.

Concentrating on keeping her footing on the wet
sidewalk, she was not aware of his presence until she
heard his voice. "Welcome back, Karen. You might know
it would be raining."

Karen didn't even stumble. One part of her mind wondered why she was not surprised. Another part moaned, oh, well, what's one more disaster on a day like this? Aloud and quite coolly, she said, "Hello, Mark. I'm sorry I missed you earlier."

"Like hell. Where were you, hiding behind a garbage can in the alley?"

"What makes you think—"

"I was right, wasn't I?" It was a crow of triumph. "That's always been your technique—hiding. And usually behind something rotten. Like Jack Nevitt."

"I would appreciate it if you wouldn't say things like that."

"Don't tell me you're still defending him. Weren't ten years of serfdom long enough?"

Anger is nonproductive, Karen told herself. Anger accomplished nothing. "What did you do with your friend?" she asked.

"Put her in a cab and sent her home. Don't worry about anyone overhearing; this is just between us."

It was raining harder. Water dripped off the brim of Mark's hat. (Mark wearing a hat? In the old days he went bareheaded in all weather, his hair darkened to carnelian by wet or frosted whitely with snowflakes.)

"There's no point in this, Mark," she said wearily. "I don't intend to invite you to come in—"

"I haven't time anyway. Dinner engagement."

"Oh. Then why—"

"Did I stand in the rain waiting for you?" Mark pondered the question with the same gravity he had once bestowed on serious issues of foreign policy. He had majored in foreign affairs; had been one of Jack's students.

After a moment he said, "I yielded to an impulse. I don't often do that anymore, but . . . Julie had said you

59

were in the office. I knew you must have seen or heard me and bolted out into the alley in order to avoid me. It made me angry."

They had reached the house. Karen stopped by the low wrought-iron gate. Mark reached a long arm over it and unlatched it, with the careless ease of someone who had performed the same action many times. But he did not open it for her. He wasn't finished.

It was on this exact spot that their final confrontation had taken place. It had been raining that day too—a soft spring rain. The sidewalk was sprinkled with catkins from the budding maples and the young leaves shone as if freshly painted. In the gentleness of April Mark's hoarse, angry voice had echoed like an obscenity. She would never forget the things he had said. She had slapped him—the first and last time, the only time she had ever struck anyone.

He was remembering too. A faint ghost of old anger tightened his lips and narrowed his eyes.

"I thought you had come to gloat," Karen said.

"Maybe I did. I hope not. It would have been a lousy thing to do. You don't need to have your nose rubbed in it, do you?"

She had been sure, only a few minutes earlier, that her spirits had sunk as low as they possibly could. She had been mistaken. Mark's eyes moved deliberately from her limp, straggling hair down to the hem of her shapeless old raincoat. Warm brown eyes, almost the same shade as his hair; but they weren't warm and smiling now, they were as cold as the amber whose color they shared.

He had a right to be angry, a right to gloat. Every prediction he had made that spring day had come true. "He likes them young and pretty and intelligent. He likes to pick their brains and cut them down to size—his size.

You have a lot going for you, Karen, you can be somebody. Don't let him use you. He only wants you because you're my lady, he's hated my guts ever since I raised a stink about that paper of mine he tried to steal, he's getting back at me through you—"

That was when she had slapped him. That was the one thing she couldn't accept—the humiliating suggestion that revenge and spite, not love, had prompted Jack's proposal. She still could not accept it. But Mark had been right about everything else, including Jack's ability to destroy her identity and her ambition.

All at once, like a thin demonic voice inside her head, she seemed to hear Mrs. Mac's screech. "And what is he doing? Seems to me he's no better than your husband. Don't stand there and take it!"

She raised her drooping head and blinked the raindrops from her lashes. "No, I don't need to have my nose rubbed in it! I don't need any more—any more crap from anybody, Mark Brinckley, especially from you. You've had your fun and I hope you enjoyed it, because you aren't going to get another chance. Good-by."

She reached for the gate, but he held it firm, moving slightly to block her way. "Fun?" he repeated, his lips twisting in a wry curve that certainly held no suggestion of amusement. "If you think I've enjoyed this . . . Maybe it's impossible for either of us to forget the past—even the past five minutes—but can't we at least be civil to one another? I'm very fond of your aunt and uncle, and I'd like to go on being friends with them. Ruth canceled an invitation a while back because she thought you wouldn't want to see me."

So he had renewed his old friendship with Ruth and Pat. Ruth hadn't mentioned him. Neither had Pat, whose tactlessness was proverbial.

61

Compared to the other emotional blows she had endured that day, this news should have been only a minor slap in the face, but to Karen it was almost the last straw. At least Mark was honest. He wanted to forgive and forget (and give him credit, she thought bitterly, for avoiding the time-worn and hideously inappropriate cliché) only because hostility between them would threaten a cherished relationship.

One last effort, she thought. I've come this far without cracking. . . . "Ruth was mistaken," she said coolly. "I don't care whether I see you or not. As for being civil— if I understand you correctly, my problem has always been an excess of civility rather than a lack of it. You're the one who has trouble being polite to people. If you intend to change your ways you can start by letting me get in out of the rain."

Meekly Mark opened the gate and stood back.

"Karen?"

Something in his voice stopped her as she started up the walk. She turned. He was smiling—a genuine smile this time, the rare, well-remembered expression that had once made her very bones melt. Ten years vanished like blown smoke.

"Congratulations," he said. "When did you learn to start fighting back?"

CHAPTER THREE

❖❖❖❖❖❖❖❖❖❖❖❖❖❖❖❖❖❖❖❖❖❖❖❖❖❖❖❖❖❖❖

THE rain continued all night, dripping mournfully from dull skies, but for some reason Karen didn't wallow in chocolate as she had planned. Supping virtuously on soup and salad, she realized that the encounter with Mark had actually lifted her spirits. Perhaps it was simply that she had finally sunk so low there was no way to go but up. However, she knew she had been subconsciously dreading the possibility of such a meeting ever since she returned to Washington. Had she but known Mark had renewed his former acquaintance with Ruth and Pat, she would have had greater cause to be concerned. There was nothing surprising about it; they had once been close friends. But to think that Ruth, sly Ruth, hadn't mentioned Mark...

No, that wasn't fair. Ruth was never sly. Tactful, sensitive, considerate of other people's feelings...Why should Ruth suppose it mattered to her? The mere fact that Ruth had avoided the subject—hadn't mentioned the invitation or its cancellation—that, in itself, implied an assumption Ruth had no right to make.

At any rate, the worst was over and, as is so often the case, the reality had not been as bad as the anticipation. Besides, she was proud of herself for standing up to him in the end. Two head-to-head confrontations in one day, first with Julie and then with Mark, and she hadn't done badly. Thanks in part to the inspiration of a bossy old witch! I could have sworn I actually heard her voice, Karen thought, smiling.

Mrs. MacDougal might not be a genuine witch, but she was unquestionably a canny lady with a profound understanding of human nature. In the next few days Karen suffered frequent spells of depression, but as Mrs. Mac had predicted, something usually happened to shake her out of them. Mrs. Mac administered a lot of the shaking herself. She nagged Karen unmercifully about the shop, and kept her so busy she had little time to brood. She made appointments with friends who might have things to sell, and bullied Karen into keeping the appointments. She introduced her to realtors in Maryland, Virginia, and the District, bought and borrowed books for her to read, and quizzed her on the contents. There were times when Karen wished she could tell Mrs. Mac to go to Borneo— or someplace even hotter—and she developed a nervous habit of reaching for her notebook every time the telephone rang. Mrs. MacDougal had given her the notebook; she never failed to ask what progress Karen had made, and Karen knew she had better be able to report progress.

It wasn't easy. If she had realized how many endless and diverse details must be covered before she could even open for business, she would never have had the courage to begin. What terrified her most were the practical aspects—keeping books, borrowing money, arranging for permits, dealing with realtors, regulations, and taxes. Sheer nerves would have kept her awake nights if she hadn't been so tired that she often fell sleep over the book she was reading.

The books were the ones Mrs. Mac had supplied, on the care of antique textiles and the history of costume. At first it was only fear of the old lady's acerbic tongue that made Karen give up her favorite mysteries and romances, but before long she became genuinely fascinated. Her ability to conquer a new subject increased her shaky self-confidence. After all, research was what she had been trained to do; the basic methods were the same for any field. But in this case she could actually touch and feel the objects of her study, and apply the methods she read about. The clothes themselves thrilled her. It was not only their beauty and their charm that moved her, but a growing sense of identification with the past. "Jumping Jack" MacDougal had showered his pretty young bride with jewels and furs and lovely gowns, the best money could buy. As she and Karen sorted the clothing, Mrs. Mac's reminiscences brought to life a world that had been as remote to Karen as ancient Greece—the last lazy summer afternoon of aristocracy before the Great War.

Mrs. Mac had worn the chiffon-and-lace evening dress at the captain's dinner on a 1913 voyage of the *Lusitania,* two years before the luxury liner was sunk by German bombs, precipitating the United States' entrance into the war. The black lace over oyster satin had attended the first performance of *The Three-Cornered Hat,* with Léonide Massine, at London's Alhambra Theatre in 1919. (And what, Karen wondered, had Jumping Jack thought of the ballet? Had he slept through it—had he snored?) The Schiaparelli suit, with huge hand mirrors in lieu of jacket buttons, had dazzled the dignitaries at FDR's first inaugural. Karen could almost see Mrs. Roosevelt's well-bred eyebrows rise at the sight of it. She felt as if she were touching history itself.

Not that Mrs. MacDougal wasted time mourning her lost youth. The expectation of playing one last practical joke on her son had given her a burst of demonic energy; she dashed around the house chortling and chuckling and driving her assistants wild. Karen was not one of them; her offers of help had been politely refused, and she soon realized they were unnecessary.

Though Mrs. Mac blandly denied it, she had obviously been planning the move for months. The larger, more valuable antiques were going into storage until their owner returned. If, as she cheerfully remarked, she survived the trip, she would then select the things she wanted to keep or give away. The rest would go to Sotheby's. Since an inventory had been kept up-to-date, this part of the moving process was relatively simple.

What wasn't simple was the question of how to dispose of the thousands of less valuable odds and ends Mrs. MacDougal had accumulated over the years. These ranged from modern pottery to Spode and Royal Prussian dinnerware, from paperback novels to first editions—and included, of course the clothing and accessories. There were enough of the latter to stock a small shop in themselves—hats, shoes, handbags, scarves, gloves, belts, costume jewelry. Karen's last compunctions about taking them vanished when she saw the piles of discarded miscellany grow to mountainous proportions.

The clothing dated from around 1910, when Mrs. Mac had attained debutante status—and a millionaire husband. However, several of her cronies had garments that had been stored away since their mothers' and grand-

mothers' day, and before long Ruth's neat little house resembled a flea market. Every wardrobe was full, the
bedroom furniture was heaped with fabric, and dresses
hung from temporary stands. Karen was glad Pat was not
there to see it, and comment on it.

Something else happened that week to stiffen
Karen's sagging spirits—the arrival of a United Parcel man
with several boxes. The surgical precision of the wrapping
told Karen who had packed them; the folded corners of
the paper looked as if they had been measured with a ruler
and pressed with a hot iron. Inside one box was a typed
note. It was cool and formal, and very forgiving. It de-
plored her impetuous and ill-considered action in leaving
so precipitously and requested—implicitly, if not in so
many words—her humble appreciation for the consideration that was being shown her. The boxes contained her
clothes and personal belongings, swathed neatly in tissue.
Not a scrap had been overlooked, including a couple of
limp bras she had meant to throw away, and a pair of
sneakers with holes in both toes.

Karen methodically tore the note into tiny bits and
flushed them down the toilet. Then she threw the piece
of chocolate cake she had been about to eat into the disposal and went out and jogged for four miles.

She did not see or hear from Mark. She didn't expect to. (At least that was what she told herself.) Nor did
she expect the encounter that took place one afternoon
toward the end of the week.

Julie had left early, to finish shopping for her approaching vacation. Not five minutes after Julie took her
departure Rob followed her, with a look that dared Karen
to object. She was at the back of the shop, checking a shelf
of costume jewelry over which one customer had lingered
long without buying—it was all right, everything seemed

to be there—when the door chimes rang. Half concealed by a hanging tapestry, she looked up to see the girl who had been with Mark on his first visit.

She knew she should emerge at once, smiling and helpful. Instead she hunched her shoulders in a half-crouch, hoping the shadows would hide her, while her thoughts raced in uncontrolled confusion.

He's not with her. Of course not—he won't come again. It's probably the armoire she wants. She's attractive, but not as glamorous as I thought. . . . Her hair is beautiful—lovely curling red-gold. It looks real, too. Get out there. Stop skulking. She'll see you in a minute and you'll feel like a fool. Say something. Something witty, intelligent . . .

She edged out from behind the tapestry. "Hello."

The girl turned with a start. "Hi. I didn't see you at first. It's so dark in here."

It was a common complaint, and Karen seized with relief on the memorized response. "I'll be glad to turn on more lights if there is something you want to examine closely. I'm afraid Julie has stepped out for a moment, but if you need help—"

"I know she isn't here, I saw her leave. I wanted to see you. You are Karen, aren't you?"

"Yes."

The girl came toward her, smiling, her hand out. "I'm Cheryl Reichardt. Mark's sister."

"Sister," Karen repeated blankly.

Cheryl laughed. "I don't blame you, everybody reacts that way. We don't look one bit alike."

The statement was certainly correct. Cheryl was as fair as Mark was dark, and her round face and dimpled cheeks were the antithesis of Mark's austere features.

Karen gathered her scattered wits and took the outstretched hand—just in time, for Cheryl, flushing slightly, had started to withdraw it. "I'm glad to meet you. Are you visiting, or do you live in Washington?"

"I live with Mark, actually. He asked me to come and keep house for him after my husband died."

"I'm so sorry." Karen's response was genuine; it seemed impossible to think of this cheerful young woman as a widow.

"It's been a couple of years," Cheryl said, her lifted chin and determinedly matter-of-fact voice assuring Karen that sympathy would be unwelcome. "But I don't know what I would have done if it hadn't been for Mark. Joe left a few thousand in insurance, but we didn't have much saved, and my folks are living on Dad's pension, and with a baby to support..."

She paused to draw breath. "You have a child?" Karen asked.

"Little Joe. He's not a baby, he's four now. Want to see his picture?" Without waiting for a reply she reached in her purse and took out her wallet. "This was taken on his last birthday."

Karen's heart gave a queer, painful lurch. The little boy had his mother's mop of fair curls and a funny turned-up nose, but his shy smile reminded Karen of a look she had sometimes seen on Mark's face.

"Do you have any kids?" Cheryl asked.

"No." Jack had not wanted children. He never actually said so, but somehow it was never the right time.

"That's too bad. I was hoping I could borrow one." Cheryl giggled. "One of these days I'm going to be arrested. Whenever I see a kid in a grocery store or someplace, it's all I can do not to grab it and squeeze it. I miss Little Joe so much."

"He isn't with you?" Karen returned the wallet,

adding, "He's adorable. I don't see how you can stand to be away from him."

"I didn't have much choice. He'd just got comfortable with Mom and Dad and I didn't want to uproot him again. Besides, it wouldn't have been fair to Mark. He's renting a town house in Foggy Bottom, all neat and shiny and modern, but not very big; and he's always having people in for drinks and talks and dinner and stuff. I'm pretty busy myself, trying to adjust to Mark's schedule and going to school. I'm studying bookkeeping and computer science."

"Good for you."

"Well, I don't want to be a checker in a grocery store all my life." Cheryl leaned against the counter, arms crossed; she seemed quite prepared to stand there for the rest of the afternoon. "I never went to college and I don't have any training—"

"No marketable skills," Karen said with a wry smile.

"Yeah, doesn't it make you feel small when they say that? Like you were a sack of potatoes that's gone bad. I'm doing pretty good in school, though. I think I'm going to get an A in accounting."

Karen offered appropriate congratulations; Cheryl's beaming smile of pride was as irresistible as her cheerful chatter. "So you don't want to become a Washington hostess?" she said.

"Hell—I mean, good heavens, no. All this protocol and formality drives me crazy. Besides, Mark is sure to get married someday. He's got women chasing him all the time."

Karen could think of nothing to say to this. Cheryl realized that she had been tactless and she flushed again, and said awkwardly, "Say, isn't it just about closing time?"

"Don't let that worry you. Take your time—"

"I came to see you. I was glad when that other woman left. I know I shouldn't talk about a friend of yours, but she gives me the pip. I thought maybe if you had time we could have a cup of coffee or a drink or something."

"I'm afraid..." The refusal was instinctive, but the words were scarcely out of her mouth when Karen realized, with some surprise, that she didn't want to refuse.

Cheryl was too sensitive to miss the implication. She blushed more deeply. Her skin had the translucent pallor that goes with red hair and that shows every emotion in the ebb and flow of the blood.

"Mark said I shouldn't come. He said I'd open my big mouth and put my fat foot in it. But I thought... well, she's like me in a lot of ways, she hasn't lived here for a long time and probably most of her friends have moved away, and could be she's a little lonesome—like me...."

She stuttered to a stop, her cheeks flaming. She's shy, Karen thought in surprise, shy and a little insecure, under that chatty façade of hers. That was something else they had in common. And although Cheryl had described herself as tactless, she had not mentioned another thing they shared—their loss, by one means or another, of the men who had dominated their lives.

"I'd love a cup of coffee," Karen said. "But why don't we go to my house? I only live a few blocks away, and the cafés around here charge an arm and a leg."

SHY was not exactly the word for Cheryl. She was acutely aware of her inadequacies as a hostess for Mark, but the rueful humor with which she related some of her funnier faux pas made it clear that they didn't keep her awake nights. Since her failures had been the result of a

blunt tongue, a kind heart, and a complete lack of hypoc-
risy, Karen was inclined to agree, and to hope, that her
new acquaintance would never become a successful political wife.

It was obvious that Cheryl wanted to become a
friend, not just a casual acquaintance. Her confession that
Mark had tried to talk her out of visiting the shop removed
one of Karen's reservations; she was damned if she wanted
Mark to think she was running after him, trying to pick
up their former relationship, but she was also damned if
she was going to let him decide with whom she could
associate. After the rudeness of her old classmates, and
Julie's barbed malice, Cheryl's candor and lack of false
pride was very refreshing.

If she had not already been predisposed to like
Cheryl, the latter's breathless interest in her new project
would have won her over. Karen had not intended to talk
about it, but the subject inevitably arose during the tour
of Ruth's house that Cheryl requested. "I'm trying to get
Mark's place fixed up for him; most of the furniture is
rented and it looks tacky, but I don't know what's right."

When they went upstairs Karen apologized for the
state of the bedrooms. "This isn't the ambiance you want
for Mark, believe me. It looks like a junk shop. But you see,
I'm in the process of opening a vintage clothing store—"

"Vintage? I thought that was wine."

Karen explained. She would have left it at that, but
Cheryl peppered her with questions and her answers took
on the length and the style of brief lectures. When at last
they went to the kitchen for the coffee Karen had offered,
Cheryl carried a lacy garment with her, and she was still
asking questions.

"What did you say this is?"

"A combing jacket. That's what the lady wore

when she sat at her dressing table while the maid arranged her hair."

"It looks like a fancy blouse." Cheryl stroked the filmy ruffles admiringly. "Can you imagine wearing a thing like this just to get your hair combed? You couldn't throw it in the washer and the dryer, it would have to be washed by hand, and starched, and ironed, and all that."

"*You* didn't do any of those things if you were the mistress of the house," Karen said. "The maid did the dirty work. Or the laundry maid; some big establishments had one girl who did nothing else."

"That would have been me," Cheryl said with a grin. "I sure wouldn't have been the lady of the house. I wouldn't mind that kind of work, though, it's a pleasure handling something as pretty as this."

The comment prompted another lecture, on cleaning methods, to which Cheryl listened with openmouthed interest. "You are just fantastic, Karen. I can't tell you how much I admire you. It takes a lot of gumption to start your own business."

"Gumption or stupidity. Sometimes I think I've bitten off more than I can chew."

"Oh, no, if anybody can do it, you can. This is all new to me, and you seem to know everything about it."

"A few weeks ago I didn't know vintage chic from a hole in the ground," Karen admitted. "I still have a lot to learn."

"I guess there is a lot to it. Have you found a place yet?"

Though Cheryl had been in Washington less than a year, she had a number of sensible suggestions about good locations—so sensible, in fact, that Karen wondered whether she had considered opening a business of her own. When she asked, Cheryl admitted she had thought of it.

"It was just wishful thinking, though. I don't have the experience or the qualifications yet. Joe's insurance is stashed away, and if I'm lucky I won't have to use it for an emergency; so some day . . . But I'll never be able to get into anything as glamorous and exciting as what you're doing. You're so lucky."

"Lucky," Karen repeated thoughtfully. "Yes, I am."

"Oh, I didn't mean it was just luck. Without brains and hard work—"

"You were right the first time," Karen said, smiling. "It was luck—and a lot of help from my friends—that got me started. The brains are questionable, and the hardest work is yet to come, but I'm going to give it my best shot."

Cheryl was clearly reluctant to leave. "I can't miss class, though, not if I want that A. Thanks for letting me bug you, Karen. I haven't had so much fun since I came to Washington."

Karen stood at the door watching as Cheryl trotted through the long shadows of early evening toward Wisconsin and a taxi. Cheryl certainly was easy to please. A woman who found a few hours of idle talk more entertaining than embassy dinners and cocktail parties would be thought hopelessly stupid by most observers.

I had a good time too, Karen thought—and then, with a self-conscious smile—probably because I monopolized the conversation.

She had been a little lonely, though not for former friends. The faculty wives with whom she had associated were almost all older than she, with interests and careers of their own. Jack didn't approve of her getting too friendly with academic inferiors. She knew what Jack would say about Cheryl. Not our kind. Her grammar, her manners, her lack of education...

What a snob Jack is, Karen thought casually. She went back inside and closed the door, never realizing that a landmark had been reached, a bridge had been crossed. She was thinking how quiet the house was, and how she really ought to get back to work on her records and lists.

ON Friday Karen went with Mrs. MacDougal to the airport. She did not offer to drive; this was to be the penultimate, perhaps the last, voyage of the 1938 Rolls Silver Cloud that was as much a Washington landmark as its owner. Karen half expected a motorcycle escort.

They had said good-by to Joseph and the other servants, who were about to leave on well-deserved vacations. A security agency would watch over the house. But Mrs. MacDougal was not setting off for Borneo alone. "I may be old, but I'm not senile," she said tartly, when Karen expressed her concern. "I'm taking Frank."

As if Frank were a suitcase. He was, in fact, the grandson of a friend of Mrs. MacDougal's, a graduate history student who had jumped at the chance of earning a substantial salary for gallivanting around the Eastern Hemisphere all summer. Karen made a point of meeting him and decided he had the necessary qualifications: intelligence enough to deal with schedules and officials, strength enough to pick Mrs. Mac up bodily if she fell down. He treated the old lady with a burlesqued gallantry that did not attempt to conceal his genuine affection.

All the same, Karen felt a mournful foreboding as she watched her friend walk toward the terminal on Frank's arm. Mrs. MacDougal did not look back. She had refused to let Karen come to the gate with her. At the last moment she had thrust a small shabby box into Karen's hand and said brusquely, "A little something to remember me by. No, don't start crying, dammit. I hate long, mushy good-bys." And she glanced at the elaborate leather carrying case in which Alexander reposed.

She certainly had not received any mushy farewells from the dog. Alexander knew something was going on and he thoroughly disapproved of it. All that could be seen of him was his hairless rump, for he had turned his back on the proceedings.

The big glass doors of the terminal building glided smoothly aside; the comically ill-matched pair, tall young man and withered old woman, passed through. The tears Karen had been forbidden to shed blurred her vision, but she saw Mrs. Mac stop to greet a man who was offering her something . . . flowers? Yes, long-stemmed red roses.

An upstart Volvo, impatiently awaiting its turn to unload passengers, had the effrontery to sound its horn, and the chauffeur put the Rolls in motion. Karen turned and craned her neck for a last look, without success; people and cars obscured her view. She could have sworn the man with the flowers was Mark.

It was possible. Mark had met Mrs. Mac while he and Karen were dating. Mrs. Mac had taken a fancy to him because he would argue with her about everything from politics to religion, giving back as good as he got without making polite concessions to her age and dignity.

Pat had liked him for the same reason. The degree of Pat's approval could be measured by the loudness of his voice and the number of times he banged on the table during a heated debate.

Pat had never argued with Jack. The antipathy was mutual; after the first few visits Jack always found an excuse for not accepting Ruth's invitations. He had tried to keep Karen from going, but that was the one issue on which she stood up to him. Even after they moved to Iowa she managed to get to Washington every year or two— when Jack was also out of town, so her absence wouldn't inconvenience him. . . .

With an effort she forced her mind away from thoughts of Jack, and from the inevitable corollary the memory had induced—"How could I have been such a wimp?"—and leaned back, enjoying the luxurious ride. It was unlikely that she would ever occupy such an elegant vehicle again. The Rolls was on its way to storage, and a long list of potential buyers was anxiously awaiting Mrs. Mac's final decision.

Gliding in air-conditioned, velvet-cushioned comfort through the summer countryside, Karen began to feel more cheerful. The feeling that she would never see Mrs. Mac again wasn't a premonition of approaching disaster, only a normal reaction to seeing an elderly friend off on a long trip. Whatever happened, she could rejoice in the knowledge that Mrs. Mac was doing precisely what she wanted to do, and would certainly have a wonderful time doing it.

To be sure, the ominously silent presence of Alexander was not calculated to lift her spirits. She avoided looking at the carrier; in any case, Alexander's rump was not a pretty sight.

Through the glass partition that separated the front and back seats, she could see the chauffeur's head and his heavy shoulders. She had met him for the first time earlier in the week, when he helped Joseph deliver Mrs. Mac-Dougal's clothing. He was the only one of the servants who had not been with her for many years. He seemed to be good at his job; the huge car slid sinuously through the traffic, with no change in speed and no delays.

Not until then did Karen remember the worn leather case Mrs. MacDougal had given her. It lay on her lap, forgotten in the turmoil of departure. An amused, affectionate smile curved her mouth as she turned it in her hands, seeking the catch that would open it. Heaven only knew what Mrs. Mac would consider an appropriate farewell gift; the box might contain anything, from diamond earrings to a Mickey Mouse watch.

Her fingers found and pressed the catch. The lid fell back. There were earrings, and a matching necklace; but not, thank goodness, of precious stones. The earrings were long dangles, heavy and ornate; the necklace choker length. Sections of black enamel edged in gold scrolls formed a background for flower-shaped insets made up of small pearls and sparkling stones, pale green and colorless. Karen detached one of the earrings from its mount and turned it over. Antique jewelry was one of the subjects she was still learning about, but she knew enough to feel sure the set was not particularly valuable. The gold wash had worn off in places, showing a lighter metal beneath. Ordinarily she would never wear anything so ornate, but the necklace would look nice with some of the Victorian clothes.

When they left the parkway and started up Wisconsin, Karen reached for her purse. She would never have dreamed of offering a tip to Joseph, but this young man was not of the old school. What was his name? That at least she could offer, some acknowledgment of the fact that he was not simply an anonymous machine. Hawkins? Higgins? No—Horton.

There was no parking space open near the house. Horton double-parked and was out of his seat and opening

Karen's door before she could move. He lifted Alexander's carrier.

"I can manage it," Karen said.

"There are the other things, miss."

"Oh, yes."

Horton unloaded Alexander's bed, his food and water dishes, and his toys. A three-month supply of Alexander's favorite foods had already been delivered, but it was unthinkable that Alexander should be deprived of his toys for so much as a second.

"Just leave them," Karen said, as the pile increased. "I don't want you to get a ticket—"

Horton's lips parted in a small, amused smile. They were full, fleshy lips, of the sort some women might consider sexy. His other features and his bulky, heavily muscled body also fit the exaggerated macho image made popular by certain film stars. The trim jacket didn't actually strain across his broad chest—no subordinate of Joseph's would ever be seen in public in improperly fitted clothing—but the fabric looked as if it wanted to stretch.

"I have my instructions, miss," the chauffeur said sedately. "Please allow me."

Of course, Karen thought, watching him lift the boxes as effortlessly as if they had been empty. Of course— Mrs. Jackson MacDougal never gets parking tickets.

Horton followed her into the hall. "Where would you like me to put them, miss?"

"Miss" instead of "madam." Was that because Joseph couldn't break his habit of referring to her as "Miss Karen," or were they all obeying instructions from Mrs. Mac, who would be delighted to see her resume her single status? Mrs. Mac had never liked Jack. . . .

Irrelevant and immaterial, Karen thought. Aloud she said, "Anywhere. Here. It doesn't matter."

"The carrier is rather heavy, miss. Perhaps in the kitchen?"

His manner was perfectly respectful, but suddenly Karen realized that she didn't want him to go any farther into the house. His body seemed to fill the entire hallway.

"No," she said. "Just leave everything here."

"Yes, miss." Horton touched his cap and turned to go.

Karen thanked him and held out a folded bill.

She was not sure she was doing the right thing, and was prepared for a well-bred rebuff, of the sort Joseph would have given her. Horton's reaction was even more disconcerting. His full lips parted in a broad, uninhibited grin. "Save it, doll. You probably need it worse than I do."

Karen gaped at him as he strutted—there was no other word for it—down the walk, his hands in his pockets, his uniform cap pushed rakishly askew. As the car glided away, he put his arm out the window and gave her an impudent wave.

Karen laughed and waved back, though she knew Joseph would have fainted with horror at the gesture and her response. Horton must have had a hard time conforming to the formal standards the butler insisted upon. This was his last day on the job, his final public appearance; he had nothing to lose by letting go.

She forgot Horton as soon as she closed the door. There had been no comment from Alexander, but his face was now visible behind the grilled front of the carrier. Both eyes were hidden by hair, but something about his pose told her Alexander was not in a good mood.

Nerving herself for the encounter, she opened the carrier. "Okay, Alexander, this is it. I don't like it any better than you do, so don't give me a hard time."

She retreated behind the carrier, hoping it would

blunt the fury of Alexander's attack. To her surprise he gave her only a cursory glance and then set out on a tour of the house. Because of his short legs and poor vision, this took an interminable time, necessitating the prolonged sniffing of every piece of furniture. Karen was tempted to hurry him along with a well-placed kick, but she was afraid to press her luck, even though she felt like an attendant pacing with measured steps behind some arthritic-ridden dowager empress.

Not until he had inspected every room did Alexander return to the kitchen, where he sat down with a thump and gave a hoarse demanding bark. Karen ran to get his food dish.

After eating, Alexander went outside and smelled the yard, pausing long enough to lift his leg and sprinkle one of Ruth's prize roses. Karen was too intimidated to protest. At least Alexander knew what needed to be done; she wouldn't have to stand in the doorway exhorting him as she had heard Rachel do. Rachel was so nice-minded she refused to use even the polite euphemisms. "Now be a big doggie," she would cry, in a horrible falsetto. "Be a good, big doggie, Alexander."

Karen had hoped Alexander would prefer to spend the day out-of-doors. The yard was fenced and shady; but it was a hot day and Alexander didn't like hot weather. Before she could close the back door, he had returned. This time he went straight to the parlor, where he collapsed with a thud and a grunt on Ruth's treasured pastel needlepoint hearthrug.

Karen made an involuntary movement of protest, but before she could order him off the rug Alexander shook his head vehemently, producing one eye that fixed itself on Karen with the clearest message she had ever seen in a single optic. She stepped back. Alexander wriggled into a comfortable position and began to snore.

Annoyed as she was by the dog's air of aristocratic hauteur, an air that accorded strangely with his distinctly plebeian appearance, Karen was also amused. Alexander had good taste. Perhaps the elegance of the room appealed to him. When Ruth was at home there were always flowers in the big silver bowls, according to the seasons—tulips and narcissus followed by lilac and sprays of dogwood, then roses and baby's breath, and, to round out the year, great bunches of chrysanthemums in the pink and lavender shades Ruth favored.

The dog's snores were rather soothing. I'll make up his bed for him later, in the kitchen, Karen told herself. In her heart of hearts she knew she had already lost the fight. Alexander had chosen his place and there he would stay. She would probably find herself arranging flowers in the silver bowls, to please his aristocratic tastes.

The soft chime of the clock on the landing reminded her that she was late. She hurried upstairs, tugging at the belt of her dress. Julie had grudgingly given her a few hours off so she could accompany Mrs. Mac to the airport, but this was Julie's last day; she was leaving for New England that evening, and for the next two weeks Karen would be in charge of the shop.

Alexander was still asleep when she left the house, feeling decidedly self-conscious in the vintage dress Julie had insisted she wear. It was an Edwardian afternoon gown, formal enough for a modern wedding, with a high, boned collar and a semi-train edged with lace. Karen had spent much of her spare time that week washing and ironing and mending and altering the dress. It was still too tight, but, she thought hopefully, not quite as tight as it had been when she first tried it on. One of Julie's customers was coming in from Potomac to see the dress and the other gowns Karen carried, chastely enclosed in a garment bag.

Karen had to give Julie credit. It was decent of her to let an employee use the premises to sell her own merchandise. Not that Julie's motives were entirely altruistic. She got her cut. Besides, Mrs. Mac had graciously allowed Julie to acquire a few bits of bric-a-brac, china, and crystal. Julie hoped for more—much, much more. It had been her idea that Karen should model her wares whenever possible, and Karen had been forced to agree that it never hurt to advertise.

In fact, she attracted less attention than she had expected. Georgetown was blasé about unusual costumes. A few people stared, and one girl stopped her to ask where she had bought the dress. So Julie was right, Karen thought; one potential customer in a three-block walk wasn't bad.

Her positive mood didn't last, though; Julie's behavior that afternoon would have driven a saint to homicide. She showered Karen with instructions as confused as they were impossible to carry out; and when, for the sixth or seventh time, she clutched her flyaway hair and moaned, "Oh, God, I must be crazy to leave town!" Karen's temper snapped.

"Then don't. Lord knows I've got enough to do without running your business for you!"

"Oh, sweetie, don't pay any attention to me," Julie cried. "You know how I am—"

"To my sorrow. You don't even need me, Rob could handle things here. And if an emergency should arise, you're only a few hours away."

"Don't you dare call unless it's a real emergency." Julie's eyes took on a faraway look. "I have a really interesting two weeks planned, if you know what I mean."

"Nothing will go wrong," Karen said. "Why don't

you leave right now? You aren't accomplishing anything except driving both of us up the wall."

"And me," came a voice from the rear of the shop. "Listening to you two screaming at each other is absolutely shattering my nerves. I shall burst into tears if I hear one more unkind word."

Julie paid no attention to this pathetic speech. She glanced at her watch. "I can't leave until Mrs. Schwarz comes, she'd be horribly offended. Damn the woman, where is she? She said three, and it's already three-thirty."

Mrs. Schwarz arrived at 4:10, apologizing and complaining about the traffic on the bridge. It was a handy excuse for anyone coming into the District, because it was usually true.

She shrieked with rapture at Karen's dress and asked to try it on. Karen complied, though one look at Mrs. Schwarz's comfortable contours convinced her the customer hadn't a prayer of getting into the dress. She did get into it, with a great deal of assistance from Julie and Karen, and the collapse of only one side seam. However, the dress refused to meet at the back.

Mrs. Schwarz said wistfully, "Perhaps if I wore a tighter girdle..."

"I'm afraid not," Karen said, looking at the six-inch gap.

"You couldn't let it out?"

"I've let it out as far as it will go." Karen added, "I shouldn't wear it either; it was made for a girl with a tiny waist and hardly any bust. You know, it's impossible to wear clothing like this if it's even the teeniest bit too small. The fabric is old and fragile, and the styles weren't designed for active women."

"I suppose you're right." Mrs. Schwarz was appeased by the tactful phrase "teeniest bit too small," though

84

it most certainly did not apply in her case. "Oh, well, such is life. I hope I haven't damaged the dress, dear. If I have, I'll be happy to pay—"

"No, that's all right," Karen said, carefully skinning the dress over Mrs. Schwarz's head. "One of the seams gave a little, that's all. I just basted it."

"Oh, you do your own alterations? That's nice to know. I must tell my friends about you."

Mrs. Schwarz bought one of the other dresses, a turn-of-the-century day dress of gold linen, hand-embroidered at the neck and hem. After she had departed in triumph, promising a return visit when Karen had more clothes ready, Karen stared in disbelief at Mrs. Schwarz's check. It was made out for two hundred and fifty dollars.

"I wouldn't have dared ask that much," she exclaimed. "I must say, Julie, I admire your nerve."

"You won't get prices like that out in the boonies," Julie said sourly. "That's fifty you owe me. I ought to get more, actually, since I set the price, but since it's you..."

"She must be crazy," Karen said. "The dress didn't even look good on her."

"That may be your opinion and it may be mine, but I suggest you keep such opinions to yourself. And remember, don't accept a check from anyone except the people on that list I gave you. Not even if the customer arrives in a chauffeur-driven Mercedes and is swathed in mink. Some of the richest people are the biggest crooks."

"I remember."

"And if I find a charge that hasn't been okayed, I'll take it out of your salary."

"All right, all right!"

Julie wrung her hands. "Oh, God! I must be mad to do this!"

CHAPTER *FOUR*

❖❖❖❖❖❖❖❖❖❖❖❖❖❖❖❖❖❖❖❖❖❖❖❖❖❖❖❖❖❖❖❖

*B*Y the time she finally persuaded Julie to leave, Karen had a splitting headache. Almost immediately Rob pranced away, golden curls agleam—"I anticipate a most interesting evening, my dear; I must save my strength!"— leaving the task of locking up to Karen. It was a complex procedure, involving an alarm system and an arrangement of steel grilles, and she performed it with painstaking concentration. It did not improve her mood to realize that if Rob's evening was as interesting as he hoped, he would probably be late to work next day.

As she headed homeward, holding her flounces high above the dirty sidewalk, she wondered uneasily what Alexander had been up to during her absence. Mrs. MacDougal let him roam freely among her treasures, and even Rachel admitted grudgingly that he was not destructive; but it was impossible to predict what he might do in a new environment, particularly if he resented the change.

Karen's steps quickened, even though she knew it was silly to hurry now. Alexander had had all afternoon to work his will.

He was not on the hearthrug, nor was that precious article damaged except for the inevitable accumulation of dog hair. Karen called. There was no answer.

She found Alexander in the kitchen standing by the back door. It wasn't difficult to deduce what he wanted, and she praised him effusively as she let him out. By a simple twitch of his shoulders Alexander expressed his contempt for this transparent attempt to win his approval.

He seemed content to stay outside, so Karen thankfully removed her elaborate and uncomfortable dress and settled down at the kitchen table with a glass of iced tea and the mail. Most of it was for Pat—professional journals, appeals for money from various causes worthy and unworthy, and a few bills. Karen put these aside to be dealt with later; her aunt and uncle had set up an account in her name so that she could pay the household expenses. She drew on it for her own needs, because she had to— the wages Julie gave her barely covered expenses—but she was keeping track of everything she spent on herself, with the intention of paying it back as soon as she could.

The only thing for her was a letter from a lawyer in Dubuque. It was the fourth such epistle she had received. She had not opened any of them, and after hesitating for a moment, she laid this one aside. Her headache was subsiding, but she was in no mood to cope with the painful emotions the letter would undoubtedly arouse. Except for the brief note in the box of her clothes, Jack had not communicated directly with her. Perhaps it was unfair to blame him. She hadn't written or called him either.

I suppose I ought to find a lawyer, she thought listlessly. Another unpleasant duty she had put off....

Well, she couldn't do anything about it until Monday. Offices were closed on the weekend and office workers, including lawyers, were relaxing at home, picnicking, entertaining friends. Enjoying themselves. Unlike some people, who had nothing to look forward to except the company of a homely, malevolent dog, and a pile of old clothes to mend.

At least she could get out of the house that evening. She had an appointment with another of Mrs. Mac-Dougal's friends, who had old laces and linens and a few pieces of clothing she might be willing to sell. Such visits had all the fascination of a voyage of exploration into unknown lands; one never knew what would turn up, junk or jewels, treasure or trash. In this case Karen's anticipation was tempered with mild trepidation, for Mrs. Mac had warned her that Mrs. Ferris was a very old friend indeed—"practically gaga" had been her appraisal.

Karen had protested. "I can't take advantage of someone who is senile. And suppose she changes her mind later, and accuses me of cheating or robbing her?"

"Oh, she has her lucid moments. Just make sure she signs a receipt and get the housekeeper to witness it. Betsy is a good soul, she's been with Joan Ferris for years."

Alexander demanded entry, so Karen let him in and fed him. He was only supposed to eat once a day, but she had no intention of trying to enforce rules Alexander didn't choose to obey. It was far too late in the game to turn him into a well-behaved, well-trained dog, even if she had felt strong enough to make the attempt. He deserved a little extra treat anyway. He must be missing his owner; he hadn't lunged at her ankles yet.

There was nothing wrong with his appetite. He polished off his food to the last crumb, belched, and then headed for the parlor, where he lay down on the rug before

Karen could stop him. I'll do something about the rug later, she told herself cravenly. There's no time now, I mustn't be late. Mrs. Ferris probably goes to bed at sunset.

However, before she could leave the house the telephone rang. Karen had been thinking about the letters from the lawyer; it came as something of a shock to hear the speaker identify himself as a member of the same profession.

"I don't suppose you remember me, miss—I beg your pardon, it's Mrs., isn't it? I'm afraid I can't recall your married name."

"Nevitt. But it won't be my name long."

"I beg your pardon?"

"That's why you called, isn't it? About my divorce? I do remember you, Mr. Bates, and I had planned to call you, but I must say I'm surprised Ruth would take it upon herself to talk to you without consulting me first."

"You refer, I presume, to the younger Mrs. MacDougal?"

"You are her lawyer, aren't you?"

"Our firm represents Mr. and Mrs. Patrick Mac-Dougal, yes. We also represent Mrs. MacDougal senior." He waited just long enough for Karen to realize that she had jumped to conclusions. Then he went on in tones of freezing politeness, "I assure you that no one has approached me on the matter of your domestic difficulties. I called about another matter entirely."

"I'm sorry," Karen muttered. "I'm a little upset, Mr. Bates, or I wouldn't have said that. Please excuse me."

"Certainly." The lawyer's voice thawed slightly. "I understand. Ordinarily we don't handle divorce cases, but if you would like me to recommend someone..."

"I would appreciate that. Perhaps I might call you

89

one day next week. I do hope nothing has happened to Mrs. MacDougal?"

"So far as I know, she is winging her way westward," the lawyer replied poetically. "It is not Mrs. MacDougal but her automobile that is the object of my concern."

"The Rolls? What's happened to it?"

That, Mr. Bates explained, was the problem. The car had not been delivered to the garage at the appointed time. The owner of the garage had not become concerned for several hours. He had been busy, and like everyone else in Washington, he considered traffic delays part of the normal scheme of things. Mr. Bates had not been notified until midafternoon, and it had taken several more hours to convince the alarmed lawyer that the car had indeed been stolen.

"But that's impossible," Karen exclaimed. "The Rolls is unique. How could anyone make off with it?"

"*How* it was done is still unknown. *That* it was done is, unfortunately, beyond any shadow of doubt. The chauffeur's quarters have been cleared out and the man himself has vanished. A Virginia state trooper saw the car heading south on Route 95 shortly after one P.M. The Virginia police are presently making inquiries along all the local routes leading off 95 between Occoquan and Fredericksburg, but they hold little hope of success. It is likely that the automobile was driven into a large closed van, which may now be well on its way to . . . anywhere."

"Oh, dear."

"You may well say so," remarked Mr. Bates morosely.

"Joseph—poor Joseph! How is he taking it?"

"Very badly indeed. He blames himself. Quite unnecessarily; it is no one's fault. All precautions were taken."

"Yes, I'm sure they were. Is there anything I can do? Look at mug shots, or—"

"No, no, certainly not. The young man had no local criminal record. I hired him myself; you can hardly suppose I would neglect to check that."

"I'm sure you did everything you could."

"I hope Mrs. MacDougal shares your sentiments," said Mr. Bates. "I telephoned you only to inquire whether you have in your possession any of Mrs. MacDougal's property."

"Well, really, Mr. Bates!"

"Pray don't misunderstand. I expressed myself badly; I am, I confess, somewhat distraught." Karen could almost see the lawyer mopping his brow. She didn't blame him; Mrs. MacDougal might not hold him responsible, but she could certainly be annoyed, and she was not in the habit of mincing words.

The lawyer went on, "It is necessary to assume that this was not, in police parlance, a one-man job. Whether the others involved were professional thieves or only amateurs is as yet unknown. It is probable that the automobile was the sole object of their interest. However, the police are keeping a close eye on the house, on the remote possibility that the miscreants may take advantage of Mrs. MacDougal's absence to loot the place. Mercifully the most valuable of the antiques have been stored and Mrs. MacDougal's jewels and silver are in her vault at the bank; but, knowing her eccentric habit of generosity, I thought it possible that she might have given you something to keep for her, or perhaps—"

Karen couldn't endure the careful, pedantic speech any longer. She knew what the lawyer was driving at, and she didn't like the idea at all.

91

"You mean they—he—that big hulk of a chauffeur—might try to break in here?"

"No, no, you mistake my meaning. I consider it most unlikely. Quite unlikely indeed. I have no desire to alarm you—"

"Well, you have!"

"Then she did give you—"

"Just her clothes."

The lawyer emitted a sharp bark of laughter. "I hardly think thieves would bother about a bundle of old clothing. That is all?"

"Yes. Oh, and the jewelry—a necklace and earrings. But it's not valuable, just semi-precious stones and enamel. She handed it to me when she got out of the car this morning—a little memento—"

"Jewelry." Mr. Bates' voice sounded hollow. "It isn't, by chance, of black enamel bordered in silver-gilt, set with rosettes of pearls, emeralds, and diamonds?"

Karen's hand flew to her throat. "Diamonds? Emeralds? I thought they were peridots and rhinestones—"

"The stones themselves are not valuable," said Mr. Bates. "However, the jewelry belonged to Dolley Madison. It is depicted in the Warren portrait, and its pedigree is authenticated."

"Oh, my—oh, good Lord! Honestly, I had no idea— I'll bring it right over to your office. I don't want—"

"Please calm yourself, Mrs. Nevitt. If Mrs. Mac-Dougal gave you the jewelry, she wants you to have the jewelry, and therefore you must keep the jewelry. I do suggest that you place it immediately in your safe-deposit box—"

"What safe-deposit box? I don't have one."

"Then you had better get one," said Mr. Bates dryly. "Is that all? You are certain she didn't give you the Beall emeralds or ask you to store her collection of Revere silver? I am relieved to hear it. Though the necklace and earrings are historic treasures, they are not intrinsically valuable, so I don't believe you need worry."

After he had hung up Karen took off the necklace and sat staring at it. So much for her expertise on the subject of antique jewelry! She hadn't even dated it correctly. It wasn't Victorian but Georgian, dating from the early part of the nineteenth century, before Victoria ascended the throne.

So Mr. Bates didn't believe she needed to worry. He was fairly sure the necklace and earrings would not attract a thief. It was nice that Mr. Bates was so unconcerned.

Even if the gang to which the chauffeur belonged decided to go after Mrs. MacDougal's other property, they might not be interested in the jewelry. The individual stones weren't worth much, and the set could not be pawned; it would be instantly recognized. But the same thing was true of the Rolls. And Horton knew she had the jewelry; not only had he seen Mrs. Mac give her the case, but she had removed one of the earrings during the drive back from the airport—held it up in full view of anyone who might glance into the rearview mirror.

Her fingers moved respectfully over the smooth surface of the enamel, the settings of the small gems. James Madison, fourth President of the United States, might have fastened the clasp around Dolley's plump neck. Dolley had worn it or carried it with her when she and the President escaped from Washington with the flames of the burning city reddening the sky behind them—the only time the capital had been sacked and destroyed by an invading enemy. Dolley had taken it all in her stride—a plump, pleasure-loving little woman who liked to wear turbans because they made her look taller. Washington Irving, among other admirers, had praised her beauty and contrasted it with the feeble face and diminutive figure of her husband. Pretty Dolley, with a pretty woman's fondness for nice clothes and jewelry...

The only reason Karen knew these things was that, by a strange coincidence, she had been reading about Dolley Madison only the night before, in the Georgetown legends book Julie had given her. Dolley wasn't really a Georgetown ghost, but she was certainly one of the most peripatetic of Washington's revenants, and as the author frankly admitted, distinguished spirits lent a book a certain cachet. Among other places, Dolley had been seen(?) in one of the old mansions on Dumbarton Avenue, where she must have danced and partied a number of times.

Karen put the necklace back in the case and checked to make sure the earrings were solidly fastened. She couldn't get to the bank tonight. Where could she hide the jewelry in the meantime? Then she remembered the secret drawer in Ruth's wardrobe. It wasn't very secret, since the hinges could be seen by anyone who looked closely, but it was the best she could do for Dolley at the moment.

Not that she really thought she was in danger of being burglarized. Horton had not struck her as the type who went in for esoteric objets d'art. Cars, yes. Perhaps he had simply fallen in love with the glamorous old automobile, as a woman might with a gown or a jewel, and had persuaded a few friends to join him in what must have seemed an irresistible opportunity. If she had not been so distressed on Mrs. MacDougal's account, Karen could have laughed when she remembered Horton's sudden descent from the formal manners of a hired employee. And the sheer effrontery of his last remark.... The five-dollar tip must have seemed a howling joke to him when he was about to make off with a car worth hundreds of thousands.

But as she showered and dressed she kept seeing Horton as he had stood in the hall, grinning down at her— his heavy features and massive chest; his hands, twice the size of hers. Harmless enough, no doubt; but not the figure one would like to meet in a dark alley. Or in a room of one's own house.

THE telephone call had delayed her. She arrived breathless and perspiring on Mrs. Ferris' doorstep. Externally the house on Thirty-sixth Street resembled Ruth's— a red brick Georgetown Federal of approximately the same age. Unlike its neighbors which it also resembled, it had a forlorn appearance; the small front yard was filled with weeds and the windows on the ground floor had draperies or shades drawn, like blind white eyes.

Karen's knock was promptly answered by a stout, smiling woman with gray hair arranged in an astonishing beehive coiffure. She drew Karen inside. "I'm sure glad to see you, honey. Glad to see anybody, to tell the truth! You don't mind if I call you Karen, do you? Miz MacDougal talks about you so much I feel like I know you. She's about the only human soul that ever comes here, God bless her. I'd just about go loony from lonesomeness if it wasn't for her—and my soaps, of course. Couldn't live without my soaps."

The vestibule was a gloomy cavern lit only by a single bulb in the chandelier. "Sorry about the dark," the housekeeper went on in a lower voice. "She"—with a significant nod at a shadow-filled doorway—"she doesn't like to waste electricity. Old age takes some people that way. Miserly. Don't let her cheat you on them old scraps she's trying to sell."

"I won't." Karen was grateful for an ally.

A quavery, querulous voice issued from the cavernous darkness of the parlor. "Who's that? Who are you talking to, Betsy? Is it that girl? Bring her in, bring her in; don't stand out there whispering about me. I can hear you. I can hear you saying things about me."

At first glance Mrs. Ferris was only a shapeless bundle, swathed in shawls and lap rugs despite the stifling heat of the room. The housekeeper turned on an overhead light and the bundle took on identity. The face that peered at Karen was a mass of wrinkles, the head almost hairless except for a few dry white wisps; but the eyes that met hers were alive and aware.

"Turn that off, Betsy," the old woman croaked. "Waste, always waste!"

Betsy winked at Karen. "Now, Miz Ferris, how can the young lady look at your junk in the dark?"

Mrs. Ferris acknowledged the truth of the statement with a grunt. Her clawed hands fumbled at something on her lap.

Blinking in the light—dim enough in itself, but dazzling after the gloom that had prevailed before—Karen was afraid to move from the doorway. The room was so cluttered with furniture, there was scarcely room to pass between the little tables and the overstuffed chairs, the horsehair sofas and the bookcases and bureaus and desks. And every surface was strewn with fabric. Crumpled silks and ragged linens draped the chairs, scraps of embroidery and lace black with dirt lay heaped on tables and footstools.

Karen's heart dropped down into her sandals. Junk

was right. How was she going to get out of here without buying something she couldn't use?

Mrs. Ferris raised her hands. Suspended from her twisted fingers was a web of creamy lace. "My wedding veil," she croaked. "Valenciennes. Worth a fortune. How much?"

The transaction took hours. At first the old lady haggled over every item and told interminable stories about each scrap. The stories, some tragic, some touching, some frankly slanderous, would have fascinated Karen if she had known any of the people concerned, and if she had not been so hot. She couldn't decide whether Mrs. Ferris was too stingy to turn on the air-conditioning, or so old she needed heat to keep her body functioning. *She* didn't perspire, but sweat beaded Karen's face and made her blouse stick to her body. As time went on, she would have been glad to pay any price just to get away, but the house-keeper's nods and winks confirmed her suspicion that Mrs. Ferris was enjoying the company, and the bargaining.

At last she began to tire and to wander down path-ways into the past, addressing Karen as Susie ("Her daughter," the housekeeper whispered. "Just say, 'yes, Mama.'") When Karen offered a flat sum for the last few boxes, sight unseen, she nodded wearily.

She perked up, though, when Karen handed over the money—Mrs. MacDougal had warned her she would be expected to pay cash— and scribbled her name on the prepared receipt. Karen had to call a taxi to carry away the loot, and when she left the room Mrs. Ferris was chuckling to herself as she counted the bills and silver, briskly as a bank cashier.

As she stood on the step with Betsy, waiting for the taxi, the housekeeper said, "You gave the old dear a real shot in the arm. She'll squirrel that money away before I get back in the room; Lord knows how much she's got tucked away, under chair cushions and behind pillows. And she'll talk for days about what a sharp bargainer she is."

"I hope I didn't cheat her."

"Good land, honey, that stuff has been rotting in the attic for thirty years or more. I'm glad to get it out of the house."

"But won't her children resent her selling family heirlooms? I mean, the wedding veil—"

"Well, honey, it's hers, isn't it? Seems to me she's entitled to do what she wants with it. There's no family except a daughter and granddaughter, and they sure don't put themselves out any for her; one of 'em comes by every month or so, and it's downright indecent how disappointed they are when they find she's still alive and kicking. Here's your taxi, honey."

The cabdriver good-naturedly helped Karen carry the overflowing cartons to the door and then left, his headlights cutting twin beams through the darkening street. Alexander ambled to the door and Karen began tugging the boxes into the house. She was anxious to examine her purchases in a decent light. Either she had made an excellent deal or she had just wasted $78.50. If it was the former, she had no qualms; she had had to work for every penny.

As she dragged the last of the boxes inside, the dog made a sudden dart for the door. Karen grabbed and missed; Alexander scampered down the steps and ran to the gate, barking furiously.

Thank goodness she had closed the gate. She went after the dog. He had stopped barking, but he seemed to be intent on something across the street.

A pool of darkness had gathered there, equidistant between two streetlights. The windows of the opposite house were unlighted. After a moment Alexander turned and went back into the house.

Until that moment Karen had forgotten her conversation with the lawyer. She was sorry to have been reminded. Not that Alexander's aggressiveness was significant; he might have been barking at a squirrel or a shadow. Nevertheless she retreated quickly into the house and locked the front door.

Alexander was sniffing at the cartons. A violent sneeze indicated his opinion; he stalked off, shaking his head.

Karen pulled the boxes into the dining room. She had cleared the long table and covered the surface with thick layers of newspaper so she could use it as a work table. She began unloading her purchases.

At first she was inclined to agree with Alexander, and her heart sank. Seventy-eight dollars wasn't much money, she supposed, but from the point of view of someone who had none at all, it was too much to waste on material that could never bring a profit. Just touching the fabrics made her want to scrub her hands. She reminded herself that she had been spoiled by the superb condition of Ruth's and Mrs. MacDougal's clothes. The things she had bought from Mrs. Mac's other friends had not been up to that standard, but neither had they been as bad as this. Most of the cloth reeked of mold and mustiness. Some appeared to have been stored without being washed. She shook out a long pink organdy dress stained all down the front; it looked as if it had been wrapped around a rusty iron frying pan.

But there were treasures among the trash. The laces were beautiful, ranging from separate pieces of edging and insertion only a foot long to big sections large enough to have been overskirts or dress panels. Most were of cotton; they would respond well to plain soap and water.

She took a double handful of laces, some of the ones that would require what her pamphlets called "heroic treatment," and carried them upstairs. Filling the basin in the bathroom with warm water and detergent, she left them to soak overnight. Tomorrow she would rinse them thoroughly and wash them again, adding a small amount of ordinary bleach to the water.

It was still early—early on a Friday night, the beginning of the weekend. Karen raised the window in the master bedroom, which looked over the street. The house across the way showed lighted windows now; the sound of voices drifted across to her. A puff of stale, hot air warmed her face and she lowered the window. Georgetown gardens were beautiful, but she didn't envy the people who were sitting in the one across the street, talking and drinking and having fun, in spite of the heat. At least she didn't envy them much. . . .

She went downstairs. Alexander raised his head when she turned on the lights in the parlor, but he did not move. He had refused to occupy his bed—antique basketry, lined with crushed velvet—when it was in the kitchen, so Karen had given up and put it in the parlor, on the hearthrug.

"Come on," she said. Her voice sounded strange in the empty room. "You're not much, Alexander, but you're better than nothing. How about coming upstairs with me?"

A rude sniff was the only reply. Karen had been prepared for a refusal. She held out the chicken breast she had taken from the refrigerator. Alexander was passionately fond of chicken—only the white meat, of course.

100

It took a while, but she finally got Alexander, and his bed, into her room. The only book on the bedside table was the Georgetown legends book. The phantom of Dolley Madison held no charm for Karen that night; she found a children's book in one of the bookcases in the hall.

Little Women was as bland and harmless as a piece of literature could be, and it finally put Karen to sleep. Yet she dreamed that night, for the first time since Ruth and Pat had left. She dreamed Horton was waltzing with Mrs. Ferris, he in his chauffeur's uniform, she swathed in her wedding veil like a mummy in its wrappings. The dance grew wilder and Horton lifted the fragile old woman clear off her feet, whirling her around like a withered leaf; and as the music swelled she shriveled and turned brown, until she *was* a leaf, sere and dead, but giant in size. Then Horton, grinning till his gums showed, let her go and she fluttered in diminishing circles around the room until someone opened a window and out she blew into the darkness. A faint shriek, like the squeal of a rusty hinge, shivered and died into silence.

KAREN had never believed in the virtues of being early to bed and early to rise, but in Washington, in the summer, the second part of the adage made good sense. From dawn to midmorning—sometimes earlier, during a severe heat wave—the temperature was at least tolerable.

It was a surprisingly sociable time of day, too. Joggers and runners and exercise buffs were out in full force, not only because of the relative coolness but because most of them worked during the day. Karen had been jogging, or trying to, for over a week. The first time she emerged from the house into the pale light and long, soft shadows, she had been self-conscious and a little uneasy. Now she enjoyed it. There was a camaraderie among the would-be healthy, a pleased awareness of their superiority over the slothful majority who were still snoring in their beds. The ruly dedicated ran in a state of profound detachment from reality, their eyes fixed in vacancy, their faces bright-red and streaming; but there were plenty like Karen, who had time for a friendly wave or grin, or gasped greeting, as they stumbled along. The tree-lined streets seemed cooler than they really were, and the towpath along the old B and O Canal was delightful at that time of day, shaded by surrounding buildings, with the water rippling gently under the footbridges.

Julie had given her a copy of the "new diet." Julie collected diets, though as far as anyone could observe she followed none. Karen was trying to stick to this one, though she found cottage cheese for breakfast an abomination difficult to accept, much less enjoy.

It was only a few minutes after eight when she returned to the house; time enough to do a load of laundry before she went to work. She couldn't believe how much she enjoyed washing clothes—not even in a machine, but tediously and carefully by hand.

The pamphlets she had obtained from the Smithsonian and the book Mrs. Mac had supplied intimidated her at first, with their dire warnings and their insistence on distilled water and special cleansing agents. In fact, they were singularly lacking in practical, precise advice. Most were written by or for museum curators, whose chief concern was preservation rather than appearance or wearability; Karen got the distinct impression that if these experts could have had their way, the garments wouldn't even have been displayed, but would have been packed away forever in special containers, safe from damaging light and touch.

The few books written for wearers and sellers of vintage clothing went to the opposite extreme. If the clothes can't be washed and cleaned by ordinary methods, don't bother with them, was the gist of their advice. Karen had had to rely on her own judgment and common sense in most cases. Anxious experimentation had proved to her that the white linens and cottons responded beautifully to soap and water and a careful use of bleaching agents. She learned to detect worn spots that might give way when wet, and she found that some long-set stains such as rust could not be removed without destroying the cloth itself. She tried the old methods—sun-bleaching, or lemon juice and water with a pinch of salt. One of Mrs. Mac's friends, delighted at finding an interested listener, told her how the frilly voluminous undergarments had been laundered when she was a girl—scrubbed by hand on a ridged wash-board, starched and sprinkled and rolled and ironed with heavy irons heated on the stove. Karen wasn't moved to buy a washboard or give up her handy electric steam iron, but she searched the stores for old-fashioned Argo starch and followed the directions on the box, boiling and strain-ing and diluting it as directed. It gave a better finish than spray starch, her mentor assured her, and lasted through several washings.

Part of Karen's pleasure was purely sensuous. It was good to handle the natural fabrics, linens and cottons and silks, and to see them transformed as if by magic from dingy, crumpled wads of cloth to garments dazzling in their whiteness and perky with starch.

There was another reason why she enjoyed a job she would once have considered unworthy of her intelli-gence. This job had visible, tangible results. They hung in lacy elegance from hangers and rods, and danced on the drying lines strung across the garden. They were the product of her own labors and her own good sense, and they would mean money in the bank—money she had earned. All she had ever gained from her long hours of labor for Jack was an occasional line in the finished book. "And finally I must thank my wife, who typed the manuscript...."

In the morning light the laces she had bought the previous night looked even better than she had hoped. She washed and bleached and rinsed again; by midmorning the clotheslines in the garden were full. Karen rewarded herself with a second cup of coffee—black—and sat down on the terrace to relax for a few minutes and admire the results of her labors.

She wondered how long it would be before the neighbors complained. The look was definitely not Georgetown, and even though the high fence ensured a degree of privacy, old Mr. DeVoto, who lived in the house to the north, was a first-class busybody. Let him object, she thought defiantly. But it would be nice to have her own place, in the country or in a small town, where the air was free of exhaust fumes and smog. She couldn't go on living with Ruth and Pat. Even if pride had not forbidden such a course, her uncle's temper would surely crack if he had to fight his way through dangling linens and laces every time he wanted to sit on the terrace or use the bathroom.

Karen arrived at the shop promptly at eleven, to find that Rob had already opened for business. Her surprise and pleasure at this unexpected development were cut short when Rob informed her that he was taking the afternoon off. He brushed her protests aside with an airy wave of the hand. "Darling, you must have more confidence in yourself. It's a piece of cake. I mean, sweetie, what's the problem?"

The problem was that Saturday was the busiest day of the week, when it would have been advantageous to have two people on duty. Rob knew this as well as Karen did, but although she was sorely tempted to give him a piece of her mind, she decided it was not worth the effort. She had no authority to hire or fire employees; if Rob took umbrage at her criticism and quit she would be left with no help at all. Like Alexander, he wasn't worth much, but he was better than nothing. She wondered how he managed to keep his job. He must have some hold over Julie, to get away with such a casual attitude; she had seen him do the same thing before. She couldn't believe Rob and Julie were lovers, though. Surely Rob wouldn't flaunt his affairs so flagrantly if that were the case. Perhaps there had been something between them in the past.

Rob left at two, reeking of some strong, supposedly sexy aftershave, and smirking in a way that made Karen want to throw something at him. Business was brisk. She didn't sell much, but the shop bell never stopped tinkling and she didn't have a moment to sit down. Finally, at around four, the traffic began to slow. The sunshine without was hazy with heat, and most people were heading for Happy Hour.

Karen had just collapsed into a chair when the telephone rang. Instead of reaching for it she eyed it warily; she was still smarting from the last call, from a dealer who had some urgent business with Julie—an appointment she had obviously forgotten, since she had said nothing about it. The dealer, not a well-bred man, had taken his ire out on Karen and she was in no mood for another such encounter.

However, the phone had to be answered. The voice

that replied to her formal "Old things. May I help you?" was familiar.

"Karen? This is Cheryl. Mark's sister."

"Oh, hello."

"Hello. I just happened to be in . . . I mean, I was wondering . . . I thought maybe you'd like to go to dinner or a movie or something tonight. I know it's awfully short notice—"

"That's no problem," Karen said. "I'm not exactly the most sought-after female in Washington."

"That makes two of us. Anyway, we're not alone; what's the ratio of women to men in this town—three to one?"

"More like ten to one, I think."

"I guess it feels that way to lots of women," Cheryl agreed. "Look, you don't have to say yes just for politeness. If you had other plans—"

"To tell you the truth, I had planned to spend the evening washing and ironing clothes. Not exactly a wild and frivolous time."

"It sounds absolutely thrilling compared to what I was looking forward to."

"I suppose Mark is busy," Karen said. Just like Mark, she was thinking—bringing the poor girl here to cook and keep house for him while he goes to all those glamorous parties. . . .

"He has to work tonight, the poor guy. I try to keep out of his way when he's preparing a speech or writing a bill, or whatever it is they do up there on the Hill. He wanders around the house talking to himself and running into the furniture—"

"Here comes a customer," Karen said, as the door opened. "Can I call you back?"

"Well, uh . . . I'm at a phone booth, actually, and . . ."

"Which just happens to be in the neighborhood?" Karen remembered Cheryl's first unfinished sentence. "Why don't you come to the shop and we'll decide what we want to do."

The customer was looking for antique jewelry. Karen displayed Julie's few pieces of Art Deco and Art Nouveau, and the customer, who was only interested in Victorian and Georgian jewelry, departed. The next person to enter was Cheryl. Karen realized she couldn't have been more than two blocks away when she called.

Her curls were limp with damp and her perspiring face shone like a mirror, but her smile would have cheered the most confirmed misogynist. You can't help being glad to see her, Karen thought; she's so openly glad to see you.

"Boy, it's hot out there," Cheryl announced, with the air of someone who has just made a new scientific discovery. "Are you all alone? Where's your assistant?"

"It's a moot point as to who is assisting whom, or if anybody is assisting anybody," Karen said.

"That bad, huh?"

"Oh, not really, I'm just in a bitchy mood. This is my first day without Julie and Rob decided to take the afternoon off. I guess I'm a little nervous. It's a big responsibility."

"Good experience, though," Cheryl said. "For running your own place."

"It's teaching me what not to do, at any rate. All this clutter and confusion isn't my style. It's too hard to keep track of things and people."

"Do you have much shoplifting?" Cheryl sounded as if she were genuinely interested.

That was all Karen needed. She didn't stop talking until she was interrupted by another customer, and after

107

she had dealt with him she was surprised to see that it was after five.

"We haven't even discussed what we're going to do this evening," she said, adding apologetically, "I didn't mean to monopolize the conversation. It's just that I have so much to do and it's on my mind all the time—"

"And it's so fascinating!" Cheryl said enthusiastically.

"I wouldn't say that." Karen began the complicated process of closing up. "The clothes themselves are fun, I love that part of it, but when I think about finding the right location and getting more stock and all the business end ... I guess that's it. We can go now."

"What computer system are you going to get?" Cheryl asked, helping Karen pull the grille across the door.

"Oh, God, don't mention computers! I'm going to start with a few old-fashioned ledgers. Maybe I can deal with them, I know I can't learn how to handle a computer."

"But that's—" Cheryl stopped suddenly.

"All set," Karen announced, dropping the keys into her purse. "I have to go home to check on the dog anyway; why don't we have a drink there and discuss our plans?"

They never did discuss plans for the evening; they didn't get to a movie or even to a restaurant. By the time they reached the house Karen was talking nonstop, her half-formulated plans and unexpressed worries pouring out in a verbal flood. Missing Mrs. MacDougal for her laughter and her companionship and her support, she had not realized how much she also missed a sounding board for new ideas. Cheryl was a perfect audience, asking an occasional question at just the right moment.

Alexander was waiting at the door, and not until she actually saw his featureless furry face did Karen remember she had failed to warn Cheryl of his habits. She tried to grab him as he charged, missed as she always did; cried out in warning. . . .

Cheryl's lifted foot caught Alexander square in the chest and tipped him gently onto his backside. For a moment he balanced, paws flailing in the air, jaws still moving; then he toppled over backward.

"I didn't kick him," Cheryl said earnestly. "He just ran into my foot; he isn't hurt."

"Only his dignity," Karen said, laughing as Alexander rolled over and strolled away. "Serves him right. He's not my dog, I was conned into keeping him for a friend."

"Mrs. MacDougal?"

"Why yes. How did you know?"

"She's a friend of Mark's. I've met her a couple of times; she's a sweetheart. Say, what's this story about her car being stolen?"

So it might well have been Mark she had seen at the airport, saying good-by. With red roses, yet. . . .

Karen explained about the Rolls as they trailed an aloof Alexander to the kitchen and tended to his needs. She found that Cheryl already knew the details, for Mark had called the lawyer that morning after seeing a paragraph in the newspaper.

"I don't think that lawyer appreciated having Mark call him," Cheryl said seriously. "I couldn't hear what he said, of course, but Mark answered him back in that cold, cutting way he has when he's mad. He said he never trusted that man—the chauffeur—and he wouldn't have hired him to look after a used Chevy, much less a car worth half a million bucks. I figure he must have been exaggerating, don't you? How could any car be worth that much?"

"He may have exaggerated, I don't know about

such things; but it was valuable—custom-built, and very expensive to begin with."

"You saw the guy, didn't you? Did he look like a crook?"

Karen was not anxious to discuss Horton, but the naive question made her laugh. "Crooks come in all shapes and sizes. Horton was definitely a large size. Handsome, if you like bulging muscles and wet red lips and fleshy cheeks. . . ."

"Which you obviously don't. Did he say any-thing—do anything—unusual?"

"He didn't make a pass at me, if that's what you mean." Karen knew that was what she meant, but she wondered what had prompted Cheryl to ask. Was it pos-sible that Mark . . . No, it wouldn't have occurred to him to worry about something like that. He was only concerned about the car.

She went on to tell Cheryl how Horton had reacted to her offer of a tip, adding, "Looking back on it, I realize why he was so amused, but I couldn't possibly have an-ticipated what was going to happen."

"Of course not."

"Anyway, it's no great tragedy. I'm sure the car was insured. Mrs. Mac would really be upset if someone had been hurt, but fortunately that wasn't the case. Would you let Alexander in, please, and we'll decide where we're going to go."

When Cheryl opened the door she saw the linens draping the clotheslines in back, and offered to help bring them in. Two hours later they were still sitting in the kitchen eating crackers and cheese and talking clothes, and it was Karen who finally changed the subject. "I'm being very rude. You must be starved."

"Not really. But you—"

"I'm trying to diet anyway. I'm sure I can find something here—salad, tuna. . . ."

"I couldn't impose on you like that."

Karen smiled. "Cheryl, you don't really want to go to a movie, do you?"

"Sure, if you do."

"There's nothing around I want to see."

"And everyplace is so crowded on Saturday night. . . ."

"It's such a pain getting dressed to go out. . . ."

Karen couldn't keep her face straight, and after a moment Cheryl grinned back at her, albeit somewhat shamefacedly. "I'm so damned obvious. You knew all along I invited myself over here so I could play with your toys."

"Saturday night is a bad night to be alone," Karen said, sobering. "You did me a favor. I am getting hungry, though. Let's see if there is anything fit to eat in the fridge."

Alexander approved of their staying home. He followed them upstairs of his own free will after supper and settled down in his velvet-lined bed. When Cheryl stooped to fondle his head he emitted a strange sound like a hoarse, magnified purr.

"He's a sweet little doggie," Cheryl said.

"He is not a sweet little doggie. But he seems to like you, for some reason. . . . Don't get me wrong, that wasn't an insult to you, but to Alexander. He hates everybody except Mrs. Mac."

"I expect he misses her."

"It's hard to tell what Alexander thinks or feels. His manners seem to be improving slightly, though. Maybe a good swift kick now and then is what he needs."

"I'm glad you have a dog," Cheryl said. She glanced at the windows, now black with unrelieved night. Moon and stars had little chance of penetrating the cloud of smog and humidity that hung over the city. "You aren't nervous here alone?"

"No."

"I didn't mean you should be. There's nothing to be scared of, nothing at all—"

"There's plenty to be scared of," Karen said bluntly. She began taking clothes out of the wardrobe, for she had promised Cheryl a fashion show of Mrs. MacDougal's designer gowns. "Burglars and muggers and rapists and perverts. But that's true of any big city, and if you spent all your time worrying about what might happen, you'd never accomplish anything."

Cheryl, who had stretched out across the bed, rose up with a shriek. She was not disagreeing with Karen's remarks, but reacting to the Schiaparelli Karen held.

"Oh, Lord, it's the most beautiful thing I ever saw! Is that real mink?"

"Try it on," Karen invited.

"Could I? Oh, no, I shouldn't. It's too delicate—"

She allowed herself to be persuaded. The dress was too big for her, but as she pirouetted and turned in front of the mirror her face shone with delight. "I never in my life wore anything this classy," she breathed. "I never expected I would. How much is it worth?"

"A thousand dollars, maybe more. A Vionnet sold at auction a few years ago for about eight thousand."

Cheryl's eyes grew round as silver dollars. "Jeesus! Here, get it off me."

"Don't be silly. Everything has to go to the cleaner before it's sold; they've all been hanging in an attic for decades. Actually," Karen added, "I'm glad you inspired me to get these things out. According to the books I've been reading, some of them shouldn't be on hangers. See here, on this Poiret, how the weight of the beaded skirt has pulled the threads loose."

"If you can't hang them up, how do you store them?"

"Lying flat, and unfolded. They ought to be wrapped in cotton or acid-free paper, because regular tissue contains chemicals that will eventually damage the fabric. I got out some old muslin sheets of Ruth's—she saves everything!—to put around them, but I just haven't had time."

"Can I help? Please?"

"Twist my arm," Karen said, smiling.

As they folded and wrapped the dresses, Cheryl said hesitantly, "I'm awfully dumb. I never heard of Vionnet or some of those other people."

She stumbled a little over the name. Karen didn't correct her. "I'd never heard of them either, until I started reading. Oh, I knew a few names—don't ask me how, I guess if you like clothes you absorb some information without realizing it. Worth, for instance; he was the first of the great designers. An Englishman, surprisingly enough; we think of haute couture as French. He did open his salon in Paris, and most of his successors were French. Paul Poiret, Callot Soeurs—they really were sisters—and Jeanne Lanvin were among the first. Madeleine Vionnet was another great designer who wasn't really successful until the twenties, but she has been called 'the architect among dressmakers.' Her clothes looked soft and flowing, but they were so cleverly constructed that they emphasized all the wearer's good points and glossed over the defects. This is one of hers; isn't it a lovely blue? Supposedly the color was her own special discovery."

Much as she admired the designer clothes, it was the "whites" that pleased Cheryl most. "They're more my kind of clothes. Simple cottons and crochet, like my grandma used to do. I don't feel as if I was a bird in borrowed feathers."

"They look good on you," Karen said, admiring the sleeveless camisole and full, ruffled petticoat Cheryl was modeling. "I think it's because you have the right kind of figure."

"Big boobs and a fat tush," said Cheryl, making a face.

"The Edwardians wouldn't have put it that way. An hour-glass figure, madam, nicely rounded as a woman should be. Now I look ridiculous in clothes of that period. I'm too tall and I'm practically flat fore and aft, with no visible waistline."

"This is your style." Cheryl held up a shimmering peach nightgown, cut low in front and clinging across the hips. "What do you call it?"

"It's a bias-cut satin nightgown from the thirties. The Jean Harlow look. I might have been able to wear it once. . . ."

"Try it on. Come on, you have to play too."

Karen had to tug the gown down over her hips, but it was something of a boost to her ego that she could get it on at all. "If I don't breathe I'm all right," she said, sucking in her stomach.

"You look absolutely super. That's your style all right, lean and slinky. You know, you may have something with this idea of analyzing women's figures according to historical periods. Maybe we—I mean, you—could start a fashion-guidance salon, like the color-analysis business. You know, winter, spring, fall, summer colors?"

"The world is full of opportunities," Karen said ironically, peeling the nightgown cautiously over her head.

Later, as she sat cross-legged on the bed watching

Cheryl rummage through a box of odds and ends, she was still thinking about what she had said, and regretting her lapse into cynicism. Cheryl had not complained or asked for sympathy, and heaven knew she had a right. She had obviously been deeply in love, and to lose a young husband so unexpectedly, to find herself poor and untrained, with a child to support, was a much more difficult situation than Karen had to face.

"Some of these things are awful dirty," Cheryl remarked, still rummaging.

"They aren't as bad as the lot I acquired last night. I dropped a few off at the cleaners today, but I doubt he can do much with them."

"This would be real pretty if it was clean."

"Let's see."

Cheryl tossed it to her—a lavender crepe-de-chine blouse with cap sleeves and a scalloped hem.

"I'll try washing it," Karen said doubtfully. "Some silks wash in cold water and turn out well, but in this case the fabric is so worn it will probably tear. What's that one?"

Cheryl straightened, holding a short jacket with leg-o'-mutton sleeves and a high collar. The fabric was silk taffeta with tiny black-and-white checks, and a complex scrolled pattern of black braid edged the lapels and waistline. From top to bottom the entire garment was cut by parallel slashes. Only the stitching at the shoulder and around the hem held them in place; they fluttered like strips of bunting as Cheryl lifted the garment.

"That's beyond repair," Karen said. "Too bad; it was a pretty thing once. Shattered silk."

"Shattered? It looks like it had been slashed by a knife."

Karen laughed. "Nothing so dramatic. It's a condition you sometimes find in silks from around the turn

115

of the century, when manufacturers used a finishing process to weight the fabric and improve its appearance. The substance contained metallic salts; eventually they rotted the fabric, but only along the warp—hence the parallel tears."

"Can't it be repaired?"

"According to one of my books, 'there is no remedy.'"

"What a sad phrase!"

"It is, rather. True, though. Just toss it into the wastebasket."

"You're going to throw it away?"

"Might as well. 'There is no remedy.'"

"Can I have it?"

"Why . . . Of course you can. Though what you are going to do with it—"

"The trimming can be salvaged," Cheryl said, examining the jacket with a pensive expression. "The braid and the cute little buttons."

"You're welcome to it. It's of no use to me."

From Cheryl's grateful thanks one would have thought she had had a Chanel gown bestowed upon her. She really does love these things, Karen thought.

"I guess I'd better get going," Cheryl said reluctantly. "Mark said to call him when I was ready to leave. . . ."

She looked doubtfully at Karen, who said calmly, "That's a good idea. It's not easy to get a cab on Saturday night."

But the suggestion had cast a slight air of constraint, and when they went downstairs to wait for Mark, Cheryl was obviously ill at ease. "I don't suppose you'd be interested in going to an auction tomorrow," she said.

"An auction?"

"Yes, up in central Maryland. You mentioned you'd

have to start finding other sources of merchandise and I just thought . . . But I don't suppose you want to."

Karen had not realized until that moment how much she had dreaded the long Sunday alone. "That sounds like fun."

Cheryl's eyes lit up. "Does it really? Would you really like to go? I'm crazy about auctions, but it's not so much fun going alone. I've been buying some things for Mark. You wouldn't believe the junk that boy has, and a man in his position needs classy furniture, don't you think? And I've seen old clothes—what do you call them, vintage?—at auctions, and you said you'd be needing jewelry and other things too. . . . Oh, that's great. I hate Sundays, there's nothing to do except study, and I've already done my next assignment. I'll see if Mark needs the car."

"I have a car. It's my uncle's, actually; he made me get a D.C. license so I could keep the car in running order while he's gone. I've only driven it once since he left, so I guess I ought to take it out again."

"That's good, because then we can stay as long as we want. I know how to get there. I made Mark take me once, but he hates auctions."

"I'll pick you up," Karen said slowly. She had just realized what she had gotten herself into by admitting she had a car.

"You don't have to do that." Cheryl's exuberant grin faded. "I'm being pushy again," she muttered. "I should have waited for you to call me, I'm always the one who . . . But I thought maybe you didn't like . . . I don't know what happened with you and Mark, he never said, honest he didn't, but I wondered . . . So that's why I keep inviting you all the time."

It may have sounded like a non sequitur, but Karen had no difficulty in following Cheryl's train of thought.

She laughed lightly. "I don't know why you should think I want to avoid Mark. We were ... we were good friends once, but that was a long time ago. My feelings toward him are ... are perfectly amiable. Casual, but—er—amiable."

"Really?"

"Really. What time tomorrow?"

"We ought to leave early so we can be there when it starts. But you don't have to come get me, it will save time if I take a cab here, then we can get right onto the parkway. Suppose I come at eight. Is that too early?"

"No, that's fine."

"There's Mark. I'd better run. I hope they have some old clothes! But even if they don't, it will be good practice for you, bidding and all that. You have to be very sly and tricky."

Karen laughed. Cheryl being tricky was a sight she wanted to see.

She stood watching as Cheryl got into the waiting car. Mark didn't get out, or wave. I got more attention from Horton, Karen thought wryly. But of course Mark's windows were closed because of the air-conditioning. The night air was hazy with mist and close as a steam bath.

He did sound the horn, though, as he drove off— a familiar syncopated signal that sent a stab of memory along Karen's nerves.

A lurid pinkish glow lit the sky. Faintly to her ears came the sounds of revelry by night—isolated shrieks of laughter, the beat of music, the throb of automobile engines. As usual, every legal parking space along the street was filled. People were more cautious about parking illegally these days; the District police didn't fool around, they booted or towed violators instead of issuing meaningless tickets. Shadows passed along the sidewalk; people hurrying to and from the night spots on Wisconsin, residents walking dogs or taking a late-night stroll. Lots of people around. Nothing to be nervous about.

She went back in and followed Alexander through his nightly routine—the final trip to the comfort station in the back yard, and the reward for good behavior, a gourmet dog biscuit. He didn't linger over his outdoor activities, and Karen was glad to close the door against the shrouded night. There were lights outside the back door, but they did not extend far into the darkness.

She handed over the biscuit and then dropped her hand onto the dog's head in a brief caress. "No squirrels out there tonight, Alexander? Let's hit the sack, okay?"

CHAPTER FIVE

❖❖❖❖❖❖❖❖❖❖❖❖❖❖❖❖❖❖❖❖❖❖❖❖❖❖❖❖❖❖❖❖❖❖

K*AREN* cut her jogging short next morning, but Cheryl was early and she was still rummaging through her clothes trying to decide what to wear when the doorbell rang. She had no idea what constituted proper attire for a country auction; presumably pearls and mink were not appropriate, which was just as well, because she possessed neither. Except, of course, for the tiny pearls in Dolley's necklace and the mink trim on the Schiaparelli gown.

She ran downstairs to admit Cheryl and apologize for being late. When she explained her dilemma about what to wear, Cheryl looked surprised.

"The coolest thing you've got. It's already pushing eighty degrees. And comfortable shoes."

She was wearing sneakers almost as battered as Karen's, and her legs were bare. A sleeveless white blouse and a dirndl skirt almost old enough to qualify as vintage completed her costume, and as Karen dashed back upstairs to finish dressing she thought how relaxing it was to be with someone who dressed for comfort instead of style— and who wouldn't make malicious remarks about how other people looked.

When she came back down, Cheryl was sitting on the stairs talking to Alexander, who sat with his fuzzy head tilted to one side as if listening.

"I'm sorry, I didn't even offer you a cup of coffee," Karen said.

"No time; we'd better get going if we want to be there before the auction starts. Do you have a couple of lightweight stools or lawn chairs? This place doesn't have seating, and it could be a long day."

Carrying the chairs, they walked to the garage where Pat kept his car, several blocks from the house.

"Wow," Cheryl said admiringly. "What a car! It's a Porsche, isn't it?"

"Yes. The MacDougals have a weakness for fancy automobiles. Frankly, I hate sports cars, I always feel as if I'm sitting right smack on the pavement, and trucks look like cliffs. Can you squeeze in, or shall I back out?"

"No problem. There's not much trunk space, is there? I hope we don't fall in love with anything bigger than a breadbox today. I suppose you'll be getting a station wagon, or a van?"

"Oh, Lord, that's another problem I hadn't considered." Karen eased the car carefully out of the garage. "I don't know what made me think I could go into business for myself, I'm so damned disorganized...."

"Nobody who was disorganized could do those things you did for your husband—taking notes and reading all those books."

"I didn't do anything a halfway competent secretary couldn't do. And according to Jack, I didn't do it very well. Do I turn right or left at M Street?"

Cheryl gave her a peculiar look but said only, "Right. Then straight on."

Traffic patterns had changed in the past ten years and Karen was a little nervous about Pat's valuable car. Not until she had left the Washington Beltway and was heading north on 270 did she really relax.

"The worst is over," Cheryl said encouragingly. "You're a good driver."

"That kid in the pickup didn't think so. What was it he said?"

"Don't ask. He was drunk anyhow."

"This car is Pat's baby," Karen explained. "He'd kill me if anything happened to it. And I haven't done much city driving lately. Jack always..."

She fell silent; she had determined she wasn't going to say anything that could be interpreted as a complaint or a demand for sympathy. After a moment Cheryl said, "I had the same problem."

"You did?"

"Sure. The trouble with being married is that you let the other guy do so many things. You share. Then, when you're alone...I suppose it's just as hard for men. They feel as helpless about cooking and cleaning as we do when we have to fix a leaky faucet or put oil in the car."

"Help," Karen said. "Don't remind me of all the things I can't do! I don't think I've ever put oil in the car."

"I'll show you, it's easy. The only thing to remember," Cheryl said solemnly, "is that the oil doesn't go in the same little hole the dipstick is in."

"Dipstick?"

"I'll show you that too." Cheryl grinned, then sobered again. "There were times when I thought it wouldn't be the big tragedy that defeated me, but the constant little aggravations, day after day. At least you can learn to handle the little things. You can't fix a broken heart or a broken spirit so easy. . . . The next exit is ours."

Though they were in good time, with a quarter of an hour to go before the auction was to begin, there were already cars parked on both sides of the narrow road leading to a graveled lot next to a low, sprawling building. A man directed them into a field, and Karen guided the car over bumps and humps to the end of a row of other vehicles. She gritted her teeth and prayed for Pat's muffler; the field had been roughly mowed, but not leveled.

"Looks like a big crowd," she said, as they got out.

"There are two kinds of people here," Cheryl explained. "Dealers like you—this is their business, after all—and people who just get a kick out of attending auctions."

Karen felt a small thrill at the matter-of-fact tone in which Cheryl had said "dealers like you." It was, however, partly a shudder of trepidation. "I don't know what I'm doing," she groaned.

"Well, you have some idea of what things are worth," Cheryl said. "What prices you can ask, I mean. You just figure out how much you can afford to spend and don't go over that amount when you bid."

"It can't be as simple as that."

"Just about." Cheryl gave a wriggle of pleasure. "This is such fun. I'm one of the second group. If I didn't have other things to do, I'd be at an auction or flea market or yard sale every darned day."

Innocently delighted at being able to display her knowledge, Cheryl explained the arrangements. The auction building, open on one side, contained the choicer

123

items that were to be sold. The auctioneer's ·podium, at the front, was flanked by long tables piled with small items—glasses and china, clocks and lamps, linens and ornaments. Furniture was stacked around the perimeter, leaving the center open for the bidders. This space was already half-filled with portable chairs, some occupied, some empty.

They set up their own chairs in a strategic spot and then Cheryl led Karen outside. Here the less valuable merchandise was arranged in parallel lines. It was a motley, shabby collection—chairs with no seats, tables with no finish, chests of drawers with half the drawers missing, rusty tools and pieces of machinery, and dozens upon dozens of cardboard cartons filled with everything from books to empty jelly jars.

"This is just junk," Karen exclaimed.

"Junk to you, treasure trove to people who are willing to do some painting and repairing. Come on, he'll be starting soon, probably with these box lots. I want to have a look at the linens. You never know...."

That phrase, Karen soon realized, was the bidder's creed. You never knew what might have been overlooked by a busy auctioneer or an ignorant seller. Among the dime-store ornaments might be a Sèvres saucer; a hand-knit cotton-warp bedspread could be hidden under piles of moth-eaten blankets. Watching Cheryl as she squatted and rummaged, her skirts trailing in the dust, Karen began to get the urge too.

When the auctioneer's voice rose over the hubbub, announcing the sale was about to begin, Cheryl rose to her feet and dusted off her hands. "We'd better get our numbers. There's nothing here you want, is there?"

Karen agreed that there was not. The most exciting thing Cheryl had turned up was a set of kitchen towels embroidered with puppies in strident shades of green and red.

They stood in line to register. After displaying her driver's license and giving her telephone number, Karen was issued a piece of cardboard with a number scrawled on it. The process struck her as extremely casual, but when she said as much to Cheryl, the latter shrugged.

"I guess the big expensive places ask for bank references and like that, but there isn't a lot of money involved in these small auctions. If you pass a bad check, the word gets around and then you can't play anymore. They don't usually take out-of-state checks, though, so it's lucky you have a local driver's license. The District is considered local, here and in Virginia. What you really ought to get is a dealer's number, then you wouldn't have to pay state sales tax."

Karen rolled her eyes and threw up her hands at the reminder of another chore to be done, and Cheryl laughed self-consciously. "There I go again. Why don't you just tell me to shut up when I butt into your business?"

They returned to the scene of the action, which had warmed up considerably in both senses of the word. A crowd surrounded the auctioneer; they attached themselves to the fringes.

At first Karen found the proceedings confusing. Microphone in hand, the auctioneer, a tall, rawboned man wearing a Western-style straw hat moved slowly down the line of merchandise. Sometimes one of his assistants held up the item being auctioned, but Karen was not always sure precisely what was about to be sold, and the bidding went with terrifying speed—or so it seemed to her. She had never attended an auction before. It was a popular avocation with some faculty wives, but she had never had time for such things. There was always a paper to be typed

125

or a set of references to check, and besides, Jack despised secondhand merchandise. He didn't even like antiques, only neat, clean reproductions.

"Here's a nice lot, folks," the auctioneer drawled as his assistant lifted a cardboard carton. "Sheets, towels, hardly used. Who'll start it off with ten bucks? Seven-fifty, then. Five..."

The bidding started at two dollars and went up by fifty-cent increments. "That was a good buy," Cheryl said, as the box was finally knocked down for eight dollars. "But it's early yet, the crowd is just getting started."

"Good buy? Who wants sheets other people have used?"

"You sleep on 'em all the time in hotels," Cheryl said practically. "Do you know how much new sheets cost, even on sale? How're you doing—getting the hang of it?"

"I need to scratch my chin," Karen said nervously. "But I'm afraid to move. Some of these people seem to bid by raising an eyebrow, or wriggling their ears."

Cheryl grinned. "No problem. Fred's a good auctioneer; he knows a serious bidder from a nervous twitcher. Just hold up your card when you want to bid. But watch out for auction fever."

"What's that?"

"Bidding on things you don't want and don't need."

"Why would anybody do that?"

"It's like a disease," Cheryl said seriously. "It still happens to me sometimes; comes on without warning. You find yourself going higher and higher and you can't seem to stop. If you see me doing it, just take my card away from me and don't let me have it back, even if I beg."

Karen laughed, thinking she was joking. Nothing like that would ever affect her! She decided, though, that she would rather accept some unwanted article than admit she had made a gesture in error; many of the bidders were known to the auctioneer, and he interspersed his droning spiel with jokes and friendly insults. "Sam, if you don't want the stuff, stop waving your hat; I don't care if the flies are driving you crazy. Lady, you're raising your own bid; it's okay by me, but try to keep track, will you?"

Cheryl bought a box of bedding for six dollars, and Karen regretted her earlier snobbish comment. The sheets weren't for Mark's expensive town house; they were for the home Cheryl hoped to establish for herself and her little boy.

The sun rose higher and the complexions of the bidders turned pink and shiny with sweat. A few people left, having attained their hearts' desires or lost them to higher bidders, but the crowd increased as late-comers arrived. The auctioneer turned his mike over to a colleague and retired into the shade.

Karen was about to suggest that they emulate him when the attack Cheryl had warned her of occurred. It came on her with the suddenness of a sharp pang of indigestion, when a box of odds and ends was about to be knocked down for two dollars. Before she knew what she was doing, she was waving her cardboard ticket high above her head.

"Two-fifty," the auctioneer droned. "Do I hear three bucks?"

He didn't hear three bucks, for the excellent reason that there was nothing in the box except two rusty license plates and a red plaster dog with a chipped ear. The auctioneer's assistant deposited the box at Karen's feet, and Cheryl giggled. "What did you do that for?"

"I don't know," Karen admitted.

She and Cheryl contemplated the red plaster dog. "A rare example of antique folk art," said Cheryl.

127

The two exchanged glances and dissolved into laughter. "I warned you," Cheryl gasped, wiping her eyes. "Give me your card."

"No, no. I'm all right now," Karen assured her, clutching the magic ticket. "I won't do it again, I promise."

When the auctioneer started on the last row of decrepit furniture, Cheryl glanced at her watch. "Let's get something to eat and check out the things inside. It should take him about half an hour to finish this lot."

"No, wait a minute," Karen said abstractedly. "I want to see how much he gets for that old rusty stove."

"No, you don't. Aren't you hungry?"

"No. I just might be able to use that—"

"Karen!"

"Oh, all right," Karen grumbled, and let herself be led away.

Karen was glad she had a knowledgeable companion; she would not have thought to bring something to sit on, and now that her fit of auction fever was subsiding she realized her legs were wobbly with weariness. They found their chairs and Karen collapsed with a sigh.

"I should have told you to bring a hat," Cheryl said, looking anxiously at Karen's flushed face.

"I'm fine. Just let me sit a minute."

"You stay there, I'll get us something to drink."

She returned with cold drinks and sandwiches and two pieces of cake. Karen decided to forget about her diet; the cake was homemade and delicious. Refreshed and revived, she got to her feet and headed purposefully for the tables at the front of the shed, followed by an amused Cheryl.

Karen was tempted to linger over the dishes and glassware. Some of the pieces, especially the hand-painted Bavarian and Austrian bowls, were quite charming. However, after having watched Julie sell a single goblet for three hundred dollars and another that looked identical for twenty-five, she had decided she would not deal in such items. She simply didn't know enough about them, and she couldn't become an expert in every field of antiques.

One table was piled with linens and quilts. The choicer of these items were displayed on wooden racks, and Karen reached a covetous hand toward an appliquéd quilt, each square of which had a different pattern.

"That's an album quilt," Cheryl said. "The squares were made by different friends—"

"I know, Julie had one. She sells these things for five and six hundred dollars. If I could get it for two hundred—"

"You won't," said another woman, who was subjecting the quilt to a searching scrutiny.

Karen stared at her. She was a pleasant-faced person, about Karen's age, with brown hair pulled back into a ponytail and laughter lines around her mouth; but Karen's viewpoint had changed. All other bidders were now potential rivals, and she was prepared to dislike each and every one of them.

"Are you going to bid?" she asked suspiciously.

"Probably. But I won't get it either. See that gal over there?" A flick of her thumb indicated a tall, white-haired woman dressed elegantly and incongruously in a knit dress, hose, and heels. "That's Liz Nafziger. She's got more money than God, and she collects linens and quilts. She can top any offer I could make, because I have to make my profit."

"You're a dealer?" Karen asked.

The woman nodded. "I have a shop in Harper's Ferry. Quilts, coverlets, old lace, vintage clothing."

"My friend is a dealer, too," Cheryl said proudly. "She specializes in vintage."

"Oh?" The other woman's smile faded; she and Karen studied one another warily. "Where's your shop?"

"I don't have one yet," Karen admitted. "I'm just starting. To be honest, I don't know what I'm doing."

"Sisters under the skin." The other woman held out a tanned dusty hand. "Helen Johnson."

Karen introduced herself and Cheryl. "I don't want to bid against you," she began.

"Boy, do you have a lot to learn," Helen said bluntly. "You bid against anybody and everybody, dear, and the devil take the hindmost. Don't bid against Liz, though, unless you want to run the price up just for spite. And speaking of spite, there's one you want to watch out for— see that fat little dumpling with the rosy cheeks and the sweet smile? She's got a place in Baltimore and she'll rearrange the boxes while you aren't looking."

"I don't understand."

Helen nudged the cardboard cartons under the table with her sandaled toe. "Well, suppose you scrounge around in these boxes and find something you'd like to have. You're bidding on the whole lot, but that one piece makes it worthwhile. So when your box comes up, you bid, and you get it cheap, and you think, hip hip hurrah— until you take a closer look and discover the one item you wanted isn't there. By a strange coincidence it happened to work its way into the box Margie just bought."

"It's very nice of you to tell me these things," Karen said humbly.

"You'll find it pays to stay on good terms with your colleagues in crime," Helen said. "We can help each other out now and then because we aren't competing, in the usual sense; our merchandise is one of a kind. If a customer comes in who is looking for a particular style or size I don't have, I'll send her on to you, and you do the same for me. If a check bounces on you, you warn me, and vice versa. Once you acquire a reputation for square dealing, people will be more likely to deal fairly with you. Don't expect any special favors, though," she added with a smile. "Not even from me."

"But doesn't it make sense for dealers to agree beforehand not to bid against each other—taking turns on the items they all want?"

Helen tried to look shocked. "Why, Karen, that's considered unethical, if not downright immoral." The amusement she had attempted to suppress surfaced in an unexpected dimple; grinning, she added, "I'm sure you wouldn't dream of doing such a thing, any more than I would. At least you shouldn't discuss it aloud."

She turned with apparent casualness to a heap of linens that had been left in a hopeless tangle by inquiring buyers. Helen's tanned, capable hands sorted swiftly through them.

"Nothing here," she announced. "Actually, I seldom buy at auctions. The merchandise is usually in terrible condition."

"Where do you get your stock?" Karen asked innocently.

Helen moved on to another pile of fabrics without answering. Karen was about to repeat the question when Cheryl nudged her. "Would you tell other dealers about your sources?" she whispered.

"Oh," Karen whispered back.

There were a few old dresses and bits of wearing apparel in the pile Helen was examining. One caught Karen's eye, and after Helen had tossed it aside she picked it up.

It was a dress made of ivory silk, the body unfitted, the modest neckline bordered with lace. A deep flounce of lace trimmed the hem, and rows of pearls, some of them missing, edged the neck and hipline. The rotted remains of a silk flower clung horribly to the left hip, like a big brown spider.

"How pretty," said the romantic Cheryl, seeing the dress as it had once been, not as it was now. "What period is it, Karen?"

Karen glanced at Helen. "Late twenties or early thirties, I think," she said timidly.

Helen nodded. "It's in terrible condition. The lace is hopelessly rotted and most of the beads are gone."

"But the fabric of the dress is in good shape," Cheryl said.

She was right; there were not even perspiration stains, which, as Karen had learned, made a silk garment useless to a dealer. Perspiration rotted silk and left a stain that no cleaner could remove.

"It's a wedding dress," she said.

Cheryl laughed. "She must have got married in January, in an unheated church. Or else she was the calmest bride in recorded history."

"But who would sell her wedding dress, or her mother's?" Karen asked. "I bought a veil from someone the other day; honestly, it's enough to make you a cynic about marriage."

"It was mine," said a voice behind them.

An arm reached out and seized the dress. The arm belonged to an elderly woman wearing a cotton house dress and faded sneakers. Her lined, deeply tanned face was bare of make-up and her hair had been pulled back into a tight, ugly bun. Her eyes, deep-set under bushy gray brows, fixed on the dress with strange intensity.

"Mine," she repeated in a crooning voice. "I wore it in 1931. I was seventeen years old. Henry was thirty-eight. Quite a catch, Henry was. A member of the legal profession, from a fine old family. I poisoned him in 1965."

With no change of tone or expression she tossed the dress onto the table and stalked away.

"What did she say?" Karen gasped.

Helen chuckled. "Mrs. Grossmuller is a little ... " She twirled her finger alongside her ear.

"She didn't really poison him, did she?" Cheryl asked, fascinated.

"Who knows? He was a judge, and reputedly one of the meanest bastards in the state. Mrs. G. was never arrested, anyhow."

Helen wandered off, with a casual flip of her hand. The shed was filling up and the auctioneer came in to start the sale.

As Karen had expected, Helen bid on the wedding dress. So did Mrs. Grossmuller. She started the bidding at "two bits" and kept repeating the same amount in a stentorian voice, which the auctioneer blandly ignored. He knocked the dress down to Karen for twenty-five dollars. She knew she could replace the rotted lace from pieces in Mrs. Ferris' collection. Repaired and restored, the dress would probably sell for two hundred dollars or more. Vintage wedding dresses were popular with young brides who went in for the nostalgic look.

She bought a few other garments and had to be forcibly restrained from bidding on a Bavarian chocolate set to which she had taken a fancy. It went for a price at least as high as anything Julie would have asked. Helen had been right about the album quilt; the collector she had pointed out bought it for $675.

It was late afternoon before Karen and Cheryl decided there was nothing else they wanted. They paid for their purchases and gathered up their belongings. As they left the building, Helen Johnson raised a beckoning hand, and they stopped to speak with her.

"Here's my card," she said, handing it to Karen. "Come by or give me a call sometime."

"That's very kind of you," Karen said.

Helen shrugged. "As I said, we can sometimes give one another a helping hand."

"I don't have a card yet." Karen dug in her purse, found paper and pencil. "Here's my address and phone number. . . . Thanks a lot, Helen."

"Don't thank me till I do something for you. Oh-oh, here comes Mrs. Grossmuller; excuse me if I make myself scarce. I've heard that story about her poisoning dear Henry too many times."

She glided gracefully out of the danger zone, but Karen, trying to pick up the chairs and clothing she had set down when she wrote her address for Helen, was fairly caught.

"Changed my mind," Mrs. Grossmuller announced. "I don't want to sell my dress. Give you two bits for it."

"But I paid twenty-five dollars," Karen protested.

She expected a scene and was not looking forward to an argument with the old woman who was, despite her age, heavy-set and formidable-looking. To her relief and surprise, Mrs. Grossmuller suddenly changed her mind.

"Oh, well, that's all right then. You might's well have it as anyone. What did you say your name was?"

Somewhat reluctantly, Karen told her. "How do you do," said Mrs. Grossmuller, in an abrupt change to stateliness. "I am Mrs. Henry Grossmuller. Judge Grossmuller's widow. I poisoned him, you know. In 1965."

Mrs. Grossmuller trailed them to their car, chatting amiably. Except for occasional references to the murder of her husband, her conversation was perfectly lucid until Karen and Cheryl were in the car and Karen had started the engine. Then Mrs. Grossmuller thrust her head in the open window and grinned fiendishly at Karen.

"Twenty-five dollars, eh? Thank you, my dear, I admit the money will not be unwelcome. But you're loony, you know; the dress isn't worth two bits."

The last they saw of her she was wandering down the line of parked cars.

"You don't suppose she's driving, do you?" Cheryl exclaimed.

"How else could she get here?" Karen steered carefully across the bumpy field. "Just because she has a little bee in her bonnet doesn't mean she's incompetent."

"So you say," Cheryl remarked skeptically. "One thing about this business, Karen: you sure meet some fascinating people."

THEY stopped for supper at a country inn, to avoid a sudden thunderstorm that rumbled through, turning the road into a shallow, running stream. Karen felt self-conscious about entering a restaurant in her sweat-stained, rumpled clothes, but when Cheryl explained to the hostess that they had been auctioning all day, the woman nodded understandingly. "Fred Behm's? Hear he had a good crowd. Hope you were lucky."

They shared a half carafe of wine in the low-ceilinged, candlelit dining room and Karen found herself talking about things she hadn't even told Ruth. Cheryl did not need wine to loosen her tongue; she talked to everybody, including the waitress, in a way that would have left Jack in a state of horrified disgust. The conversation bore useful fruit; the waitress knew of a place in Woodsboro that might be for rent, all fixed up; it had been a craft shop.

She also knew Mrs. Grossmuller. "Poor old soul, she's a little strange. Not crazy nor nothing, she can take care of herself all right. Just kind of—well—strange. They say she's got millions stashed away, but the way she acts you'd think she was dirt poor. Want your coffee now or later?"

"I like places like this," Cheryl announced. "People are so friendly. Not like Washington."

She admitted she missed her friends back home. Some of the people she had met through Mark were nice enough, but they weren't interested in the things she cared about. Karen sympathized; but when she hinted that Mark should not have forced such an incompatible role on his sister, Cheryl was quick to defend him.

"He doesn't make me do anything I don't want to do. I never go to those really formal parties with him; I don't know the right way to act, and I'd just embarrass him. But I owe him so much, and I like to do everything I can to help him."

"I'm surprised you don't want to rush back tonight to get his dinner," Karen said. She regretted her sarcastic tone as soon as she spoke, but Cheryl appeared not to notice it.

"Listen, I'm in no hurry to get back, believe me. Tonight is the Murder Club, and those guys—"

"The what?"

Cheryl giggled. "That's what I call it. It's just Mark and a buddy of his sitting around drinking beer and arguing. They argue about everything under the sun, actually, but Tony is a cop—a detective—and he's interested in crime."

"I suppose he would be," Karen agreed. "But isn't that rather a busman's holiday for him? I'd think he would get enough of crime at work."

"Yeah, you would, wouldn't you? But the cases they discuss are old ones—classic unsolved crimes, Tony calls them. One time I remember they spent the whole night arguing about some king of England who murdered his two little nephews. Only Mark said he didn't."

"Richard the Third?"

"I guess so. That's right, you know all about history." Cheryl looked at her respectfully. "It was all Greek to me. But you know, some of them are kind of interesting. I'm real squeamish—I never would go hunting with Joe, even though I am a damned good shot—but there's something about those old cases, they happened such a long time ago they don't seem real. More like a book."

"So Mark thinks Richard the Third was innocent," Karen said, amused.

"Oh, you know Mark, he'll argue about anything. He takes the opposite side just to get Tony mad. There was one time when they had a big fight about something that happened back in the 1850s—the Bell Witch, I think it was—"

"Witch? That's not crime, that's pure superstition."

"Sure, you know that and I know that—and Mark knows it too. He likes to get Tony riled up. Tony says everything has a rational explanation, and when Mark starts talking about poltergeists and haunted houses, he just about blows his stack."

"I think I'd like Tony."

"You'll have to meet him. He's a nice guy."

"But not when the Murder Club is in session. I

can't imagine how anyone could find that sort of thing entertaining."

"Really? I couldn't help noticing that book on your bedside table...."

At first Karen couldn't imagine what Cheryl was talking about. "Oh, the Georgetown legends book," she exclaimed. "Julie foisted that off on me the other day; either she hoped it would give me nightmares, or she expected the story about Mrs. MacDougal would upset me."

"Swell friend," Cheryl said. "Don't tell me Mrs. MacDougal has a ghost. But I guess if there was such a thing, it would hang out in a house like hers."

"It wasn't a ghost story, it was an old scandal," Karen said distastefully. "Fifty years old. According to the book, some idiot shot himself in Mrs. Mac's billiard room —killed himself for love of her."

Cheryl grinned and quickly sobered. "I'm sorry! But it sounds so silly when you put it that way."

"It sounds pretty silly any way you put it," Karen agreed. "But you're right about the deadening effect of time; it's impossible to get emotionally involved in something that happened so long ago."

"You wouldn't say that if you could hear Tony and Mark arguing about that King Richard," Cheryl said darkly.

The storm had passed by the time they left the restaurant. There was little traffic on the quiet country road, and they drove in companionable silence for a while as stars blossomed in the darkening west. Then Cheryl, who had been stroking the soft silk of the old wedding dress, said dreamily, "I know you must get sick of hearing me say it, but I really do admire you, Karen."

"I'll be older than Mrs. Mac before I get tired of

hearing that. But if you're referring to my business plans, such as they are, I haven't done anything worthy of admiration; it was pure good luck and the good will of friends that got me started."

"But it's such a fascinating business. The old dresses and underwear—excuse me, lingerie—it's as if they were alive, you know? They have histories just the way people do."

"To me they're just merchandise," Karen said, touching the brake as a pair of bright circles reflected her headlights. The rabbit prudently withdrew into the brush at the side of the road.

"Watch out for—oh, good, you saw him. You can't mean that; you have lots of imagination. Like this wedding dress. Can't you picture that poor girl, barely seventeen, standing there in front of the minister—cold as ice, because she was marrying a man she feared and hated...."

"What a romantic you are," Karen said amiably. "Just because the lucky lady didn't perspire—"

"She hated him," Cheryl insisted. "I know she did."

Karen was silent. Cheryl nudged her. "You're thinking about something. I can practically hear you thinking. What?"

"I was remembering something that happened last week," Karen admitted. "A girl came in and wanted to try on the flapper dress I had in the window. Light-pink chiffon with sequins and crystal beads. It fit her well—she was one of those skinny little things, practically anorexic—but she barely had it over her head before she began trying to tear it off. I could have killed her; you can't be rough with clothes like that, they're too old and fragile. I said something rude—well, not really screaming rude, cold and nasty. She stared at me with big, pale-blue eyes, just like a dead fish, and said, 'Can't you feel the vibes? Some-

139

thing awful happened to the woman who wore that dress! I wouldn't have it if you gave it to me.'"

"Geez," said Cheryl, impressed.

"I thought she was just being dramatic. And," Karen added firmly, "I still think so."

"Oh, right. I wasn't trying to suggest there was anything spooky about it. Like Tony says, everything has a rational explanation. The way I feel about this dress comes from meeting Mrs. Grossmuller and hearing her talk about—about her husband. But the clothes themselves can give you clues about the people they belonged to, can't they? Suppose the seams are all pulled and stretched; you figure the woman was either too poor to buy a new dress after she gained weight or too vain to admit she needed a bigger size."

"Clothes are historical artifacts, like pottery and tools," Karen agreed. "I suppose they have an additional mystique because they actually touched and were shaped by the people who wore them. A historian can learn a great deal about a culture from costume—not only the bare facts of fashion, but the social and political attitudes of the period. The clothing women wore in the late nineteenth century directly reflects their status; tight corsets and heavy, cumbersome fabrics and long skirts prevented the wearers from engaging in any useful activity whatever."

"You sure know a lot of fancy words," Cheryl said.

Her voice was noncommittal, and in the darkness Karen could not see her face. "I didn't mean," she began.

"Oh, hey, I like it." After a moment Cheryl added, "You don't talk down to me. I appreciate that."

Karen decided to park on the street that night rather than carry their purchases all the way from the garage.

She had to drive around the block several times before she found a legal parking space. Except for streaks of sullen crimson low in the west, the skies were dark; the streetlights sent shimmering reflection across the wet pavement.

Karen had not expected they would be so late, and she had neglected to leave any lights burning. As they felt their way carefully along the short stretch of sidewalk between the gate and the steps, the carton Cheryl carried slipped from her arms, spilling the contents onto the ground.

"Damn," Cheryl said. "Oh well, they needed washing anyway. Don't try to help me, Karen, you've got your arms full. How about turning on some lights so I can see what I'm doing?"

Karen ran up the steps, trying to find her key without losing her grip on the chairs and the armful of clothes. Cheryl was still crawling under the boxwood that lined the walk when Karen opened the door and stepped into the darkened hall.

Before she could reach for the light switch, something grabbed her. The attack was so unexpected that pure shock froze her for an instant—time enough for the fumbling, anonymous hands to find her throat and close around it. The door slammed shut with a crash like a rifle shot, and from somewhere in the house came the frenzied, muffled barking of a dog. Those sounds, and the thick hoarse voice whispering were all she heard before the roaring of the blood in her ears drowned out sound altogether.

Light dazzled her eyes when she forced them open. She was lying on her back staring up at the chandelier in the hall. No one else was there except Alexander. He was sitting a few feet from her, and although his eyes were invisible as usual, she deduced from his alert pose that he

141

was staring at her. As she turned her head he let out a sharp peremptory bark and went trotting off.

Running footsteps heralded the arrival of Cheryl, breathless and pale. She knelt beside Karen.

"He got away, dammit! Are you all right? Just lie still. I called the police; they should be here any minute."

"Don't believe it." Karen clutched her throat. "I'm all right. Help me get up."

With Cheryl's assistance she staggered into the parlor and dropped onto the sofa. Cheryl peered anxiously at her.

"How about a cup of tea?"

"How about a stiff drink?" said Karen.

"Right." Cheryl went in search of refreshment and Karen rearranged her skirt, and her scattered thoughts. Physically she was not in bad shape. A lump on the back of her head and a sore spot on her throat seemed to be the extent of the damage. But for some reason she couldn't stop shaking. The sight of Alexander wandering nonchalantly around the room infuriated her.

Cheryl came back with a glass in each hand. "I could do with a little something myself," she announced. "But I'm not so sure about you. How many fingers am I holding up?"

"None. You've got all ten of them wrapped around those glasses. I don't have a concussion, Cheryl, I just bumped my head when I fell. There's nothing wrong with me except—except..."

"Shock," Cheryl said gently, steadying her shaking hand. "Here. Take it slow."

She had brought brandy—the conventional remedy for swooning females. Karen hated brandy, but she didn't say so. The beverage lived up to its reputation; after a few sips her hands stopped quivering.

She let Cheryl take the glass and then leaned back against the cushions. The color had returned to Cheryl's face; she had been as white as a bleached petticoat. Sipping her own brandy, she said, "We're going to make a great impression on the cops, both stinking of alcohol."

"Don't expect the cops to show up for a while. The weekend revelers are winding up their celebrations, and a little old break-in isn't going to impress the boys in blue."

However, it was not long before there was a vigorous pounding on the front door and Karen said in surprise, "Such enthusiasm. Cheryl, would you—"

Cheryl rose slowly. "I think maybe," she began.

"Oh, wait. Where's Alexander?"

"In the kitchen, I guess. Karen, I guess I should tell you—"

"You had better let them in before they kick the door down. I hadn't expected such zeal."

As she should have known, from the vehemence of the knocking and from Cheryl's hesitation, it was not the police. Naturally, she would call Mark, as well as the cops, Karen thought. He's her brother, after all.

There was another man with Mark, a muscular youngish man whose Hispanic ancestry showed in his olive complexion and opaque dark eyes. He was almost too handsome to be believable; one expected to see a make-up person hovering, and hear a director shout, "Ready for Take 2." A heavy mustache only partially concealed his delicate, finely cut lips. Like Mark, he was wearing jeans and a short-sleeved shirt open at the neck. Compared to Mark he looked as dapper as the male model he resembled. Mark had not shaved that day and his shirt was streaked with stains. Beer stains, Karen thought, remembering Mark's habit of using a beer can as a baton, waving it in the air to orchestrate his arguments, banging it on the table to emphasize a point. He was always very apologetic when it splashed on the furniture and people's clothes....

No one spoke for a few seconds. Then, with an irritated glance at his silent, staring companion, the dark man smiled in an embarrassed fashion. "I'm Tony Cardoza—"

Karen was still shaky and disoriented. "You can't be. Tony the cop? Tony the rationalist? Tony who spends his spare time arguing about old murders?"

Cardoza's smile faltered, and Mark found his voice. "What's the matter with you, Karen?" His eyes moved to the two glasses side by side on the coffee table and his eyebrows rose. "I might have known. Sitting here getting sloshed—you never did have any head for liquor—damn it, Cheryl, don't you know better than to give alcohol to an injured person? She could be concussed, or—or—"

Karen interrupted with a yell. "Watch out! Cheryl—grab him—"

It was too late. Alexander had only hesitated for a moment because he could not decide whom to bite first. His leap was one of his best ever. He caught Mark square in the calf and hung there, slobbering and growling, while Cardoza stared and Mark swore and Cheryl burst into a peal of slightly hysterical laughter.

The police arrived shortly thereafter. Cheryl carried Alexander away in disgrace, and although Cardoza identified himself to the patrolmen, he effaced himself thereafter, following Cheryl to the kitchen. Mark sat stiff and scowling, his arms folded, while an officer took down Karen's statement. The dignity of his demeanor was only slightly marred by his scruffy cheeks and chin and by the loose flap of denim that bared a sizable patch of hairy leg.

The statement didn't take long. There was little Karen could add to the bare facts: "I walked in the door and somebody grabbed me by the throat." Mark followed the policemen out. He had not spoken to Karen since his initial outburst.

Left alone, she drowsed off, and did not awaken until she heard Cheryl say softly, "Poor baby, she's worn out. I'm going to put her to bed. Mark, could you—"

Karen's eyes popped open. "I don't need to be carried. Mark, if you dare—I'm too heavy—"

"That's okay, I've been working out." His smile recalled an old, almost forgotten joke between them. His slim build and lack of inches had caused a lot of people, including Karen herself initially, to underestimate his wiry strength. In spite of herself, her stiff lip curved in an answering smile. But she stiffened again when his arms lifted her and held her close. Mark's smile faded.

"Relax, will you? I'm not about to take unfair advantage of you, not with a cop right at my elbow...."

"I—uh," said Cardoza. "I guess I'll be running along."

"Please don't," Karen murmured. "I mean—I'd like to talk to you, about what happened."

Mark started up the stairs, moving as lightly as if he were carrying an empty dress. Karen could feel the hard muscles under his thin shirt, but for all the emotion he displayed he might as *well* have been carrying an empty dress. Why did I do that? Karen thought wretchedly—and then, with a spurt of anger, And why does he have to be so supersensitive?

"I'm not even here officially," Cardoza protested.

He was still at the foot of the stairs, still talking, when Mark carried Karen into her room. Her shriek brought him bounding up. "What the hell—"

"Look—just look!" Karen cried. "Look what he did!

All my things—all over—I spent hours washing and ironing—"

"Please—stop—kicking," Mark gasped. "I don't want to drop you on your—"

"Put me down!"

"Where?"

It was a reasonable question. The mattress had been dragged off the bed, trailing sheets and blankets. Every drawer in the dresser and chifferobe stood open, the contents tumbled as if by a giant beater or tossed helter-skelter onto the floor.

Cardoza leaned against the doorjamb breathing heavily. "Don't scare me like that," he said furiously. "I know the room is a mess, I saw it. So are the other bedrooms—"

Karen burst into tears and buried her face against Mark's shoulder.

"Crying over a bunch of clothes," Cardoza said, shaking his head. "I'll never figure women out. There I was thinking what a cool lady you were, kidding me and smiling sweetly—"

"That's a chauvinist speech if I ever heard one," Cheryl snapped. "It was delayed shock, that's what it was. I'd like to see how you'd behave after somebody choked you half to death and scared the fits out of you. And what's more, Tony Cardoza—"

"Okay, okay." Cardoza smiled at Cheryl affectionately, as he might have smiled at a pretty child. "I should have warned her, I guess. You too, Cheryl, I thought you were going to start bawling too."

"If you knew how much time and effort it took to get those clothes so nice and pretty, you'd be more sympathetic. No, put that down; it's sweet of you to try and help, but you're just making more of a mess."

Karen was in her bed, which had been restored to its proper state. Murmuring distressfully, Cheryl was smoothing and folding the crumpled garments. Mark was sprawled in the one comfortable overstuffed chair, his legs stretched out, his expression dour. Cardoza occupied the desk chair; arms folded, one ankle resting on the other knee, he looked quite at home. In fact, there was something insanely cozy about the whole business, and they were all drinking tea—which Cheryl seemed to consider a universal panacea—except Cardoza, who held a can of beer.

"I'm not driving," he had explained gravely. "But Mark can't have any."

Karen felt rather like a medieval monarch holding court, as those gentry were wont to do in their bedrooms, but even more like a sick child being visited by the grown-ups. Cheryl had bundled her into the least crumpled of the white nightgowns; it had long sleeves with ruffles on the cuffs, and it buttoned clear up to its ruffled neckline.

"So he got in through a window," Mark said.

"Must have. The back door was standing open, but we can assume he unlocked it after he entered the house—in preparation for the conventional quick getaway. The lock hadn't been tampered with, and one of the downstairs windows was unlocked."

"Stupid," said Mark, looking at Karen.

Cardoza came to her defense. "Those old window locks are easy to force. Too bad people around here are so set on their antiques; the wooden frames are so warped you can get a crowbar in the crack between the sashes."

"Fingerprints," said Mark. "Footprints."

"Mark, we've been over this a dozen times," Cardoza said patiently. "The back yard is all grass and graveled paths and nice neat mulch. Not a patch of handy mud

147

anywhere. The guy got on the roof of the garden shed and went over the wall. As for fingerprints—sure, they'll check, but most crooks know enough these days to wear gloves."

"In the middle of the summer? Your favorite junkie, who is supposedly too strung-out to know which end his head is on?"

"What are you trying to suggest—that Mrs. Nevitt has a secret enemy who's out to strangle her?" Cardoza demanded.

Karen's eyes opened wide. "Hey, wait—"

"No, of course not," Mark muttered.

"He was alone," Cardoza said. "Cheryl only saw one person—nothing more than a shadow, actually. If there had been two of them or more, they might have ... well, they might not have run away. So it wasn't a gang. Gangs go after TV sets, hi-fi's, things like that. This guy tore up the bedrooms, not the downstairs. He was looking for money or for jewelry—something small and portable he could hock. That's the obvious, rational conclusion, and I'm damned if I can see why you're trying to make something more out of it."

"I'm not. I just don't understand why—"

The telephone rang, and Mark reached across Karen and picked it up. "Hello? Yes, she's here, but she isn't able to talk right now. May I take ... What? My name is Brinckley. Mark Brinckley. Who is this?"

In the silence that followed they heard the far-off voice quacking unintelligibly. A wave of dull crimson moved slowly up Mark's face from the base of his throat to his hairline.

Karen sat up. She had seen the phenomenon before. It was not a sign of shame or embarrassment; Mark was never embarrassed. It was pure red rage.

148

"Give me the phone," she said, and took it from his hand. "Hello, Jack."

"I've been trying to reach you all day. Where have you been?"

"Out."

"Obviously. Why haven't you answered the letters from my lawyer?"

The cool incisive voice, with its peremptory tone, affected her as it always had. Instead of replying in kind, she heard herself mutter feebly, "I haven't been . . . I was a little upset. . . ."

"Not too upset to console yourself, I see. It was rather careless of Brinckley to answer the telephone at this hour of the night. Adultery is still grounds for divorce in this state, and some judges are influenced by it when it comes to alimony."

"But I didn't—"

"Not that I have any objections. Being a fair-minded man, I felt obliged to point out the legal complications you may incur. Personally I'm relieved that you have found a protector. You are quite incapable of managing your life by yourself. It's decent of Brinckley to take you back. Some men might be more particular about secondhand goods. But he never was very fastidious."

His voice had risen in pitch and in intensity. "Hang up," Mark said suddenly.

"What?" Karen felt dazed. Jack was still talking; he sounded shrill and hysterical.

"Hang up the phone."

"Oh." Karen obeyed. She wiped her hand on the bedspread.

Said Cardoza, staring into space, "You can get a restraining order, you know."

The telephone rang again. Mark picked it up. He

was about to slam it back into the cradle, unanswered, when Cardoza said casually, "Do you mind if I..."

Mark's angry color subsided. Smiling grimly, he handed over the telephone. Karen said nothing. She felt bruised and sick with shame. She had a good idea of what Jack had said to Mark.

"This is Detective Cardoza of the D.C. police," Cardoza announced. "Who's this?"

The reply was inaudible. Cardoza grinned and winked at Karen. "Mrs. Nevitt's home was broken into tonight and she was assaulted. Where did you say you were calling from? I see. You have witnesses who can verify that, I suppose?"

The quacking began again. Cardoza's smile broadened, displaying even white teeth. "Yes, I'm sure you are concerned. I'll tell her that. Good night, Mr. Nevitt." He hung up. "That should take care of him."

"Mr. Cardoza," Karen said earnestly, "I think I love you."

"In that case, you'd better start calling me Tony."

"If you two have quite finished the compliments," said Mark, through tight lips, "I'd like to return to the case at hand."

"There isn't any case," Tony said, his patience wearing thin. "At least there's nothing we can follow up. If we had a description..."

"I didn't even see him," Karen said. "He grabbed me from behind and it was pitch-dark in the hall."

"You're sure it was a man?"

"Well, of course...No. No, I'm not sure of anything except that he, she, or it had two hands."

"No distinctive smell? After-shave, unwashed body..." He glanced at Mark. "Marijuana, alcohol?"

"I can't remember."

"Did you feel anything other than the hands? Cloth, hair, mustache, fur? Big hands or small? Calloused?"

Karen kept shaking her head. "I didn't see him or smell him or feel him or . . . Oh!"

Tony sat up alertly. "What?"

"I heard him," Karen said slowly. "He whispered. Right in my ear, the same words over and over, like a recording. 'Where is it, where is it, where is it?'"

C*HAPTER* S*IX*

❖❖❖❖❖❖❖❖❖❖❖❖❖❖❖❖❖❖❖❖❖❖❖❖❖❖❖❖❖❖

T*HE* memory of that obscene whisper was Karen's last coherent recollection. She was vaguely aware of voices and movement as Cheryl shooed the men out of the room, and she half-heard Cheryl's statement that she intended to spend the night. She was too drowsy to protest the offer even if she wanted to, which she emphatically did not. Once recalled, the whisper went on echoing in the corridors of her mind; she was almost afraid to go to sleep for fear it would follow her into her dreams.

However, she slept heavily and dreamlessly until she was awakened by a thud that shook the bed, and by a hot and not particularly sweet-smelling breath on her face. It was, of course, Alexander. The sight of his prize-winning ugliness only inches from her eyes was so horrible she promptly closed them again. Alexander bit her on the nose. Karen sat up with a shriek. Alexander retreated to the foot of the bed, where he sat down and began to bark.

The gist of his comments would have been plain to the slowest intelligence. When Karen looked at the clock she was forced to agree he was right. It was after nine o'clock. This was a workday, and she was supposed to be at the shop at eleven.

She got out of bed. Except for a sore throat, she felt remarkably well, and the sight of the confusion that still reigned in her room filled her with a burst of anger that sent the adrenaline pumping healthily through her veins. Cheryl had not had time to do more than fold and hang the crumpled garments over the chairs and bureau. The empty dangling sleeves and limp skirts looked pathetic. Most would need washing and ironing; at the thought of all her hours of wasted work, Karen stamped her foot and swore.

The door opened a crack before she had finished swearing and Cheryl's voice remarked, "I don't blame you, but maybe you should save your strength. Ready for breakfast?"

"You shouldn't have gone to all that trouble," Karen said.

"No trouble." Cheryl put the tray on the desk, which was practically the only uncluttered surface in the room. Sadly surveying the confusion, she shook her head. "It sure is a mess. But you know, you're lucky in a way; they're just dirty and wrinkled. I've heard of cases where the burglars got mad because they couldn't find drugs or money and they slashed everything with knives and—well—got them dirty. . . ."

"I know." Karen sniffed appreciatively. "That coffee smells great. You are going to join me, I hope."

"I brought two cups." Cheryl pulled up a chair. Alexander, smelling bacon, came out from under the bed and squatted at her feet.

Karen scowled at him. "My, my, how charming you are when you smell food."

"He doesn't bite people out of meanness," Cheryl assured her. "It's just a habit. He sure is devoted to you, he wouldn't leave your room last night."

"That's a new twist. He's been barely civil."

Alexander put his front paws on Cheryl's knee and barked. Cheryl meekly handed over the strip of bacon she had been about to eat, and Alexander retreated under a chair, growling over his prize.

"He does look more cheerful today," Karen said. "I guess he needed an interest in life. There's nothing like a burglar to perk a dog up. But I can't give him any prizes as a watchdog."

"It wasn't his fault. He was shut up in the dining room. You look pretty cheerful yourself for someone who was half strangled last night. How do you feel?"

"My throat is a little sore, but otherwise I feel fine." Karen forced down a mouthful of scrambled eggs. Her stomach was still queasy, but she was grateful for Cheryl's efforts, and even more for Cheryl's willingness to pretend that nothing more distressing than an attempted burglary had occurred the previous night.

"I might be in much worse shape if you hadn't rushed to the rescue," she said. "It was very brave of you, Cheryl, but it was also very foolhardy. How did you get in? I seem to remember hearing the door slam. . . ."

"Well, that was how I knew something was wrong. I figured you wouldn't slam the door in my face and leave me out there in the dark! Luckily you had left your keys in the lock. All I saw when I opened the door was something dark and shapeless, fading away into the shadows. By the time I turned on the light and made sure you weren't badly hurt and let Alexander out of the dining

154

room, he'd gone out the back door. I should have chased him right away."

"Good Lord, no, you shouldn't have," Karen said sharply. "You did exactly right."

"You aren't mad because I called Mark?"

"No, I'm not mad at you." Karen took a deep breath and plunged into the subject she had avoided. It felt like jumping into a pool, not of water, but of some viscous slimy liquid. "I'm only sorry you had to overhear that telephone conversation."

"I didn't really hear anything."

"You heard enough to realize what was going on. You know Mark as well as . . . you know him better than I do; you've seen him look like that, you can imagine what was being said. Jack has a tongue like an adder; it leaves welts that sting for days. At least," Karen said, with a dreary little laugh, "Mark can derive some satisfaction from having his accusations confirmed. I called him paranoid and egotistical when he told me Jack's principal reason for marrying me was to get back at him. Now I know he was right. I ought to tell him so. It's the least I can do after subjecting him to that—that garbage."

"Stop it," Cheryl said sharply.

"Stop what?" Karen had expected sympathy; she had not expected to see a scowl darken Cheryl's face and hear the anger in her voice.

"Stop blaming yourself for everything. So you made a mistake. Everybody makes them. It's not your fault that your husband is a mean bastard. And Mark is a big boy. He's heard a helluva lot worse than your husband can dish out. He hears worse every day." Then she clasped her hand over her mouth. "I shouldn't have said that," she mumbled, behind it. "I'm so tactless. . . ."

"You are tactful to a fault," Karen said, recovering

from her surprise. "You've known about Jack and his—his little foibles all along, haven't you? And Mr. Cardoza—Tony—too. He wouldn't have been so quick to react if he hadn't heard plenty. I guess I can hardly blame Mark for sounding off to his best friends. He has good reason to detest me."

"There you go again. Have you always been little Mrs. Martyr? What did that man do to you?"

"It wasn't all Jack's fault," Karen said slowly. "I let him do it. I never was a very aggressive person. My sister was the tough one; she was smarter, prettier, older, taller. . . . Cheryl, don't you dare laugh."

"I'm not laughing."

"Well, maybe you should. It sounds pretty silly, doesn't it? Sara was—is—just great. She couldn't help being taller, older . . . What was she supposed to do, cut her feet off at the ankles and fail exams to make me feel more secure? Funny; I couldn't see that at the time—that it was my problem, not hers. Then she married Bruce, and they were so happy. . . . Jack sure as hell didn't help. Not that he ever laid a hand on me. He just . . . cut me to ribbons inside, where it didn't show. Like that old jacket. Shattered silk . . . Slow corrosion, attacking the fabric at its weakest points."

"Oh, come on, don't be so dramatic." Cheryl's smile took the sting out of the words. "There's no remedy for shattered silk—right? You're cured—"

"Not yet. But I think I'm on the road to recovery. It may take a while."

"I'm glad you told me," Cheryl said.

"So am I. Now we can forget about it. But I wish," Karen said wistfully, "that I could have seen Jack's face when Tony practically accused him of attacking me."

Cheryl giggled. "I guess Tony probably shouldn't

have done that. It was like intimidation or exceeding his authority or something. But he got a kick out of it, I could tell. He likes you. Oh, he said to tell you he'd let you know if they got any leads, but don't count on it."

"He still thinks it was an amateur—someone looking for money to buy drugs?"

"Well, he claims a professional thief would have gone for the antiques and the silver. I guess your aunt's things are pretty valuable?" Karen nodded, and Cheryl went on, "He says the man must have been high on something or he wouldn't have behaved so inconsistently—throwing everything around but not damaging or taking anything, trying to choke you and then running like a scared rabbit when I came in."

"But you don't agree?"

Cheryl looked doubtful. "It sounds too convenient. You know what I mean? Like saying, I don't know why he acted that way, so I guess he was out of his mind. Seems to me Mark has a point—"

"If Mark thinks there's a maniac out there with my name at the top of his list, I don't want to hear about it."

"Oh, no, it's just the opposite. He doesn't think the man intended to hurt you; he just panicked when you walked in on him unexpectedly. Karen, are you sure you heard him say, 'Where is it?'"

"I'm sure."

"He was looking for something, then," Cheryl said.

"He might have meant money. He sounded..." Karen searched for a word. Even the memory of the hoarse whisper made her shiver. "...not normal," she finished weakly. "That fits Tony's theory of someone on drugs."

"I guess so. But Mark says it's too much of a coincidence that this should happen so soon after Mrs. Mac's car was stolen. He wondered if the guy was after something of hers."

Karen jumped up. "Good heavens. I completely forgot..." She ran into the master bedroom.

The burglar had turned that room into a shambles too. The furniture was heaped high with the crumpled clothing Cheryl had picked up from the floor. But he had not found the secret drawer. The panel slid aside under Karen's pressure and there was the shabby red morocco case, just as she had left it. She opened it, to make certain the contents had not been disturbed, and carried it in to show it to Cheryl.

"It's pretty," Cheryl said politely. "But it doesn't look like the kind of jewelry a burglar would care about."

"It's the only thing of real value I've acquired lately, though. Anyhow, if that's what he was looking for, he didn't find it. Cheryl, you have a very peculiar look on your face. What are you thinking?"

"I was remembering that weird old lady."

"Mrs. Grossmuller?" Karen's voice rose incredulously.

"I guess you think I'm silly."

"Why, no. I just—"

"He did." Cheryl's cheeks flamed. "He practically laughed in my face."

It wasn't difficult for Karen to deduce the identity of the person referred to. "You told Tony about Mrs. Grossmuller?"

"Yes, I did. I'm sorry if you didn't want me to."

"I don't mind. But it is pretty far out, Cheryl. Even admitting she's that disturbed, which I doubt, how could she track me down so quickly?"

"Your address was on your check," Cheryl said. "She could have gotten it from the auctioneer. And we stopped for supper, that took a couple of hours. Mrs. Grossmuller is a big, stout woman, in spite of her age. And insane people are supposed to have unusual strength."

THE manic strength of the insane . . . Karen didn't know whether it was true or not, but the idea accompanied her through the day like an unwelcome guest who will not go home. She could not decide whether she preferred to be the victim of a hopped-up young thug or a crazy old woman—or, if Mark was right, the unwitting possessor of a valuable object that might or might not be still in the house. On the whole, Tony's theory was less threatening; random violence was not likely to recur.

Rob saw the scratches on her throat and demanded to know what had happened. When she replied briefly that she had been mugged, he shrugged—"Welcome to the club, sweetie—" and went on to tell her in laborious detail about his own encounters with crime.

Monday was usually a slow day, and Karen's boredom was increased by her desire to get back to the house and deal with the chores that awaited her—not only the endless laundry but a number of other tasks she had allowed to accumulate. One, which she might not have thought of doing, had already been done for her. Mark had called a locksmith and asked him—or ordered him—to make an emergency call. The man had telephoned just before she left the house to say he'd be there between one and three.

Cheryl had offered to wait until he came. "I hope you're not mad," she began guiltily.

Karen smiled. "You're a fine one to lecture me about

159

apologizing for the things other people do. I'm grateful—
to you and to Mark. Please thank him for me."

But neither of them had mentioned one unpleasant
corollary implied by the need for additional locks—that
the intruder had not had to force a window because he
had a key to the house. It was only an unproved theory,
after all.

Karen had not had time to take the necklace to the
bank, or to call Mr. Bates. The latter task at least she could
do now. She wasn't keen on having Rob eavesdrop, which
he would undoubtedly do, but if she waited till she got
home, Mr. Bates might have left for the day. She couldn't
keep putting things off. Jack's vicious verbal attack had
shattered her apathy and inspired her with an urgent need
to be done with him.

Knowing Mr. Bates' busy schedule, she expected
she would have to leave a message and wait for him to
call her back, but when she gave her name, the secretary
put her straight through.

"I had expected to hear from you before this" was
Mr. Bates' only greeting. "In fact, I tried several times to
reach you, without success."

His critical tone filled Karen with resentment, probably because it followed a similar complaint from Jack.
Really, people had a lot of nerve yelling at her because she
wasn't available when it happened to suit their convenience.

"I've been busy," she said. "There are several questions—"

"Do you still have the Madison jewelry?"

Karen was still annoyed, and his peremptory tone
did not soothe her feelings. "I haven't hocked it yet, if
that's what you mean."

"I am glad," said Mr. Bates, in a tone that flatly

160

contradicted his words, "that you can joke about it. One would think that after having been physically assault-ed—"

"How did you hear about that?"

"I received a telephone call from Congressman Brinckley."

"Oh."

"The jewelry—"

"I have it." Karen heard an audible sigh of relief. She went on, "That was one of the things—"

"I strongly suggest that you bring it to me imme-diately."

"Now?"

"Immediately."

"I can't. I'm in charge here, and we don't close until five. After that—"

"After that I am attending a cocktail party." Mr. Bates brooded briefly. Karen fancied he must be looking through his appointment book. "I will return to the office afterward," he announced. "Can you be here by seven-thirty?"

"I—yes, I suppose so. Why not tomorrow?"

"The answer to that should be self-evident. Not that I subscribe to Congressman Brinckley's fantastic the-ory that your assailant was a member of the gang that stole the Rolls—"

An uncomfortable prickling sensation touched the nape of Karen's neck. "Wait a minute," she said. "Wait just a minute. . . . It didn't dawn on me at first. . . . How did Mark—Mr. Brinckley—know I had something of Mrs. MacDougal's? Did he mention the jewelry?"

"Why, yes. I assumed you had—"

"No. I didn't tell him."

"Then Mrs. MacDougal must have done so. Really,"

the lawyer said impatiently, "this is all beside the point, Mrs. Nevitt. Although I am convinced there is absolutely no connection between the two events, I do most strongly urge—"

"Yes, all right," Karen said abstractedly. "I'll come at seven-thirty. I also need the name of a good divorce lawyer."

"I will have the information for you this evening."

"Have you heard anything from—" Karen began. But the lawyer had hung up.

He was definitely annoyed with someone, and Karen suspected it wasn't she. Mark must have read him the riot act. It would be like Mark to concoct a wild theory just for the fun of getting the lawyer's back up. Mrs. MacDougal must have told Mark what she planned to do with Dolley's jewelry. Or possibly Cheryl had mentioned it to him.

She hung up and went back to the office. His feet on the desk, Rob was busily reading a paperback novel— one of the popular best-sellers focusing on the lives of the rich, dissolute, and famous. His look of profound concentration would not have deceived a child.

"I hope I talked loudly enough for you to hear without straining yourself," Karen said.

Rob put the book down and smiled sweetly. "It was fascinating, darling. I'm so pleased you've decided to press on with your divorce; it's a fatal mistake to delay these things. But what's all this about Mrs. MacDougal's car, and necklaces and urgent appointments?"

Karen couldn't remember having mentioned the car. Rob must have been listening in on the extension in the office. Rather than allow him to speculate and invent preposterous stories, she explained briefly.

Rob admitted he had heard about the Rolls. "So

thrilling, like one of those super crime films." The necklace, which Karen described only as a relatively inexpensive personal memento, didn't appear to interest him. However, Karen made a point of mentioning that she intended to hand it over to the lawyer that evening.

In fact, Rob was the last person she would have suspected of trying to throttle her. He would have been more likely to scream and run when she caught him in the house. As for the Dolley Madison jewelry... Oh, surely it was absurd to think it was involved. The fact that the intruder had not found it was no proof that he had not looked for it, but no ordinary thief would be aware of its presence. No ordinary thief... Her assailant had been no ordinary thief. That thick, hoarse whisper... There were only two people, aside from Mr. Bates and Cheryl, who knew she had Dolley's jewelry.

No, Karen thought. It couldn't have been Horton. Horton would not have run from Cheryl. Horton's big-muscled hands could have snapped her neck like a twig.

At five o'clock she left Rob to lock up and hurried home. Alexander was waiting; he led her directly to his empty food dish. Not until the dog's demands had been satisfied did Karen see the note Cheryl had left. The locksmith had come and gone; the keys were on the hall table.

Karen went to look. The keys made a formidable heap; there were three for each new door lock, front and back, and several more for the elaborate latches that had been added to the downstairs windows.

It must have taken the locksmith most of the afternoon. Congressman Brinckley's influence, Karen thought; usually it took days to get a service person to come, even in an emergency. But who was she to complain?

She went back to the kitchen and finished reading

Cheryl's note. "I hope you don't mind, I did a little mending and washing. Love working with those things. Have to go to some boring party tonight, will call if we aren't too late getting home."

The telephone rang while Karen was getting supper. It was Western Union with a cable for her and a complaint, rather than an apology, that they had tried to reach her earlier, without success. The cable read, "I'll get you for this someday, you traitor. Ruth sends love. I don't. Pat."

Karen decided she could safely conclude that Mrs. MacDougal had arrived on her son's doorstep, by gnu or some other means. Grinning, she put a diet TV dinner into the microwave and went upstairs to see what Cheryl had done. "A little" mending and washing turned out to be ludicrously understated. Many of the petticoats and chemises had been meticulously laundered and returned to their hangers. Across the bed lay several pieces of lace; all had been washed and ironed and one tattered strip had been neatly mended.

She was eating supper when the doorbell rang. Before she could get up she had to dislodge Alexander, who was sprawled across her feet. He had insisted on sampling the fish in her frozen dinner and had promptly spat it out. Now he followed her to the door, hoping for something that tasted better.

Instead of opening the door, Karen looked out through the small spy-hole. Though grotesquely distorted, the figure outside was definitely that of a woman.

There was nothing to be afraid of. It was still broad daylight outside, and whoever the caller might be, she was certainly not Mrs. Grossmuller. No distortion, however extreme, could make Mrs. Grossmuller's stocky figure look so slim.

But Karen left the chain in place when she opened the door. Alexander promptly lunged for the opening. The frown on the visitor's face deepened as she looked down at the furry muzzle trying to push through the crack.

"Shut that damned dog up," she said sharply.

Karen stared. What was Shreve Danforth—no, Shreve Givens now—doing on her doorstep? She was dressed for a formal dinner or party, in a glittering white dress that set off her deep tan. Diamonds winked at her throat and twinkled in the auburn hair that half-covered her ears. Shreve, who had been so rude the day she visited the shop; Mark's latest lady.

Shreve's silver shoe began to tap impatiently. "Well, are you going to let me in? I'm in rather a hurry."

"Oh. Oh, yes. Of course. Just a minute."

Karen scooped up the dog and shut him in the kitchen. When she returned to the door, Shreve's foot was tapping faster and she was glancing ostentatiously at her watch.

Acutely conscious of her faded housecoat and bare feet, Karen admitted her visitor. She wished she could have thought of an excuse for refusing to do so; something like "Sorry, I think I'm catching the plague." The old habit of courtesy had prevailed, and it was too late now.

"I'm sorry it took me so long," she said. "I'm rather wary of letting people in until I'm sure who they are. Someone broke in here last night—"

"Oh, really?" Shreve's lips stretched into an expression that was not quite a smile. "I do hope nothing was taken."

"No. I had new locks put on, though. Mark was kind enough to send a locksmith around this afternoon."

Now why had she said that? Karen knew the answer, but she could have kicked herself for challenging an

165

opponent like Shreve. The other woman's smile widened as she looked Karen over, from her unkempt hair to her dusty feet. Gently she said, "Mark has such a kind heart. He spends a lot of time with old Mrs. MacDougal too."

Well, I deserved that, Karen thought. I should have known better; I can't fight her on her terms.

With freezing politeness she said, "Can I offer you something to drink?"

"No." Shreve reached into her bag and took out a checkbook. "I just stopped by to get those things of Granny's. She had no right to sell them to you. The old witch is completely goofy. I believe you paid her seventy-five dollars?"

The amount she mentioned gave her bewildered listener the essential clue. "Mrs. Ferris is your grandmother?"

"Yes, didn't you know?" Shreve uncapped a gold pen and began to write, resting the checkbook on the hall table. "Seventy-five..."

"It was seventy-eight fifty, to be precise." Karen braced herself. "But I won't take your check."

"How much do you want, then?" Shreve asked coolly.

"Nothing. Not from you. I haven't had a chance to inspect all the merchandise yet, but that's what it is to me—merchandise. It was an honest business transaction—"

"Business," Shreve murmured. "I suppose it is good business to take advantage of a senile old woman."

Karen was so angry she felt lightheaded. The sensation was rather agreeable. "It's called free enterprise, Shreve. I'm surprised you haven't heard of it. Your husband is such an enthusiastic supporter of the system...."

Shreve blinked rapidly, as if someone had aimed a

blow at her face. It *was* a low blow, Karen thought, as her anger gave way to self-contempt. Congress had finally confirmed Mr. Givens' appointment, but not until after a long and acrimonious debate over certain "questionable business practices."

"Is there anything of yours in the boxes?" Karen asked.

"Good Lord, no." This suggestion seemed to outrage Shreve even more than Karen's refusal to sell. "What gave you that idea?"

"I only meant that if your grandmother had sold something that wasn't hers, I would of course return it."

"I see." Shreve bit her lip. "I think I will have a drink after all. Do you have Stolichnaya vodka?"

"I don't know."

"Vodka and tonic, with just a squeeze of lime. If you don't have Stolichnaya I'd prefer plain Perrier and lime."

"I'll see," Karen said. "Excuse me."

By the time she had ascertained that Pat preferred another, cheaper brand of vodka, and had unearthed a lone bottle of Perrier from the back of the liquor cabinet, she was—she fondly hoped—in control of her temper. There wasn't a lime in the house, nor did she bother looking for one.

She had not asked Shreve to sit down, but she found her in the parlor, poised on the edge of the sofa and looking about her with cool interest. "Ruth really ought to replace those draperies," she remarked. "They are quite faded. Maybe it's just as well she didn't; by the time the dog gets through with them she'll need new ones."

Karen handed her the glass and a coaster. She was determined to behave like a lady if it killed her, but she wanted to get Shreve out of the house as soon as she could.

The very sight of her, poised and slim and elegant, was like a shoe rubbing a blister.

"Was it your grandmother's wedding veil you wanted?" she asked.

"Wedding veil?" Shreve looked blank. "I don't give a damn about Gran's junk. I just don't like the idea of its being displayed in some cheap shop window, where people can see it and say that Gran was so poor she had to sell her clothes—that her family wasn't taking proper care of her."

The secret was out. All Shreve cared about was what people would say. Karen found it more believable than sentiment, a quality Shreve obviously lacked. It did not make her feel any more kindly toward Shreve.

"No one would recognize your grandmother's things. And anyway, if Mrs. MacDougal isn't embarrassed at having her clothes in a shop window, it shouldn't bother you. Hers are very distinctive and very valuable, and she told me I could—"

"I'll give you a hundred and fifty."

"No."

"Why not?"

"I hope to make a good deal more than that."

Shreve's eyes narrowed unpleasantly. "How much more?"

"I'm afraid you are missing the point," Karen said. "I am in business to make as much money as I can. The value of the merchandise I sell depends on a number of different factors, primarily on what people are willing to pay." Shreve continued to stare at her, lips pressed tightly together, and some imp of perversity made Karen add, "When they are ready for sale, cleaned and pressed and mended, I'll let you know. If you care to pay the price, they're all yours."

"I see," Shreve said slowly. "I'm to be allowed to bid—is that it?"

"No bidding, no haggling. I set the price; you pay it or someone else will. And now, if you'll excuse me, I have an appointment and I've barely time to change."

SHE really was late, but instead of dashing upstairs to dress she did a clog dance down the length of the hall, to the consternation of Alexander, whom she freed from bondage as she passed the kitchen door.

"I'm sorry," Karen said breathlessly. "That was a dance of triumph, Alexander. You wouldn't understand, and anyway I haven't time to explain it to you."

Talking to the dog was only one step better than talking to herself, but she had to crow to someone. A month ago she would not have been able to handle Shreve as ably as she had. She would have meekly accepted the check and handed over the merchandise, as Shreve had expected she would. Shreve wasn't accustomed to having people bite her back, especially someone she remembered as quiet and yielding. It would have been a fatal mistake to give in, for it would have set a precedent, for herself if not for her customers. She might end up doing something as asinine as letting Mrs. Grossmuller buy her wedding dress back for two bits.

What was more, she had not lost her temper, though the provocation had been extreme. As she came downstairs, neatly if hastily attired, she remembered Shreve's insolence, and the anger she had suppressed boiled up stronger than before. How Mark could fall for such a vulgar, arrogant woman . . . But it wasn't Shreve's personality that interested Mark. He was kind and charitable to old

169

friends and former enemies, but he liked his women slim and sexy and influential.

Stop it, Karen told herself. She concentrated intently on locking the door. The new keys were a trifle stiff, but they would probably loosen up in time.

It was lucky for Karen that she approached her interview with the lawyer in such high spirits, for he did everything possible to depress her. He looked exactly like the picture she had formed of him in her mind—a little man, short and spare, with a narrow, closed-in face. His eyes were obscured by thick glasses and his thinning hair had been carefully brushed across his bald spot. He held a chair for her, but she had barely seated herself before he made his chief concern evident.

"The jewelry, Mrs. Nevitt. May I—"

"I didn't bring it." Karen settled herself more comfortably.

"You didn't. . . . May I ask why not?"

His tone was only too reminiscent of the one Jack used to demoralize and intimidate her. This time Karen refused to yield. She was getting tired of being pushed around; instead of explaining and apologizing, she went on the attack.

"What are you worried about, Mr. Bates? The jewelry or me?"

"Why—I—"

"Because if it's the jewelry, that's no longer your responsibility. It belongs to me, and I intend to wear it and enjoy it as Mrs. Mac meant me to, not lock it up in a bank. And if you are afraid I might be in danger from someone who wants it—"

"Nonsense," said Mr. Bates shortly.

"Okay, it's nonsense. So why the fuss? Anyway, there is no point in my getting rid of a potential danger unless the presumed thief knows I've gotten rid of it. I should have come here carrying a sign? 'Attention, everybody: Dolley's jewelry is being handed over to Mr. Bates'?"

"Really, Mrs. Nevitt—"

"If anyone is watching me, my visit to you this evening will suggest to them that I've handed the jewelry over. What further precautions could I take, short of putting an advertisement in the newspaper? Now, if you don't mind, I'd like to discuss something more important."

Mr. Bates sighed, adjusted his glasses, brushed his hair back from his high forehead, and gave her his full attention.

He took a dim view of her plans. A young woman with no business experience had, in his opinion, little hope of success. But Karen was moved almost to tears when he grudgingly informed her that her uncle by marriage had cabled to put a large sum of money at her disposal, to be drawn upon at need.

"You have heard from Pat, then," she murmured, reaching for a tissue and pretending she was blotting away perspiration. "That was one of the things I wanted to ask you."

Mr. Bates eyed her warily. He knew perfectly well that emotion rather than heat had necessitated the tissue, and he obviously disapproved of women who wept.

"Yes. Only the information I have just given you, and the news that Mrs. MacDougal senior has arrived safely. I must add that had Profesor MacDougal consulted me before arranging for a transfer of funds, I would have counseled him—"

"You needn't worry," Karen cut in. "I have no intention of abusing Pat's generosity. Now I wonder if you would mind reading these letters from my husband's lawyer. It may be a few days before I can get an appointment and they sound very peremptory."

Her quick recovery from ill-conceived emotion brought a frosty gleam of approval to Mr. Bates' pale-gray eyes. As he read the letters his nostrils quivered. "Hmph," he said. "It appears you may have a fight on your hands, Mrs. Nevitt. The offers are outrageous. I beg you will not reply in any way until you have consulted the attorney I will recommend to you."

Karen assured him she was not that stupid, and Mr. Bates looked as if he would like to have believed her but couldn't quite manage it.

There was no news about the missing automobile or the missing chauffeur. The police investigation had fizzled out—Mr. Bates didn't use the word, but that was what it amounted to. Yes, he had cabled Mrs. MacDougal about the car. He had not yet received a reply. He would let Karen know when he got word. He would give them all her love. And would she please—implicit in his manner, if not expressed—get the hell out of his office and let him go home?

The long summer twilight was dying as Karen stood on the corner waiting for a bus. The air was gray, not with twilight but with exhaust fumes, and according to an electric sign on a nearby corner, the temperature was still in the high eighties. No wonder Washingtonians fled the city in late July and August. The only wonder was that they had functioned so long without air-conditioning. The affectionate phrase, "the Federal Swamp," though it had acquired other connotations, had originally been a literal description of geographical fact.

A bus lumbered into sight but stopped half a block away as the traffic light turned red and cars and trucks barred its further progress. Karen glanced casually at the poised traffic, and suddenly froze. A brand-new bright-red, Ferrari convertible, in the middle lane . . . The top was down. The twin mufflers throbbed as the driver jiggled the gas pedal, ready to take off the instant the light changed.

As if the intensity of her stare sent out palpable waves, the driver turned his head and looked directly at her. His full red lips pursed like those of a girl expecting to be kissed. They shaped words. She couldn't hear them, but she knew what he had said. Before she could react, the light changed and the convertible took off like a bullet, narrowly avoiding a crossing van that had run the last second of the yellow.

Karen turned and bolted back into the building she had just left.

Mr. Bates drove her home. He could hardly avoid doing so; she had caught him as he emerged from the elevator, his car keys in his hand.

He felt sure she had been mistaken. "There are many men of that type," he said distastefully. "We had been speaking of the matter, so it was on your mind. I assure you, Horton is miles away by now. He would not be so foolish as to remain in the city."

"I know it was Horton. He knew me. He said, 'Hi, doll.'"

"But you informed me you could not hear—"

"I read his lips. He called me doll once before. Oh, for heaven's sake, Mr. Bates, can't you at least notify the police? It was a new red Ferrari with Virginia plates, and the first two letters were BV. You know whom to talk to, and they'll pay more attention to you."

"Very well. However, I feel certain they will inform me that Horton has been seen in three other places, all miles from Washington."

173

Despite his skepticism he insisted on going to the door with her and on waiting until she had opened it. He didn't have to insist much. This time she managed to catch Alexander's collar while he was in mid-leap as Mr. Bates, obviously only too familiar with the dog's habits, skipped nimbly aside.

"Thank you," she said, as the lawyer cast a keen if seemingly casual glance inside. "I hope I haven't taken you out of your way."

"Not all all. I live in Chevy Chase; I can as easily go up Wisconsin as Connecticut."

Then why didn't you offer to drive me home in the first place? Karen wondered. Mr. Bates might make light of her identification of the chauffeur, but he wasn't altogether easy in his own mind or he would not have accompanied her home after hearing her story. Horton knew where she lived; he might even have a key to the house. Mrs. Mac probably had one, and she was notoriously careless with her possessions.

Thank goodness for the new locks, Karen thought. The darkening air was still breathlessly hot, but a shiver ran through her as she pictured Horton's big brown hands and fleshy, smiling mouth. She still could not believe Horton had been her attacker. But now he had a reason to seek her out. If he thought he could silence her before she told the police she had seen him...

She knew she was overreacting. Anyone who drove breezily around the city in a car as conspicuous as that one obviously wasn't concerned about being seen. Either Horton was extremely stupid, or he just didn't give a damn.

Alexander growled. He did not enjoy being hugged. Karen carried him back into the house and locked the door.

She wandered restlessly through the various rooms, turning on lights, checking and rechecking the locks on the doors and windows. The house was very quiet, very empty. She found herself hearing sounds that were not there—the ghostly echo of Pat's booming laughter, Ruth's quiet voice. If only they had been in some civilized part of the world she would have been tempted to call them. There was no one she could call, no familiar voice that was reachable by telephone.

Karen knew what was wrong with her. It had different names, some simple, some ponderous and scientific—shock, post-stress syndrome, whatever. It was, simply and starkly, an awareness of her own vulnerability. She was no more open to attack than she had ever been—less so, in fact, thanks to the new locks and her heightened awareness of danger. But her sense of safety had been violated; her private place had been entered by those who had no right to intrude. She had heard other victims of crime speak of the sensation. Now she knew how it made people feel—naked, exposed, helpless.

She went to the kitchen and put the kettle on. The refrigerator clicked; she jumped and cried out. I've got to stop this, she thought. I'll drive myself crazy if I go on this way. Find something to do, something to occupy my mind. . . .

She made the rounds once more, compulsively relocking doors that were already locked, touching window latches, looking out into the street and the garden. Alexander ought to go out once more. Alexander would have to take his chances, that was all. Before she lured the dog upstairs with a handful of his favorite dog munchies, she pushed a chair against the back door and piled it with pots and pans.

She felt more relaxed after she had locked herself in her room and climbed into bed with a book. Pat had an enormous collection of mysteries; he favored the tough-

private-eye variety, and Karen hoped the exotic and unlikely perils encountered by those fictitious heroes would
distract her—rather like hitting oneself with a hammer to
forget the pain of a broken leg.

It was not long before she knew she had made a
mistake. The tough, wise-cracking PI was captured by
members of the drug ring he was investigating. The author
lingered with loving affection on the tortures inflicted by
the chief villain—"a big, hulking character with a pretty
pouting mouth like that of a girl expecting to be kissed."

Karen threw the book across the room and turned
on the television, only to encounter another cynical wise-
cracking PI being beaten up by members of a drug ring he
was investigating.

She was relieved to be able to settle for the late
news. Forest fires in the Western states, drought in the
Northeast, tornadoes in the Midwest; breakdown of the
arms talks, plane crashes, riots, and murders. But the giant
pandas were making love. Thank God for the pandas.

Sleep was still out of the question, and since TV at
its most engrossing occupies only half the mind of the
beholder, she looked around for something else to do.

There was more than enough to do. Jack's caustic
comments about her lack of organization had not been
entirely unjustified. She hated keeping records, making
lists, balancing accounts. But accurate records were essential for the business she hoped to start. At Mrs. Mac's
suggestion (i.e., order) she had bought a looseleaf notebook and some paper. It took her quite a while to find
them, and when she did, she was dismayed to see so many
empty pages. She hadn't meant to fall so far behind. Leafing through the book, she realized she had not even finished listing the items from Ruth's attic.

The idea was to have a separate page for each article, giving the source and the price paid, plus notes on repairs, restoration methods, and—ultimately—the selling price. Not only would she need the information for tax purposes, but it would be an invaluable reference.

Karen grimaced. Oh, well; there was nothing like concentrating on a hated, boring job to get her mind off other worries.

While the anchorman's voice droned on, she dragged out a box of miscellaneous linens and got to work. They had come from Mrs. Ferris, and they reminded her of Shreve. So Shreve wanted Granny's things, did she? If she could see the condition of the pieces she wouldn't touch them with the tip of her fastidious finger.

Karen shook out a tattered petticoat and sneezed violently as dust billowed up around her. The old lady must have worn it to scrub floors or climb fences; the fabric was torn, and covered with ugly black spots. But the deep flounce of the lace might be salvageable. Karen found a pair of scissors and cut it off, then wadded the rest of the garment and threw it into the wastebasket, wrinkling her nose at the sour smell of mold.

She forced herself to finish sorting and listing the contents of the box. She was getting sleepy, and she felt as if she would never get the smell of mold off her hands. Cheryl had not called. One more chore, Karen thought, and then I'll go to bed. She won't call after midnight— but it's not quite midnight yet.

The flounce she had removed from the old petticoat might be right for Mrs. Grossmuller's wedding dress. For some reason the mold had not affected the lace. Perhaps it had something to do with the type of fabric.

After a prolonged search she finally located the dress at the back of the wardrobe. Cheryl must have picked it up off the floor of the hall, along with the other things

Karen had bought at the auction—and dropped when the fumbling hands found her throat. Yes, the rest of them were there—the frayed petticoat with the crocheted trim, the absurd bloomers, and the linen nightgown.

A muted howling from without rose and fell—Mr. DeVoto's cat, seeking romance and/or a fight. Karen identified the sound, but her skin prickled, and Alexander twitched and mumbled in his sleep.

She decided she had better list the auction items while their origin was still fresh in her mind. "Lace-trimmed bloomers, circa 1910," the name of the auctioneer, and the date. She entered the dress last, and her writing faltered. But she had the information; it would be ridiculous to omit it. "Wedding dress of Mrs. Henry Grossmuller, 1931." Mrs. Henry Grossmuller, who poisoned Henry in 1965 and who claimed the dress wasn't worth two bits.

"I will not write that down," Karen said aloud. No need to, she would never forget it. Damn the old woman, and damn Cheryl too, for talking about the romance of old clothes and the tragedy of a terrified young bride. . . . No, that wasn't fair. Cheryl had not blathered on about auras and vibes, she had better sense. It was Karen's own imagination that invested the innocent fabric with an almost palpable coating of some dark, slimy substance.

The lace was certainly dark, and as Karen inspected it she knew her first assessment had been correct. The lace was beyond repair; the staining substance had had a corrosive effect, leaving great rents in the delicate web. Into Karen's mind popped a vivid, most unwelcome picture of Mrs. Grossmuller kneeling by her husband's body, the flounce of her wedding dress trailing in a pool of his blood.

She really must get her imagination under control. It would be an effective scenario for a horror film—the abused wife putting on the dress she had worn as an

178

unwilling bride before wreaking her vengeance on her torturer. But Mrs. Grossmuller hadn't stabbed Henry, she had poisoned him.

Karen let out a gasp of laughter. One day she might be able to tell the Mrs. Grossmuller story and find it genuinely funny. But at best it would always be black humor, for there was something sad and twisted behind the old woman's insistence—guilt or fear or frustrated anger. Like the anger she herself had felt, and was only now beginning to acknowledge?

Resolutely Karen turned her mind back to business. The lace she had removed from the petticoat was just right. It was the same width, and there was so much of it that she could remove the damaged sections and still have enough left to edge the dress.

She took the lace into the bathroom and dunked it in warm water, to soak overnight. Now all she needed to restore the dress were pearls (hers wouldn't be genuine, but the originals hadn't been either) and a silk flower to replace the limp brown specimen on the hipline. She cut off a pearl bead to serve as a sample and began a list of needed materials on a page at the back of the book. As she had already discovered from her earlier attempts at mending the old garments, ordinary cotton and polyester sewing thread was often too coarse. Shops specializing in fine fabrics carried silk thread. She ought to lay in a supply, in a variety of colors, and get needles to match. Buttons— old ones, if possible. They wouldn't be easy to find, but there must be sources for such things.

She kept glancing at the clock. At twelve-thirty she decided Cheryl wouldn't call so late. At any rate, she was now tired enough to sleep soundly. As she had hoped, the need to concentrate on a specific task had quieted her nerves.

179

There was nothing wrong with Alexander's nerves, but unfortunately his bladder was not as good. He wanted to go out and he would not take no for an answer. When he started to lift his leg against the bed flounce, Karen gave in. There were too many things Alexander could ruin if he chose, and unless he got his own way, he probably would choose.

She had to disassemble the tottering structure of pans in order to open the door. Alexander shot out like an arrow from a bow. The night air was still and hot, with trails of ground mist curdling among the shrubbery. A furious rattle of foliage and a feline squawl explained the dog's haste; the cat paused on top of the storage shed to address a rude remark to its pursuer. Karen saw its eyes glow eerily red. A Siamese cat. Mr. DeVoto always had Siamese.

Alexander returned the cat's compliments in his own tongue. Not until the Siamese left, melting into the darkness with only a rustle of leaves to prove it material, did Alexander go about his business. He took his own sweet time about it, probably to punish Karen for being so reluctant to let him out, and she swore at him under her breath as she shifted uneasily from one foot to the other. There was no sense in yelling at him and disturbing the neighbors; and he wouldn't pay attention anyway. She did not want to go out after him. The mist was thickening, and although there was not a breath of air stirring, the pale trails of fog seemed to sway and shift, with a motion of their own.

Alexander finally gave up—she assumed he had been backtracking the cat—and came in. Karen double-checked the locks again, and rebuilt the tower of pots. Alexander followed her from room to room whuffling irritably. He knew he was entitled to a dog biscuit but Karen held off giving it to him until after he had gone upstairs with her.

In the dream that quickly seized her she was picking her way across a landscape covered with tumbled ruins, cyclopean columns, and fallen blocks of stone. The stones were carved with reliefs; but though she examined them with an absurd and nightmarish intensity, she could not make out their meaning. At last, dim in the purple distance, she caught a glimpse of some intact structure towering high above the plain. She ran toward it. A tottering column crumpled and collapsed; the fragments struck the earth, not with a solid thud, but ringing like metal.

The dog's barking shot her out of sleep, every muscle knotted. Alexander was at the window. The scraping of his claws on the glass made her skin crawl.

Karen fumbled for the lamp. It seemed to take forever to find the switch. The dog was getting frantic. He ran to the door, clawed at it, trotted back to the window.

The cat, Karen thought. He must have heard the cat. Siamese have loud voices. Audible through closed windows, the hum of air-conditioning?

Clinging to the idea of the cat as to a lifeline, she got out of bed and went to the window.

The mist had condensed into a layer of solid fog. The roofs and chimneys of the houses on the street behind the garden were invisible; nearer shapes shone ghostly, soft gray tree trunks pearly with wet, garden chairs gleaming like silver thrones in the glow of the lights by the back door.

Something was sitting in one of the chairs.

It was on the terrace, close enough to the lights so that she should have been able to identify the shape that occupied it—filled it, rather, like a giant featherbed that had been punched and pummeled into a rough imitation

181

of a human form. It might have been the fog that softened its outlines so that they appeared to melt into nothingness.

Alexander was still trying to bark, but he was so short of breath the sound came out in weird little squeaks. It was probably this touch of low comedy that kept Karen on her feet. The sound that came from her taut throat was a rather pathetic echo of Alexander's squeak, but she meant it for laughter, and the hands she raised hardly shook at all. She unfastened the window and threw up the sash.

The thing in the chair rose up and drifted across the yard. It was quite opaque. However, its means of locomotion were as uncanny as its general appearance, for it seemed to float, without haste, threading a path around the rose bushes and the trees until it was swallowed up by the fog.

Alexander ran to the door.

I can't open it, Karen thought.

But neither could she remain in her room without knowing what might be outside the locked door. Alexander sounded like one of his own squeaky toys, but his small size and shortness of breath did not deter him; he wasn't cowering or hiding. How could she, a member of a supposedly superior species, do less?

Karen unlocked the door, but she let Alexander go first. Not until she heard a horrible crash from the kitchen did she realize she had made a mistake. Alexander had flung himself head-long into the pile of assorted hardware, and now she would never know whether some or all of them had already fallen, producing the far-off ringing sound that had entered her dreams and had, perhaps, wakened Alexander from his.

The lights in the hall burned steadily. She took a poker from the set of fireplace tools and went out of the room.

By the time she reached the kitchen Alexander was pushing the pots around with his nose looking for something edible. He had clearly lost interest in going out. The door was locked.

She gave Alexander the treat he deserved and they went upstairs together. The dog was sound asleep within minutes, but Karen sat by the window looking out until the sounds of morning traffic began and sunrise brightened the blanket of fog muffling the garden.

CHAPTER SEVEN

✤✤✤✤✤✤✤✤✤✤✤✤✤✤✤✤✤✤✤✤✤✤✤✤✤✤✤✤✤✤✤

*K*AREN sat at the dining room table. On it lay an antique petticoat she was shortening and altering for a customer who had been visibly disconcerted when the waistband didn't begin to go around her purportedly twenty-five-inch waist. Since the petticoat was too long anyway, the solution was simple—take off the waistband and shorten the garment from the top—but the execution was not so easy, for the measurements had to be accurate and the fabric of the new waistband had to match the time-softened muslin of the original.

The scrap of material Karen held in her hand was not designed to be a new waistband. It was the wrong shape and size—roughly triangular, about three inches at the base. Nor, unless her recently acquired knowledge of fabrics misled her, was it old. A polyester-and-cotton blend, brand new and unstained except for a smear of rust from the nail on which it had been caught. It might have been torn from a bed sheet.

Karen had found it that morning, hanging from a nail on the back fence. It was the only visible evidence that someone had been in the yard the night before. As Tony had pointed out, the garden was too neatly tended to take footprints.

Pat and Ruth had a part-time gardener who came several times a week. Apparently his working hours coincided with Karen's, for she had never set eyes on him. Perhaps the gardener would know if there was any sign of disturbance, but it was hardly worthwhile trying to locate him. She had no intention of telling anyone of the incident, including the police. They had already heard from her twice in the last two days, assuming Mr. Bates had passed on the information about Horton. It wasn't exactly a case of the boy who cried "wolf," for there had definitely been a wolf of sorts in her hallway; but she had a feeling the police would get a trifle blasé about her complaints if she called them every day. Anyway, the scrap of cloth wasn't evidence—the police would probably think it had been torn from one of her laundered garments—and the story sounded worse than silly, it sounded demented. A ghost in the garden, lady? Well, you know these old Georgetown legends.

Her lips tightly set, Karen put the scrap in an envelope and laid it aside. There was no doubt in her mind that the affair had been designed for one purpose only—to frighten her. After trying the door and discovering he could not get in, the unknown had roused Alexander—perhaps he had thrown gravel at the window—and lingered until the light in her bedroom went on, so that she would be sure to see him. The fog had been a helpful but not essential adjunct to his performance; and the weather forecast would have informed him that some such meteorological phenomenon could be expected that night.

Instead of reducing her to a state of quivering terror, the incident had had precisely the opposite effect. She was getting tired of people trying to intimidate her; and a clumsy, childish trick like that one added insult to injury.

Rob was late to work. She had to unlock the shop herself. Damn him, she thought, surveying the unemptied ashtray on the front desk and the tumbled folders scattered across the table. It wouldn't have taken him five minutes to tidy up. She straightened the folders, observing that a scant half dozen of the Georgetown book remained. It had been selling like hot cakes, all right; Julie's cynical assessment had been accurate. Maybe I'd better have another look at it, Karen thought. Maybe I can find a nasty scandal about someone else I know. Not mentioning any names . . . Wouldn't it be funny if Shreve were anxious to retrieve Granny's things because somewhere in the lot was evidence of an antique misdemeanor Granny had committed?

Rob finally sauntered in, magnificent in designer jeans and shirt, his hair newly styled. "Like it? There's the dearest little person in a new place on M Street; he could do wonders for you, duckie, you ought to give him a try."

He then retreated to the office and his paperback. Karen watched him go, lean hips swaying, muscles rippling, hair gleaming, and smiled ruefully as a familiar sensation rippled through some of her own muscles. No wonder women found Rob so devastating. He must work like a fiend to keep that body looking the way it did. Too bad he had such a feeble little mind to go with it.

During the next lull in business she opened her notebook, which she had decided to carry with her—as if it were a magic talisman promising success, or as if some variety of osmosis would magically transfer onto its blank pages the information she needed to put there. Lists, she thought. Why is it I can't make lists? Some people love to make them. Sometimes they even get around to doing the things on the lists.

She had accomplished one thing that morning; she had called one of the lawyers on the list Mr. Bates had given her, and she had an appointment for the following day. But her brief sense of accomplishment faded when she began listing her other chores. They weren't small chores, quickly done. Find a suitable building; see what work needs to be done; call contractors, plumbers, electricians; apply for a permit—permits, rather—heaven only knew how many she would need and for what. . . .

Karen groaned and dropped her head into her hands. That was just the beginning. She ought to be attending auctions and flea markets and yard sales. Visiting museums. Reading her reference books. Washing, mending, finding sewing supplies.

And dealing with the most basic question of all: What was she going to use for money?

The solution slipped into her mind so smoothly and gently that she knew it must have been there all along. What she needed was a partner. Any business enterprise—including marriage, she told herself wryly—requires two people if it is to succeed. Two bodies, since one person can't be in two places at the same time; two pairs of hands to lighten burdens and carry twice the number of loads.

Cheryl's talents complemented her own. Cheryl had, or would soon have, the business training she lacked. Cheryl didn't wince when the word "computer" was mentioned. She was fascinated by the old garments, good with

187

a needle, intelligent. She was easy to get along with. She had a sense of humor. (After dealing with Julie, Karen appreciated the importance of the last two attributes.) Cheryl had even mentioned that she had a little money saved and that eventually she hoped to invest it in her own business.

It was the perfect solution. In fact, as she remembered some of the things Cheryl had said, Karen realized that she had dropped several broad hints. So why had it taken her so long to recognize it?

She knew the answer. One word. A name.

It was high time she got the name and the complex, difficult emotions it aroused, out of her system. She could now admit that Mark also had some right to feel injured. If he could forgive and forget, she could do no less. There was no reason why they couldn't be friends. "Friendly" was the word for his behavior the other night. Strange that a word so warm and comforting when applied to one person should sound so cold when applied to another.... Men seemed to prefer the kind of life he was presently leading, without commitments, flitting from woman to woman as the King of Siam had advised, having casual extramarital flings with the wives of colleagues and associates.

There's plenty of that going on, Karen reminded herself with a sour smile. Men weren't the only ones who had no qualms about the Seventh Commandment.

She decided she would talk to Cheryl that evening. Of course she might be mistaken; Cheryl might not be interested. But even the possibility lifted Karen's spirits. She gathered up her despised lists with new determination and carried them back to the office, ordering Rob to man the shop.

She was at Julie's desk scribbling busily when she

heard the doorbells tinkle, and Rob's saccharine coo, which he reserved for old customers. "Darling, how divine to see you. I do hope you want to buy lots and lots of expensive goodies."

Rob had a lot in common with anchovies—either you adored him or he made you slightly nauseous. Karen decided she had better go out and see which category the customer belonged to.

Judging by her expression, she belonged to the second category. Her frown smoothed out when she saw Karen, and then Karen recognized her. The old school ties were strengthening; it was Miriam Montgomery, who had been with Shreve on an earlier visit to the shop, and who had snubbed her almost as thoroughly as Shreve. Though she wore a well-cut linen dress, she didn't have Shreve's style; the garment hung from her slumped shoulders like any cheap copy from a department-store rack. Her flat, rather doughy features showed the same combination of expensive equipment improperly employed; her mascara was too dark for her pale-blue eyes and her lipstick was smeared.

She returned Karen's cautious greeting and then gave Rob a casual, dismissive glance as definitive as a royal "We give you leave to go." Rob winked at Karen and discreetly faded away.

"How can you stand working with that man?" Miriam asked. Her voice was high-pitched and rather whiny. "He's such a poseur."

"Oh, Rob's not so bad," Karen said, knowing full well that the office door had been left open a crack. "Are you looking for something in particular, Miriam, or would you rather browse in peace?"

"I came to talk to you." Miriam frowned at an almost invisible spot on her white handbag. "I hope you don't think I was rude the other day."

"Why, no."

"I'm afraid I was. I didn't mean to be. It's Shreve's fault. Of course she's an old friend and I'm terribly fond of her, but she is awfully bossy. And tactless. You'd think that after all these years in Washington she would have learned a little discretion. But no, she just charges straight ahead like a bull in a china shop, without realizing that she antagonizes people."

Nothing like an old friend who is terribly fond of you to cut you down, Karen thought. Aloud she said carefully, "Shreve always had a—a strong personality."

"Anyway, I thought I ought to explain why I behaved so rudely."

"You weren't rude. Don't give it another thought."

"I don't like people to think badly of me," Miriam murmured.

Karen reassured her again. Miriam seemed to require a lot of reassurance. Who would have supposed that a woman so richly endowed with worldly goods could be so insecure? According to Julie, Mr. Montgomery was one of the wealthiest men in the Southeast.

"I'm so glad you understand," Miriam said. "Now I hope you can help me. I'm thinking of giving a little party next month. Everyone seems to be into nostalgia these days—though I can't imagine why...."

Her voice trailed off indecisively.

"The good old days," Karen said.

"What was so good about them? I wouldn't want to live my high school years over—would you?"

"No," Karen said, with an involuntary grimace. "I guess not. So you want a theme for your party, is that it?"

"How clever of you! And I suppose I'll need a dress, won't I?"

"From the seventies?" Karen asked doubtfully. She was getting used to customers who took forever to tell her what they wanted, possibly because they didn't know themselves.

"I need something really smashing. I guess the seventies aren't really 'in,' are they?"

"Not in terms of vintage clothing, no. I have a few fifties and sixties dresses, but I wouldn't call them smashing. Some of the younger girls like those styles, but they aren't old enough to be vintage or quaint."

"What do you recommend?" The spot on Miriam's handbag seemed to bother her; she picked at it with a manicured nail.

"What about the twenties? I have some gorgeous dresses from that period. And you have the right figure for them."

Miriam smoothed her flat stomach complacently. "I try to keep in shape. The twenties? Yes, that could be fun. Jazz and prohibition and—and that sort of thing."

Like bootleggers and gang wars, Karen thought. Oh well, nostalgia is in the eye of the beholder.

"I have several beautiful flapper dresses," she said. "But they aren't here; they are designer originals and very expensive."

"I assumed they would be," said Miriam.

She wanted to see the dresses and she wanted to see them right away. She was perfectly pleasant about it; her excuse for insisting on immediate service—that she lived in Middleburg and did not get into the city often— was eminently reasonable. Karen did not hesitate long. She suspected Miriam was trying to do her a favor, as a way of apologizing for her rudeness the week before. If

191

she didn't strike while the iron was hot, Miriam might change her mind, and she would lose a sale. Besides, Rob owed her for several long lunches and early departures.

At Karen's suggestion they walked to the house. This time she remembered Alexander and managed to collar him before he could sink his teeth into Miriam's leg. Miriam did not care for Alexander. She was rude enough to refer to him as a "hideous creature," and Alexander, resenting the insult, growled and struggled to free himself as Karen bore him away.

Miriam's attitude was now much more that of customer to shopkeeper; she seated herself regally in the parlor and let Karen trot up and down stairs with the dresses. They had to be carried one at a time, for the weight of the crystal drops and beads was so great that they cast a strain on the fragile fabric. Miriam seemed pleased and a little surprised at the beauty of the gowns; she wavered for some time between two that bore the names of famous designers. Both were the standard straight chemises with slit skirts. One was covered from neckline to hem with white crystal beads, on white silk. The other had iridescent Venetian glass beads on pale-aqua crepe de chine; the slightest movement bathed the wearer in a soft shimmer, like a mermaid in the moonlight. The color was flattering to Miriam's washed-out complexion, but she seemed loath to give up the white.

Finally she shrugged. "I may as well take both. How much?"

"Don't you want to try them on?" Karen asked in surprise.

"No, there's no need. You'll pack them for me, I assume."

"Oh, I can't let you have them today," Karen exclaimed. "Some of the beads are loose, and you can see they need cleaning—"

"Oh." Miriam thought for a moment. "When will they be ready?"

"I'm not sure. I'll have to ask the cleaners how long it will take. Shall I let you know?"

"All right." Miriam reached for her checkbook. "How much?"

Karen took a deep breath. "The Hattie Carnegie is nine hundred and fifty." There was no reaction from Miriam except a slight movement of impatience as she sat with her pen poised. Karen went on, "The white one is— is thirteen hundred. That comes to two thousand, two hundred and fifty. Plus tax."

Miriam stared at her. "You've got to be kidding."

"I know it seems like a lot, but the white one was handmade by Callot Soeurs."

Miriam's face was as blank as a doll's. Karen said firmly, "I could probably get more from someone else, Miriam. I'm giving you a break because I hope you will want other things—and recommend me to your friends. You don't have to pay me now. Or you can give me a deposit, if you like."

Miriam bent her head over the checkbook and began to write.

AFTER Miriam had left, Karen stood admiring the check she held. Two thousand two hundred and fifty dollars, plus tax. The full amount. That had been really decent of Miriam. One couldn't blame her for her initial protest. A woman who could casually dash off a check for over two thousand dollars might not be expected to balk at such a sum, but Karen knew from experience that the richer the customer, the more likely she was to haggle.

Of course a third of the money belonged to Mrs. MacDougal, and today's sale was an unusual event, one that wouldn't happen often. All the same, it deserved a celebration. Karen decided she would not go back to work. It was four-thirty and she felt sure Rob had already closed up.

She went flying down the hall to release Alexander from the kitchen. He almost fainted with surprise when she snatched him up and hugged him. "Steak for you tonight, my boy. And champagne for me!"

Alexander's ears pricked up. He had an extensive vocabulary, and "steak" was a word he knew.

Karen put a bottle of champagne into the refrigerator and reached for the telephone.

Cheryl was almost as excited as she was, but she reluctantly refused Karen's invitation to supper. "I've got a class. I don't dare skip it, there's a test tonight. Unless— would it be all right if I came over afterwards? I could be there by nine, unless you're set on getting drunk right this minute."

"I think I can hold off for a few hours," Karen admitted.

After inspecting the larder, she decided there was nothing on hand worthy of the occasion. Snatching her purse, she ran out to shop, treating herself to veal chops (two very small chops) from the Georgetown Market. She did not buy Alexander's steak at the Georgetown Market. She hoped he couldn't tell the difference between supermarket fare and that of a French butcher, but she did not count on it.

Cheryl arrived at 9:10, brandishing a bottle. "I figured one bottle of champagne wasn't enough for your first big sale. Let's open it right this minute."

They drank with simulated solemnity—"to Miriam and her millions." Karen filled the glasses again. "I'd like to propose another toast. Feel free to throw the wine and the glass out the window if you hate the idea, but . . . How about drinking to our new partnership?"

Cheryl stopped with her glass halfway to her lips. She stared at Karen; then her eyes suddenly brimmed with tears. "I thought you'd never ask," she said.

AT midnight they were halfway through the second bottle and neither one of them had stopped talking.

"Might as well finish it," Cheryl said seriously, pouring the wine. "It'd be a shame to let it go flat. Here's another toast. To the greatest business brains in the state—"

"This isn't a state," Karen said, with only the slightest difficulty over the sibilants.

"And a damn shame, too," Cheryl cried. "Here's to self-gov'ment for the District of Columbia!"

"Right on!"

"No, but I mean we are the best business brains in whatever it is," Cheryl insisted. "Do you realize that in the last three hours we've figured out everything we're gonna do, even the way we're gonna decorate the shop?"

"We haven't got the shop yet."

"But I'm gonna start looking tomorrow. In all those places we talked about. You know, this town closes down and dies in August, after Congress lets out. My classes are over the end of July, and soon as your friend gets back you can give her your notice and work at this full-time."

195

"I think we can do it," Karen agreed. They looked at one another, at once sobered and exhilarated by the prospect. "I really think we can do it, Cheryl."

"Sure we can do it. You know, Karen, you don't know what this means t'me. I can't tell you—"

"You did tell me. About ten times."

"An' I'll say it ten more times," Cheryl declared. "Can't say it too often."

For some reason this struck both of them as hilariously funny, and they laughed until they were breathless.

"We're drunk," Karen said, in surprise.

"Maybe you are, but I'm not. I'm just a little tipsy. Here we go—this is the last. A final toast?"

"To us," Karen said.

"Couldn't've said it better myself."

They had retired to Karen's room to inspect the merchandise and go over the books. "I tell you what," Karen said, trying to collect her wits. "You better not go home in that condition. Oh, I know you aren't drunk. But neither of us is exactly sober, now are we? Why don't you spend the night?"

"Okay," Cheryl agreed. "I better call Mark. Ask him if I can spend the night."

"What do you mean, ask him?"

"You're right, you're right. Don't ask him—tell him. Only . . ." Cheryl's mouth drooped. "Only I don't have my toothbrush or my nightie."

"No problem. Ruth is one of those perfect hostesses who always has extra toothbrushes for guests. And if you want a nightgown—" Karen walked, none too steadily, to the wardrobe and threw open the door. "Take your pick. Victorian with handmade eyelet ruffles, Edwardian with pin tucks and tatting, bias-cut peach satin—"

"What, wrinkle the merchandise?" Cheryl's eyes

widened in horror. "I'll sleep in my skin. First, better call ol' Mark."

Cheryl pulled herself together enough to sound relatively coherent when she announced to her brother that she would not be home that night. Karen, preparing Ruth and Pat's room for a guest, overheard enough to deduce that Mark had been properly congratulatory about the partnership and rather pleased than otherwise that he would not have to deal with a giggling, tipsy sister.

After she had tucked her new partner into bed, Karen went downstairs to let Alexander out. It was not until she looked into the darkened garden that she remembered her ghost. "Nothing like cash in hand to scare away spooks," she thought with a smile as she called Alexander in, checked the doors and windows, and went up to bed.

"Karen! Karen!"

Muzzy with sleep and champagne, it took her a while to recognize the voice. She struggled to sit up, muttering, "Whazzamatter?"

Cheryl stood in the doorway, silhouetted against the light from the hall. She had been persuaded to wear one of the older, more tattered nightgowns; it was too big for her and puddled around her bare feet.

"What's the matter?" Karen repeated.

"There was somebody in my room."

The only body in Cheryl's room belonged to Alexander, who was engaged in a thorough sniff of every corner. Someone had certainly been there, however, or else Cheryl was guilty of walking in her sleep. The wardrobe doors were flung wide, and most of the clothes had been removed from the hangers.

"What happened?" Karen gasped, reaching for some of the garments that littered the floor.

Cheryl caught her arm. "Don't touch anything yet. Did you feel a draft when we came through the hall?"

They stared at one another. Then Karen ran for the stairs, with Cheryl close behind. The draft of air became stronger as they descended. Karen heard Cheryl stumble and swear as Alexander scooted between her legs. He passed Karen, tumbled down the last few steps, and scrambled wildly on the slippery floor before achieving a right-angle turn and vanishing in the direction of the kitchen.

When Karen reached the room he was gone. The back door stood wide open.

She stopped to catch her breath, and Cheryl caught up with her. "For God's sake, Karen, wait a minute. You don't know what the hell is out there."

Clinging to one another, they ventured cautiously out the door and onto the terrace. A faint, far-off rumble of thunder shivered in Karen's ears, and a gust of wind hot as a breath from an inferno stirred her hair. There was a storm brewing; but the stars overhead were still bright, and a sliver of moon hung low in the sky. The white forms crowding the garden shone faintly in the starlight, stirring feebly like victims of a massacre who had been thrown in broken, distorted attitudes across the bushes. A limp sleeve fluttered, as if in a last futile appeal for help.

They got the clothes in before the storm broke. Thunder crackled overhead as Cheryl made coffee, just in time; the electricity went out soon after the kettle had boiled. The telephone was also dead. They sat at the kitchen table with candlelight throwing gruesome shadows across their strained faces.

"I shouldn't have shut Alexander in with me,"

Karen reproached herself. "When I think what could have happened—"

Cheryl was equally angry with herself. "Lord knows how long he was in there rummaging around before I woke up. If only I hadn't had so damned much to drink!"

"Thank God you did. If you had screamed, or made a sudden move..." She couldn't finish the sentence, or decide what horrified her more—the thought of what the intruder might have done to Cheryl, or Cheryl's appalling nonchalance.

"Try the phone again, Karen," Cheryl urged. "The storm seems to be letting up."

"I'm not sure I want to call the police."

Cheryl's jaw dropped. "Why not? This is the second time—"

"That's just it. It isn't the second time I've complained to the police, it's the third; and it would be the fourth if I had reported what happened last night...Damn. I'm so shaken up I can't keep my mouth shut. I wasn't going to tell anyone about that."

"Well, you'd damned well better tell me. Honestly, Karen, I can't figure you out. You're too brave for your own good. What happened last night?"

Karen hoped Cheryl would laugh at the bed sheet incident. She didn't laugh. "There's something funny going on, all right," she said soberly. "All the more reason why you should notify the police."

"But don't you see, they're going to get sick of hearing from me! They get calls all the time from nervous women who think there are burglars under the bed—"

"Men, too," said Cheryl, loyal to her sex. "Tony told me about some screwball who is convinced aliens from outer space are tapping his phone. What does that have to do with you? You aren't imagining things. I saw what happened tonight—"

"You did have a lot to drink tonight. I could have crept into your room and cleaned out the wardrobe—done all the rest of it—before I went back upstairs and made noises to waken you."

Cheryl studied her gravely. "You're your own worst enemy, Karen. It's as if you were still blaming yourself for everything that happens to you. You can't just sit here wringing your hands and letting people hassle you."

"You think that's the motive behind all this?"

"I don't know. It doesn't make sense. I guess I don't have the right to boss you around, but..."

"You want me to call the police."

"I sure as hell do. After all," Cheryl said. "I've got a half interest in that merchandise."

It was late morning before an officer finally arrived in response to the call they made after the storm had ended and telephone service had been restored. The bad weather had produced flooding and innumerable minor traffic accidents, and he was obviously in no mood to sympathize with their complaint. One of the first things he did was scold them for disturbing the scene of the crime.

"What were we supposed to do, leave the door wide open with a thunderstorm going on?" Cheryl demanded, looking like an indignant hen with her ruffled yellow curls and bright eyes. "Let the clothes get soaked? They're our merchandise!"

The officer looked with polite incredulity at the limp blue negligee she was waving at him. "If you say so, ma'am. But there's not much I can do except file a report."

After he had gone, Karen could not resist. "What did I tell you?"

"We did the right thing, anyhow." Cheryl yawned.

"Why don't you go back to bed for a few hours?"

"Who, me? I'm going to Gaithersburg to see that realtor."

"What realtor?"

"Anyone I can find. We talked about it last night, remember? Or have you changed your mind?"

"About the shop? Of course not. I thought perhaps you might have had second thoughts."

"Me? Why?"

"I wouldn't blame you, after last night."

"Oh, that." Cheryl grinned, obviously relieved. "What's a partner for?"

"A partner isn't obliged to set herself up as a sitting duck."

"I'm no sitting duck," Cheryl stated, her jaw protruding. "I may not be big, but I'm tough. I've taken a few karate lessons, and I'm a dead shot."

"I fondly hope those skills won't be required."

"Back where I come from, every kid learns to handle a gun. Do you have one?"

"I think Pat did have a gun, once upon a time. He kept it in the drawer of his bedside table."

"There's no gun there now. Not if that's the room I slept in; I opened the drawer this morning, looking for tissues."

"Then it must be somewhere else—or he got rid of it. I know Ruth never liked having it around. Cheryl, what are you getting at?"

"Why, I'm going to move in with you," Cheryl said calmly. "Unless you object, that is."

"But—"

"I won't be any trouble. I'll do the cooking and the

cleaning, and we're going to be so busy getting the shop started that I'd be here a lot of the time anyway."

"You don't have to sell yourself. But—"

"Mark doesn't really need me. He only asked me to move in as a favor to me, and now that the session is ending he's too busy to do much entertaining. Can I have a key?"

"There are extras on the hall table. But—"

"But me no buts. You'd better get dressed. Didn't you say you had an appointment with a lawyer this morning? I'll feed Alexander and lock up before I leave. Hurry, you're going to be late."

Karen started up the stairs, feeling as if she had been adopted by some strong-minded female head of state who combined the motherly concern of a kindly old lady with the role of general in chief of the armed forces. On the whole, she thought she was going to like it.

ROB was late to work again. When Karen spoke to him about it, he replied with poorly concealed insolence and retreated to the office.

Could Rob be the one responsible for what appeared to be a deliberate campaign of petty persecution? He had the right personality traits; he was eccentric, small-minded, and capable of harboring a grudge for fancied wrongs. He had pretended to be airily amused by Julie's refusal to leave him in charge, but perhaps he resented the person who had, as he believed, replaced him in Julie's trust.

Karen dealt with a minor flurry of customers and then sat down with the petticoat she was altering. Rob's temper had improved; she could hear him crooning to himself from the office, where he was supposedly un-packing china. He only hummed when he was in a good mood. Was he looking forward to another conquest that night or congratulating himself on another trick success-fully carried out?

She was holding the petticoat up to make sure she had not missed any rents when Rob came out of the office.

"Mmm, yummy," he remarked. "I know a little lady who'd look gorgeous in that. Want me to steer her in? For the usual commission, of course."

"It's already spoken for," Karen said. "That's why I brought it in; I told the buyer it would be ready today."

"How much?"

There was no reason why she shouldn't tell him, so she did. Rob clucked appreciatively. "You're really mak-ing a killing at this, aren't you, duckie?"

"I'll be happy if I can make a modest living."

"'Twill be more than modest if you go on as you began. Who's the buyer, one of your rich friends from Middleburg?"

"I don't have any rich friends," Karen said shortly. "If you are referring to Mrs. Montgomery, she's only an acquaintance and—I hope—a good customer." Realizing that her tone had been repressive, she tried to make amends. There was no sense in irritating people need-lessly. "She wouldn't buy anything like this. It's the young girls who go for the Victorian whites."

"Well, I'm sure it's just terribly fascinating, but I'm glad I don't have to worry about pin tucks and edging and all that. I'm going to run next door for a snack. Can I bring you anything?"

Karen declined with thanks and a pleasant smile. Her customer came while Rob was out; the remodeled petticoat was a perfect fit, and after the girl left, Karen studied the check with a satisfaction she had not felt even with Miriam's extravagant purchase. This money represented almost pure profit, for the petticoat was one she had found in old Mrs. Ferris' motley collection, and its pristine perfection was due to her own labors. Few people would have given it a second glance in its original condition.

Rob returned with an ice cream cone wrapped in a paper doily, which he presented with a bow. "Champagne ice," he announced. "Just the thing for you."

"Why?" Karen asked in surprise.

Rob's blue eyes widened. "To celebrate your sale, duckie. What else? I'm too poor to go for the bottled bubbly."

Karen laughed and thanked him and reminded herself she must not be paranoid, seeing sly hints in innocent remarks. But her annoyance revived when Rob appeared shortly thereafter wearing a blue silk shirt that set off his eyes. "You don't mind if I leave a bit early," he announced breezily. "Heavy date tonight—and I do mean, my dear, hea-vy!"

The chimes above the door tinkled mockingly as he opened it. "I may be late getting in tomorrow," Karen said. "Will you be sure—"

"But of course, darling." Rob's teeth shone like ivory. "That's fine with me. Be as late as you like."

He really is a maddening little bastard, Karen thought. Neither the adjective nor—as far as she knew— the noun was strictly accurate; but one tended to think of Rob as little, despite his inches. It was descriptive of his personality, anyway. But she could hardly scold him for taking time off just before she announced she intended to do the same. She wasn't paying his salary.

She hoped to join Cheryl next morning in her search

for a suitable location. Cheryl was right, that was really the first order of business upon which everything else depended, and the sooner they got at it, the better. When Cheryl called later that afternoon it was to announce that she had found several likely prospects, but that she thought they ought to look farther. "I'll tell you about them tonight. I'm at home now, packing my things; okay if I go right to the house?"

"Yes, fine."

"Are you very tired?"

"Why? Are there some places we could inspect this evening?"

"Well, not exactly. We've been invited to dinner. I said I'd let him know. That maybe you were too tired after last night."

"Him," Karen repeated. "You told Mark what happened?"

"Wasn't I supposed to?" Cheryl asked innocently.

"Oh, it doesn't matter."

Cheryl appeared not to notice her ungracious tone. "He's really pleased about the partnership. That's why he's taking us to dinner, to celebrate."

"It's very nice of him," Karen said dryly.

"Would you mind if Tony joined us?"

"Of course not."

"Good. I'll tell him. See you later."

She hung up before Karen could answer.

So Cheryl had barely waited till her back was turned before running to her brother for help and sympathy. The fact that Karen felt a sneaking, cowardly sense of relief at Mark's involvement only made her angrier, not with Cheryl but with herself. She should never have agreed to letting Cheryl move in with her. It was tantamount to inviting a friend to join you in a cage of lions. Or perhaps a cage of rats—the attacks thus far had been more frightening than physically dangerous, but part of the terror was not knowing precisely what threatened her, or why.

Naturally Mark was concerned about his sister. The talk of celebrating the partnership was only an excuse; including Tony Cardoza in the party gave Mark's true motive away. She and Cheryl were about to attend another meeting of the Murder Club. Only this time, instead of idly arguing about classic crimes, the two men would be discussing a real case.

It was probably the sort of case Mark would relish if Cheryl were not involved. He had undoubtedly tried to talk her out of staying in a house where so many peculiar, possibly threatening, things had happened. He had failed, of course. Cheryl was as stubborn as she was loyal. What else could Mark do but take all possible steps to protect his sister?

I shouldn't let her do it, Karen thought. But how can I prevent her? Especially when I don't want to prevent her.

CHAPTER EIGHT

KAREN closed a few minutes after five, practically pushing a last lingering customer out the door. The woman had been in the shop for half an hour and obviously had no intention of buying anything; she was just killing time. Cheryl wasn't at the house when Karen got there, but she arrived soon afterward, by cab, with several suitcases.

"I left the car for Mark," she explained. "He said he'd pick us up about six-thirty."

While she waited, Karen had tried to summon up courage enough to tell Cheryl she had changed her mind. Though she paced up and down rehearsing different approaches, she couldn't find one that sounded convincing. If she denied being afraid, Cheryl would tell her she ought to be. If she admitted she was terrified at the idea of staying alone, Cheryl would be all the more determined to stick to her side. And she couldn't bring herself to admit the truth—

that she did not want to be obligated, even indirectly, to a man who had been forced, against his will and his wishes, into the conventional role of male protector by her friendship with his sister. He might even think she had encouraged that friendship in order to see more of him.

She had not decided how to tackle the subject when Cheryl arrived, but it didn't matter; Cheryl never gave her a chance to introduce it. She talked steadily while they showered and dressed, with only a few brief interruptions as she dashed in and out of the bathroom. "... the one in Poolesville is kind of cute. Cheap, too. But it needs a lot of work, and I think we'd be better off in an area that already has some craft and antique shops. Not New Market or Alexandria, rents are too high, but maybe Kensington or Falls Church. Suppose we try Virginia tomorrow. There's a town in Prince William County...."

Karen gave up—at least for the present. She decided defiantly that she might as well enjoy her evening out, a rare chance to wear pretty clothes and dine at a nice restaurant with two good-looking men. Even if both of them were more interested in burglars than in her.

It had been Cheryl's idea that they model some of their merchandise. "We should always do that when we go out, Karen, especially to someplace fancy. I told Mark he had to pick the best restaurant in town."

Karen had agreed, primarily because she had nothing else suitable. Never again would she appear in public wearing the disastrous silk dress Jack had called homemade. If she could ever afford a cleaning woman, she would emulate Mrs. Mac and give the dress away.

She had selected a dress from the thirties that hung straight from the shoulders to the irregular, calf-length hemline. Its chiffon skirts were frosted with overlapping rows of black sequins and tiny rhinestones. She was struggling with the snap fasteners along the side when Cheryl came in.

"Oh, Karen, you look sensational! Here, let me do that."

While Cheryl coped with the snaps, Karen studied her reflection in the mirror. It was certainly a considerable improvement over the one she had seen a few weeks earlier. She looked thinner, but that might be the dress; black is notoriously slimming. The greatest change was in her expression—lips curved and cheeks flushed with laughter at Cheryl's breathless compliment. The shadow girl was laughing too; but now there was no mockery in her smile.

"Don't you think the dress is too stagy?" Karen asked doubtfully.

"You can look at me and say that?" Cheryl struck a pose. She was wearing a strapless fifties prom dress with a bouffant net skirt, in which she looked no more than eighteen. "Anyhow," she went on, "that's just how we want to look. Eye-catching. Stand up straight. Throw your shoulders back. That's better."

Mark arrived promptly at six-thirty, wearing a conservative dark suit and tie. After explaining that Tony had been delayed and would meet them at the restaurant, he examined his sister and broke into rude, uninhibited laughter. "What are you supposed to be, the sweetheart of Sigma Chi?"

"Sneer all you want," said Cheryl, unperturbed. "Do I look cute or don't I?"

"You look sweet sixteen and ready to be kissed. If that's a compliment..."

"Now tell Karen how gorgeous she is."

Karen stiffened self-consciously as Mark gave her the same careful inspection he had given Cheryl. "She's beautiful. Even more beautiful than..." He checked himself and then went on smoothly, ". . . than Mrs. Mac when she wore that dress. Ever see pictures of her when she was young? You wouldn't call her beautiful, but she was a knockout in her own way."

He turned away to help his sister with her wrap. The quintessential politician, Karen thought sourly. The compliment hadn't ended the way she expected; she only hoped her expression had not betrayed her feelings. She wondered how he had known the dress was one of Mrs. MacDougal's. It was hardly likely that she had shown it to him. Perhaps she had worn it in one of the pictures he had mentioned. Or perhaps he had simply assumed it had been hers, after hearing Cheryl chatter about Mrs. Mac's designer dresses.

The restaurant was new to Karen—not surprisingly, since fads in eating places came and went in Washington—but Cheryl nodded approvingly. "Good choice, my boy. It's one of the 'in' places. We'll be seen by everybody who is anybody. Too bad we don't have our cards printed, Karen, we could pass them out to people."

"That would be just dandy for my image," said Mark. "I've got trouble enough being seen in public with somebody who looks like Debbie Reynolds."

They did attract a few stares as the headwaiter led them to a table. Its position was indicative of Mark's status as a fledgling Congressman—not one of the cozy banquettes that were reserved for real celebrities, but in a location where they could see and be seen.

"We may as well order," Mark said, after they had been seated. "No sense waiting for Tony; he never knows when he can get away."

"I suppose he's stuck with another murder," Cheryl said.

"Murder?" Karen repeated. "Let's hope it's just a nice harmless breaking and entering."

"No, it would be murder," Cheryl said absently, her attention fixed on the menu. "That's Tony's job—homicide."

Karen was content to drop the subject.

Cheryl did most of the talking. Descriptions of the properties she had inspected carried them through the cocktails, and she had just launched into an animated lecture on bookkeeping methods when the appetizers arrived. She stopped talking and inspected her oysters on the half shell with visible disgust.

"I don't know why you order oysters when you hate them," Mark said, spearing one and swallowing it.

"They're classy. Besides, this way you can eat twice as many. Look—isn't that the TV announcer—Channel 4—I forget his name—"

"Quit staring," Mark ordered. "That definitely is not classy."

"Someone's waving at you," Cheryl said delightedly. "I can't see who... Oh!"

The sudden change in her voice would have been amusing if she had not been so visibly embarrassed. Mark was not embarrassed—when had Mark ever been?—but the rising tide of color in his face betrayed his annoyance with his sister—not because she had pointed Shreve out, but because her exaggerated reaction underlined a situation that could, and should, have been passed off as a casual social encounter.

On a sudden impulse, Karen waved back. The look of surprised indignation on Shreve's face pleased her enormously.

"There's Tony," Mark said with relief. "It's about time."

Theirs were not the only eyes that followed Cardoza's progress across the room. Again Karen was struck by his astonishing good looks. His colleagues must kid him unmercifully about being so beautiful.

"Sorry I'm late," he said, pulling out a chair. "A policeman's lot..."

"Bad?" Mark asked. At close range the signs of strain on Tony's face were visible to all of them.

"Yeah."

Though Mark was obviously curious, he took the hint. "Drink up, then. You're behind."

"I'll stick to wine, thanks. Have to toast the new enterprise."

After Tony had ordered he leaned back and smiled at them. "This is a pleasant change from my usual stale sandwiches and TV dinners. If you had told me the ladies were going to be so dolled up, I'd have gotten my tux out of mothballs."

"Just don't mention the sweetheart of Sigma Chi," Cheryl warned him.

"You look cute."

"Thanks for nothing."

The affectionate older-brother smile Tony had given Cheryl faded as he turned his attention to Karen. After a moment he said unexpectedly, "'She walks in beauty, like the night of cloudless climes and starry skies....'"

Karen felt her cheeks grow warm. She could think of no appropriate response to a compliment so gracefully expressed, so obviously sincere. How long had it been, she wondered, since she had blushed at hearing the open admiration in a man's voice?

Mark broke the silence. "If there is anything more revolting than a literary cop—"

Tony grinned. "Hey, pal, if you can't hack it, don't

knock it. Here's luck to the lovely lady, and her partner, and their business." He raised his glass.

"Thanks," Karen said. "We're going to need it."

"Especially if people keep messing up the merchandise," Cheryl added. "We've washed and ironed some of those nightgowns twice in two days."

Her blue eyes widened innocently as she spoke, but as Karen had realized, her new partner was not as ingenuous as she appeared. Cheryl did not believe in wasting time, or resources. To her surprise, Karen found that her initial reluctance to imposing on Mark—and Tony— had faded. Tony's charming tribute had nothing to do with it, of course. Neither man appeared averse to discussing the matter. In fact, Mark looked more alert than he had all evening.

"That's one explanation," he said. "Have you got a jealous rival, ladies?"

"A couple of dozen rivals, I guess," Cheryl answered. "But if someone is trying to discourage us they're going about it the wrong way. It will take more than a little washing and ironing to stop us."

"If the low-down rat knew what a menace you are when you're riled up, he wouldn't mess with you," Tony said, smiling at Cheryl. "I agree with you. Anyone who wanted to put you out of business would burn or destroy your stock. There's something else involved. Karen, can you think of anyone who might have a grudge against you?"

"No. Tony, I appreciate your concern—and Mark's—but we don't have to talk about this. It's not your responsibility. And I'm sure you are very, very sick of crime."

"Honey, this isn't a crime." The endearment slipped out smoothly and naturally; Tony appeared not to notice

213

he had said it. "Not the kind I'm accustomed to deal with daily, at any rate. It's more like an interesting little problem."

"A case for the Murder Club?" Karen asked with a twist of her lip.

"Oh, hey," Tony said quickly. "Don't get the idea that this is just an academic exercise for me. It might be if I had read about it or heard about it. But when it happens to someone I know and like . . . You aren't going to tell me to stay out of it, I hope?"

"I'm very grateful," Karen said quietly.

"There's nothing to be grateful about. That's just the point. No serious crime has been committed, and in my expert opinion there is no danger of a serious crime. This looks like a case of simple harassment. It may not even be directed against you personally. Kids playing tricks, picking a victim at random—"

"Trying to strangle someone is a hell of an unfunny joke," Mark said.

"Shut up and let me be the detective. That's what they pay me for, you know. The first incident may or may not be connected with the others. Whether or not, it's obvious that the guy was not lying in wait for Karen; he was caught by surprise, and lost his head. As for the enterprising young man who made off with Mrs. Mac-Dougal's car—I'm sure you thought you recognized him, Karen, but we have a reliable report of his being seen in Cleveland. It's his home town and he is not unknown to the police there."

He smiled at Karen, who shrugged resignedly. If he was trying to prove that he knew all about her recent adventures, he had convinced her. But he had not convinced her she had been mistaken about Horton.

"The next episode is particularly interesting," Tony

went on. "We might call it 'the ghost in the garden.' A bed sheet is certainly a weird disguise—"

"It's a damned good disguise," Mark broke in. "It conceals not only the face but all other identifying characteristics, even height and build. I admit a person wearing it would be somewhat conspicuous out on the street, but in a secluded back garden nothing could be better, and once he leaves the premises he can just roll it up and carry it under his arm. What's suspicious about dirty laundry?"

"Okay, okay. The trouble with you, Mark, is that you talk too much. I still think the bed-sheet disguise suggests someone's peculiar idea of a joke. And a pretty childish joke at that—I mean, who in this day and age believes in the old-fashioned sheeted specter? We've seen too many special effects in too many horror films to be frightened by anything so primitive. Hell, if I decided to play ghost, I could come up with a much more ingenious costume."

"I'll bet you could," Cheryl said.

"Which is precisely my point," Mark insisted. "It wasn't meant to frighten Karen. . . . You weren't frightened, were you?"

"Who, me?" Karen gave a hollow laugh.

"Well, I don't mind admitting I'd have been scared to death," Cheryl announced. "Seeing something like that, in half-fog, half-darkness. . . . You big brave heroes can jeer all you want, but I'll bet you'd have been shocked out of your socks too—at least for a few seconds."

"Exactly," Mark said triumphantly. "Those few seconds could make the difference between capture and escape."

"I don't know what the devil we're arguing about," Tony said. "There was no danger to Karen in that incident—right? The next one, last night's, is a little more serious. The joker actually got into the house. Now are

215

you girls absolutely certain you locked up? I got the impression you were both a little—well—"

"You have a lot of nerve calling us drunks," Cheryl exclaimed.

"I didn't say you were drunk, I implied you were careless. Did you lock all the doors and windows?"

"Certainly," Cheryl said loftily.

"I'm sure," Karen said. "Well—ninety-nine percent sure."

"You'd better be a hundred percent sure," Tony said soberly. "Because if you did lock up, it means your visitor has a key to the house."

"Or that there is a way in we don't know about," Mark said.

"Come off it," Tony grunted. "Next thing you'll be talking about secret passages. Look, ladies, I'm not trying to cast aspersions on your sobriety, but it doesn't seem possible that someone could have a key. You just had new locks installed, didn't you? So. The next question is, did anyone know Cheryl was staying overnight?"

"No," Cheryl said without hesitation. "It was a last-minute decision. I didn't know myself until after midnight."

"You didn't call Mark?"

"Well, of course. You know I did."

"Just a damned minute," Mark said. "Are you suggesting—"

"I am trying to conduct a proper interrogation," Tony said. "And I'm having a hell of a hard time doing it. Did you tell anyone Cheryl was going to be at Karen's?"

Mark's cheeks darkened. "What do you think, that I called everybody I know to tell them the cat's away and now little brother can play?"

"I don't know what you're so uptight about," Tony

said in an aggrieved voice. "Relax. I am simply trying to establish that Cheryl's presence in that room and in that bed was known only to Cheryl and Karen."

"Oh." Mark sat back.

"Nobody knew," Cheryl said. "For goodness' sakes, you men make such a fuss about the simplest things."

"So," Tony continued doggedly, "the guy went into what he assumed was an empty room. He opened the wardrobe. He probably got the shock of his life when Cheryl started stirring and mumbling. He ran—with an armful of clothes. Now if he was startled, scared, he might have held on to them for a second or two. But why didn't he drop them on the stairs or in the hall? Why carry them out to the garden and spread them around? Why bother with a lot of rags in the first place?"

"They aren't rags," Cheryl said indignantly. "They are valuable—"

"Yeah, sure, so you keep telling me. But come on, ladies—how much are they worth? A couple of hundred bucks? A couple of thousand?"

"Closer to a hundred thousand," Karen said.

"What?" Tony was obviously taken aback.

"I've never really thought of it in those terms," Karen said slowly. "But I have—oh, thirty or forty of Mrs. Mac's dresses. They aren't all designer originals, and their value varies a lot; but when you consider that a Poiret evening dress sold at Christie's in 1981 for fifty-five hundred dollars—"

"Five thousand bucks for a dress?" Tony exclaimed incredulously.

"Some are worth more," Karen assured him. "Some less, of course. . . . I almost wish you hadn't brought it up, Tony. I guess I don't have the mercantile mentality."

"That's what I'm supposed to be contributing to

217

this partnership," Cheryl sputtered. She smacked herself on the forehead with the flat of her hand. "Insurance. My God, insurance! Why didn't I think of that? First thing tomorrow—"

"Hold it," Tony said. "I'm glad I reminded you of your forgotten duties, kid, but we're wandering off the subject. I didn't realize—"

"Throws your theory into a cocked hat, doesn't it, buddy?" said Mark with a mocking smile.

"What about yours, buddy?"

"Doesn't affect mine." Mark leaned back and folded his arms.

He obviously wanted someone to ask him what his theory was. No one obliged. Tony swallowed, pondered for a moment, and then said firmly, "No, it doesn't have anything to do with what I was thinking. Because the clothes weren't stolen. They were arranged—deliberately arranged—around the garden. That reminded me of something. I'm surprised it didn't strike you, Mark."

"You mean the Stratford case," Mark said.

"Uh—right." Tony looked crestfallen. In the hope of a more appreciative audience, he turned to Cheryl. "It happened in 1850, in Connecticut. Started with the standard poltergeist phenomena: objects flying through the air, fires breaking out with no apparent cause. But there was one unusual feature. One day when the family came home from church they found a lot of their clothes in the parlor, stuffed with pillows and arranged in strange positions, like dummies in a tableau. One was kneeling in front of an open Bible."

When he had finished, there was a profound silence that lasted until the waiter had removed the plates and requested their choice of dessert.

"I'm having those little cream puffs with chocolate sauce," Cheryl said. "Tony, are you out of your mind?"

"You don't get it," Tony said. "No, thanks, no dessert for me."

"Nor me," Karen said. "I'm afraid I don't get it either."

But it had been a curiously disturbing image and it increased the eeriness of what she had seen the night before—the white shapes fallen in helpless abandon, like victims of a massacre.

"This is serious, Tony," Cheryl said reproachfully. "And you start rambling on about haunted houses and poltergeists!"

Tony glanced at Mark, who was not trying to conceal his amusement. "I'm not rambling on about poltergeists," he said, in the strangled voice of a man who is controlling his temper under extreme provocation. "I don't believe in poltergeists. Everything has a rational explanation, including the Stratford case. The dummies were set up by someone—"

"Everyone in the household was in church," Mark said gently. "Including the servants. They alibied each other."

"Then they lied, or they were misled," Tony said. "There was malice in that case, and that's the motive here too. The parallels—"

"Are purely coincidental," Mark said. He was no longer smiling. "The motive in this case is so obvious it hits you in the face. I can't imagine why the rest of you don't see it. Somebody wants something Karen has. It's that simple."

"Ruth's silver," Karen began. "Her antiques—"

"Not Ruth, you. This nonsense didn't begin until you started collecting old clothes."

219

Karen laughed. "Are you suggesting a competitor is trying to steal my stock? The most valuable things haven't even been touched, much less taken. Or maybe it's someone who has a mania for dressing up in antique women's clothing."

Mark looked thoughtful. "I hadn't thought of that one."

"But I'll bet you've thought of things that are just as far-out," Tony jeered. "A will in the pocket of an old coat? A diamond bracelet some woman just happened to forget she had left in her purse?"

Cheryl began waving her hands. "He's right, but he's all wrong," she said excitedly. "I mean, it must be something Karen bought. But don't forget the trouble began the day we went to the auction. And what happened at the auction."

Mark had obviously heard all about Mrs. Grossmuller. He let out a whoop of laughter. "I suppose the old lady stitched a confession of murder into her wedding dress—thirty years before she bumped the judge off."

That ended any hope of a sensible discussion. Even Tony got carried away; it was he who postulated a treasure map embroidered onto a tablecloth. Paste gems that weren't paste but genuine, diamonds disguised as buttons—they covered the gamut of absurd theories. They were laughing over Karen's suggestion—a lost Edgar Allan Poe manuscript cut up and used to line a lady's bodice—when a voice behind Karen said brightly, "I had to stop and say hello."

Tony was on his feet. Mark started to follow suit; Shreve put her hand on his shoulder and held him in his chair. "Don't get up; I wouldn't disturb such a pleasant group for the world. So nice to see that you're having an evening out, Karen."

"Like the maid, you mean?" Karen turned. "Have you met everyone?"

She performed the introductions. Shreve nodded slightly at Cheryl—"I've met Mrs. Reichardt"—but her eyes returned immediately to Cardoza. "Detective?"

"Yes, ma'am," said Tony, trying to look stolid.

"Charming," Shreve murmured. "What a pretty dress, Karen. Is it for sale?"

"I'm afraid it wouldn't suit you," Karen said. "But if you are interested in a dress, come by any time. All customers welcome. I'll even take your personal check."

"How adorable of you." Shreve's hand moved from Mark's shoulder to his cheek. She patted it gently. "Well, I'll say good night. Don't let this poor boy work too hard."

"I'd say the honors went to Karen," said Tony critically, as Shreve joined the rest of her party.

"Is that her husband?" Cheryl asked, staring unabashedly.

"No," Mark said. "Does anyone want coffee?"

"At three bucks a cup?" Tony shook his handsome head. "Now if someone were to offer me a cup later, after I had escorted her home . . ."

"Good idea," Cheryl said. "And then you guys can help us look for the missing treasure."

"I was just kidding about that," Tony protested.

"I wasn't." Mark reached for the check. "I tell you, he's looking for something. Don't forget what he said to Karen."

"'Where is it?'" Cheryl repeated. "I had forgotten that. I think you're on to something, Mark."

Tony was not so easily convinced. Pressed by Mark, Karen was forced to admit that the idea was not as far-fetched as their joking discussion had made it sound. She had heard of dealers finding old letters and diaries, even jewelry, in a bag or a pocket. They argued back and forth most of the way home, and in the end Tony grudgingly conceded that there was a possibility Mark was right. Only a possibility, though.

"It will be like looking for a needle in a haystack," he grumbled. "If the purported missing object were something obvious, you'd have found it by now. You've looked in the pockets and in the toes of the shoes?"

"I never thought about the shoes," Karen said.

"Oh, hell," said Tony.

They had reached the house; Karen took out her key and inserted it in the lock. "Damn," she said, twisting. "It sticks."

"Let me." Mark unlocked the door.

"Aren't you going to open it?" Cheryl demanded.

Mark stepped back. "You go first."

"Our hero! What are you afraid of?"

"The dog," Mark said simply. "This is my best suit."

Tony seemed equally disinclined to volunteer. With a scornful sniff Cheryl opened the door and demonstrated her technique. After he had been tipped over, Alexander got to his feet and walked away with the abstracted air of a philosopher pondering one of the great universal questions.

"I've got to get out of this dress," Cheryl announced, leading the way into the house. "It's so tight I can hardly breathe."

"You ate too much," her brother said rudely.

"You ate my oysters."

"Oysters aren't fattening. What did it was that mountain of profiteroles."

"I shall ignore that," Cheryl said. "Shouldn't you change too, Karen? Remember our rule: Don't wrinkle the merchandise unnecessarily."

"I'll make the coffee," Mark said. "I take it the merchandise is upstairs? Yell when you're decent and we'll come up. This way, Tony."

Loosening his tie, he strolled toward the kitchen with the confidence of someone who knows his way around a house and feels at home there. Which of course he did, Karen thought. At one time he had been a frequent visitor, welcomed with the total hospitality Pat extended to people he liked. Memories warm as summer and clear as actual sight filled her mind—Mark and Pat sitting in the kitchen, elbows on the table, sleeves rolled up, scattering crumbs and leaving beer and coffee stains on the cloth; Ruth scolding both of them with affectionate impartiality as she mopped up the mess. . . .

"Hey, Karen," Cheryl called from the top of the stairs. "I need help with this zipper."

"Oh, yes." Karen came back from ten years in the past. "Coming."

The search began with a certain amount of enthusiasm. Even Tony looked hopeful as he examined the shoes, most of which had belonged to Mrs. MacDougal. They had been neatly stuffed with tissue paper—but only with tissue paper. Mark seemed fascinated by the dresses. He kept repeating, "Five thousand dollars? Five thousand?"

Finally Karen lost patience. "They are like any other kind of antique or collectible, Mark; the price depends solely on what people are willing to pay. Here, give me that. You're going to loosen the crystals pulling at them."

"I can't believe they aren't diamonds," Mark said, giving up the dress—one of Mrs. MacDougal's more heavily beaded creations. "There's no place to hide anything in these dresses—no pockets, no collars, no sleeves."

Tony's interest had declined, but he stuck to the

223

job, methodically examining handbags and purses, feeling the linings to make certain they were intact, turning them upside down and shaking them.

"What's this?" Mark reached into the wardrobe and took out a small cream-colored box.

Karen launched herself at him with a shriek and snatched the box from his hands.

Mark recoiled. "What the hell—"

"That's my Fortuny!"

"I don't know what a Fortuny is, but I can assure you I wasn't about to wipe the floor with it."

Karen peered cautiously into the box. "It's one of his Delphos dresses. Nobody knows to this day how he got those tiny pleats, covering the entire garment. They had to be returned to him to be re-pleated, and they were sold in boxes—like this one—rolled and twined around like a skein of yarn. I was afraid you were going to take it out. I haven't dared touch it, because I know I'd never get it back the way it was."

"How much?" Tony asked, as Mark contemplated the small box with a mixture of disbelief and respect.

"A couple of thousand—but that's just a guess. As I told you, the price depends on the market at any given time."

"Holy Geez." Tony shook his head.

"All right," Mark said. "We won't unwind your Fortunato."

"Fortuny."

"Whatever. I trust this isn't another sacrosanct item?" He took out a black velvet evening cloak and ran his hands over the fabric. "Hey—there's a lump under here—"

"That's a shoulder pad, you oaf." Cheryl snatched the cloak from him. "You'd better leave this to us, Mark.

You're getting everything all wrinkled, and you don't know anything about clothes. We're more likely to notice something unusual than you."

"I'm running out of steam," Mark admitted. "And out of ideas." He ran his hands through his rumpled hair. "What about that jewelry of Mrs. Mac's, Karen?"

"How did you hear about that?" Karen asked.

"She told me she was going to give it to you," Mark said readily.

Apparently this was one piece of information he had not passed on to Tony; the latter demanded to know what they were talking about, so Karen explained, and brought out Dolley's necklace and earrings. The gleam in Tony's eyes faded when he saw them, however. He shook his head. "No."

Karen was beginning to feel protective about poor Dolley's jewels. "What do you mean, no? They are historic treasures."

"Maybe so, but they aren't worth much to your common garden-variety thief. I was expecting big shiny diamonds."

"I thought you were going to let Bates take charge of them," Mark said.

Karen repeated what she had told the lawyer. Her tone was aggressive; she rather expected Mark would tell her she was wrong, and demand that she put the jewelry in safekeeping. However, he nodded and said agreeably, "Right. It's not a question of whether you have it, but whether someone thinks you have it. Why don't you give me the case? I'll carry it conspicuously out of the house— drop it and take my time finding it—"

Tony hooted. "Drop-kick it into the street, maybe. Or I could go out for a pass."

Cheryl didn't smile. Karen could see that she too

225

was disturbed by the suggestion that someone might be watching the house. She said sharply, "If you think we're under surveillance, you had better take a couple of shopping bags too. We don't know what this character wants."

"If anything," Tony agreed. He yawned widely. "We'll leave you ladies to your well-earned rest. I don't admire your bedtime reading, though, Karen. Guaranteed nightmares."

He picked up the Georgetown legends book. Karen explained its presence, adding, "You know about it?"

"Oh, yeah." Tony's eyes twinkled. "The local precinct got a couple of calls from irate citizens. They wanted the author arrested."

"I wouldn't mind giving him or her a few swift kicks," Mark said. "Resurrecting those old scandals can only hurt people. The one involving Mrs. Mac..." His thin lips curved in a reluctant smile. "She thought it was funny. Laughed till I was afraid she'd choke."

"Can I read the book?" Cheryl asked.

"Help yourself. It's only on my bedside table because I've been too lazy to put it away. Maybe I had better get rid of it before Pat comes home; he's likely to go after the author with a horsewhip when he reads that libel about his mother."

"It's not libel," Tony said. "That's why the author is safe from the heavy hand of the law. Most of the information comes from old newspaper stories and other published sources; the rest is innuendo, and the author was smart enough to skirt the edge of the actionable. Besides, nobody seems to know who he is."

"Pat is just as likely to consider it the best joke since Watergate," Mark added. Rising, he stretched and yawned. "Feel free to call at any hour, girls, if you find the diamonds."

"Don't worry," Cheryl said. "We will."

"Is someone going to escort us to the door?" Mark inquired.

Cheryl flatly refused, with a few pointed remarks about big strong men and little helpless dogs. Karen offered to do guard duty. Tony lingered; she heard him say something to Cheryl, who replied with a peal of laughter and a comment whose tone was decidedly caustic.

As they descended the stairs Karen said, "I'm sorry you were dragged into this, Mark. It wasn't my idea."

"I'm sure it wasn't."

"If you could persuade Cheryl to leave—"

"No one can talk Cheryl out of, or into, anything. She's a grown woman; she makes her own decisions." They had reached the door; Mark turned to face her. "Are you seriously suggesting that I remove Cheryl and walk away, leaving you to the tender mercies of some wandering lunatic—or that muscle-bound chauffeur whose pretty face you admire so much? What kind of cold-blooded bastard do you take me for?"

His voice cut like a knife. Before Karen could reply, Tony came running down the stairs, and Mark turned away.

Tony took Karen's hand. "Thanks for an interesting evening. It isn't often I get a chance to search for lost diamonds and literary manuscripts."

Without turning, Mark opened the door. "If you're going to start quoting, keep it short and snappy," he said, and went out, leaving them alone.

"I want to hear the key turn and a lot of clattering of chains and bolts," Tony said softly. "Not that I think there's anything to worry about—"

"I know. Thanks, Tony."

Abruptly he bent his head and touched her lips with his. Brief though it was, the kiss had nothing tentative

227

about it; the brush of his mustache along her upper lip sent a tingle through her body. Then he was gone, closing the door after him. She heard a soft voice say, "Locks."

Karen did as she was asked. There was no further comment from Tony. Peering through the spy-hole, she saw only his broad back, retreating.

Mark was waiting for him on the sidewalk, strategically situated in the light of a street lamp. Karen's view was limited and distorted, but as she watched she realized Mark was putting on the promised performance with the jewelry case. He did everything but drop-kick it, and although his gyrations were exaggerated to the point of farce, Karen was not particularly amused.

She made a detour into the kitchen and prepared a pot of tea. The rumble of Alexander's snores followed her up the stairs; really, she thought, there must be something wrong with his sinuses. Considering that his entire face was wildly out of sync, it would not be surprising.

Cheryl looked up from the ledger she was inspecting and smiled. "I was just thinking a cup of tea would hit the spot. Are you tired? Want me to get out of here so you can go to bed?"

"I'm still keyed up. I need to unwind. But if you're sleepy—"

"We've got to stop being so damned polite," Cheryl said. "To tell the truth, I'm dying to go over your records. Unless you mind—"

"Who's being overly polite now? I'd be delighted to have you take over the damned books. I'm absolutely hopeless about keeping records; I keep forgetting to write things down." Karen curled up in the chair Mark had occupied. "What I really want to do is sit here and watch you work."

"That's right. You're the artistic half of the team

and I'm the business end." Cheryl frowned at one of the entries. "Did you itemize Mrs. MacDougal's dresses? All I can find is an entry that says, 'Misc. clothes, Mrs. Mac.'"

"Oh, dear. I meant to do it right, only..."

"You've been distracted," Cheryl said, with a wry smile. "Let's start with the two dresses you sold that friend of yours."

After she had made the entry she asked, "When did you tell her you'd have them ready?"

"I didn't. But we must get at it right away. Some of the beads are loose, and then they have to go to the cleaners'."

"I'll do that tomorrow afternoon. What cleaner do you use?"

"It's someone Mrs. Mac recommended. What's more," Karen added, "I had to be recommended to him. He is not, if you please, taking new customers. But he knows how to handle delicate things. Be sure you explain to him—"

"I get it. Throw Mrs. MacDougal's name around and insist he handle these items personally."

"While you're at it, you could pick up the things I took in a few days ago. I think the ticket is here somewhere." Karen rummaged in her purse and finally came up with the receipt. "Be sure you keep track of the cost. And speaking of money—"

"Why talk about something we don't have?" Cheryl grinned. "This is a hand-to-mouth operation, Karen. Sooner or later we'll get a proper accounting system set up, but right now it's grab it while you can."

Karen refused to be amused. "It's going to be touch and go for a while, I know that. It looks as if I may have to take advantage of Pat's offer and borrow from him until—and if—I can get a settlement from Jack."

229

"That's right, you saw the lawyer today. I'm sorry, Karen, I didn't even ask how it went. There was so much to talk about."

"He was nice. He's just starting out, that must be why Mr. Bates recommended him. I'm sure his fees are a lot less than Bates, Bates, and Whoever. But he wasn't terribly encouraging. These things take time, said he profoundly—especially when, as seems evident, Jack is not inclined to be generous. Well, damn it, I don't want generosity, I just want what's fair. Lord knows I earned it."

"It's definite, is it? You aren't going to change your mind?"

"About the divorce? Not on your life. Even if I were dumb enough to stick my head back in the noose, Jack wouldn't take me back. It was his idea in the first place."

Cheryl studied her earnestly. "I'm sorry if you are; I'm not sorry if you're not. Don't get me wrong; I just wouldn't like to be left without a partner before we even get this show on the road."

"No fear of that. Even if both of us had complete changes of heart I'd still go on with the shop. I have to do it. It means a lot to me. Actually, I was about to ask you the same question. You'll marry again one day—"

"No."

"You may feel that way now, but—"

"No. I'm never going to get married again."

Her head was bent over the book, and her tumbled hair hid her face. After a moment Karen said gently, "How long has it been?"

"Two years. I know what you're going to say." Cheryl turned to face her, tossing her hair from her forehead. Her face bore an expression Karen had never seen on it before, a blend of dedicated exultation and of pain. "Everybody says the same thing. You'll get over it, time heals all wounds.... But I won't. My life isn't ruined or anything like that. I'm a very happy person, really. But I'll never love anyone but Joe."

The flat finality of her voice would have forestalled argument, even if Karen could have thought of anything to say. She was astounded. To think that Cheryl, outwardly so cheerful and matter-of-fact, nourished this unrealistic, sentimental delusion...

Karen had no doubt that it was a delusion. Love was not eternal, grief did not endure. "Men (and women) have died, and worms have eaten them, but not for love." She was as convinced of those clichés as she was sure the sun would rise next morning. All the same, she felt a dull ache of envy.

"I'm so sorry," she began. "I shouldn't have raised the subject—"

"Oh, it's just as well we got it out in the open," Cheryl said calmly. "People are always trying to fix me up with other guys. It's a waste of time; you might as well know that from the start."

"So that's why Tony..." Karen stopped and bit her lip.

"Tony is a good friend."

"He is also the best-looking man I've ever seen. A real hunk, as they say. I wondered why you hadn't mentioned that little detail."

"I guess he is handsome," Cheryl said indifferently. "Joe wasn't. I mean, most people wouldn't consider him good-looking. Tony likes you, Karen. I could tell."

"I'm not so sure," Karen murmured. She was seeing several things in a new light.

"You're the one who is likely to remarry. A beautiful, educated person like you—"

"I doubt it. I didn't like being married."

231

The statement surprised her almost as much as it did Cheryl. "Really? Wasn't there anything—"

"No. Now that I think about it, there wasn't much about being married that I liked. I didn't own anything. Everything I had was a gracious, patronizing gift—money, clothes, food, the house, even my time. Jack's work came first, and I got what was left over."

"Not all men are like that," Cheryl said earnestly. "And there must have been something. . . . I mean, don't you miss . . ."

Cheryl's delicacy amused Karen. In her new role as partner she was trying to be more refined. "Sex? Yes, I do miss it. But, to put it as nicely as possible, there wasn't much to miss."

"That's putting it nicely, all right. But I get the picture. You mean he . . ."

"I think the word would be competent," Karen said musingly. "Marginally competent. It came as a shock too, I can tell you. He was very amorous before we got married. Once it was legal, he seemed to lose interest."

Cheryl let out a gurgle of laughter. "You're funny, Karen. You say things so elegantly, but they sound much more insulting than if you'd cut loose and used a lot of four-letter words."

"I should be ashamed of myself," Karen said with a smile. "We're always complaining about men thinking of women as sexual objects, and here I am doing the same thing."

"Was Mark . . ." Cheryl stopped with a gasp, and turned away. Karen had a glimpse of a beet-red, horrified face before Cheryl's hair swung down to hide her features.

"I'm sorry," said a muffled voice from behind the hair. "Me and my big mouth. I should have it amputated."

"Forget it." Karen laughed and put an affectionate

arm around Cheryl's hunched shoulders. "This is like those old college bull sessions, where we all sat around and let our hair down."

"I never went to college," Cheryl muttered.

"I never finished. So what?"

Cheryl looked up. Her face was still crimson. "Pretend I never said that, okay? I don't want to know anyway. I mean, my own brother . . . He never told me any personal things, Karen. Honest."

"I said it's all right." Karen had no intention of answering the implied question. It had set off a sharp stab of memory that was humiliatingly physical in its intensity. "Was Mark . . ." Oh, he was, she thought. He certainly was.

"We'd better get to bed," she said lightly. "We should be bright and sharp tomorrow for our session with the realtor."

"Right. Listen, how would you feel about a place with living quarters upstairs or at the back? For us, I mean. I'd pay a bigger share of the rent—"

"Why should you pay more if we share . . ." Karen's breath caught. "I'm a selfish, thoughtless jerk. I keep forgetting about your little boy."

"I don't talk about him much. But I think about him all the time."

The words were quiet and unemotional, but they struck a chord that vibrated deep down in Karen's very bones. Her fingers closed over Cheryl's shoulder. "We'll do it. Come hell or high water, burglars or bankruptcy, you'll have him with you in time for kindergarten this fall."

It was an extravagant promise, a promise she had no right to make; factors over which neither of them had any control could make it impossible to keep. But she was filled with shame at her selfishness. Preoccupied with her own emotional problems, she had failed to consider Cheryl's.

Yet who would have supposed that beneath the other woman's smooth, bright façade there was a layer of sensibility as fragile, and as damaged, as the shattered silk lining of an antique garment?

She ought to have known, or at least suspected. Friendship deserved more than she had given.

CHAPTER NINE

*F*ALLS CHURCH was, as Cheryl put it, a bust. The buildings they inspected were too expensive, too rundown, or in the wrong area. They left their names with a realtor who promised to notify them if anything turned up and headed for home, feeling somewhat deflated.

"We've just begun," Cheryl said consolingly. "Shall we have a quick look at Alexandria? You never know..."

Karen consulted her watch. "I'm afraid there's not time. Rob is totally unreliable, and I'm going to be late as it is."

As matters turned out, she was even later than she had expected. They finally found a parking place several blocks from the house; and as they approached it they saw something on the doorstep. It resembled a pile of rags rather than a human being, and Cheryl said pitifully, "Oh, it's one of those poor old bag ladies, shopping bags and all. I feel so sorry for them."

"That's no bag lady." Karen came to a stop and clutched Cheryl. "That's Mrs. Grossmuller!"

"My God, it is!" Cheryl clutched back. They stood huddled together, staring, until Karen let out a nervous laugh.

"What are we going to do? We can't stand here like a couple of Victorian damsels in distress."

"Let's walk around the block. Maybe she'll go away."

But Mrs. Grossmuller had seen them. Rising with monolithic dignity, she beckoned. She wore what must have been her "town" clothes—a rumpled, tarnished black suit of decidedly antique vintage, and the most incredible hat Karen had ever seen. It measured a good two feet across and was heaped with limp pink moire bows, with an almost naked ostrich feather crowning the pile.

"Don't laugh," Karen said out of the corner of her mouth, as they obeyed the summons.

"Laugh? I'm more likely to howl like Alexander. Why, hello there—Mrs. Grossmuller, isn't it?"

"I have been waiting a considerable time." Mrs. Grossmuller brushed at her dusty skirt. "You are very late."

Her dignity was so extreme it was difficult not to apologize; but Karen managed to refrain from doing so. Being at a loss for words, she fell back on the formula she used with customers. "Can I help you with anything?"

"Brought you some stuff," said Mrs. Grossmuller, in one of her sudden descents from formal English to western Maryland accent and colloquialism. "You gonna ask me to come in or do you want I should dump it out on the sidewalk like a common vendor?"

She pushed past Karen as soon as the latter had unlocked the door, and Karen's cry of warning came too late. "Watch out for the dog!"

Mrs. Grossmuller stood looking down at Alexander, who was squirming at her feet in unbecoming admiration. "Homely, ain't he? I guess that's the homeliest dog I ever seen."

The insult did not affect Alexander in the least. He continued to grovel and Mrs. Grossmuller added grudgingly, "Nice little feller, though. Friendly."

"He likes you," Karen exclaimed incredulously.

"Most dogs do. Well? Where's the sitting room? I could be persuaded to partake of a glass of sherry if it is not too sweet."

Mrs. Grossmuller got her sherry. She then spread her wares out across the furniture. They weren't quite as bad as Karen had feared, but they ran the gamut from a pair of pretty Victorian petticoats to faded calico aprons and sunbonnets. Some could never have fit Mrs. Grossmuller, at any stage in her life; Karen deduced that she had been looting her neighbors' attics, spurred on by her successful sale, and only hoped she had had their permission to do so. Being a receiver of stolen goods had a certain piratical ring to it when the stolen goods were gems and precious metals, but it would be demeaning to be arrested over a calico sunbonnet.

For once it was she who had to put her foot down on the outlandish prices Mrs. Grossmuller asked. Cheryl, who had not spoken a word since Alexander's astonishing performance, seemed absolutely hypnotized.

Her worst fears were uncalled for; after a reasonable amount of dickering Mrs. Grossmuller accepted her offers and repacked the merchandise that had been rejected. "You're smarter than I thought," she remarked. "Couldn't take you in. Figured it was worth trying, though."

She settled back with a pleased smile and thumbed through the money Karen had given her.

"How did you find me?" Karen asked.

The answer was the one she expected. "Your address was on your check. I'll bring you some more stuff another time."

"No, don't do that," Karen exclaimed. "I mean— I'll be moving soon."

"Where?"

"I don't know yet. Why don't you give me your address and phone number and I'll call you."

"Makes sense," said Mrs. Grossmuller agreeably. She reached into her capacious purse. "My card."

It really was a calling card, yellow with age and frayed around the edges, but handsomely engraved.

"Thank you," Karen said. "Well. I'll be in touch."

"Oh, I'm not leaving yet," said Mrs. Grossmuller, settling herself more comfortably. "You still got my wedding dress?"

"Uh—no. It's not here. It's—it's at the cleaners'."

"Oh. Too bad. I'd have liked to look at it again."

Karen glanced at Cheryl, who was staring at Mrs. Grossmuller with the dumb fascination of a chicken under the cold, hypnotic gaze of a snake. She herself was conscious of a desire to burst into wild, uncontrolled shrieks of laughter.

"I'm sorry we can't ask you to stay, Mrs. Grossmuller. We are going out."

"When?"

"Right now," Karen said firmly.

"Oh. Well, I guess you couldn't ask me to stay to lunch then. Were that not the case I might be offended by the omission." Mrs. Grossmuller gathered up her shopping bags and rose, stepping carefully over Alexander, who was sprawled at her feet, licking her shoe. "I guess I'll just hike down Wisconsin and look in the windows. Maybe have lunch out, seeing as I'm so rich. Is there a McDonald's around?"

Karen showed her out and then ran into the parlor, where she and Cheryl stood watching out the window, as Mrs. Grossmuller walked to a car parked—illegally—across the street, and got in. The vehicle swung abruptly out into the traffic, ignoring a Camaro that had to slam on its brakes to avoid a collision, and wove erratically away.

"Are you all right?" Karen asked, nudging her paralyzed partner.

"Pinch me," Cheryl gasped. "I don't believe it. Did you see that car? It was a Mercedes. And Alexander... She put a spell on him!"

"Cheryl, get hold of yourself. She's a poor, senile old woman. Why does she affect you that way?"

"Listen, I know a lot of senile old ladies. None of them acts like that. I can't help it. She gives me the creeps. Be honest, Karen; what would you think if you woke up in the middle of the night and saw that face looking in your window?"

"I'd think I was dreaming. She couldn't get up to a second-story window without a ladder—"

"Or a broomstick," Cheryl muttered.

"I'm sorry I can't stay and protect you from witches, but I'm horribly late already. I haven't even time to change. Are you sure you won't be nervous?"

Cheryl gave herself a shake. "Don't be silly. I've got plenty to keep me busy. But I'm going to lock all the doors."

"You do that. I wish I could stay and help you. Oh, well, it won't be long; Julie will be back in a few days."

Julie was back sooner than that. Karen was not

unduly surprised, though she was angry, to see that the shop was dark and that the grille across the door was still in place. Not until she started to unlock the padlock did she realize that although the hasp had been inserted into the hole, it had not been pushed home.

"*THIS* is getting monotonous," said Tony Cardoza.

Hands on his narrow hips, he looked down at Karen, seated at Julie's desk.

"It's not my fault," Karen growled. "And if you've called Mark..."

"I have not called Mark." Tony sat down on the corner of the desk.

"Then don't. I won't have him dashing to the rescue everytime something happens."

Tony grinned and pushed his hat back on his head; then he remembered and whipped it off. "Sorry about that."

"Oh, for heaven's sake, who gives a damn about formality? Just tell those idiots to stop spraying powder on the merchandise. It will take me all day to clean it up."

"They are looking for fingerprints," Tony said mildly.

"I know. I'll never get the damned ink off my hands."

"If you're through yelling, maybe I can ask you some questions. I have a few other things to do this afternoon, little unimportant things like investigating some murders."

"Okay, okay." After a moment Karen added, "I'm sorry, Tony. I appreciate your coming so quickly."

"Oh, listen, I've developed a conditioned reflex. I've seen your name on so many call sheets lately I automatically jump into action. Did you call what's-er-name— the owner?"

"She was out. I left a message for her at the hotel."

"The name of which is..."

"I told the officers."

"Then tell me."

"What are you up to?" Karen asked curiously. "Cheryl said you're Homicide, so this isn't even your case."

"I'm on my lunch hour," Tony said. "What I do in my spare time is none of the Department's business. Now, then, you were about to give me the name of that hotel."

Karen leaned back in her chair. She was recovering from her evil humor; Tony's calm, friendly professionalism was comforting to overstrained nerves.

"I thought of Julie when you asked me if someone had a grudge against me," she admitted. "She was furious when I refused to let her have the clothes for her own shop. I gather you know all about that; you seem to know everything else about me."

"Cheryl talks a lot," Tony said. "Look, Karen, I'm doing this because I want to—okay? Nobody's forcing me. So why don't you relax and let me do it?"

"Well..."

"Here comes one of the boys in blue to ask you what is missing. Talk nice to him."

"I don't know what's missing. The place is so torn up. ... Oh, damn! Julie is going to blow her stack."

Julie did. It was late afternoon before she telephoned, and it was clear that she had already heard the bad news, for she burst into a scream of vituperation as soon as Karen picked up the telephone. Karen had been prepared to sympathize, but the unreasonable accusations

of negligence and worse made her angry; after trying un-
successfully to get a word in, she finally hung up. Then
she closed the shop and went home.

Cheryl administered iced tea and sympathy, and
Karen expounded her own theory. "Rob has to be the
guilty party. He never showed up, and when I called his
number nobody answered. I told Tony, but that man just
smiled mysteriously and wouldn't say a thing."

"I could call him," Cheryl began.

"No. And don't call Mark, either. Tell me about
your day. I'm sick to death of Julie and her problems. One
good thing—I'm through with her. After the things she
said to me I don't feel any obligation about staying
on."

"You should have told her you quit," Cheryl said
loyally.

"I did. Three times. But I don't think she heard me.
She'll probably show up here later; don't be polite and
leave us alone, I'll need your moral support."

"I'll slug her if she gives you a hard time," Cheryl
promised.

"Oh, damn," Karen said, hearing the telephone.
"I'll bet that's her now."

It was Mark. He asked to speak to Cheryl, and
Karen handed over the phone. Cheryl covered the mouthpiece with her hand. "Can I—"

"Oh, sure, go ahead. Tony has probably talked to
him already."

She stamped out to the kitchen and began peeling
potatoes. Cheryl followed her a few minutes later. "Mark
was wondering," she began, "if we'd like to go—"

"He'll have to settle for hamburgers and potato
salad." Karen gestured with her paring knife at the pile of
vegetables. "And tell him to bring that closemouthed friend

of his. Maybe when Tony is off duty and full of food he'll be more communicative."

TONY was perfectly willing to talk. "It's not a secret. You didn't have to bribe me. But I'm glad you did," he added, accepting a second serving of potato salad.

They were sitting around the kitchen table. It was still too hot for an outdoor picnic, and Ruth's formal dining room didn't seem appropriate for hamburgers and the beer Mark had brought. He and Tony were in their shirt sleeves and the latter was very obviously off duty. He paid Karen outrageous compliments on her cooking; when she accused him of looking unusually pleased with himself, he was prompt to admit it.

"I think we've solved the identity of your ghost, Karen. Since he's probably well on his way to parts unknown, you shouldn't have any more trouble."

"Rob?" Karen asked.

"You don't sound surprised."

"I am—and I'm not. I knew he didn't like me, but I can't believe he would be so vicious."

"You're jumping to conclusions," Mark said, tugging absently at a lock of hair. "What makes you think it was Rob?"

"This was found on the floor of the office, where it might have fallen out of someone's pocket, and been kicked into a corner. I persuaded the boys to let me have a copy."

He handed the paper to Karen. Mark reached for her hand and moved it into a position from which he could see too. His fingers tightened over hers, and he muttered something under his breath.

243

The original had been a group photograph. Karen recognized it immediately. "It's from my college year-book," she said in a strained voice. "I made the tennis team the first year—by a fluke, really, everybody got sick or broke an ankle or something. That's Anne—I forget her last name ... Susan Reeder ... and (strange how hard it was for her to pronounce the name) ... and Shreve."

"And the hole in the middle is you?" Mark asked. He snatched the paper from her numbed fingers and examined it closely.

"The names are printed underneath," Tony said. "That's how I knew. The face has been obliterated. Slashed with a knife or a pair of scissors."

"How do you suppose Rob got hold of this?" Cheryl asked. Some of the pretty color had faded from her cheeks.

"Julie brought the yearbook in one day," Karen said. She had to clear her throat before she went on. "She was pretending to play 'do you remember?' games; but I think she wanted to rub it in—how much I had changed. She showed it to Rob and—and to other people. He made a few of his cute little cutting remarks. ... I thought she had taken it home after the joke wore thin."

"She may have. The book wasn't at the shop." Tony retrieved the paper from Mark, who was holding it by the tips of his fingers, his lips curled in disgust. "This is proof of malice—"

"Malice?" Mark's hair stood up in agitated tufts. "This is sick."

Tony looked uncomfortable. "I didn't realize how it would affect you. Guess I've become hardened; some of the things I see make this look like a harmless joke. Sorry, Karen."

"It isn't only the photograph," Karen said. "It's the total accumulation. I feel as if I've been walking blindly along, doing my thing and trying not to get in people's way—assuming I was on solid ground—and all of a sudden I look down and see there is nothing under my feet except a narrow plank over an abyss. And someone is sawing the plank. I've never deliberately hurt anyone. . . ."

The movement Mark made was so slight no one except Karen noticed it; it affected her like a bolt of lightning that cast a sudden garish illumination into dark corners of her mind. She had never thought of her actions as hurting Mark himself, only his pride—his ego. There had been no commitment broken. . . . At least that was what she had believed.

"Sure, I know that," Tony said. "You're a natural victim, that's all."

It was Cheryl, not Karen, who exclaimed in indignant repudiation. Karen was struck speechless by this second burst of enlightenment. She felt as if someone were not only sawing the plank on which she walked, but knocking down all the protective walls she had built up. Was she really a natural victim, the helpless object of random violence, the scapegoat for resentment and hatred she had done nothing to deserve? The idea was humiliating and repellent.

Tony had tried to redeem his error by explaining. "Most women are passive victim types. . . ." This had only enraged Cheryl more, and they got into a heated argument which Tony ended by snapping, "Nobody would ever accuse you of being passive."

"Leave him alone, Cheryl," Karen ordered.

Cheryl looked at her in surprise, and subsided. Tony let out a martyred sigh. "Thanks, lady. As I was about to say—with the obviously mistaken intention of relieving everybody's mind—the robbery was an inside job. Your friend Rob tried to make it look like a break-in, but it was

245

a clumsy effort that wouldn't fool a baby. Now he's disappeared. One of the other tenants in his building saw him go out last night about midnight. He was carrying a couple of suitcases."

Frowning and unconvinced, Mark continued to tug at his hair. Tony added, "He has a record. Petty larceny, procuring, immoral acts—"

"What kind of immoral acts?" Cheryl asked, her eyes bright with curiosity.

"Uh—you know. The usual."

"Porno films and dirty photographs," Mark said, his tight lips relaxing into a half-smile. "She's of age, Tony, you don't have to be so prim and proper. How about drugs?"

"He used 'em. But we never picked him up for dealing."

"Burglary? Breaking and entering?"

"No."

"Assault? Armed robbery?"

"No. Now look, Mark, I know what you're getting at and I'm here to tell you it doesn't mean a damned thing."

"It's the wrong profile," Mark insisted. "You used the word passive—that's the word for little Robbie and his little misdemeanors. He wouldn't have the guts to break in here or attack Karen."

"You don't know what he would do. That's the trouble with you armchair detectives, you think real life is like the cases you read about, all neat and tidy and tied up with a ribbon."

They glowered at one another. Tony's brows were drawn down until they almost met in the middle of his forehead; Mark's face showed the familiar dark mantling of anger. This wasn't one of their usual friendly arguments; Karen could almost feel the tension between them.

Mark turned his head slightly. His eyes met Karen's for a brief, electric moment before he looked away and made a visible effort to control his temper.

"I'm not trying to tell you your job, Tony, but there are some big gaping holes in your theory. If Rob decided to take off after robbing the shop, why didn't he do a thorough job of robbing it? According to Karen, none of the major items were taken, only odds and ends. He knew how to turn off the alarm; he could have pulled a truck up to the back door and loaded it. Why leave the most valuable pieces?"

"You said it yourself," Karen replied, before Tony could speak. "He's a coward. He was afraid he'd be seen."

"Whose side are you on?" Mark demanded.

"Tony's," Karen said.

"I knew this woman had brains," Tony said, relaxing. "You have a point, Mark, but again you're assuming this guy was behaving rationally. After we've talked with the owner—"

"You're about to have that pleasure," Karen said, as the doorbell set up an angry, persistent clamor. "That sounds like Julie. I thought she'd come here looking for me. Somebody hold on to the dog."

She never knew whether the request was deliberately ignored, or whether Alexander's escape was accidental. He arrived on the scene just in time to turn Julie's angry greeting into a scream of pain. It was Mark who removed the culprit and sent him flying with a whack on his hairless rump.

Mark's appearance halted Julie's outcries. Smiling and brave, she allowed herself to be escorted to the kitchen, and accepted a beer.

"You can't blame me for being upset," she said plaintively. "Karen understands; she knows how I am.

247

Darling—" She fumbled for Karen's hand and clasped it tightly. "Darling Karen, I'm so relieved you weren't hurt. That was my first thought: Thank God Karen wasn't there, she might have been hurt."

Karen freed her hand. "It's not likely that I would be at work in the middle of the night."

"Oh," Julie murmured. "Was that when it happened?"

"So we assume," Tony answered. "Do you mind answering a few questions, Ms. Kerchak? It's not official procedure, but since we're both here..."

"Do call me Julie." She smiled at him, lips tremulous, lashes quivering. "And please ask any questions you like."

At first Julie refused to believe Rob was the thief. She defended him so vehemently that Karen wondered again whether their relationship was more intimate than she had believed.

Yet Julie's arguments were not those of an infatuated lover. "He might sneak things into his pockets—he's done it before—but he wouldn't risk his job. He's got a soft deal with me and he knows it, lots of perks on the side..."

"Like meeting wealthy women customers," said Mark.

Julie's lids veiled her eyes. "That's not my business. I tell you, Rob will turn up in a few days. He's gone off with one of his women, that's all."

"The locks weren't forced," Tony said. "Who else had keys?"

"Why, no one. Except Karen, of course..." Her indecisive tone and the quick, sidelong look she gave Karen virtually amounted to an accusation.

No one spoke. Cheryl was crimson with anger, but

Tony's hand on her shoulder kept her quiet. After a moment Julie threw up her hands. "I'm so upset I don't know what I'm saying. I won't sleep a wink tonight, I just know I won't. I'm afraid to go home. What if someone is there, waiting—"

"I'll take you home if you like," Tony said.

"Oh, would you? That is so sweet of you. I'd appreciate it more than I can say. Good night, all. Karen, I'll see you tomorrow."

Karen cleared her throat. Even after Julie's latest outrage she felt some qualms about what she was planning to do, but Tony's casual comments still rankled. A helpless victim type, was she? Not if she could help it.

"You won't see me tomorrow. I quit, remember?"

"Quit? Oh, but Karen—"

"I quit three times."

"I thought you were joking. You didn't take those things I said seriously, did you? Karen, you know how I am!"

"You also fired me. Right after I quit the first time."

"Oh, Karen." Julie clung to her hands. "You can't leave me in the lurch. You can't abandon me when I need you."

"I'll try to help you out now and then, until you find someone else. But I can't come in tomorrow. I'm busy."

Julie looked as if she were choking on the words she had to hold back. It was Tony's presence that restrained her; taking the arm he had not offered, she drooped and clung her way out of the house.

Cheryl immediately opened the back door. "Place needs airing out. What a bitchy broad! I was afraid for a minute you were going to let her talk you into going back to work."

249

"I'm not quite as big a sucker as everyone seems to think," Karen said shortly.

"Hey, I didn't—"

"I know. I wasn't referring to you." But even Cheryl had a protective big-sister attitude at times. That could be charming—if one wasn't overly sensitive about one's passivity. Mark did not protest. Instead he said mildly, "She's the kind of friend immortalized in the classic saying about not needing enemies. Has she really been out of town the past week?"

"I have no reason to suppose she was lying," Karen said.

"Right. Well, Tony will find out."

"Is that why he was so gallant about offering to take her home?" Cheryl asked.

"It wasn't because he's wild about her company. She's not his type." Mark spoke abstractedly, as if his mind were on something else.

"Well, if it was her, she'll be too tired to try anything tonight," Cheryl said. "And if it was Rob, he's long gone. Looks as if we can get a good night's sleep, Karen."

"Is that a hint?" Mark asked, without moving.

"No, just an announcement. You two can sit here all night if you want. I'm going to bed."

Mark got to his feet. "What's on the schedule tomorrow?"

"Virginia," Cheryl said with a grin. "Not all of it, just as much of it as we can cover. Why, were you about to make us an offer?"

"Just curious. Drive carefully, hmmm?" He gave her a quick kiss on the cheek and nodded casually at Karen. "Good night."

Karen stayed in the kitchen when Cheryl went to the door with Mark. He had made it clear he wasn't interested in her company. Why was he so determined to deny Tony's theory? Tony was the professional; and Tony felt sure the trouble was over. Rob and/or Julie were certainly the most likely suspects. It was almost as if Mark wanted her to be afraid.

OCCOQUAN, the town in Prince William County Cheryl had mentioned, was charming—small in size, fronting directly on the river, with a disproportionate number of craft and antique shops. According to Cheryl, its other advantages included restaurants with liquor licenses and lots of salads on the menu.

"That's important," she insisted, when Karen laughed at her. "I went antiquing a couple of times with some of those high-class Washington women—friends of Mark's, being nice to his poor relation—and I'm telling you, they consider the day a dead loss if they can't get their booze at lunchtime."

However, the only available building had no living quarters attached and the structure was in poor repair. They left their names with the realtor and inspected a few other properties in nearby towns before heading northward, following a route Cheryl had mapped out.

Shortly before noon they were in Leesburg, which Karen remembered as a quiet country town with a number of fine eighteenth-century houses. It also had several antique shops and restaurants that met Cheryl's specifications. However, Cheryl was pessimistic about their chance of finding anything in their price range.

"Loudon County is getting fashionable, which means expensive. There's a new shopping mall in Leesburg, one of those restoration projects like Harborplace and Faquier Square; that will drive prices up too."

They found one house that tempted both of them. Though the original structure was much older, turn-of-the-century additions had turned it into a late-Victorian gem with a wide veranda supported by white pillars and a profusion of gingerbread trim. The third floor had been converted into a separate suite with its own kitchen and bath, and there were two other bedrooms in an annex that overlooked a sunny, tree-shaded yard. The moment Karen saw the twin drawing rooms, one on either side of a wide, handsome hall, she knew they were the perfect ambiance for her gowns and linens. They were so like the mental image she had formed that she had an eerie sense of déjà vu.

The owner didn't think he wanted to rent. He had not quite made up his mind, but he was in a hurry to sell and would give them a price they couldn't refuse.

"We should have known it was just a come-on," Cheryl said disgustedly, as they drove away from the realtor's office. "These people will do anything and say anything to get you into a house. They think you'll fall in love with it and forget it doesn't meet any of your specifications."

"It almost worked, didn't it?" Karen, in the passenger's seat, twisted around for a last look as they passed the house. Wicker furniture and ferns on the front porch, she thought; in fine weather we could have dressed-up dummies sitting in the chairs, like ladies having tea.

Dressed-up dummies reminded her of her plundered wardrobe and the case Tony had mentioned. It was not a pleasant thought. At least they had passed a quiet night, with not so much as a growl from Alexander to alarm them. It must have been Rob, she thought. I wonder where he is now.

Cheryl glanced wistfully around as they drove through the quiet streets toward the highway. "It's a pretty town. I bet the schools are good, too."

"Maybe we could afford to buy."

"No, we couldn't." Cheryl gave her an affectionate smile. "I was just dreaming out loud. Doesn't cost anything to dream. What do you say we head south on Route 15? Then we can take 50 back to the Beltway."

Karen glanced at the map. "I hope you aren't dreaming about finding a place in Middleburg. Even in my day it was a haven for the horsy rich."

"It's even more so now. But it can't do any harm to look. Maybe one of the nearby towns will have something."

Almost the first thing they saw in Middleburg was a little shop specializing in vintage clothing. The owner was not overly gracious; either she spotted them as prospective competitors or she was unimpressed by their rumpled appearance.

"You shouldn't have asked her about her overhead," Karen said, as they walked along the street toward a realtor's office. "That was a dead giveaway."

"Well, we have to find out about those things. Most of the other merchants I've talked to have been nice and helpful."

The realtor was nice but not very helpful. As they had suspected, rentals in the center of town were beyond their means, and the few properties she had listed in outlying areas had other disadvantages. They left the office with a handful of Xeroxed papers to add to the other listings they had collected.

"I've had it," Karen announced, as they got back into the car. "Let's quit for the day."

"What do you say we go home by back roads? We can avoid some of the highway traffic and scout out the area."

"You're driving." Karen settled back. "Lord, it's hot. Turn that air-conditioning up, will you?"

The countryside steamed under a hazy sun. From the cool comfort of the car it looked very attractive, the lush greenery of trees and pasture forming a perfect setting for the white-pillared and soft red brick façades of handsome old houses. Cheryl drove easily and competently, undisturbed by the slow-moving farm vehicles that sometimes slowed their pace to a crawl. Fields of ripe hay glowed like golden tapestries; the corn was tassled and breast-high, and beyond white-painted fences horses grazed in the green meadows, their coats of black and russet shining in the sunlight.

"What a way to live," Cheryl said, glancing at a mansion high on a knoll beside the road.

"If you don't mind living with security guards and Dobermans," Karen said, indicating the closed gates and the two fierce dogs behind them.

Cheryl flicked on the turn signal. "I'm going to pull into the next driveway and let that Cadillac pass. It's been driving up my tailpipe for the last couple of miles, and I don't want to take any chances with your uncle's car."

As she suited the action to the words, the following car suddenly picked up speed and shot past, narrowly missing their rear bumper. Cheryl swore, and Karen exclaimed, "That looked like Miriam Montgomery."

"That friend of yours who bought the flapper dresses? She's a lousy driver."

"She's also no friend of mine. Just an acquaintance

and, I hope, a good customer. She said she lived in Middleburg."

"Then I won't tell her she's a lousy driver. I'm going to turn and go back to the main road. I don't have the faintest idea where we are."

THEY got home in the late afternoon, after stopping at the cleaner's.

"Let's not entertain this evening," Cheryl said, as Karen opened the gate. "We really do have lots to do."

"I had planned to invite the President for drinks, but since you insist..."

"Karen—Mrs. Nevitt!"

Karen turned to see the next-door neighbor in his doorway. He came trotting fussily toward them, the sun glaring on his bald head and winking off his glasses.

"Hello, Mr. DeVoto." Karen introduced Cheryl, adding, "Mrs. Reichardt is staying with me."

"Ah, I see. I am glad to know that. I had wondered who she might be." He turned his bespectacled gaze on Cheryl and explained seriously, "We watch out for one another here, Mrs. Reichardt. We are concerned citizens. In times such as these—the old values crumbling—crime rampant—moral and ethical standards deteriorating—and a young lady alone... You follow me, I am sure. I was only too happy to assure her aunt and uncle I would keep my eyes open."

Remembering Pat's reference to his neighbor as a fussy, prurient old fuss-budget, Karen was hard-pressed not to laugh.

"It's very kind of you," she said. "How is Mrs. DeVoto?"

"Keeping her spirits up, as always." He turned again to Cheryl. "My wife is bedridden, I am sorry to say. But always cheerful, always interested in the world around her. As a matter of fact, it is she whom you must thank for observing the incident I am about to relate to you. She insisted I tell you about it as soon as you returned home. She takes a great interest in young people. Karen is a particular favorite of hers."

Since Karen had seen Mrs. DeVoto twice in the past ten years, she took the statement with a grain of salt, but offered the apology that was obviously demanded. "I've been meaning to call on her, but I have been awfully busy. I work, you know."

"What incident?" Cheryl asked.

"A very peculiar-looking person came to your house today. Mrs. DeVoto happened to be at the front window. She is a keen student of human nature and enjoys watching people pass along the street..."

Mr. DeVoto was finally persuaded to come to the point. The very peculiar person had been a woman—"an elderly female, shabbily dressed; one of the sort they call street people, I believe, for she carried a number of parcels."

After knocking several times she had tried the front door, banging on it and rattling the knob. She had then gone to the back and banged on that door. When Mr. DeVoto spoke to her from his garden—"my wife had called me to the window, and of course I felt obliged to see what the woman was doing"—she had said something rude and gone away.

"Perhaps I should have called the police," he finished. "But since I am not acquainted with all your friends..."

"I'm glad you didn't," Karen said. "I think I know

who it was. She's perfectly harmless, but a trifle eccentric. We mustn't keep you standing out in the heat, Mr. DeVoto. I do appreciate your concern."

Mr. DeVoto was not that easy to dismiss, but after it had become apparent that he had learned all he was going to learn, he retreated into his house to pass the information on to his wife.

"That's a relief," Karen said, closing the door behind them. "I was afraid he was going to lecture me about hanging laundry all over the garden."

"I am not relieved," Cheryl announced. "Hi, Alexander, did you miss us? I don't like the idea of that crazy old lady hanging around here."

"What's the harm? She can't get in. Mr. DeVoto and his wife are terrible busybodies, but I suppose they don't have much else to do, poor things. Oh, all right, Alexander, it's early, but I guess you may as well have your supper, you'll go on bugging me until you get it. I can hardly wait to get into the shower!"

"Go ahead, I'll feed Alexander."

When Cheryl came upstairs Karen was in her room, hair dryer in hand. "What are you doing?" Cheryl asked. Instead of applying the dryer to her damp hair, Karen passed it carefully over a dress spread across the bed.

"Killing mildew. This is satin, it can't be washed; according to that book, the mold can be dried, and then brushed or vacuumed off."

"New book?" Cheryl picked it up and began leafing through the pages.

"I sent away for it. It came in the mail today."

"Hmm. Well, I know you're the intellectual half of the partnership, but I think this stuff is a waste of time. These people are so pompous! Listen to this: 'Historical costumes should never be worn for any occasion.' If we followed that rule we'd never sell anything."

"Most of the books are written for museum curators and conservators," Karen said. "But you know..." Absently she turned the dryer onto her head and reached for a brush. "I understand how they feel. It's true that the great majority of the clothes we'll be handling won't be unique or museum quality, but when I think of those dresses of Mrs. Mac's I get a pang of conscience. They're real works of art, one of a kind. And I'm selling them to rich idiots with no appreciation of their beauty who will ruin them in one wearing and throw them away."

"If it were my dress, I'd want someone to wear it— and look pretty, and have fun in it," Cheryl said. "I wouldn't want it to be stuck up in a case in some museum."

"That's because you are a hopeless romantic," Karen said, smiling. "My romantic side agrees with you. I wouldn't mind so much if they were going to someone who appreciated them. Miriam doesn't care about anything except how much they cost."

"If you really feel that bad about it—"

"Don't suggest we keep them. We simply can't afford to. Maybe someday, when we're rich and successful, I can start collecting for myself. But right now we need every cent we can get our hands on."

"I was going to say, before I was so rudely interrupted, that maybe we could sell them to collectors. Like museums, for instance."

Karen stopped brushing; her hair stood up in a wild halo, like Frankenstein's bride. "I don't know why I didn't think of that. We could try, at any rate. The Costume Institute in New York has a terrific collection of designer dresses."

"There's a list of museums in one of your books. I'll copy it and we can write letters, or call."

"You're sensational." Karen beamed at her.

"Oh, hey, that's my job, being sensational. I'm also great at making lists, which is what I'm going to do now. I wanted to finish listing the merchandise we have."

She went into the other room, but came back after only a few minutes. "Karen?"

"I don't think this is working," Karen muttered, moving the dryer slowly back and forth over the dress. "Maybe it takes longer. . . . What?"

"Did you move any of the clothes in your aunt's wardrobe just now?"

"No, I haven't even been in that room. What's wrong?"

"I'm not sure anything is wrong. But I could swear things have been moved. The blue peignoir was on the end last night. Now it's not."

Karen followed her into the bedroom. "I can't see anything different," she said, after a brief inspection.

"Maybe I'm imagining things."

"It's the baneful influence of Mrs. Grossmuller," Karen said with a laugh. "She couldn't have gotten into the house, Cheryl."

"I guess not."

"Is anything missing?"

"How would I know? That's why I want to finish that inventory. We can't even get insurance without it. Come and give me a hand when you've finished fooling around with your moldy satin."

Karen didn't resent her brusque tone; she could tell Cheryl was still brooding about Mrs. Grossmuller. Really, Cheryl seemed to be developing a complex about the old woman. To Karen, Mrs. Grossmuller was more pathetic than frightening and more pitiful than funny. Perhaps it was because she could understand better than Cheryl the years of desperation that had driven Mrs. Grossmuller over the edge. If she had gone on living with Jack, resenting every move he made and every word he said, would she have ended up, forty years from now, with a similar idée fixe? Not the same delusion necessarily, but one that reflected the same long-suppressed anger and indignation? Mrs. Grossmuller probably hadn't killed Henry; but oh, how often she must have wanted to!

At least divorce was a more acceptable option today. Not for Mrs. Grossmuller; in her time, decent middle-class women didn't get divorced. Socially it was more acceptable to murder an infuriating spouse—assuming you got away with it—than to leave him. Easier for me, Karen thought absently. All I had to do was get fat and sloppy . . .

Her mouth dropped open as the truth dawned—the answer to a question the psychologist had asked weeks ago. *That* was why she had let herself go. She didn't have the guts to come right out and tell Jack she wanted to leave him; she didn't even have the courage to admit it to herself. So she had pushed him into taking the fatal step, by turning herself into a careless, unattractive frump.

Was she succumbing to the weakness Cheryl had accused her of, blaming herself for everything that happened to her? No; there was a difference between feeling guilty and accepting responsibility. She had been silly and cowardly, but that didn't absolve Jack of his share of blame.

The telephone rang, interrupting her train of thought. She was not sorry to have it halted; her new insight would have to be considered and absorbed before she could really accept it.

The call did nothing to calm her. When she joined

Cheryl a short time later, it was Cheryl's turn to ask, "What's wrong?"

"Nothing." Karen forced a smile. "That was Shreve."

"Oh. What did she want?"

"That's a good question. She was so busy dropping little hints and innuendoes I couldn't figure out what the hell she was driving at. Finally I just said, 'Do you want to buy something or don't you?' and she admitted she did."

"Good, another big sale," Cheryl said. She replaced a white nightgown and took out another garment. "Where did you get this?"

Karen frowned. "It's one of Ruth's, I think. Yes, it's her size."

"Blue wool suit, size 6, Garfinckel's label," Cheryl muttered, writing. "Which of the dresses are you going to sell that—Mrs. Givens?"

"I don't know. She'll want one of Mrs. Mac's gowns, I suppose. Keeping up with the Joneses—or, in this case, her dear friend Miriam. But I'm not going to let her have anything until I'm certain the museums aren't interested."

"Makes sense," Cheryl murmured, her head bent over the ledger.

It was easy to tell when Cheryl was embarrassed or uncomfortable. Karen knew why her face was averted, her comments brief and stiff. Karen didn't regret the way she had answered back when Shreve deliberately baited her in front of other people, but talking about her behind her back was a form of spitefulness she was determined to avoid. She didn't want Cheryl to get the wrong idea about her reasons for disliking Shreve.

She went on, in a voice she attempted to keep cool

and detached, "I told her my best dresses were at the cleaners'. It's true, actually."

"Yes. I forgot to tell you, he didn't have the other things ready. Try again tomorrow, he said. But he wasn't very apologetic; acted like he was doing us a favor by working on them."

"By his lights he is. He's the 'in' cleaner for the smart set. I don't intend to use him except for really good clothes, but I don't want to take a chance on some incompetent ruining a valuable item."

"Is this one of your aunt's?" Cheryl held up a pink crepe afternoon dress. She was determined to stick to business, and Karen was content to go along with her. She didn't want to talk about Shreve, or think about her, any more than she had to.

"Yes. I think that finishes Ruth's things. Now this one—"

They worked steadily for several hours, stopping only long enough to snatch a hasty meal. They made good progress, although the telephone seemed to ring incessantly—first Mark, inquiring whether they had been burglarized lately and wanting to know what Cheryl had done with his black socks; then a realtor from Gaithersburg, with a new listing she wanted to show them; then Julie, tearful and reproachful and apologetic. They were in the kitchen looking over the list of properties they had inspected thus far when Julie's call came; and when Cheryl realized who was calling she didn't pretend not to listen. Karen had barely hung up when she burst out, "Honest, Karen, you haven't got the gumption of a rabbit. After all that woman did to you, and now you tell her you'll go back to work!"

"I didn't tell her anything of the sort—just that I'd give her a hand now and then, whenever it didn't conflict with my own schedule. I'll have to go back at least once, to pick up my paycheck."

"Hmph," said Cheryl, only partially appeased. "Your big fat check. Minimum wage, I believe you said?"

"Every little bit helps."

"Well . . . I guess if you weren't a sucker at heart I wouldn't want to be your partner."

"You put things so nicely. Now where were we?"

The telephone rang again. "I'm going to take the damned thing off the hook," Karen said irritably. "Hello? Oh. Hello, Tony. Cheryl is right here if you . . . Oh."

Her altered expression and tone brought a faint smile to Cheryl's face. She gathered up the papers and retreated into the dining room, carefully closing the door behind her.

This demonstration of tact only made Karen more self-conscious. "No, I can't tonight. Oh, I understand, I know you can't always tell in advance when . . . It isn't that. I just . . . Tomorrow night? I guess so. All right. Yes."

After she had hung up she went to the dining room door and threw it open, in time to see Cheryl hastily thrust one piece of paper into the pile.

"What was the object of that?" she demanded.

"I thought a little privacy—"

"Oh, crap," Karen said. Cheryl's eyes opened wide. Karen went on, "You knew what he was going to ask me. You put him up to it, didn't you? Poor Karen, she hasn't had an honest-to-God date in ten years, why don't you give the girl a break? I don't want you, so—"

"Just a goddamn minute," Cheryl exclaimed. She bounded up from her chair, cheeks flushed, eyes flashing. "That's a lousy thing to say!"

"It's the truth, isn't it? You're not interested, so you kindly hand over—"

"Hand over? Tony Cardoza? You think I can give him away like I would a—a raw oyster? Tony?"

Her voice rose in outrage, ending in an absurd coloratura squeak. Alexander jumped up, barking insanely. Cheryl's lips twitched. "Hey," she gasped. "Look at us. We're having our first fight. And over Tony Cardoza."

Karen found it was impossible to hold on to her indignation. They fell into one another's arms, shaking with laughter.

"I'm sorry," Karen said after a while. "I don't know what got into me."

"It's more a question of getting something out of you," Cheryl said profoundly. "That awful inferiority complex. I mean, just look at the two of us. What man would pick a short, fuzzy-brained woman with a fat tush when he could have you?"

"I suspect Tony Cardoza might," Karen said soberly. "Cheryl—"

"Look, don't push, okay? I'm glad we had our fight, we were being so damned sweet to each other it wasn't natural, but one fight per day is enough."

"More than enough. Let's get back to work. What's that paper you were trying to hide?"

Since one corner was sticking out of the pile, she found it without difficulty, despite Cheryl's laughing attempt to prevent her. As she had suspected, it was the listing of the house in Leesburg.

"I was just looking at it," Cheryl explained. "No harm in looking."

"Or in dreaming. I wish we could, Cheryl. I like it too."

"Maybe he'll decide to rent after all. We could make him an offer."

"Why not?"

This time it was not the telephone but the doorbell that interrupted. Karen swore—Cheryl's uninhibited vocal habits were having a decided effect on her own—and Cheryl said, "If it's that Julie, don't let her in."

"I'm not letting anybody in," Karen said, going to the door.

Mindful of Alexander, among other matters, she left the chain in place when she opened it. For a moment she thought she was hallucinating. A second look told her her eyes were not deceiving her. The wavy, silver-gray hair, the aristocratic features, even the faint frown that was his normal expression when he looked at her . . .

"Jack?" she whispered.

"Karen? Is that you? What the devil are you doing? Open the door."

"I don't open doors without looking," Karen said. "I was mugged the other night, if you remember."

"Oh, yes. Well, I'm not going to mug anyone. Let me in."

"When did you get to Washington?"

"I arrived this afternoon. I have my ticket to prove it, so don't try accusing me of anything. I came to talk to you, in the hope that we can cut through some of the legal red tape. . . . For God's sake, Karen, are you going to let me in or do you want everyone in the neighborhood to learn about our private affairs?"

"You really want to come in?"

"No, I'd prefer to stand here and shout at you through the crack," said her husband, with heavy sarcasm.

"Okay," Karen said. She opened the door and stepped back.

After Cheryl had detached Alexander and carried him off to the kitchen, Karen followed Jack into the parlor.

He sat down and fixed her with the icy stare that had so often reduced her to sick silence.

"I hope that childish demonstration made you feel better."

"Yes, it did," Karen admitted. "What do you want, Jack?"

He opened his briefcase and removed a sheaf of papers. Placing them on the coffee table, he studied her curiously. "You look different. I can't quite decide how. . . . Have you lost weight?"

"Yes. I'm rather busy, so please get to the point."

"I brought these papers for you to sign. Since you chose not to reply to the letters from my lawyer—" He broke off, staring pointedly at the doorway, and Karen turned to see Cheryl hovering, not certain whether she was wanted or not.

"Come in," she said.

"Really, Karen, this is between us," Jack protested.

"I want her here," Karen said. "She's my—er— accountant."

She had planned to say "lawyer," but thought that was putting an unfair burden on Cheryl's powers of dissimulation. Jack's eyebrows lifted in a well-remembered and thoroughly hated expression, as he contemplated Cheryl's cotton dress and her bare feet. Cheryl smiled broadly and sat down, crossing her legs in such a way that the dusty sole of one foot was visible.

"Hi," she said. "Go right ahead, don't mind me."

"Accountant," Jack repeated. After considering the options for a few seconds, he selected charm. After all, he was supposed to be irresistible to women.

"I'm delighted Karen has found someone to advise her on business matters," he said in a confidential tone. "You can tell her what a mistake it would be to let personal grievances blind her to her real interests. The sooner we settle these unpleasant but necessary financial questions, the better it will be for both of us. Lawyers merely exacerbate the bitterness in a divorce. The longer they drag things out, the more money they make—and the less there is left for the parties themselves."

"I s'pose that's true," said Cheryl, widening her eyes.

"So if you'll just sign here, and here." Jack offered Karen his pen.

Karen took it. A faint shadow of anxiety crossed Cheryl's face, but she didn't move or speak.

Karen didn't know what to do. Conflicting emotions came and went with such bewildering rapidity she was unable to focus on any one.

She opened her fingers and let the pen fall to the floor.

"You have to be out of your mind," she said. "Did you really believe you could con me into doing something that stupid?"

"Now see here," Jack began angrily.

"Excuse me." Karen rose. "There's someone at the door."

As she left the room she heard Cheryl say earnestly, "You see how she is, mister. I just can't get her to do a thing. No sense in you hanging around, is there? Hey, Karen, maybe that's your friend, that nice policeman."

Karen rather hoped it was. She didn't bother putting up the chain; hearing Jack's footsteps behind her, quick and heavy with anger, she flung the door wide.

The two men confronted one another as she involuntarily stepped aside. Mark was the first to speak. "Just leaving, were you? Don't let me stand in your way."

For a moment Karen thought Jack was going to

swing the briefcase he carried in a futile, spiteful blow; but he thought better of it. Mark was coatless, his shirt sleeves rolled to the elbow; the tendons in his forearms twitched as he flexed his hands.

Jack edged past him without speaking. Once safely on the sidewalk he turned; before he could say anything, Mark had pushed Karen out of the way and closed the door.

"I'm not sure I could control myself if he started sounding off," he explained apologetically. "My constituents would hate it if I were arrested for assault and featured prominently in the evening news—"

"I'm not sure I can control myself," Karen said. She folded her arms. "What are you doing here?"

"I just happened to be . . . No, I guess you won't buy that. So, all right, I was parked down the street. I saw him go in; when he didn't come back out, I started to worry."

"And who licensed you to worry about me?"

"Uh—Karen—" said Cheryl, from the door of the parlor.

"Keep out of this," said Karen. "I don't blame you, Mark, for taking precautions on Cheryl's account. That's between the two of you. But if you think you can come waltzing in here whenever some situation arises that you believe I can't handle . . . I didn't need you. I had everything under control."

"She really did, Mark," said Cheryl. "You should have seen her. She was—"

"Keep out of this," said Mark. Cheryl threw up her hands and vanished. "Okay, you didn't need me," Mark went on. "Fine. Great. I humbly apologize."

"Don't you see, you only made matters worse! He's already been abusive and insulting, now he's going to think—"

"I get the point," Mark interrupted. "Don't worry, I'll stay out of his way from now on. I don't want to make matters more difficult for you. Good night, Karen."

The door slammed as she stood openmouthed, her hand half-extended—too late to stop him.

He had misunderstood. Small wonder; she hadn't made it clear that she was primarily concerned about the verbal vitriol Jack could throw at him. His constituents wouldn't like to hear on the evening news that their congressman had been arrested for assault? They wouldn't be too happy about the insinuations Jack was capable of feeding the press either. He could play the injured, betrayed husband to perfection. Those who lived "inside the Beltway," as Washington was sometimes designated, were cynically casual about sexual misconduct; the small-town Midwest was not.

Karen reached for the doorknob. She didn't want Mark or anyone else rushing to her rescue all the time. Affectionate concern could be as destructive of independence as Jack's domineering contempt had been. She had to learn to handle her own problems. But she might have put it more gracefully, and expressed her appreciation for his intentions, if not his actions. An impractical, romantic gesture, and wholly typical of Mark—not the cool, calculating politician he had become, but the quixotic boy she remembered. He couldn't possibly mount guard over them every night, he had to sleep sometime! He was probably out there now, sitting in his car and sweltering in the summer heat. He wouldn't go off in a huff, however badly she treated him. She knew she would toss and turn half the night, in a turmoil of self-reproach, if she didn't set things right.

It was very dark outside. She stood uncertainly at the gate, looking up and down the lines of parked cars. Then she saw him, across the street—only a shadow moving, but the glimmer of his light shirt and the very way he moved made her certain. She called out and started after him. It was hard to find a way between the cars. Many were parked almost bumper-to-bumper. Half-running, she passed out of shadow into the patch of yellow cast by a streetlight, and went back into shadow before she found a way to cross the street.

She never actually saw the car. Without headlights it was only a shape of greater darkness, suddenly growing larger. She heard it, though—a squeal of tires, the roar of abrupt acceleration. Midway across the street, which was narrowed to a single lane by vehicles on either side, she wasted several vital seconds trying to decide whether to retreat or go forward. A voice shouted; then, as the car hung over her like a moving cliff face, she was struck and flung back. She felt his arms close bruisingly around her body; pain stabbed her thighs as she was squeezed and thrust into a space too small to admit her, between the close-parked vehicles. A rush of hot air fanned her face and lifted her hair.

Then there was nothing but the rapidly fading sound of the engine and the crumpled shape at her feet. It took her a while to extricate herself from the cramped space where she was pinned by metal and hard plastic. As she crouched beside him, fumbling with numbed, frantic fingers in the darkness, she felt the sticky wetness of blood on her hands and heard Cheryl screaming her name.

"GET away from me." None too gently, Mark pushed his sister aside. "I'm not going to the Hill tomorrow swathed in bandages. It's just a scratch."

"Suit yourself," Cheryl said. "It's your face. What's left of it."

Her pallor belied her sharp tone. Suddenly she sat down hard, her legs folded under her. "My God. I've never been so scared in my life. Hearing those tires squeal, then going down and finding the door wide open, and not a sign of either of you. . . ." She covered her face with her hands.

Karen wanted to reach out to comfort her, but she couldn't seem to move. The air in the room felt abnormally cold; she had to clench her jaw to keep her teeth from chattering.

"Calm down," Mark said. "Nobody is hurt. I knocked myself out for a second when I fell, and scraped some skin off my face. That's all. It could have been worse."

It would have been worse if you hadn't thrown yourself in the path of the car. The words formed in Karen's mind but some substance filled her throat and blocked their utterance. Cheryl took her hands from her face. She was still pale, but she had herself under control.

"Drunk driver?" she suggested.

"Could be." Mark started to shrug, winced, and changed his mind. He had fallen heavily; he'd have bruises and sore muscles next day.

"His headlights weren't on," Karen said.

The others stared at her in surprise, as if a table or a rock had spoken. She had not uttered a word since Cheryl found them—Karen sitting stupefied on the pavement, Mark trying to pull her to her feet.

"It could have been Jack," Karen said.

"It could have been anybody. I didn't get a good look at the car. All I know is it was light in color—white or tan or pale blue—and good-sized. Maybe it looked bigger than it was," Mark added with a faint smile.

"It could have been Rob," Karen said. She sounded like a parrot, even to herself.

271

"I thought of that," Mark said. He swung his feet off the couch and sat up, looking quite himself except for the scraped, raw patches on his forehead and cheek. "This was brutally direct, though, not the same style as the other incidents. It's almost as if..." He stopped and looked intently at Karen. "If I weren't afraid of being slapped down for butting into someone else's business, I'd suggest you go to bed. Since I am afraid of getting slapped down, I suggest *I* go to bed."

He levered himself carefully to his feet. Hands still folded in her lap, Karen said, "Are you going back out there to sit in your car?" Mark made a movement as if to deny the implicit accusation; before he could speak, Karen went on, "Because if that's what you are planning to do, you may as well sleep here. Cheryl, I'll leave him to you; try to talk some sense into him. I'm going to make up the bed in the guest room."

As she left the room she heard Mark say, "I'll stay on one condition. If you call Tony Cardoza and tell him to rush over because baby brother has been damaged, I'll tear you limb from limb."

Karen did not hear Cheryl's reply. She got to the top of the stairs before she broke down. It wasn't a serious collapse, only a fit of trembling and a few hard, hot tears. Then she heard them in the hall below, and hurried to find sheets in the linen closet.

Later, after the house was quiet and she lay staring into the darkness, it was easier to come to grips with the truth she had denied so long. She was still in love with him; had never really stopped loving him. If spite had been Jack's reason for asking her to marry him, her motive for accepting him had been no less contemptible. Mark had never told her he loved her, never asked for a deeper commitment. Perhaps he never would have asked. But

272

that was no reason to fall into the arms of the first man who offered her the conventional safety of marriage, who more or less demanded her acquiescence as something to which he was entitled.

Mark had saved her life, risking his own. He would have done the same for a stray dog or cat. But that did not lessen the value of what he had done.

THE hot new listing in Gaithersburg was in a shopping mall, a fact the realtor had not bothered to mention.

"I told her, no malls," Cheryl sputtered. "That's not the type of clientele we're looking for. Besides, the rents are too high, and the so-and-sos want a percentage of the gross, can you imagine such nerve?"

They were having coffee at a fast-food restaurant while they discussed their next move. Cheryl's eyes were heavy, and even her curls had lost their usual bounce.

They had not talked about the previous night. Karen had overslept; when she came downstairs, Mark had already left and Cheryl was eating breakfast. Karen had had to rush in order to avoid being late for their appointment.

"What time did you finally get to sleep?" she asked.

"Late. That damned brother of mine slept like a baby," Cheryl added bitterly. "Did you hear him snoring?"

"I closed my door."

"I left mine open so I could tend to the sufferer if he needed me. He was asleep the minute his head hit the pillow, and he never stirred." A ghost of her old dimple showed at the corner of her mouth, and she added, "I was tempted to go in there and give him a kick, along about three A.M., but my better nature prevailed, as they say."

"Then he was all right this morning?" Karen concentrated on adding sugar to her coffee.

"Oh, sure. He looked like he'd been in a fight, though. Black eye and everything. I asked him if he was going to tell people he ran into a door and he said, yes, he was, because that's what hit him. A car door."

"I'm glad you can both laugh about it," Karen said.

"What else can you do? Life is full of narrow escapes. Some drunk—"

"I don't believe that, and neither do you."

"What do you believe?"

Karen shrugged. "It wouldn't surprise me to learn it was Jack driving that car. He hadn't been gone but a few minutes. If he happened to see me crossing the street he might have yielded to a sudden impulse—not meaning to hurt me, just scare me."

"He hates you, all right," Cheryl said soberly. "You should have seen his face after you walked out on him."

"I'm not afraid of him. Not physically, at any rate. He's too cautious to take direct action. But he can do a lot of damage in other ways. . . . Oh, damn it, Cheryl, I wish you hadn't been exposed to that—and so many other horrible things."

"I enjoyed that part of it," Cheryl said with a grin. "Watching you slap him down—that was wonderful. It wasn't worry that kept me awake, actually, it was that damned book. I started reading it and I couldn't stop. Then I was afraid to turn off the light."

"Georgetown ghosts?" Karen smiled, accepting the change of subject.

"And murders. I don't know which was worse. There was one awful story about some house that's haunted by a girl who was killed by her own father during some long-ago war, because she wanted to elope with a dashing

274

captain from the wrong side. When a girl the same age moves into that house she is possessed by the ghost and tries to murder *her* father!"

Cheryl's eyes were round as pennies. "Bah, humbug," Karen said. "Sounds like a novel I read once. But I wouldn't blame the owner of the house for wanting to sue the author. Such a story wouldn't improve his chances of selling, especially to a family with a young daughter. Some people," she added cuttingly, "are hopelessly superstitious."

"It's the way the book is written," Cheryl said sheepishly. "Half serious and half kidding, like a gossip column. Then there was another one, about—"

"For heaven's sake, Cheryl!"

"...about a father and mother getting stabbed to death on the day of their daughter's graduation. Stabbed a dozen times—just cut to pieces. Now that really happened. It was in the newspapers. And they never found the homicidal maniac that did it—"

"If you don't shut up, I'm going to throw this coffee at you," Karen threatened. "I'm surprised you didn't wake me up screaming about witches at the window."

"Mrs. Grossmuller drives a big car," Cheryl said. "A Mercedes."

"A dark-blue Mercedes. That's enough of that. Where are we going next?" She pushed her coffee cup aside and unfolded the map.

Their search had been simplified by their decision to concentrate on areas that already had a number of antique and craft shops. One place in Bethesda, just off a main commuter route, boasted a small antiques mall that offered possibilities. A number of dealers shared the space, each with his own cubicle. There was space available, and the rent was within their means. They debated the pros and cons as they ate lunch at one of the many restaurants in the area—another positive point, as Cheryl reminded Karen.

"Going into a previously established place is a kind of short cut," she added. "People are already in the habit of shopping there."

"The space is awfully small, though. And it definitely lacks pizzazz—those awful cardboard dividers."

"The space limitation is a negative, I admit. We're going to have to sell other things, you know, not just clothes. What they call 'alternative selling areas.'"

"Like accessories—fans, shoes, shawls?"

"Jewelry, too. But I think we'll need more than that."

"Textiles and linens," Karen mused. "Laces and ribbons, buttons..."

"Boxes. Hat boxes, jewel boxes, button boxes..."

"Books on costume. Prints from *Godey's Lady's Book*, frames..."

"We definitely need more space," Cheryl said. "Let's go to Kensington."

Kensington also had a concentration of antique shops, with several malls like the one they had seen in Bethesda. Unlike the latter, which was in a purely commercial area, the Kensington center was surrounded by shady side streets and beautiful turn-of-the-century houses. The realtor they consulted was pleasant and helpful; they left with another handful of possibilities, but without a definite decision.

"We're going to have to settle on something soon," Karen said. "We could go on looking for the perfect place for months. Suppose we set ourselves a deadline. Two weeks?"

"Fine by me." It was Karen's turn to drive; Cheryl

slid down and rested her head against the back of the seat. "I'm enjoying this, though. It seems impossible that we've done so much in only a few days."

"Especially considering the distractions. Maybe they are finished. Maybe that was a drunk driver last night."

Cheryl sat up and knocked on the dashboard.

"That's plastic," Karen said.

"It's the thought that counts," said Cheryl.

Cheryl insisted on approaching the house from an oblique angle, but there was no one squatting on the doorstep and Mr. DeVoto did not emerge to tell them about peculiar visitors.

"What time is Tony picking you up?" Cheryl asked casually.

"He said about six. Are you sure you don't mind—"

"Staying alone?" Cheryl deliberately misunderstood. "My dear, I won't be alone. Alexander will keep me company. Just be sure you're home by midnight, dearie, and don't let him take any liberties."

"I'm not so sure about that," Karen said. "He strikes me as the type who would take very nice liberties."

"Then let him take all he wants."

Tony never got the chance. He called shortly after six to tell Karen he couldn't make it; he was working late. Rob's body had been found in a wooded area in Virginia. He had been dead for almost two days.

CHAPTER TEN

❖❖❖❖❖❖❖❖❖❖❖❖❖❖❖❖❖❖❖❖❖❖❖❖❖❖❖❖❖❖❖❖❖

MARK pounded the table with his beer can. "I hereby call the meeting to order—"

"Don't," Cheryl said, wincing. "This isn't a meeting of your awful old Murder Club, Mark."

"Well, I'm damned if I am going to go into deep mourning over Rob Simpson's demise," Mark said. "If a murder victim ever asked for it, he did. And if he was the one who's been harassing Karen, he got what was coming to him."

"I must be hearing things," Tony said. "Don't tell me you agree with me for once."

"I didn't say he was the one. I said he might be. It's possible—"

"Forget it," Tony said curtly. "I'm in no mood for your far-out theories tonight."

He looked older and more formidable as he sat hunched over the table, his hands clasped around his can of beer. Patches of wet darkened the fabric of his shirt and his black hair had curled into damp knots. There were a few wisps of dried grass clinging to it, and Cheryl gently plucked out the longest of them.

"You look exhausted, Tony. Why don't you go home and get some rest?"

Tony sat up straighter. "I'm not tired. Just hot. Those Virginia woods were like a steam bath. I thought you'd want to know what happened. But if I'm in the way—"

A chorus of protests assured him he was not, and the lines in his face smoothed out. "It wasn't all that bad. Relatively neat, as these things go. The body wasn't far from the road—"

"Buried deep?" Mark asked.

"Not buried at all, just covered with loose brush and branches. The killer probably believed he wouldn't be found for months. What he didn't know was that there's a new subdivision just over the hill, on a parallel road. Kids and dogs..."

Cheryl made a faint sound of protest. Karen knew she was thinking of little Joe and imagining the shock a child would feel, stumbling over such a horror.

"Julie," she exclaimed. "Has she been told?"

"She was the first to be notified," Tony answered. "In fact, she identified him. Not that there was any doubt; his wallet and ID hadn't been taken. But there are formalities to be observed, and he didn't have any relatives in town, so..."

Karen rose. "I'm going to call her."

Cheryl started to speak, but then subsided with a shrug. "I have to," Karen said, answering the implicit objection. "I'll use the phone in the other room; you just... just go on talking."

But her cowardly hope that she might not hear the

gruesome details was in vain; when she returned, the others were sitting in silence, waiting for her. At the sight of her face, Mark's brows drew together. "What did she say to you?" he demanded.

"She wants me to come tomorrow," Karen said wearily. "Well, what could I say? She was ... very upset."

"Can't blame her," Tony said. "Her boyfriend was not a pretty sight."

Mark's was the only face that did not mirror Tony's distaste. "So the motive wasn't robbery," he said coolly. "How was he killed?"

"Multiple stab wounds, back and front. Some shallow and glancing, some deeper; it was one in his throat that did the job, tore the carotid artery. But a couple of the others—"

He stopped with an apologetic glance at the women.

"They won't thank you for treating them like shrinking violets," Mark said.

"That's right," Cheryl agreed. "I've heard worse from the two of you when you were dwelling on the gruesome details of your favorite murders. It's different for Karen, though. She knew him."

"Yes, I knew him. I didn't like him very much, but he enjoyed living so enormously, and it's horrible to think of someone you've met and talked to ... But I'd rather know the facts than imagine things."

"The facts aren't very pleasant," Tony said. "He had been stabbed repeatedly, with a razor-sharp knife— not a switchblade, something longer and heavier. There were cuts on his forearms. The doc thinks he was on the ground by then, trying to shield his face and throat." He raised the can to his lips and drank deeply before continuing. "And more cuts on his back. Presumably he rolled over onto his face in the final moments, and the killer just—kept on slashing him."

Karen thought that after all she could not have imagined anything much worse. The shadowy charade was so vivid she could almost see it—the dim forms moving and whispering in the darkness under the tangled trees; the sudden lunge, the strangled cry, the fall and the struggle—and a featureless blackness stooping over the prostrate man, stabbing and stabbing and stabbing again, in a blind frenzy of hate.

"There must have been a lot of blood," said Mark.

"There was," Tony said, "a lot of blood."

"Then the killer would be splashed with it."

"Yeah, well, that would be a useful clue if we had any suspects," Tony said dryly. "We can't examine every closet in the Washington area. The killer has had time to change and destroy his clothes by now."

"It reminds me of something," Mark muttered. "Some case we discussed a year or two ago. Damn. My brain's gone sour."

Tony was not as hardened as he appeared. His reaction to Mark's remark was exaggeratedly violent. "Goddamn it, Mark, don't give me your crap about poltergeists and homicidal maniacs! I'm in no mood for academic discussions."

"You were the one who mentioned poltergeists the last time," Mark said mildly. "I'm talking about a murder case, one of the classic unsolved crimes. Something you said reminded me of it, but I can't pin it down."

"Huh," said Tony, only half-appeased. "You can find parallels to everything, Mark. There's nothing new under the sun. Especially these days, when half the killers we haul in are high on something or other."

"Your favorite junkie again?" Mark asked.

"Well, hell, what other explanation is there? From what I've heard about this guy, he had some peculiar friends. They wouldn't have to be all that peculiar; a lot of the smart young Washington types play around with coke and the latest fads in designer drugs. Either he picked the wrong friend to assist him in his burglary, or he ran into someone later that night who wasn't dealing from a whole pack."

"What does this do to your theory that Rob was the one hassling Karen?"

"It doesn't affect it in the slightest. I know—some crazy driver came close to nailing you last night, and it sure as hell wasn't Rob. It's my belief that that had nothing to do with the other incidents."

He eyed Mark warily, as if anticipating an objection, but Mark only shrugged. "It wasn't the same sort of attack."

"Again we agree. Or is this the first time? You can't eliminate the possibility of a drunk driver, there are plenty of them around. Also"—he looked at Karen—"your soon-to-be ex is driving a rental car, a tan Olds 88. There's no use testing it for bloodstains or dents, since the car didn't actually hit you. Also..."

He hesitated. "Oho and aha," said Mark. "Don't tell me you've located pretty boy Horton?"

"He's not in Cleveland," Tony admitted reluctantly. "That lead didn't pan out. He could be anywhere, including Washington. However, I can't think of any reason, sensible or otherwise, why he would want to harm Karen. It's been a week since she saw him; he must know she'd have reported it by now."

"Hmph," said Mark helpfully.

"Believe me, there is absolutely no reason for the girls—excuse me, the ladies—er—"

"Try 'women,'" said Cheryl.

Tony scowled at her. "The female persons to be alarmed. Whether Rob was the joker or not, his murder has absolutely nothing to do with the other business. That was harassment pure and simple. The frequency of the incidents proves it—night after night, a constant battering at the nerves of the victim. I think you've seen the end of that. A certain person got the bejesus scared out of her tonight—"

"Julie?" Karen exclaimed.

"It could have been her and Rob working together. She's the right type—malicious, neurotic."

"But why would Julie—"

"Motive is the last thing we worry about, Karen. People do the damnedest things for the damnedest reasons. . . . Let's talk about something else, okay? I'm off duty—for a few hours—and I'd like to forget about crime. Tell me about your house-hunting."

"It's not very interesting," Karen began.

"It is to Tony," Mark said with a smile. "That's how the big tough cop spends his spare time—looking at houses."

"I don't know what's so damned funny about that," Tony said stiffly. "It's stupid to pay rent when you can be building up equity in a house. And our tax laws make investment property very attractive."

"Don't count on that continuing," Mark warned. "It's one of the loopholes I'm hoping to close."

"You fuzzy-minded liberals don't worry me, pal. There are too many special-interest groups fighting you. What's this one?"

Cheryl surrendered the sheet of paper, with a self-conscious glance at Karen. "It got mixed in with the others by mistake. We aren't really considering it."

"Why not?" Tony studied the fuzzy black-and-white photograph. After a moment he said quietly, "It looks like a house in one of those old-time books—*Tom Sawyer*, or *Huckleberry Finn*. Front porch, big shade trees, picket fence..."

"The photograph doesn't do it justice," Karen said. "It's a charming house. Needs work—"

"But nothing major," Cheryl said quickly. "Just painting and plastering and a little carpentry. They put in a new furnace five years ago—"

"How's the plumbing?" Tony asked.

"That was brought up-to-date at the same time. It needs new wiring—"

"That's not a major problem. The price isn't bad. You could probably talk them down a few thousand."

He and Cheryl went on talking. Karen listened in silence. Cheryl had really fallen in love with the house; it was a pity they couldn't get it, for the premises would have been ideal. If she had had the cash, or if she thought she could depend on a reasonable settlement from Jack, she might have been tempted to take a chance—a gamble, really, for it would be at least two years before they would know whether their business would turn a profit. Just as well I don't have it, she thought. I'm not going to risk Pat's money on something so chancy.

She glanced at Mark; she couldn't help it, he drew her gaze as irresistibly as a magnet attracts a nail. Whatever subject occupied his mind and furrowed his brow, it was not one that pleased him. His battered face was a silent reminder of how close they had come to death the night before. Random, coincidental, that attack? She had a feeling Mark was not convinced. She had a feeling she wasn't either.

Alexander shifted his weight across her feet, grumbling in his sleep. Across the table two heads, shining gold and dishevelled black, bent over the papers. Outside, darkness and mist pressed at the window, trying to come in—failed. Held back, not by a physical barrier of glass but by the opposing forces within—light, safety, companionship. They were more than four separate people, they were a group connected by complex, intertwining strands. It was nothing so simple as friendship, though that was an element; there were different levels of loyalty and frustration and old resentment and new caring.

Karen was reminded of the other occasions, so long ago, when four of them had sat around the same table. She and Mark, Pat and Ruth. Usually it was Mark and Pat who did most of the talking then, arguing about everything under the sun from the Shakespeare ciphers to pro wrestling; seldom agreeing, sometimes changing sides in mid-argument just for the fun of it. Occasionally Ruth would interject a comment in her quiet, ladylike voice, a common-sense, pointed remark that stopped the combatants in mid-shout and reduced them to foolish smiles. Karen had never said much. It was pleasure enough to listen and laugh, to feel herself part of such accepting warmth. Besides, it wasn't easy to get a word in edgewise when Pat was in full spate! At least that was what she thought at the time, if she thought about it at all. She had a feeling that when the group met again—if it ever met again—her voice would be heard more often, even if she had to yell to make it heard.

As if feeling her gaze, Mark looked up. Perhaps his thoughts had been running along a similar line, for he said, "Have you heard from Pat and Ruth?"

"Only a cable from Pat after Mrs. MacDougal arrived. He threatened me with nameless things for letting her get away."

"He couldn't have stopped her either. Mrs. Mac is a force of nature, like a hurricane."

"It was nice of you to visit her."

"Nice, hell. I didn't do it to be nice. I didn't keep in touch with Pat and Ruth to be nice. I don't do anything to be nice, for God's sake!"

Tony couldn't resist that. He interrupted his discussion with Cheryl long enough to remark, "You never said a truer word. Quit insulting the man, Karen."

Karen waited until the conversation across the table had resumed—Tony was asking about zoning regulations, a subject on which Cheryl was well informed—before she said quietly, "I didn't mean it to be insulting. 'Nice' is a rare quality. I wish there were more of it in the world."

"It's okay."

"Ruth was the one who told you where I was working, wasn't she?"

A reluctant smile tugged at the corners of his mouth. "As a matter of fact, it was Mrs. Mac."

"I suspected Julie."

"Not her. She wouldn't do you any..." He checked himself. After a moment he muttered, half to himself, "She fits the profile. I just can't see... What has she got against you?"

"Nothing! Oh, there were a few little irritants; she had hoped to get some of Ruth's and Mrs. Mac's antiques for her shop and she was furious when I decided to keep the clothes for myself. But Julie blows her stack about everything, and then she cools off and forgets it. Besides, she has other ways of getting at people."

"Such as?"

"Oh..." Karen gestured helplessly and laughed a little. "I was tempted to say that, being a mere male, you wouldn't understand; but after reading some of the congressional transcripts I know men are just as good at it as women. The insults disguised as compliments, the constant pricks and jabs that hit the victim's weakest point. For instance, she kept telling me..." Karen stopped. I am strong, I am invincible, she told herself, but I am double-damned if I am going to tell Mark Brinckley about Julie's comments on my weight and my dowdiness. She went on, "For instance, she gave me that awful book about ghosts and murders and hinted that there was some terrible story about this house."

"Oh?" Mark's face showed a spark of interest. "That sounds as if she were setting you up for a scare."

"But there wasn't anything in the book about this house."

"House? What house?" Tony looked up alertly.

"You've got real estate on the brain," Karen said with a smile. "We were talking about another subject entirely."

"Then I don't want to hear about it," Tony said. "I'm trying to talk Cheryl into making an offer on this Leesburg house. You know, you could probably qualify for various loans—"

"We're so damned broke we could qualify for unemployment and welfare both," Cheryl said with a wry smile. "But that's not the problem, Tony. We just can't afford to get stuck with a huge mortgage, and taxes, and repairs, and all the rest. What do you think of the Poolesville property?"

They continued their discussion and this time Karen joined in. Mark relapsed into silence; he sat brooding, as animated as a mushroom, for some time and then suddenly got to his feet.

"I'm leaving," he announced.

"What's your hurry?" Cheryl asked.

"I've got some reading to do. Try to have a quiet night, please."

"We'll do our best. See you around."

"You won't see me around until Tuesday or Wednesday. I have to go out of town for a few days."

"Oh. Well, have a nice time."

"Thanks. You coming, Tony?"

"I think I'll stick around for a while," Tony said comfortably.

Mark nodded and wandered out.

Karen didn't offer to accompany him. He seemed totally preoccupied with some absorbing problem. Perhaps he was worrying about the job that lay ahead of him that weekend. Greatly as she had resented his efforts to watch over them, Karen had been conscious of a strange, flat feeling when she heard him say he would be gone for several days.

She was getting sleepy, but she hated to suggest that Tony leave. He seemed to be enjoying himself—elbows on the table, his face relaxed and free of care. He needed an interlude like this one even more than most people.

It was Cheryl who finally yawned loudly and declared she was too tired to talk any longer, even about real estate. She was kind enough to add, "You've been a big help, Tony. Karen and I will have another look at the Poolesville place tomorrow."

"I can't," Karen said. "I promised Julie I'd work tomorrow."

"Oh, damn, so you did. I guess you have to."

"It's the least I can do. I should have asked her to spend the night here—or offered to go to her...."

Tony got up. Taking Karen's hand, he raised her to her feet. "You're a nice person, Karen. Don't worry about that one, she's a survivor. Come on, walk me to the door. Night, babe."

"Mmm," said Cheryl, returning to her fact sheets.

"I'm sorry I had to cancel tonight," Tony said, when they were outside the room.

"For heaven's sake, you couldn't help it. That's part of your job."

"Want to try again Monday night?"

"Why . . . Sure, I guess so."

"Such enthusiasm." His teeth flashed in the light, and one hand lightly touched her shoulder.

"I'm sorry, Tony. I feel . . ." She raised her hands in a small, bewildered gesture. "Unreal. So much has happened the last few days, and then this, tonight . . ."

Somehow her hands settled on his chest and his arms were quick to respond, circling her shoulders and waist. There was strength and support rather than passion in their grasp and she pressed against him, grateful for the warm strength of him under her hands.

"You're one tough little lady, Karen. What you've been through would have floored most women. Most people," he amended hastily, and she laughed and leaned closer.

"I'm not so tough," she said.

"I meant it as a compliment."

He was just the right height—tall enough so that she had to raise her face for his kiss, not so tall that the long, lingering caress put an intolerable strain on her muscles. His lips were warm and softer than she had expected; not so much tentative—for he knew exactly what he was doing, and how to do it—as inquiring. Is this what you want? How do you feel about it? And this . . .

Her lips parted and all individual sensation—the warmth of his body against her breasts, the movements of lips and tongue and hands, were swallowed up in an overwhelming wave of sheer physical pleasure. She was only vaguely aware of a voice somewhere in the background, but Tony responded to it, releasing her, reaching for the door.

"See you Monday," he said, and was gone, with a last lingering brush of fingertips across her lips.

Cheryl called again. "Yes, I'm coming," Karen called back.

But she didn't move immediately. Tony was already out of sight, lost in the darkness. The air was steamy, sticky, and hot, but it didn't warm her; for a few blissful moments she had been enveloped in comfort, like wrapping herself in a warm coat on a winter day, and now she was cold again.

There had been more to it than that. How much more she was unable to assess. She realized she was reluctant to face Cheryl. It was as if Tony's kiss had left a luminous imprint no observer could miss.

IT rained during the night. Karen didn't hear the rain, or anything else; she slept heavily and woke later than she had planned. When she went downstairs she found Cheryl dressed to go out while the radio announcer burbled happily about the weather. "... sunny and warm, lower humidity, unseasonably mild..." From the pride and pleasure in his voice one would have thought he had produced the lovely weather by praying, or casting spells.

Karen poured coffee and sat down. She felt rumpled and disoriented; though she could not remember the details of her dreams, she knew Tony Cardoza had played a prominent part in them. She was not sure what she wanted to do about Tony—or whether she had any choice in the matter.

"I thought I'd let you sleep," Cheryl said. "After the awful day you had yesterday."

"Your day was the same as mine. At least nothing happened last night. What do you have on the agenda?"

Cheryl's curls were pinned high on her head, in an attempt to make her look businesslike. She glanced at the paper in her hand. "I'm going to see a realtor in Alexandria. There was an ad in the paper this morning that sounded interesting, so I called and made an appointment. I want to check out a few yard sales and get back early to do some mending."

Her handwriting was as compact and as neat as printing. Karen wondered whether there was some connection between neat handwriting and a neat, well-organized mind. Probably. Her own writing was barely legible, even to her.

"Very good," she said respectfully.

"You might be thinking about a logo," Cheryl went on, making a precise check by one of the items on her list. "We need something eye-catching that we can use on signs and ads and business cards and promotional literature. You're the artistic half of this partnership, so that's your assignment for the day."

"Logo, my eye," Karen said. "We need a name! They go together, don't they? At least they should."

Cheryl looked at her rather blankly and then burst out laughing. "My gosh, that's right—we haven't got a name yet. That's your department too, you're the smart one."

"I don't know why you keep saying that. I have some skills you don't have, but the reverse is certainly true—and yours are a lot more useful than mine."

"I don't believe it, but I sure love to hear it," Cheryl said.

"You can't get out of it that easily. We'll both think about a name and a logo. It will distract me from Julie's moaning," Karen added. "I really do feel sorry for her, but I'm not looking forward to this afternoon. I wish I could go with you. It looks like a gorgeous day."

"It is." Cheryl got up and opened the back door, admitting Alexander, who paused to sniff at Karen's foot before heading for his bed. "They say it will be nice tomorrow too. We'll spend the whole day rambling around."

Karen was a few minutes early, but she found that the shop was already open. At first she saw no one within and assumed Julie was in the office. Then something moved behind the desk in front, and as her eyes adjusted to the dim light, Karen saw Julie's pale face. It seemed to hang bodiless in mid-air, a pale oval lifeless as a mask. The parted lips and wide eyes were like an exaggerated artist's rendering of startled fear.

Then Julie let out a long, quivering sigh. Karen saw that her eyes were red-veined and her garish clown's makeup was less than perfect.

"I didn't think you'd come," Julie said.

"I told you I would. I'm sorry about Rob."

"You never liked him," said a flat voice she scarcely recognized as Julie's.

"I didn't dislike him."

"Yes, you did. And with good reason. He was a two-timing, cheap bastard." A single tear rolled down Julie's cheek, trailing a black slime of mascara. It was an obscenely pitiful sight, all the more so because Julie's frozen look did not alter and she made no attempt to wipe her face.

"I'm sorry," Karen repeated—but this time she meant it. "I didn't realize you were—that you had—"

"I wasn't," Julie said. "But I had." A ghost of her old mocking smile touched her lips. "Along with half the other female inhabitants of D.C. and suburbs. Maybe some of the males too. Oh, hell." She got up from her chair and went to the mirror. "What a mess," she said in a more normal voice, and reached for a tissue.

"Is there something special you want me to do?" Karen asked. She couldn't offer conventional expressions of sympathy; Julie's behavior, and her relationship with Rob, were not conventional.

Julie dabbed carefully at her eyes and replied, without turning, "There's plenty to do. I'm closing for a week, maybe two. My nerves are shot to hell. And with nobody to help me..."

The complaint was an echo of Julie's old maliciousness, aimed directly at Karen; but Julie's heart wasn't really in it, and Karen did not react.

"I think that's a good idea," she said. "You need a rest. August is always slow, a lot of places close then."

"Here comes a customer," Julie said. "Take care of him. I have a lot of paperwork to clear up."

She spent most of the afternoon in the office. Karen didn't disturb her; the fine weather had brought shoppers out in large numbers and she was kept busy. One woman who had bought a Victorian nightgown from her came back, bringing a friend, and was disappointed to find Karen had nothing on hand. Karen took down her name and address and promised to notify her when she was open for business. She realized she should have started a mailing list earlier. Perhaps Julie would let her display her cards and brochures—in return for favors rendered, of course. She knew Julie's present mood was temporary; she would bounce back, bitchy and greedy as ever, after the initial shock had worn off.

The telephone kept Karen busy too. Most of the calls were inquiries she could handle herself; a few she passed on to Julie. Late in the afternoon came a call for Karen herself. With typical arrogance Shreve did not identify herself. She assumed—correctly—that Karen would recognize her voice.

"I called the house," she announced. "That woman—your partner?—said you were at work."

"That's no woman, that's Mark's sister," Karen said. "She is my partner, yes."

"Oh. You don't like to be alone, do you? Always someone hanging around."

Karen suppressed her irritation. Everything Shreve said had a heavy current of innuendo. It must be a Washington habit; even "hello" could be made to sound sinister or suggestive.

"Well, you know how it is," she said meaninglessly. "What can I do for you, Shreve?"

"We've discussed it before."

"A dress for the party?"

"The dress, yes. I'm getting tired of being put off, Karen. When can I have it?"

Karen hesitated. She knew she was being silly, behaving like a nervous mother watching a favorite child leave home for the first time, but she really hated seeing one of the beautiful old dresses go to Shreve.

Since it must be done, let it be done quickly. She said, "They've been cleaned. If you're that anxious, you can come to the house tomorrow."

"I'm going out of town. What about Tuesday?"

"All right."

"I'll be back Tuesday morning. Come about three. Do you know how to get to the house?"

"No. Why can't you—"

"Because I choose not to. Because I'm buying and you're selling. It's the good old free enterprise system— remember?"

Karen discovered she was squeezing the hard plastic of the telephone so hard her hand ached. Carefully she relaxed her fingers, one by one. Rude customers are part of the deal, she told herself. Rude customers are part of the deal....

There was some comfort in the thought that Shreve wouldn't crack the whip quite so hard if she were not angry about something else. Mark hadn't liked her overt demonstration of possessiveness the other night.

Stop it, she told herself. You're pathetic. Like a teenager with her first crush, finding signs of hope in every careless word.

"Are you writing this down?" Shreve demanded.

"Sorry. I was thinking about something else. Give it to me again."

After she had hung up she sat quietly for a moment, clenching and unclenching her fists and counting under her breath. When she looked up, she saw that Julie had come into the shop and was watching her. "Was that Shreve?"

"Yes. She wants a dress for some party Miriam is giving."

"Watch out for her," Julie said. "She can be a real bitch."

"I know. But thanks for the warning."

"She and Mark," Julie began. Karen felt her face stiffen. She met Julie's look with one of cool disinterest, and after a moment Julie turned away. "It's almost closing

295

time. I want to pack some of the smaller things, there's no sense in leaving them lying around. Give me a hand, will you?"

They filled several cartons with jewelry, silver, and the more valuable pieces of crystal, and stacked them by the door.

"That's it, I guess," Julie said. She looked so tired and forlorn, Karen put an impulsive arm around her. Julie flinched, as if her touch had been red-hot.

"I'm sorry," Karen said in surprise.

"No, I'm sorry. I didn't mean . . . I'm just so damned jumpy." She hesitated, then said awkwardly, "I didn't mean to give you a hard time, all these weeks. You've been a big help."

Karen knew that was all the thanks she was going to get. It was, in fact, more than she had expected. "I wasn't easy to get along with either," she said. "If you still need help after you get back..." Cheryl would kill her if she heard that, but Karen did not retract the offer.

"That's okay. I have somebody lined up to start the middle of August. I'll—uh—keep in touch."

"Please do." Karen reached in her pocket. "Here are the keys."

"Right." The pause prolonged itself, became uncomfortable. Then Julie muttered, "I suppose you want your paycheck."

"If you hadn't mentioned it I would have asked," Karen said calmly.

"I think you would have at that. Oh, well." Julie went to the desk and scribbled rapidly. "Don't deposit it till Wednesday, okay? My cash flow..."

"Sounds familiar."

"It will sound even more familiar once you're in business," Julie said. "I wish you luck. Here's a number where I can be reached in an emergency; I'd appreciate it if you'd let me know about future murders, break-ins, muggings, and little things like that."

"Let's hope there won't be any." Karen was standing by the table; idly she glanced down. "I see you sold out on the Georgetown book."

"I threw it in the trash." Julie came to the door. "Here."

Karen took the check and the paper on which Julie had written the telephone number. "You threw the books away?"

The surprise in her voice brought a sour smile to Julie's lips. "Yeah, imagine me throwing away money. I couldn't stand the sight of the damned things. You knew. You must have figured it out."

Until that moment Karen had not known, and yet she felt as if Julie were only confirming some long-accepted fact. "Rob wrote it?"

"Yes. To me it stood out like a sore thumb, his writing style was so much like the way he talked. I suppose it's stupid of me, but when I first heard about his death I couldn't help wondering..."

"That is silly, Julie," Karen said. "Tony ... Someone I know told me that nothing in the book was new. All the information came from newspapers and other printed sources. I did hear that people were annoyed at having old scandals revived; but what good would it do them to kill the author? That wouldn't stop the gossip, it would only exacerbate it."

"I know. I said it was a stupid idea. Did you read that story about your aunt's house?"

"There wasn't anything about Ruth's house."

"No? Rob said there was. He was giggling over it. . . ." Her face twisted, and for a moment Karen thought she was going to break down. Fond memories of an old lover, recalling the laughter they had shared over someone's discomfort and distress... Perhaps the incongruity also struck Julie, because she recovered herself without shedding any tears.

"So," she said. "I'll get the car. You can start dragging the boxes out to the curb; I'll have to double-park."

When the boxes had been loaded Julie drove off with a final wave that had almost her old panache. There was no need to worry about Julie. As Tony had said, she was a survivor. How oddly she had behaved, though, almost as if she were not only grief-stricken but...

Afraid.

Afraid of me? Karen thought incredulously. The way she flinched when I touched her.... Oh, but that was too absurd. Guilt as well as fear could produce such a reaction; if Tony was right, Julie had good reason to feel guilty about what she had done, and to regret her involvement in that grubby little scheme.

But suppose she was involved in some of Rob's other schemes? He probably had plenty of irons in the fire; he certainly had other women. The problem with tracking down Rob's killer was not a lack of motive, but an overabundance of them. Jealous husbands—and wives?—jealous lovers and ex-lovers. And blackmail? Tony hadn't mentioned that among Rob's "misdemeanors," but it fit Rob's personality. Victims of blackmail seldom go to the police. If pressed, they may take direct action to keep the secret hidden.

What if Rob's death had been the result, not of a story in his book but of a story that was not in it? Omitted, at the urgent request of one of the participants, after a sizable payment? Suppose Rob had been talking in his bright, chatty way about writing a sequel. And suppose, as well, that Rob had dropped hints to Julie, but had not mentioned names. He had been a hopeless gossip, but he would have known better than to involve her directly in something both criminal and dangerous. If Julie suspected the truth but didn't know the details, it would explain her odd behavior, including her repeated questions about Ruth's house. There was nothing in the book about Ruth's house, unless one of the stories that named no names and gave no precise address referred to some old, half-forgotten and undocumented tragedy. It didn't really matter. Rob's hints had been designed to alarm and frighten her, they need not have any basis in fact.

A story that wasn't in the book . . . That theory would explain why Julie had decided to get out of town for a while. She had not told Karen where she was going or given her an address; only a phone number.

Karen felt certain of one thing: Julie might not know who had killed Rob, but she knew more than she was saying.

KAREN hastened home to tell Cheryl about her new theory. Cheryl listened politely, but she was not inclined to take the matter seriously; she had a happy facility of dismissing problems that weren't imminent and concentrating on things she could do something about.

"Even if you're right, where does it get you?" she demanded. "It's hard enough to pick one answer out of a list of possibles, but you're trying to find one that isn't even on the list."

"True," Karen said gloomily. "There must be enough scandals in Washington to fill an encyclopedia."

"I wonder if that's what Mark was mumbling

about," Cheryl said casually. "Seems to me he did say something about that book. It would be funny if both of you came up with the same idea. You know what they say about great minds—"

"Mark called?"

"He was here, not long after you left."

"I thought he was going away."

"He is. He stopped on his way to the airport. He had some new idea," Cheryl said, with a tolerant, sisterly smile.

"Did he say what it was?"

"To be honest, I didn't ask. Mark is always coming up with wild theories. I tell him he ought to write thrillers. Margaret Truman does it, and Senator Hart, so why not Congressman Brinckley? He insisted on going through all the clothes again."

"Still looking for the diamonds?"

"Who knows? He asked me if we had anything from the late sixties or early seventies."

"There are a few things of Ruth's," Karen said curiously.

"I know, I showed them to him, but he just swore and said he was going to miss his plane—as if I was the one who was holding him up. He's speaking at some sort of fund-raiser and he didn't dare be late."

"Tonight?"

"I suppose so, otherwise he wouldn't have been worried about catching the plane."

"I only wondered because he said he would be out of town for a few days."

"I don't know what he's doing the rest of the time. Some kind of political business, I guess."

Her tone of utter indifference to the politics of the nation as exemplified in the person of her brother made

Karen smile. She didn't pursue the subject. It was none of her business what Mark did in his spare time. But she couldn't help wondering whether he was off on a quest, following up the new theory that had brought him to the house that day. It would be nice to think he cared enough to spend so much time and effort.

"So what are we doing tomorrow?" she asked, going to the refrigerator for more ice.

Cheryl pushed her papers aside and frowned thoughtfully. There was a pencil behind her ear and a pen in her hand and a smear of ink on her cheek, but she didn't look like a businesswoman. She looked like Shirley Temple, dimples and all. Karen decided not to mention the resemblance. She had a feeling Cheryl wouldn't appreciate the compliment.

"No luck with the yard sales," Cheryl said. "But I found a store in Springfield that has possibilities. I told the realtor I'd bring you to look at it."

"Okay. What's on the schedule tonight?"

Cheryl's eyes sparkled. "I was hoping we could look at the dresses we got from the cleaner. We didn't have a chance before."

Karen shook her head with a rueful smile. "You poor woman. Is that your idea of an exciting evening? We ought to treat ourselves to something special, after that less-than-thrilling Saturday night."

Cheryl's eyes went back to the papers and clippings that heaped the table. "I guess I've forgotten what Saturday night means to most people. After little Joe was born we didn't go out much. It cost so much—baby-sitters and tickets and gas—even a night at the movies ran fifteen, twenty bucks if we went for a hamburger afterward. Usually I'd pop popcorn and Joe would get a six-pack and we'd sit and watch TV, and talk. . . ."

"It sounds nice," Karen said sympathetically. She was touched, but the look on Cheryl's face—the remote, smiling glow of remembered love—also roused a degree of irritated impatience. You're just jealous, she thought; jealous because you've never had the chance, or the right, to feel that way about someone.

"Anyhow." Cheryl's voice was once more brisk and matter-of-fact. "I don't want to keep you from doing something. Do you want to go out? I'll go anywhere you want."

"I was not about to suggest a singles bar," Karen said; there had been a faint but unmistakable note of martyrdom in Cheryl's voice. "It's not my kind of scene either."

"We could go out to dinner."

When faced with a decision, Karen found she couldn't think of anything she wanted to do. "No, that's silly. It's too expensive. We'll be good little businesspersons and work tonight. Let's do something really wild and exciting and have supper on the terrace. It's a lovely evening."

They carried their tuna salad and iced tea outside— and their papers and ledgers as well. The soft, clear air affected even Cheryl's dedication to duty; leaning back, she put her feet on the chair opposite and said lazily, "This was a good idea. The garden is so pretty."

A breeze ruffled the leaves, and the dappled patterns of sunlight on the lawn below the trees shifted like flowing water. A robin hopping across the grass stopped and cocked a bright eye in their direction. Alexander, lying across Karen's feet, didn't even lift his head, and the robin proceeded to attend to his supper. Plunging his beak into the ground, he came up with a fat grub and flew off.

"We may as well enjoy the weather while it lasts," Cheryl went on. "The Gulf Stream is doing something funny—"

"Don't you mean the jet stream?"

"Whatever. Anyhow, days like this are rare, and we've got six more weeks of misery before fall."

"It's funny," Karen said musingly. "I hate this damned sticky heat, but when I look back on the years I lived in Georgetown I don't even remember it. Only the lavishness of spring—all the flowers bursting out at once and smelling like heaven—and crisp days in fall, and winter days inside around the fire."

"I mark only the sunny hours," Cheryl said. "I saw that written on a sundial. It's a well-trained memory that operates on the same principle."

"Mine must be better-trained than I thought, then. When I was talking to Miriam—"

"Who?"

"Miriam Montgomery. I told you about her, she's that friend of Shreve's."

"Oh, right. The one we toasted. How could I forget her?"

"Anyhow, she said she'd hate to live her youth over again. I agreed with her—and I still wouldn't want to go back—but neither would I want to forget these days entirely. There were some wonderful memories."

Cheryl glanced at her and then looked away. From the quirk of her lips, Karen knew she was wondering how many of those memories concerned Mark. But Cheryl was learning discretion; she didn't ask and Karen didn't elaborate.

Alexander rose with a grumbling growl and stretched. He sauntered off to investigate the garden and see if there were any new smells. Apparently he found some, for he burrowed under the azaleas and disappeared from sight.

"He must smell that cat of Mr. DeVoto's," Karen said.

"Uh-huh." Even the seductive summer air and the lovely long shadows could not distract Cheryl for long. "I hope we can have a yard someday. I don't mean right away; it looks as if we'll have to settle for an apartment and a stall in one of those antique malls at first. But maybe in a few years..."

"A yard is a lot of work. We won't be able to hire help, even in the shop, for a long time."

"I love yard work. We could buy a secondhand mower; they have them at yard sales sometimes. Your aunt sure keeps her garden nice. I suppose she has a gardener?"

"I suppose. No, I know she does, I send him a check every month. But he reminds me of the shoemaker's little elves. I never see him."

"We wouldn't want a garden as fancy as this. Roses take a lot of care. Well." Cheryl reached for a ledger. "I'd better get to work."

"Me too. There are several hours of daylight left, and a good breeze; those old linens would probably dry before dark if I hung them out right away." But Karen didn't move. It was too pleasant to sit in lazy contentment enjoying the peace of the secluded garden. Not that the future promised all clear sailing. There were patches of rough water, financial and emotional, ahead; Jack represented a big squall all by himself. But the worst seemed to be over, and she had no excuse for self-pity. Thanks to the loving help of friends old and new, she had been relieved of problems that might have sunk a vessel as heavily loaded as hers had been. But she had done some of it herself; at least she had the gumption to take advantage of the opportunities presented. Julie was off her back, and so was Rob. Poor Rob. She could pity him, but she still could not understand why he had done such cruel things. One could only feel sorry for a mind so burdened with malice—and be guiltily relieved that it was no longer a factor in one's life.

"You're looking pleased with yourself," said Cheryl. "What are you thinking about?"

"I'd be ashamed to tell you. I just had a bad attack of smugness. I guess I'd better drown it in hot water and bleach."

A telephone call from Jack later that evening was another salutary antidote to smugness, reminding Karen that he could not be airily dismissed with an apt metaphor. She was seething with rage when she hung up.

"Can you believe him?" she demanded of a sympathetic Cheryl. "He asked me to lunch tomorrow. He still thinks he can talk me into signing those papers."

"You turned him down, I hope."

"Naturally. It's getting dark; I'll bring in my laundry and then you can have your treat."

"Oh, goody. The cleaning."

"The cleaning. You may enjoy it, but I won't; I've got to pick out a dress for Shreve."

"You are going to sell her one, then."

"I have to. There was never any question of that. Those designer originals are my sole source of capital, Cheryl. It's only thanks to Mrs. Mac that I have them, but somehow it doesn't seem quite as bad as borrowing from Pat. Two or three more sales like the one to Miriam will bring enough money for me to contribute my half of our opening costs."

"Okay, okay. I'm on your side, remember?"

Karen bit her lip. "Sorry."

"I told you to stop apologizing. What time is she coming for the dress?"

"She isn't coming. I said I'd deliver it to her, at her house. Well, what else could I do, when she insisted?"

"Nothing," Cheryl murmured, following Karen to the door.

"She's so busy and so important," Karen went on. "And I'm just a scruffy little tradesman, after all. Lord, how I hate to hand over one of those gorgeous dresses to that..."

"Don't do it if it bugs you that much. There will be other buyers."

"I can't do that. If I begin getting sensitive about rudeness and bad manners, I'll never survive in business."

"Right."

Karen opened the back door. "I'll be right back. Put the kettle on, would you, please? We'll indulge ourselves in an extravagant cup of tea while we look at clothes we can't afford to wear ourselves."

I must stop doing that, she told herself, as she took the linens off the lines. I must have repeated every damn word Shreve said to me, twice over; Cheryl is sick of hearing it. No more bitchiness, no more sarcasm, no more self-pity. At least not tonight!

The bed in her room was stacked with boxes. Karen had determined to pretend she was as thrilled as Cheryl at the prospect of inspecting the dresses; when she lifted the lid off the first box she didn't have to pretend.

"Oh, gorgeous! He did a super job, even if he did charge an arm and a leg. Just look."

Silvery cloth glimmered under the light, the sleeveless, draped bodice molded by underlying tissue. A wide hip sash was studded with paste gems, ruby and emerald topaz surrounded by patterns of tiny jet beads. The sash ended in a two-foot fringe of the same jet beads.

"I cannot let her have that," Karen moaned, forgetting her recent resolution. "It's a Poiret original—one of his Egyptian models. That very dress is shown in one of my books."

In painful silence they replaced the lid and went on to the next box. "He said you wanted them stored flat," Cheryl said. "Not on hangers."

"That's right, you can't hang these beaded dressed without some support; it's too much of a strain on the fabric." Another groan came from Karen's lips as the lid came off to reveal a gown of black taffeta whose deep décolletage was framed by wide bands of intricately patterned crystal beads. The full skirt was looped and held in front by a glittering waterfall of beads lying in petaled festoons. "Lanvin," Karen murmured.

Cheryl snatched the lid from her and replaced it. "There are limits beyond which no woman can be expected to go," she announced firmly. "I'd just as soon cut off one of my fingers as give this up. What did the museums say, or did you have a chance to call them?"

"Museums prefer donations," Karen said. "A couple of them said they'd be in touch; the Costume Institute wants me to bring them to New York so they can have a look."

"Nuts to the Costume Institute. I don't even want the museums to have them. You know, Karen, we don't have to let all of them go. In fact, we'd be crazy to get rid of them. They could make the difference between our being just another old-clothes store and one of the top vintage clothing boutiques in the country. Which is what we're aiming to be, right?"

"Well, of course. But I don't see—"

"A collection like this is worth thousands in publicity, Karen. We can have fashion shows, and display these dresses in the shop as part of the décor; rent them, on rare occasions, to special customers—and charge the earth for the privilege—get write-ups in newspapers and magazines, maybe even TV interviews."

"Do you really think so?"

"Knowing we have things of this caliber will attract not only customers, but people who want to sell similar clothes. I'm telling you, we'd be making a big mistake to let them go."

"Do you mean it, or are you just being noble? I admit it's disgusting to see a grown woman cry over a dress, but..."

"I mean it, you dimwit. You'd have seen the possibilities yourself if you weren't so busy bending over backward to make yourself miserable."

They indulged themselves for a while, gloating over the glow of silk and satin, the rich softness of fur, the glitter of crystal and paste, and the sheer structural brilliance of the designs. The thought that they could keep the best of the beauties reconciled Karen to the approaching sale. "I'll have to offer her something good," she said finally. "Something I can really soak her for. I think I could bear to part with this one. It's Louiseboulanger, but it isn't one of my favorites."

"How about this black taffeta with the big fat silver flowers?"

"That's Cheruit," Karen mumbled. "Oh, well. I'll take these two and give her her choice. Okay, that's it. I don't know how you managed to get all this in the car," she added, surveying the piles of boxes on the bed and the floor.

"Ask how I paid for it," Cheryl said, grimacing. "I thought I'd need smelling salts when he handed me the bill. No, don't worry about that, it's a business expense; I put it in the book, broken down by item. There are a few more things in the wardrobe. They only rated the usual hangers and plastic bags. He said to tell you he couldn't get the stains out of some of them."

"But I'm sure he charged for them." Karen stripped off the cleaners' bag. "Hmmm. I was hoping this would clean."

"Another evening gown? We seem to be heavy on formal clothes."

"Evening and wedding dresses were only worn once—maybe twice—so they didn't wear out. And people were more inclined to save them." Karen laid the burgundy lace dress aside. "I may be able to cut the bad part out and take the skirt in; it's a large size. I got it from one of Mrs. Mac's less affluent friends."

"Which friend?" Cheryl reached for the ledger.

"Uh . . . I have it written down somewhere. . . ."

Cheryl tactfully dropped the subject. "What's that?"

"That, my dear, is a total loss. Look at those stains; they're all over the front, bodice and skirt both. I don't know why I sent this to be cleaned, it must have gotten in by mistake."

She tossed the dress aside, and Cheryl picked it up. "I could try that new cleaning stuff."

"It's not worth the effort. The fabric is a synthetic. It's practically impossible to get set-in stains like rust out of polyester-cotton."

"The label says Saks."

"But it's not a designer dress; it isn't even very old. Just throw it in the wastebasket."

"I don't suppose I should ask where you got it."

"No, please don't. I seem to remember it was in a box with a lot of other things, all crumpled and rolled up. So we aren't out much except for the cleaning. I didn't pay much for any of the box lots. Oh, damn, here's another failure. The silk did disintegrate."

"Shattered," Cheryl said.

"Yes. He warned me it might, I'll say that for him." Karen threw the bodice aside. "This one . . . Yes, the lining shattered. But the velvet is in good shape. We can make another lining."

They finished looking through the rest of the things and Karen set two of the big white boxes aside. "These are the ones I sold Miriam. I ought to call her and tell her they are ready. She's been very patient, not like . . . Perhaps I should call her now."

"She's probably out on the town tonight. Isn't there some big gala at the Kennedy Center?"

"I don't know. I fear my invitation was misplaced in the post."

"Mine too. But there is, and she'll be there, because her husband contributed a million or two to the President's re-election campaign." Cheryl turned on the television set. "Maybe it will be on the news. I want to catch the weather report anyhow."

It was a slow news night. Even the pandas seemed to have lost interest. Cheryl got bored and went downstairs to make herself a sandwich. Alexander went with her. They missed the coverage of the gala, but Karen was rewarded by a glimpse of Miriam, standing in the background as the President waved and beamed.

Karen braced herself to hear some reference to Rob's murder. She had gone out of her way to avoid newspaper and television reports of the case; hearing it discussed in the impersonal and yet ghoulish style characteristic of the media would have brought the horror of it closer to home. However, new crimes had taken precedence. Day-old news was stale news, and apparently there were no new developments in the case.

Cheryl came back with Alexander in hot pursuit. "He's been out," she told Karen. "And he's had his biscuit. And all the doors are locked and double-locked."

"Fair and pleasant again tomorrow," Karen reported. "You missed Miriam."

"Oh, was she on?"

"Only a fleeting glance. She looked bored to death. Shall I turn it off?"

"Okay by me. Dammit, Alexander, give me a break. You had your treat, this is my sandwich."

Karen was a moment too late or just in time, depending on one's viewpoint. As she reached for the knob, the screen showed the interior of the terminal at National Airport and the announcer began interviewing the head of a group that was attending a fund-raiser in Atlanta. Cheryl leaned forward with a squeal of surprise. "Hey, there's Mark, right behind the speaker. Doesn't he look..."

He looked as if he wished he were somewhere else. It took him a moment to realize that the cameras were aimed in his direction and only another moment for him to get out of their reach. The movement was swift and smooth but not quite fast enough. Shreve had not been indiscreet enough to cling to him in public, but she was standing so close and watching him so narrowly that she might as well have been holding his arm.

CHAPTER ELEVEN

MONDAY lived up to the forecast. They had breakfast on the terrace and lingered over a second cup of coffee, while Cheryl described the yard sales she had investigated the previous day.

"They all sound marvelous," she said, with the worldly-wise voice of experience. "But they usually aren't. You have to learn to read between the lines, and plan your route so you can cover as many as possible."

"We'll try again next week. If we split up, we could cover more of them."

"But it wouldn't be as much fun. Half the pleasure is making rude remarks about the tacky merchandise."

"I'd like to go to a few, just for the sake of curiosity. I've never been to a yard sale."

"Boy, have you led a sheltered life. It's fun if you don't have anything better to do. But the chance of coming across anything in our line is practically nonexistent these days."

There was a certain feeling of constraint in their camaraderie that morning. Neither had referred to the news broadcast. Cheryl had tried—"I was surprised to see how large that delegation—"

Karen had not let her finish the sentence. "That wasn't a delegation, that was a typical Washington boon-doggle, complete with sisters, cousins, and aunts. Do you want orange juice or grapefruit?"

Cheryl had selected grapefruit, her lips pursed as if she were already tasting the fruit, without sugar. As Karen prepared it, she tried not to think about Mark, but did not succeed. She also tried to believe she was angry with herself and not with him. How fatuous and naïve she had been to hope his preoccupation the other evening had been with her affairs and her safety. He had probably been looking forward to his weekend—thinking of Shreve, an-ticipating their time together. . . .

The knife slipped, slicing into her thumb, and she reached for a paper towel to stanch the bleeding. Like all good cooks, Ruth kept her knives razor-sharp. It was my own fault, Karen told herself; I went at that grapefruit as if it were. . . . She managed to cut that thought off, and concentrated on what she was doing.

By the time they reached the realtor's office, Karen had—she believed—forgotten her ill humor and the event that had caused it. The shop had possibilities; they added it to their list.

They also investigated a few antique shops—a good many were closed on Monday—but came away empty-handed.

"Honestly, the prices people want for their junk," Cheryl grumbled.

"Junk to you and me, bargains to some," Karen said philosophically. "I suppose it all depends on what you're looking for. Our requirements are a bit esoteric."

"Yeah, that's right. Let's head out into the country. Maybe we'll find some innocent little old lady who is cleaning out her attic and hasn't heard the word 'antiques.'"

They did not, however, and they soon became surfeited with costume jewelry, empty Avon bottles, and oak furniture. Finding a roadside market, they stocked up on tomatoes and melons, corn and peaches, and headed homeward.

It made Cheryl's day when they arrived to find they had missed Mrs. Grossmuller. They didn't need Mr. DeVoto to tell them she had been there, for she had left a bulging shopping bag on the doorstep. A note fluttered coyly from the string handle. "I will come next week to pick up the money."

"It's nice that she trusts us," Karen said, as Cheryl glared at the stained, crumpled mass of fabric protruding from the top of the bag.

When they took the bag in and inspected the contents, the filthy object on top turned out to be a cutwork tablecloth, with its matching napkins wadded up beneath. In addition, there were three pairs of ladies' gloves, a calico apron, and a 1920s bathing suit of black wool full of moth holes.

"We've got to make her stop doing this," Cheryl declared grim-faced, while Karen laughed over the bathing suit.

"How? We can't complain to the police; she isn't doing anything illegal. You're right, though," Karen said, sobering. "I certainly don't want her turning up on the doorstep with her dirty clothes after Ruth gets back. Can you see poor Ruth's face? Not to mention Pat's. . . . It would almost be worth it to hear Pat explode. We'll tell Mrs. Grossmuller we're moving right away."

"But don't tell her where," Cheryl pleaded.

"If I don't, she'll come back here. Besides, I don't want to lose a source. We can use the tablecloth and napkins, and maybe the apron. She may have other things."

"I'm going to throw the whole lot in the washing machine," Cheryl announced, picking up the bag with the tips of her fingers. "Even the things we don't want. We can't leave them in this condition; the whole house will be infected. I keep feeling as if fleas are hopping on me."

"Don't put the bathing suit in with the tablecloth."

"Please! I know better than that."

Karen felt sure Cheryl's fears were exaggerated; she hadn't seen any sign of fleas or other vermin. The moths that had devoured the bathing suit had been dead and dust for decades.

Alexander displayed an inordinate amount of interest in the clothes; Cheryl had to fight him off while she loaded the washing machine. Perhaps he scented his beloved Mrs. Grossmuller. Karen had never seen him react to anyone with such doting admiration. That said something about Mrs. Grossmuller, or Alexander—or both—but she wasn't sure she wanted to know what.

Cheryl's temper improved after she had put everything in the machine, or—in the case of the bathing suit—in the basin they used for hand-washing. Wiping her wet hands, she watched Karen unload the vegetables and fruit they had bought.

"What's for supper? Those tomatoes look nice; we could have a salad."

"I'm going out for dinner," Karen said.

"Heavy date?"

"I guess I forgot to tell you."

"No reason why you should. Did you pick up a new boyfriend, or is it Tony?"

Her tone made it sound like "good old Tony." When Karen said yes, it was Tony, she smiled placidly. "I hope he makes it this time. Poor boy, he needs some amusement."

"So I'm to be the good-conduct prize?"

"Hey, Karen, don't start that again."

"I won't. I think he deserves something too, and I'm fully prepared to deliver. Not only is he incredibly good-looking, he's nice and kind and considerate and sensitive and intelligent—"

"You really like him, huh?"

"One might reasonably draw that conclusion from what I just said."

"Good." Cheryl picked up a tomato and examined it with the concentration a scientist might devote to a specimen. "Sometimes I could kill that brother of mine."

"Now don't you start, Cheryl."

"Honest, Karen, he hasn't seen that woman for over a year. She's trying to make it look like more than it was, to hurt you. She always was the one who was chasing him, not the other way around." The words bubbled out as if she had held a cap on them too long, and they could no longer be repressed. "He never talks about people— women—not to me—but I told him all the nasty things she did to you, coming here and insulting you and all that, and I could tell he didn't—"

"I would appreciate it if you would stop trying to arrange my emotional life for me," Karen said between her teeth. "I could make a few pertinent comments about your hang-ups too, if I chose."

This time Cheryl's temper did not spark when rubbed the wrong way. She lowered her head, her mouth drooping. "I know. I've heard them."

"From Mark."

"Among others. I didn't mind so much from Mark. He knew Joe, they were buddies."

"And I'm sure he pointed out that Joe wouldn't want you to cut yourself off from love the rest of your life. What kind of tribute is that to him or to your marriage? Oh, all right, I'll shut up. You let me settle my own affairs and I'll let you sit there and—petrify."

Fortunately the telephone rang, or another quarrel might have developed. At first Karen could not identify the caller.

"Miss Everley? I don't believe . . . Oh, at Mrs. MacDougal's. Yes, of course; I thought your voice was familiar. Oh, you do? Worth? Yes, I'm very interested. No, I'm afraid I can't tomorrow afternoon. Would Wednesday. . . . I see. Yes, Cannes should be delightful at this time of year. Just a minute . . ."

Cheryl's head had snapped up like that of a hunting hound at the sound of the name Worth. She began making frantic gestures.

"I can go tomorrow," she said, while Karen covered the mouthpiece with her hand. "Where does she live?"

"Clear out on the Eastern Shore. She's going abroad on Wednesday and she wants to get these things out of the way first."

"Let me talk to her." Cheryl reached for the phone.

She was beaming broadly when she hung up. "Sounds like a hot lead."

"Cheryl, are you sure? Maybe I could put Shreve off."

"You have to trust me sometime. I've got a pretty good idea of what to pay for things."

"It isn't that. But it's a long drive, and didn't you say you had to study for your finals?"

"I'll study tonight. We can't pass up a potential source—you're the one who keeps telling me that. And the old lady doesn't sound as if she would last much longer."

"All Mrs. Mac's friends sound like that."

"So we better strike while the iron is hot. What time are you going out tonight?"

"He said he'd pick me up at seven-thirty."

Karen dressed with care, pleased by the fact that the gradual decrease in her girth had produced a corresponding increase in her wardrobe. She was no longer self-conscious about wearing her vintage clothes. They were a good deal more stylish and far better made than anything else she owned.

From one of Mrs. MacDougal's sources—not old Mrs. Ferris—she had acquired a dress she was longing to wear. It had been just a trifle too tight when she sent it to the cleaner—a pale-yellow linen A-line from the late fifties, simply and flatteringly cut, with a subtly generous flare at the hips. It was no designer model, but it had a label from Debenham and Freebody, one of the better London stores. Karen was pleased to find that the dress went on without a wrinkle. The clear, bright shade was becoming to her dark hair and her new tan. Tony wouldn't be ashamed to be seen in public with her, at any rate. Good old Tony. . . . He did deserve something better than the condescending affection that was all Cheryl had to give. Fond as she was of Cheryl, there were times when Karen could have shaken her partner, and this was one of them.

She was thoroughly out of temper with both brother and sister. Good old Tony and good old Karen could get along very well without them.

"MY God, you're ready," Tony said. "I thought I'd have to sit in the parlor for half an hour with my toes turned out, making polite conversation with Cheryl and the dog."

"Don't tell me the ladies you date these days live with parents who put you through that old routine."

"No, I was just trying to be funny." He opened the car door for her and then turned to make a rude gesture at Cheryl, who was waving at them from the doorway and beaming in a way that made Karen want to repeat Tony's gesture more emphatically.

"I'm sorry I couldn't make it earlier," he went on apologetically.

"For heaven's sake, don't be so humble. You're out there laying your life on the line for us defenseless citizens every day; the least we can do is accommodate ourselves to your schedules."

"I'm glad you feel that way about it. Not all my— I mean, not all women do."

From his expression Karen suspected he was thinking of one woman in particular. A present lover or a former lover? Cheryl? She couldn't help saying "It needn't be selfish vanity that causes that attitude, Tony. What you do is unpleasant and dangerous. I can understand how a woman might find that fear too hard to live with."

"I won't be doing it all my life. I'm not one of your dedicated TV cops; my big ambition in life is to become a small-town sheriff, where my biggest problems are Saturday-night drunks and harvesting the yearly marijuana crop out of the cornfields."

The discussion had taken a more serious turn than Karen expected or was ready for. Tony didn't seem to expect an answer. He changed the subject. They made casual conversation until he pulled into a vacant space at the curb. "This is about as close as I can get," he said lightly. "Do you mind walking a couple of blocks?"

"No, of course not. It's a lovely evening."

"Actually, I could have found a parking lot nearer the place," Tony admitted. "But this way I get a chance to show you off. That is one pretty dress."

Karen was pleasantly conscious of the way people looked at them. We're a handsome couple, she thought, amused at the cliché. At least Tony is; he's handsome enough for two.

The restaurant was small and quiet, with a country décor. The headwaiter greeted Tony by name. "I hope you're impressed," he said, after they had been seated. "This is the only place in town where they know my name."

"I doubt that."

"I meant in a social capacity."

He smiled as he spoke, but Karen was sorry she had reminded him of that other capacity. Yet the subject was bound to come up, sooner or later; she decided it would be better to face it and get it over with.

"There's something I feel I ought to tell you, Tony. I hate to talk about it, and I hate even more to spoil your evening off—"

Tony's smiled broadened, and he reached for her hand. "That's one of the things I like about you, lady. You don't back away from unpleasantness."

"Little do you know," Karen said wryly. "But I'm trying."

The warm, firm clasp of his hand on hers made it easier for her to repeat what she had learned from Julie, and to mention some of the ideas the information had suggested to her.

"Interesting," he said, when she had finished. "Like you, I feel as if I ought to have known. I guess I never gave much thought to that stupid little book."

"I gather you've read it."

"Parts of it. Mark has a copy; I think he got it from Mrs. MacDougal. The blackmail angle is certainly an idea."

"You're just being polite," Karen said, laughing. "You don't really believe it."

"It's too complicated for my simple cop's brain— more in Mark's line; he loves unlikely theories. I wonder if that's what he was referring to. . . . He left a cryptic message for me—something about old and new murders. I called him back, but there was no answer. Guess he'd already left town."

"You don't take it seriously, do you, Tony? Be honest; my ego isn't involved. I've no aspirations toward being a great detective."

Tony's fingers moved caressingly across the back of her hand, around her wrist. "Thank God for that. To be honest, then, I don't. The simplest solutions are usually the right ones. I only wish we could find solid proof that Rob was the joker in the bed sheet; it would be a load off your mind to be absolutely certain. That's the way these things usually work out, though. It's a rare day in court when we can produce conclusive evidence."

"I know. We won't talk about it anymore."

"I'll tell you everything I can. The press already has most of this information, I'm not violating official security by telling you—and what the hell, I'd probably do it anyway if I thought it would help you. I guess you're the kind

321

who'd rather know the facts, however unpleasant. Not," he added quickly, "that there's much to report. We did locate his car. It had been left in the parking lot of a hamburger joint a couple of miles from the place where he was found. His suitcase was in the truck. He had a sizable stash of odds and ends—pot, coke, pills—under the seat, but I think it was his private supply. There were fingerprints all over the interior—his, Julie's, and some we can't identify. The killer's fingerprints may be among them, but unless he has a record and his prints are on file, we'll never trace him that way. This may turn out to be one of the ones we don't solve."

After that Karen was content to let him change the subject. Delicately exploring new terrain, they discovered mutual interests—jazz, Monty Python, and the Impressionist painters. Tony laughed good-naturedly when she let her surprise show. "You think we're all uncultured slobs? I'm pretty high on the fifteenth-century Tuscan painters, too. Go on, ask me something."

By the end of the meal they were talking easily. When the coffee arrived, Tony started to tighten up, and Karen wondered if there was some other ugly development he had been afraid to mention. Instead he said suddenly, "I bought a house."

"You—you what?" His sheepish grin told her the rest. "Tony! Not—"

"Yes, the one in Leesburg. Actually, I haven't bought it yet, just signed the contract. But I think the owner will accept my offer."

Karen got her breath back. "You don't waste time, do you?"

"Not when I know what I'm doing. The reason I mention it is, I wondered if you want to rent from me."

Karen lost her breath again. While she stared

speechlessly, Tony elaborated. "I told you I was looking for an investment. I hesitated about rental property, because there are so many drawbacks when you don't have the time to supervise your tenants closely. Renters can wreck a place, move out owing you money. . . . I figure you and Cheryl aren't about to throw wild parties or skip out on the rent. From your point of view it might not be such a bad deal either. I'm not going to do you any favors—this is business, pure and simple—but if you add up what you and Cheryl would each pay for an apartment, plus the rent on a small commercial property—"

Karen held up her hands. "Stop a minute and give me time to think! You don't have to tell me about the advantages of combining living and business quarters; Cheryl has already calculated the relative costs."

"Then why not take me up on it? You liked the place, didn't you? Cheryl said you were as crazy about it as she was, only you didn't want to admit it because you knew it was out of the question."

Karen said in exasperation, "Cheryl is . . . Oh, she's right. I did like the house, it's perfect. It wouldn't even need any structural changes; I could use the parlors, add portable racks and stands, curtain off an area for a dressing room. . . ."

"Tracks for movable floodlights? They're easy to install."

"Some kind of floor covering," Karen said eagerly. "You wouldn't want people tracking mud all over those beautiful yellow pine boards. . . . Tony! Don't tempt me. I can't let you do this."

"You don't understand," Tony said, and all at once his face was remote and a little sad and very vulnerable. "It would be an escape for me. A chance to get away from all the dirt and filth and sick tragedies that are my job."

323

"I do understand. Better than you realize."

"Then why won't you let me enjoy myself?" He grinned at her, and she felt a wave of pure affection sweep over her.

"I'll think about it," she said.

"That's all I'm asking. I'll let you know as soon as it's definite. Uh—maybe you'd better not say anything to Cheryl until I'm sure."

"Okay."

But he couldn't stop talking about the house. "I think we could close in thirty days; the owner is anxious to sell and there won't be any trouble about getting a loan; my credit's good. Say another month to get things set up— you could do a lot of the preliminary work beforehand, couldn't you—permits and promotion and buying furniture, making curtains, that sort of thing. Say you have your grand opening the first of October. The kid could start school on time—maybe a few days late. That doesn't matter so much in nursery school or kindergarten, does it? Being a few days late?"

"No, I'm sure it wouldn't matter," Karen said gently.

It wasn't until the yawning waiters began stacking the chairs that Karen realized they were the only patrons left in the restaurant.

"Good heavens, it's almost midnight," she exclaimed.

"So? Do you get grounded if you're late coming home?"

"I was thinking about you. What time do you have to be at work?"

"Two A.M." He smiled at her look of consternation. "I'm on the late shift this week—or maybe it's the early shift."

"You could get a couple of hours' sleep if you went home right now."

"I don't want to sleep. It's your civic duty to keep me company until I go back to the job of protecting you defenseless citizens at the risk of life and limb."

"How can I resist an appeal like that?"

"You can't. I guess we'd better leave, though. Do you get the impression that the waiters are dropping subtle hints?"

Once outside, they debated how to spend the next two hours. Karen refused Tony's suggestion of a nightclub, sensing that he was no more attracted by the idea than she was. "Why don't we take a walk? It's such a beautiful evening."

"Every man's dream—a cheap date." Tony gave her arm a squeeze. "Let's go back to Georgetown, then. Downtown D.C. is no place for a peaceful stroll."

"From what I've heard about Georgetown, it isn't overly safe either."

"I wasn't talking safe, honey. Without wishing to brag too blatantly, I can assure you there aren't many people you'd be safer with."

"If anybody bothers us, you scream 'Hiya!' and leap?"

"Something like that. Georgetown has nicer walks than downtown."

"Fine with me. Would you mind if we swung by the house? We needn't stop, just drive past."

"Are you having a premonition of impending disaster?"

"No, of course not. But Cheryl is alone...." He helped her into the car. After he had settled himself behind the wheel she went on, "No more shop talk. I promise."

"It isn't shop talk when it concerns you and Cheryl."

325

"I guess I'm being silly."

"No. It's a normal reaction after what you've been through. And it's healthy to be afraid, so long as you don't let it get out of hand." They drove for a while in silence. Then Tony said, "Here we are. I see Mama has left the lights burning for you."

The outside lights were on, but the windows were dark. Karen let out a sound of exasperation. "I told her to leave all the lights on. I suppose she's upstairs, sewing or making more of her endless lists. The bedroom is at the back, so the lights wouldn't be visible from here."

Tony slowed the car to a crawl. "Do you want to check?"

"No, that's not necessary. Everything looks just as it should."

"Okay."

Tony finally found a legal parking place, several blocks from the house and some distance from the commercial area. Instead of getting out of the car, he turned to Karen and took her in his arms. There was no hesitation this time, and she yielded willingly. After a time his lips slid away from hers, tracing the curves of her cheek and earlobe with a skill that sent trickles of electricity along every vein.

"Do you really want to go for a walk?" he asked softly.

"No. But this isn't going to work, Tony. You know it isn't."

He was silent for a time, his warm breath stirring her hair, his mouth absently exploring the soft skin of her face and throat. "Is it that obvious?" he asked finally.

"You give yourself away with every word and every look," she told him, half laughing, and more than half regretful.

"You don't. Is it Mark?"

"What a gentleman you are, Tony." Karen freed herself and settled into the curve of his arm, her cheek resting on his shoulder. "Don't tell me you didn't notice what a fool I am."

"Men are notoriously obtuse about things like that."

"I hope Mark is."

"That's dumb," Tony said, his cheek against her hair. "How's he supposed to know unless you tell him?"

Karen could think of no sensible answer. "It doesn't work that way," she mumbled.

"He's very concerned about you—"

"Sure I know. He's so concerned that he's gone off for the weekend with one of his floozies."

Tony's breath erupted in a sputter of laughter, and his arm tightened around her. "Floozies? The only other person I've ever heard use that word was Mrs. MacDougal. It may not be what you think, Karen. Give the guy a break."

"He doesn't want a break. Tony, are you sure you didn't suspect that I—how I felt?"

"I wondered once or twice. But I hoped I was wrong."

"No, you didn't. You don't really want to settle for second best."

"You aren't second best. Karen, don't think I deliberately set out to use you—"

"To make Cheryl jealous? You wouldn't be so naïve. I think you're trying to talk yourself out of a situation you consider hopeless. Give her a little more time."

"She's had a year. I haven't pushed, Karen."

"Maybe you should have."

"Swept her off her feet? I don't buy that. Maybe it works in romantic novels, but any woman who's dumb

327

enough to fall for the caveman technique is too dumb for me. I've tried everything else, God knows."

"You could get wounded and stagger in dripping blood and faint at her feet."

She felt the muscles of his cheek contract as if he were smiling, but there was no amusement in his voice. "Thanks, but no thanks. That's another conventional fictional device, but I've got my doubts about its effectiveness. Besides, I don't want to get wounded. It hurts."

"Oh, Tony, what are we going to do?" She pressed closer to him. "She must be out of her mind. You're so nice—I like you so much...."

His arm tightened. "Me too. That's not such a bad beginning, is it?"

"No..."

"We could work at it. Give it our best shot."

"You already have. Not that I didn't enjoy every minute of it."

Again his laughter stirred the hair on her temple. "I appreciate the testimonial, and return the compliment. Friends?"

"Friends," Karen agreed, and settled more comfortably into an embrace that promised and demanded nothing more than either of them was willing to give.

"Just one thing, Karen."

"Mmm?"

"You're not doing this just because you feel it would be disloyal to Cheryl.... My God. What a conceited thing to say. I didn't mean—"

"I know what you meant. Lucky for you," Karen added, smiling to herself. "No, my friend—that wasn't the reason. I made one big mistake. Not that you aren't about a million percent better than Jack; but I learned that

328

there's no substitute for the genuine article. It's better to do without than settle for less."

They did go for a walk eventually, strolling slowly along the silent streets, arms entwined. They talked in spurts, with long periods of comfortable silence in between: about the weather, about politics—and about the house in Leesburg. When Karen finally admitted her feet were beginning to hurt, Tony said he'd walk her to the house; they were as close to it as to the car.

There was no one on the street. If she had been alone, Karen would have hurried, casting uneasy glances into the shadows. She felt more at ease than she had for days. It wasn't only Tony's size or the feel of hard muscle against her arm, or the even harder bulge of the gun under his coat; it was his air of competence and of confidence. She would feel safe with this man anywhere.

As they approached the house, whose front lights still burned, she began, "I hope you aren't—"

"Ssss." Tony pulled her to a standstill.

"What—"

"Quiet. Listen."

Karen could hear nothing except the normal night noises. After a moment Tony said in a low voice, "Walk on. Past the house."

His hand moved her forward. The sound of their footsteps echoed with abnormal loudness. Karen was afraid to speak. Not until they had gone some distance at the same leisurely pace did she venture to whisper, "What is it?"

"Probably nothing." Tony's voice was equally inaudible. "I thought I heard something—a muffled thump— from the back of the house. Probably a shutter or a door banging. Turn the corner. . . . Okay. There's no alley behind the house, is there? How do you get into the back yard?"

"A side gate." Karen explained its location.

"Right. You stay here. I'll double back and have a look."

"I'm not staying here alone!"

"Quiet. Okay, come on, but don't make a sound."

He moved with a speed that left Karen hard-pressed to obey his orders. When they reached the wooden gate opening onto the passage toward the back, his hands were quick to find the bolt that held it closed, even in the dark. Karen crouched behind him, dry-mouthed and tense.

Tony started to ease the gate open. Despite his care the rusted hinges gave a squawk of protest that shattered the silence as loudly as a scream. Tony swore. "That's done it. Stay here."

He plunged into the darkness of the passage. Karen only hesitated for a moment; there were cobwebs lacing the narrow place from side to side, they felt like ghostly fingers on her face. The gate at the far end burst open under Tony's charge; for a moment she saw him, silhouetted against the lighter shape of the opening. Then he shouted and ran forward.

Karen ran too, but by the time she reached the garden it was all over. She caught only a glimpse of something moving among the tangled limbs of the maple overhanging the wall. Inside the house Alexander was barking madly. Lights flashed on in the kitchen.

All other impressions faded into insignificance under the impact of the white form thrashing and writhing on the ground not far from the garden shed. The muffled, breathless voice that came from it was Tony's.

THERE was a nightmarish feeling of déjà vu as they ministered to another injured man. Tony's language was hot enough to blister their ears, but most of his concern was for his suit. The jacket was certainly a total loss, not only bloodstained but slashed in parallel cuts.

"You've got to go to the emergency room," Cheryl said. "I think I've got the bleeding stopped, but—"

"I should hope to God you've stopped it, you've used enough bandages to wrap a mummy," Tony snarled, contemplating his arm with disgust. "Goddamn that son of a bitch! This suit cost me—"

"Oh, who cares about your suit?" There was blood on Cheryl's nightgown too. Most of it had come from a single deep cut in the arm Tony had thrown up to protect his face; the others were superficial.

Cheryl had rushed downstairs when she heard the racket in the back yard, without stopping to put on a robe. The thin fabric of her gown clung to her body in a way that would have distracted a man much closer to death than Tony. When Cheryl repeated, "You've got to go to the hospital," he let out a roar.

"I've got to call in, that's what I've got to do, and I can tell you I'm not looking forward to hearing what the lieutenant is going to say. Falling for a stunt like that! 'Sorry, Lieutenant, I got tangled in a bed sheet!' Oh, Christ!"

"He threw it over you," Karen said. "You couldn't help it."

"He did throw it over me and I could have helped it. Mark was right, damn his eyes; not only was the sheet a perfect disguise but it was so damned weird it got me off base for a second or two, just long enough ... Cheryl, I told you to cut that out. Where's the goddamned phone?"

"If it makes you feel better to swear every other word," Cheryl began.

"It does make me feel better. Not much better, but some." Tony pushed her hand away and stood up. Then he sat down, more suddenly than he had intended, almost missing the chair. Cheryl swooped on him and steadied him. "There, you see, you shouldn't go jumping around like that. Just sit still and let me—"

Tony took a deep breath. His lips moved; Karen imagined he was counting under his breath. At "ten," some of the color came back to his face. "I am going to use the telephone," he said quietly. "I am going to use the extension in the hall, not this one, because I do not want you to hear what I am going to say. Stay here. Both of you."

This time he stayed on his feet. Swaying slightly, he walked to the door. Then he turned.

"See?" he said to Karen. "I told you it wouldn't work."

"What is he talking about?" Cheryl demanded, as the door closed behind him.

Karen looked at her. Her hair was aureoled by the light, and the rounded curves of her body pushed distractingly at her thin garment. She was pale with concern—the same concern she had demonstrated a few days earlier when it was her brother who required her care. All at once Karen wanted to stamp her foot and yell at the top of her lungs—anything to penetrate the shell of sacrificial celibacy in which Cheryl had swathed herself. It wasn't Cheryl's fault. A woman is not obliged to love a man just because he wants her to. But Tony was so worthy of love. A half-step more and Karen would have been over the brink herself.

And the reason that she couldn't take that half-step was as hopelessly sentimental and absurd as Cheryl's reasons. Pots and kettles, she thought wryly. Not to mention people who live in glass houses.

Her eyes kept returning to the objects on the table—ordinary household items, harmless in their origin and function, now ominously suggestive—a crumpled, bloodstained sheet and a knife, its blade dulled and sticky. The sheet was double-sized, a polyester-and-cotton blend; at a rough guess, several hundred thousand of its duplicates presently existed in linen closets and on store shelves throughout the area. It had been roughly tailored—the trailing corners hacked off, a narrow slit ripped away so the wearer could see where he was going. The knife was almost as undistinguished—a Solingen steel-bladed carving knife, eight inches long. There was one almost like it in the rack next to the sink.

Cheryl dismissed her own question with a grumble. "Men act so silly. Here's Tony worrying about what his boss will say to him, like some kid whose mother forgot to write him an excuse, when he ought to go to the—"

Karen's resolution about staying out of other people's business vanished in a puff of smoke. "Damn it, Cheryl, are you really that insensitive? Can't you see how he feels? He went rushing out there to rescue us poor defenseless females from a maniac, and ended with us untangling him from a sheet. He feels like a fool."

Cheryl's jaw dropped. "He did not! Look like a fool, I mean."

"You may not think so and I certainly don't think so, but I have a nasty feeling the lieutenant will think so. His friends will never let Tony hear the end of this one. His theories have been knocked into a cocked hat; he'll be hearing oblique references to bed sheets for months to come; and worst of all, he has to sit here and be interviewed by the police, like any other helpless victim of crime. For a cop, a professional, that's the crowning humiliation. Compared to all that, a knife wound doesn't even hurt!"

"I never thought—"

"Maybe it's time you did, then. He's just as vulnerable as anyone else under that tough exterior, and you're ripping him to shreds emotionally. Give the guy a break."

Someone else had said that recently, Karen remembered. Tony—to her. About Mark. "Oh, Lord," she said wearily, "what's the use? I'm a fine one to talk."

But the sight of Cheryl's stricken face and quivering lips didn't make her regret what she had said.

Tony came back into the kitchen. "Someone will be here in a minute," he said curtly. He looked at Cheryl. "Go and get some clothes on. Now."

Cheryl fled without another word.

CHAPTER TWELVE

✤✤✤✤✤✤✤✤✤✤✤✤✤✤✤✤✤✤✤✤✤✤✤✤✤✤✤✤✤✤✤

*T*HE only one who had a good night was Alexander. He managed to bite not one but both policemen. Cheryl and Karen didn't get to bed until after four. Karen expected she would lie awake, but she was so exhausted she was asleep the moment her head touched the pillow.

Cheryl claimed she had slept too, but there were purple shadows under her eyes and lines around her mouth next morning. It was almost eleven before they sat down to breakfast, a meal in name only, for neither of them ate.

"Looks like rain," Cheryl said, breaking a long silence.

Karen said, "Uh-huh."

"Am I still in the doghouse?"

"What?"

"I've been thinking about what you said last night."

"I said a lot of things last night." Karen sipped her coffee, hoping a healthy dose of caffeine would clear her head. "I suppose I should apologize, but I'm not going to. I guess I owe you one," she added, with a futile attempt at a smile. "Five minutes of criticism, at your convenience."

Cheryl did not return her smile. "I'm tempted to take you up on it. You're so smart about most things and so incredibly dumb about others."

"Let's not fight now," Karen said. "I'm too tired."

"Okay."

"Cheryl."

"What?"

"I want you to move out. Go back to Mark's."

"I figured you were going to say that. Did you figure out what I'd say back?"

"I figured, yes. And I also figured what I'd say after you said what you said."

"Don't bother. Look at it this way, Karen—would you walk out on me if the situation were the other way around?"

"I certainly would."

"You're a damned liar."

Karen's lips quivered. She wasn't sure whether she was going to laugh or cry until laughter finally won out. "You're hopeless. Maybe I can hire someone to kidnap you."

"That's the only way you'll get me out of here." Cheryl's smile was almost back to normal. "They'll catch the guy, Karen. They're bound to. Tony said someone would be watching the house every night from now on. And if I know Tony, he'll be sticking pretty close too. Not to mention my only brother. I wonder what he's going to say about the latest developments. Looks as if his far-out theory was right after all."

"What theory? He never said what it was, just sat there poking holes in Tony's theories." Karen's jaw set. "If he gloats—if he says one word that can be interpreted as rubbing it in—I'll kill him. Tony feels rotten enough without that."

"Yeah." Cheryl didn't enlarge on the subject. After another silence she said, "So what are we going to do today?"

"Go bravely forward, like good soldiers, I guess. What else is there to do? We can't huddle in the house all the time. I'll take those dresses to Shreve."

"And I'll go see Mrs. MacDougal's friend. I don't know, though, Karen. Maybe you shouldn't go."

"Are you suggesting Shreve is the sheeted specter? Shreve, of all people? Climbing fences and waving butcher knives? In her Moygashel linen and her white gloves?"

Cheryl did not share her sour amusement. "She hates you."

"She has subtler methods of cutting me down. She doesn't need knives." Karen pushed her chair back and stood up. "Besides—in case you've forgotten—Shreve has the perfect alibi for last night. Vouched for by no less a personage than Congressman Brinckley, a.k.a. your only brother."

SHREVE'S directions had been clear and explicit. That didn't prevent Karen from getting lost. Stopping at a crossroads store, she discovered she was heading in precisely the wrong direction—a classic example of a Freudian slip in motion, she surmised. She was only fifteen minutes behind time, but she found Shreve pacing up and down the drive waiting for her.

"You're late," she snapped.

"I got lost. It's a long drive."

"How true. Come in, then."

"Can someone give me a hand with these?" Karen asked, opening the back door of the car. "They have to be carried carefully."

Shreve's eyebrows soared. "I'm afraid there's not a soul around, darling. I assumed you wouldn't want a witness."

"I beg your pardon?" Karen straightened, holding one of the boxes.

"And well you should. Oh, well, I'll take the other one, if you insist. This way."

Karen followed her into a room that might have been called a library if there had been any books on the shelves. It was furnished expensively and with a striking lack of originality. Shreve tossed the box carelessly onto a long leather sofa. "Is it in this one?"

Karen hesitated, not knowing what to say. She was completely bewildered by Shreve's remarks, and a faint but growing sense of uneasiness added to her confusion.

Before she could reply, there was the sound of an automobile horn—not a simple hoot, but a strident rendering of the first bar of "Dixie." Shreve scowled. "Damn. I might have known he'd turn up, just when . . . Stay here. I'll get rid of him. Don't leave this room."

Karen sat down to wait. The time stretched on; apparently Shreve was finding it difficult to dismiss her visitor. Karen shifted impatiently.

On a low table near her chair a number of glossy magazines were arranged in order, neat as an illustration out of a copy of *House Beautiful*. Karen went through them, taking a petty and malicious enjoyment out of the disorder she created. They were of the type she had expected to find on Shreve's table—*Vogue* and *Vanity Fair*, *Washingtonian*, the *New Yorker*.

One thin magazine differed from the rest. On the cover was a black-and-white photograph of a young girl dressed in white lace and pearls standing under a blossoming tree. Above the photo was a name Karen recognized—that of a prestigious private girls' school. Idly she picked it up and flipped through the pages. It appeared to be the commencement issue of the alumnae bulletin. Photos of beaming girls hugging one another and waving their diplomas; photos of commencement speakers and prominent parents. Karen was mildly entertained to learn that people actually did give children names like Muffin, Taffy, and Lolly.

Half the book was devoted to pictures of, and news about, alumnae—understandably, since the unspoken thrust of the publication was to extract money from same. There were photos of children and grandchildren and old graduation pictures. Among the latter was one of Shreve. Smirking as usual, Karen thought, studying the picture. It showed three girls, their arms around each other, with Shreve in the middle. They were wearing identical fluffy dresses with demure puffed sleeves and ruffled necklines. Karen had heard that some of the posh schools insisted all the girls wear the same dress for graduation, thus ostentatiously avoiding ostentation.

The truth didn't hit her all at once. It started as a tiny trickle of suspicion; then it widened, breaking down the walls of disbelief like a flood of evil-smelling, rancid water. The room darkened for a moment, and she had to hold tight to the arms of the chair; it seemed to be swaying under her like a swing.

She was on her feet when Shreve returned. After one quick glance at her face, the other woman turned back to the door. There was an ominous little click, which registered vaguely in Karen's mind as something she ought to worry about, but which made only a minor impression compared to the staggering knowledge she was trying to assimilate.

"It's a little late to get cold feet now," Shreve said. "You've been enjoying your little game of cat and mouse, haven't you? I must admire the way you handled it. Not a word, even in private, that could incriminate you. Everything innocent and straightforward. But I knew you'd slip up eventually. You were so damned pleased with your cleverness you got careless. Coming here alone was a big mistake. I don't suppose you were foolish enough to bring it with you, though...."

As she spoke she opened one of the boxes and tossed the dress aside with no more than a cursory glance. Karen winced as crystal tinkled and crisp pleats flattened, but she knew the condition of the merchandise was the least of her worries.

As Shreve opened the second box and rummaged among the tissues, Karen began edging toward the door. Her purse, with the essential car keys, was over her shoulder.

She can't stop me, Karen thought. She's in good shape, but I'm taller and heavier, and I don't think I'd have any scruples about hitting below the belt....

Shreve threw the empty box aside and turned, her face livid. Karen made a dash for the door. It was locked. As she fumbled for the key she watched Shreve over her shoulder, prepared to turn and resist if the other woman came after her. Instead Shreve ran to the desk and opened a drawer.

"I told you I was tired of your little games," she said coolly. "Come back here and sit down."

She held the heavy revolver the way people did in the movies—arms straight, one hand bracing the other.

Karen put her back against the door. "You wouldn't dare. Not with your own gun, in your own house."

Shreve's laugh was all the more shocking because it was genuinely amused. "Not my gun. Though I can use it—make no mistake about that. We're all frightfully, frightfully sporting here in Middleburg. No; this gun belongs to Pat MacDougal. Half of Washington knows he kept it in the drawer of the wardrobe in his bedroom. Believe me, my dear, I've thought this out very carefully. However, I've no particular desire to shoot you or anyone else. If you behave yourself and do as you're told, you'll be all right. Sit down!"

Too stunned by this latest piece of news to resist, Karen selected a chair as far from Shreve as possible. She didn't doubt that Shreve was speaking the truth. She must have taken the gun the night she woke Cheryl searching the wardrobe. She had planned this days—weeks—ago. But how had she gotten into the house?

Then Karen remembered the extra keys, conveniently left on the hall table, and Shreve's sudden request for something to drink after she learned Karen was unwilling to give up "Gran's old things."

"That's better." Shreve came out from behind the desk and sat down on its corner, her foot swinging. She rested the gun on her knee. "All I want is the dress. Hand it over and I'll leave you alone—but strictly alone, darling. Whatever gave you the consummate gall to suppose you could blackmail me, of all people?"

"I didn't. I wasn't trying . . . Honestly, I didn't know until a few seconds ago. . . ." Her voice failed as she saw Shreve's skeptical smile.

Not that it mattered. She knew the truth now, she had admitted as much. "You can't let me go," she said stupidly.

"I can, actually—once the dress is destroyed. Your unsupported word can't hurt me. Especially after your carryings-on this past week; aren't the police getting a teeny tiny bit tired of your complaints?"

"You planned that? But you couldn't have. You were out of town last night."

Shreve's smile grew fixed. "I planned it, all right," she said sharply. "The idea was to discredit you—and it worked, didn't it? Once the dress is gone there won't be a shred of evidence."

"I can't understand why you didn't destroy it long ago." Karen felt quite calm except that her mouth was so dry that her lips felt stiff and leathery. She had to keep talking, though; the longer she could drag this out, the greater the hope that Shreve would relax her vigilance.

"I didn't because I couldn't think of a safer place for it than up in the attic among Gran's filthy rags. They should have been thrown out years ago. How could I anticipate that anyone would be imbecile enough to pay money for them—and that, of all the ironic coincidences, it would be you who bought them! One of the few people in the entire world who knew what she had and was low enough to capitalize on it."

It was a pity, Karen thought, that Shreve couldn't appreciate the crowning irony—that without her own efforts to retrieve the damning evidence, Karen would never have known it existed. She had been slow enough at that. Perhaps fatally slow.

There were still many things she didn't understand, but isolated events and statements to which she had paid no attention now made a horrible sense. The scattered clothing that had reminded Mark and Tony of a famous haunting had been, quite simply, an intruder's search for one particular garment. Every statement she had

342

made to Shreve had been misinterpreted; and as she remembered what had been said, she realized that a listener
expecting veiled threats and demands could have found
them. And Rob . . . Had he known the truth before Shreve
enlisted his aid in order to enter the shop, in a final desperate search for the dress she had failed to find at the
house? Rob had researched the case and included it in his
book. Perhaps he had suspected but had not been sure
until Shreve gave herself away, somehow, on the night of
the break-in. No wonder he had packed his bags and
planned never to return to his poorly paid job and his
cheap apartment; he had counted on extracting money
from Shreve in return for his silence. His miscalculation
had been fatal—literally. Shreve wasn't the type to submit
to blackmail.

"We'd better get moving," Shreve said briskly. She
stood up and went to a nearby cabinet, from which she
took a decanter and a single glass. A little of the liquid
slopped over as she poured, left-handed; with an exas-
perated, housewifely click of the tongue she carefully
mopped up the spill with a handful of tissues. Then she
offered Karen the glass. "Here. Drink it."

"No. No, I won't."

"You stupid little twit, this is for your own good.
Would you rather be hit over the head and stuffed in the
trunk of the car?"

Karen shook her head.

"God, you're slow," Shreve said contemptuously.
"Do I have to spell it out for you? We are going back to
your place and you are going to give me the dress. I'm
not driving all that way with you sitting beside me, looking
for a chance to jump out."

"I can't give you the dress," Karen said. "I threw
it away."

"Sure you did. Drink this. Oh—you think I'm trying to poison you, is that it? Here..." She took a sip, then held the glass out again. "Drink."

There did not seem to be much choice. I can't do anything if I'm lying unconscious in the trunk, Karen thought. But as she choked the liquor down she felt the effects almost instantly. She had eaten practically nothing all day, and the frantic pounding of her heart sent the alcohol racing through her bloodstream. When she rose to her feet, prodded by the gun, she staggered and almost fell.

Her car was still in front, where she had left it. "Keys," Shreve said curtly. After watching Karen fumble in her purse she snatched it and found the keys before she tossed the purse into the car.

Karen got in the passenger seat as directed. Her head was spinning, but she knew there would be a moment, after Shreve shut the door and went around to the driver's side, when she might have an opportunity to make a break for it. There was another set of car keys in her purse. She always carried two sets in case she locked one in the car.

It was a desperate, almost hopeless risk, but she had to take it. There was a far-out chance that Cheryl had not thrown the dress in the trash; Cheryl was always trying to salvage things. But if she had done so, the dress was gone. The weekly trash pick-up had taken place that morning.

Anyway, Karen didn't believe Shreve's assurance that she would be released unharmed. Why should a multiple killer balk at murder number four? Compared to the others, this would be easy. Suicide, while in a state of depression following the break-up of her marriage, with a gun registered to her uncle—a gun that, so far as anyone knew, had never left the house. It would be said that she had arranged the false telephone call to get Cheryl out of the house—that she had played most of the tricks on herself or invented them, further evidence of a mental and emotional breakdown. Cheryl wouldn't believe it; but everyone else would. Even Tony. He had insisted all along that there was no connection between the harmless nocturnal visits and the violent incidents. And Mark...

She didn't dare think about Mark. Shreve must have had an accomplice. She could not have done everything alone....

Karen had worked most of it out while she walked to the car and fumbled for the keys, delaying as long as she could. But she had barely settled herself on the seat, one hand already reaching for the catch that would lock the doors, when Shreve raised the gun and brought the barrel down against her temple. She felt her forehead strike the dashboard and felt nothing more.

KAREN was not completely unconscious for long, but the state that followed her dazed recovery could not really be called consciousness. It was a nightmarish succession of isolated, incoherent memories separated by periods of dizzying darkness. Once or twice she must have tried to sit up, for she felt a hand shove her back into the corner of the seat. The motion of the car was erratic, sometimes smooth, sometimes jerking forward and then stopping. *Traffic is always backed up on the bridge this time of day.* The sentence floated to the surface of her mind, and her body tried to respond to the possibilities it suggested, but then something pushed her again, so hard that her bruised temple banged against the window glass and she lost track of things again.

The worst moment was when she heard voices, or thought she heard them; she never knew whether the incident really happened. "Your friend doesn't look so good, ma'am." A deep man's voice, that one, and Shreve's, replying smoothly, "I'm afraid she has had a little too much to drink, officer. I couldn't let her drive in her condition." Then something about a hospital, and Shreve's little laugh. "She'll be fine once I get her home and in bed." The hand again, covering her mouth and holding her in place with hurting strength. "Oh, darling, don't be sick here. I'll have you home in a jiffy. Officer, if you don't mind..."

She didn't remember being sick, but there was a sour taste in her mouth when she finally woke, and her head was beating like a tom-tom. Shreve was slapping her face, rhythmically and efficiently.

"Stop it," Karen croaked, raising a feeble hand to protect herself.

"Then sit up and take notice. You'll have to walk a few feet. I'll be damned if I'm going to carry you."

She dragged Karen out of the car and draped a limp arm over her shoulders. Cool wetness stroked Karen's cheeks. "It's raining," she mumbled.

"Pouring, in fact. Filthy driving weather. I hope your little friend is enjoying herself on those back-country roads."

They negotiated the gate and started up the walk. The bricks were uneven and slippery with rain; the boxwood bushes on either side glistened as if varnished. Karen's foot slipped. Instead of trying to recover her balance she let herself fall heavily to her hands and knees. Already her hair was soaked, but the cool water on her aching head cleared some of the cobwebs away. If she could just stay

346

where she was, head bowed, for a few minutes, she might be able to think. One last chance, when Shreve opened the door, her attention concentrated on the stiff lock. . . . And there was Alexander. Darling little Alexander. How could she have resented Alexander's wonderful habit of biting everyone who came in the door? Please, Alexander, do your stuff.

Shreve didn't give her a few minutes. She yanked Karen to her feet and shoved her toward the house. "Take the key. Unlock the door."

Karen dropped the keys. The gun jabbed painfully into her side. "Pick them up. And don't try that again."

She didn't have to make the threat explicit. In the gloom and the driving rain, half-hidden by shrubs, anything she chose to do would be unobserved from the street or the neighboring windows. Another chance gone. If only Alexander . . .

But when Karen opened the door there was no sign of the dog. Or of anyone else. She fell again, her wet shoes slipping on the smooth, polished floor of the hall. Shreve pushed her inside. The door slammed; the key turned in the lock, and a switch clicked. The chandelier overhead blazed into light so brilliant it cast shadows across the floor. A squat, huddled shadow and a longer one standing over the first: the shadows of killer and victim.

"Crawl if you prefer," Shreve said. "The position suits you. Where is it, upstairs?"

"I told you—"

Shreve's foot caught her in the ribs and toppled her onto her side. The light beat down, plunging fiery fingers into her eyes. Karen covered them with her hands and heard Shreve's brittle laugh.

"I'm beginning to enjoy this," Shreve said.

All right, Karen thought. That does it.

Physically she still felt as wretched as a sick dog, but the surge of anger brought a strange unnatural strength to her limbs. It couldn't last, but while it did she had better take advantage of it.

What could she tell Shreve, where could she take her that might offer a chance of escape? Not upstairs. Not any farther from the doors, front and back. Her strength was no match for Shreve's now, she wouldn't stand a chance in a hand-to-hand struggle, even if she got an opportunity to grapple for the gun. Get out of the house—that was her only hope. Once outside, she'd be safe. It was only on television that the bad guys stood out on the street blazing away at the fleeing hero.

The kitchen was one of the few places Shreve had not searched already. The kitchen possessed that most attractive of objects, a door. But there was no hiding place there that Shreve couldn't examine in a few moments.

From between her fingers Karen saw Shreve's weight shift, saw her raise her foot. The inspiration she had been searching for finally came. "I buried it. In the garden."

The look on Shreve's face consoled her a little—but only a little—for the kick. She mumbled, "It's in a cookie tin. Wrapped in plastic, sealed with tape. . . ."

"Goddamn! Where in the garden?"

"Between the Marchioness of Lorne and Frau Karl Druschki. They are roses," Karen added.

Shreve's face twisted. Rain had reduced her sleek coiffure to a straggling ruin and washed off most of her makeup. Her linen dress was rumpled and damp, not only with rain but with perspiration. Without its mask her skin looked dry and mottled; her nose was longer than Karen had realized, and her lips were thin and colorless.

"At least the ground will be soft," she said. "Easier for you to dig. Let's go."

Karen took her time about getting to her feet. Was Shreve really going to allow her to get hold of a shovel? It would be Shreve's first mistake and with any luck it would be her last. Once outside in the rain, I'll take my chances with the gun, Karen thought. Her aim won't be too good if I'm swiping at her with a shovel.

Pretending a greater weakness than she felt, she stumbled along the hall, with Shreve close behind. The kitchen door was ajar. As Karen reached out to push it open, a light within suddenly went on.

Shielding her eyes, Karen heard Shreve's breath catch in a furious hiss. For a brief, exultant moment, hope leaped like a flame. Then she recognized the figure that stood between her and the back door; and the last missing pieces of the puzzle fell into place.

For once the tables were turned; Miriam was as composed and well-groomed as her friend was disheveled. There wasn't a spot on her dress. She must have arrived before the rain began. The only details that marred her appearance were her torn stocking and the carving knife in her hand.

"My dog," Karen cried. "What have you done to Alexander?"

Miriam's pale-blue eyes touched her indifferently and moved on. "I'm surprised at you, Shreve," she said in her gentle voice. "Were you really going to let her go outside? That was a trick, you know. She didn't bury it."

Shreve did not answer. Karen could almost feel the other woman's fear, like a heavy cloud whose edges touched her too.

"Don't stand there, come in," Miriam said. She

gestured graciously toward a chair; the knife turned the movement into a grotesque travesty of courtesy.

Shreve nudged Karen. She had to nudge again, harder, before Karen moved. She had never seen anything more terrifying than the smiling, immaculate figure of her old classmate.

Shreve cleared her throat and made an attempt to reassert her authority. "Miriam, I told you not to come in the house. You were supposed to wait for me and drive me home."

"But that would have been silly. I wanted to search the house one more time. Now I'm sure. It isn't here. She must have given it to someone to keep for her. We'll have to make her tell us where it is."

"She will, Miriam. She will. Let me—"

"She's already told you a lot of lies, Shreve. You don't know how to question people. The only way you can be sure they aren't lying is to hurt them. That's how I was sure Rob was telling the truth when he said he didn't know about my dress."

Karen took a quick, involuntary step back. Shreve didn't look at her. She said urgently, "Miriam, put the knife down, okay? You'd better leave this to me. You know you get . . . you get too excited sometimes—"

"Please don't talk to me that way, Shreve," Miriam murmured. "I don't like it when you talk to me that way. As if I were irresponsible or something."

"Give me the knife, Miriam." Shreve stepped forward.

The blade made one brilliant, flashing move. Shreve's hands went to her breast. They could not hold back the flood; it bubbled out, staining her gloves and spreading across the crumpled linen of her dress. The sound of her body striking the floor made an appalling noise; it seemed to Karen as if the entire house vibrated with it.

"She shouldn't have done that," Miriam said. "She's so damned bossy."

"We've got to call a doctor. The telephone—"

"I'm afraid not." Miriam's voice was politely regretful. "I cut the wires, you see. Why don't you just give me the dress, Karen? Then I'll go, and you can do what you want about Shreve. I don't know why you're so worried about her, she always was nasty to you."

"But, Miriam . . ." Karen's voice failed. Was Miriam really so far removed from reality that she failed to see the old dress no longer mattered? Whether that was the case or whether Miriam intended to kill her too and hope she would be blamed for Shreve's death didn't really matter. The result for her would be the same, because she couldn't give Miriam the dress. Shreve was still alive—the ghastly stain was still spreading—but she would bleed to death if she didn't get help soon.

There were three doors in the room—one into the dining room, one into the hall, and the back door, the one closest to Karen. The way to it was barred, not only by Miriam, but—Karen realized with a jarring shock—by the dead-bolt lock. She would need a key to open it, and the same thing was true of all the ground-floor windows. She'd have to break the windows to get out, not only the panes of glass, but the connecting wooden strips. It looked easy in the movies, when the hero flung himself at a window and it exploded in fragments that left only a neat little cut on his cheek, but she had a feeling it wouldn't work so well in real life.

There was only one viable means of escape, then—the front door. She was almost certain Shreve had locked it from the inside, but the key would still be in the lock. She started edging toward the dining room door.

Shreve's purse had fallen too, spilling a clutter of objects across the floor. Miriam pushed them around with her foot. "She really shouldn't have done that," Miriam repeated, in a querulous, complaining voice. "She had it coming. So did he. He did it for years, you know. It started right after Mother married him. I was thirteen. I told her, but she didn't believe me. She must have known, though. She wouldn't stop him because she cared more about what people thought than she cared about me."

"Oh, God," Karen said involuntarily. "That was why . . ."

"I thought after I got out of high school I could go away to college and get free of him," Miriam said conversationally. "But he wouldn't let me. He said it was better for me to live at home and go to Georgetown. So I had to do it. And then, when she came in and saw what happened, I had to do it to her too, or she would have told someone it was me."

The sensation that froze Karen's limbs and came dangerously close to making her forget her own peril was not fear. It was a paralyzing blend of horrified pity and of mindless terror—terror of the irrational and the unknown. Miriam was beyond reason or appeal. Part of her mind was back in the past, reliving her torment and the double murder it had caused. Even her voice changed.

"Of course after I did it I was all splashed with blood. I knew the dress was the main thing. I had to get rid of it. Then I remembered Shreve was next door, visiting her grandmother. We were all going out someplace afterward, to celebrate. To celebrate . . ." A sudden, obscene giggle blurred her voice. Then she went on, "Shreve stopped to see the old lady because she'd told her she had a graduation present for her. We thought it would be a check, but it was only some tacky little cameo pin. Shreve had a change of clothes with her because we were going to meet her folks at the restaurant and we wanted to get out of those stupid pink dresses right away. So mean of them, making everybody wear the same dress. But it turned out to be lucky for me, so I guess I shouldn't complain.

"Anyway, I went out the back into the garden and signaled Shreve—we had a special place where we could climb the fence, we used it when she was at her grandmother's and we wanted to get together without anybody knowing. We changed clothes right there, in the yard. Nobody could see us, you know how high those walls are." She giggled again. "Shreve looked so funny standing there in her underwear holding that nasty, dirty pink dress of mine at arm's length. Her grandmother was half senile even then, and she knew she could get changed and hide the dress up in the attic without anybody seeing her, and that's what she did. I just went straight to my room by the back stairs. The maid had gone to the store to get liquor. She was the one that found them. She got hysterical, so I had to call the police. I think they were suspicious, all right. There was one horrible man with a big fat stomach and eyes like marbles who kept asking me questions. He shot his mouth off to the reporters, that's where they got that Lizzie Borden stuff, but my uncle threatened to sue the papers, so that stopped that. You see, the doctor said the killer must have been covered with blood, and they couldn't find any bloodstains on my clothes, except for the ones I got when I knelt by Mother after the police arrived. I thought I had better do that to cover up any spots on my shoes or under my fingernails. The dress got most of it, though."

A faint, bubbling moan stirred the air. Miriam

353

glanced casually down at the still form at her feet. Her expression didn't alter, and Karen nerved herself for the final appeal.

"She was a loyal friend, Miriam. She helped you. She'll die if you don't get a doctor for her."

"Loyal to herself, you mean. Oh, sure, she helped me at first. I think she was so surprised and—well—excited, she just acted without thinking. But once she'd done it, she was an accessory, wasn't she? If the story ever got out, it would finish her husband's career. And Shreve wants to be First Lady someday. You know how this town is, every bit of mud sticks. I wonder what she did with..." Her foot nudged Shreve's purse.

Karen turned and ran.

The swinging door slapped shut behind her. She had never realized how long the dining room was; it seemed to take her forever to reach the farther door. It was closed. She lost several seconds there, because her hands, slippery with sweat, couldn't get a firm hold on the knob. The door opened outward. Shelter for a moment; but she dared not stop, and as she flung herself at the front door, reaching for the key, she saw out of the corner of her eye that Miriam had come out of the kitchen and was standing at the back of the hall.

The bullet smashed into the door, missing her head by only a few inches, sending splinters flying. Her body reacted before her dazed mind; falling, rolling as she fell, she cursed herself for not remembering the gun. Miriam had not forgotten about it. For a crazy woman Miriam was thinking and functioning very efficiently.

She was shooting well, too. The second bullet hit the floor on the spot Karen had just left as she scrambled, rolled, crawled through the doorway into the parlor.

Now which way? There were two doors, the one

at the front through which she had come, another at the back of the room opposite the kitchen door. It was like some horrible game, the Lady and the Tiger—pick the right exit you win, pick the wrong one you're dead. She stayed down, crouching between the two big sofas. Through the thin curtains at the back of the room she could see the gray, rainswept garden. The entrance to Paradise could not have looked more seductive. If only she could get out of the house! The walls that had once formed shelter were now those of a prison, shutting her in with her own death. Once outside, she could make a run for it, risk a bullet. She remembered Pat telling her that hand weapons weren't accurate except at close range. Inside, the range was close enough.

Two shots fired. How many did the damned gun hold? She knew absolutely nothing about guns except the one important fact: they fired hard little pellets that killed people. If only Cheryl were here...

Thank God Cheryl wasn't here. It would be over, one way or another, by the time Cheryl finished searching the back roads of the Eastern Shore and realized she had been sent on a wild-goose chase. No wonder the voice on the telephone had sounded familiar.

A board in the hall creaked. She wished she knew which one. There were several that protested when a foot pressed them. If Miriam had the sense to stay where she was, she had it made. From the hall she could cover both doors and cut off the stairs. Karen would have welcomed a chance to get upstairs now. Those windows weren't locked. It was a long way to the ground, but the boxwood under the windows of the master bedroom would break her fall.

Another creaking board. The same board, or another? Was Miriam moving or standing still, waiting, shift-

ing her weight impatiently? Think, Karen told herself. Do
something. You can't squat here forever.

But there was a false and dangerous illusion of
safety in silence, immobility. She knew how a rabbit or a
mouse must feel when it crouched motionless in the open,
hoping to escape the cruel eyes of a predator. She scanned
the room, trying to find something that would help her.
There was a poker in the set of tools by the fireplace. She
could have used something like that earlier, when the only
weapon she faced was a knife. No good now.

As her eyes continued to search the room she saw
something half hidden by the rose-pink draperies at the
front windows. It looked like a muff or a moth-eaten fur
collar torn from one of the old coats she had bought. It
didn't move.

A stab of anguish as surprising as it was intense
brought her to her feet. The heavy brass stand with its
collection of fireplace tools fell with a crash as she snatched
the poker. Had she heard a shot? She thought so; it was
hard to tell, the ringing reverberations of the tumbling
metal kept echoing, drowning out other sounds. She felt
the pull of her lips, drawn tight over clenched teeth, and
as she circled the couch on the way to the door at the back
of the room she found a fleeting irony in the thought that
it was Alexander—not Shreve, not even her own shrinking flesh—that had moved her to a fury so intense it swallowed fear. When the third—or was it the fourth—bullet
shattered a vase inches from her elbow, she kept moving,
straight through the door into the hall.

The thing that stopped her in her tracks was not
the sight of Miriam standing half in and half out of the
parlor and facing directly toward her. It was the sound of
someone at the front door.

Miriam had to raise her voice to be heard over the

fusillade of knocking. "They can't get in. They'll have to go away pretty soon. I'm getting very annoyed with you, Karen. Why don't you stop this nonsense?"

Karen pulled back into the shelter of the doorway. This latest development was almost too much for her reeling brain and her aching body to absorb. She knew who was at the door, even before she heard the peremptory voice demanding entry.

Mrs. Grossmuller. Mrs. Grossmuller come to collect the money owed her—banging on the door, yelling....

Mrs. Grossmuller would not go away pretty soon. Would Mr. DeVoto see her, and come out to ask what she wanted? It was still raining; he might not even notice she was there. And she, Karen, had told him not to call the police. She knew she ought to turn the old lady's presence to her advantage, but she couldn't think clearly.

Miriam was getting rattled. Another bullet smashed into the door; Mrs. Grossmuller's voice soared into a high-pitched shriek. Surely the bullet could not have penetrated the heavy door. She must have cried out in surprise, not in pain. Karen wondered how crazy Mrs. Grossmuller was. She'd have to be pretty far gone if she failed to realize that something peculiar was going on inside the house. Would she have sense enough to go to the police?

I can't risk it, Karen thought despairingly. It would take Mrs. Grossmuller forever to convince the police she had not been imagining things. And Mrs. Grossmuller was just as likely to go to the window and peer in, offering Miriam a clear shot.

Karen screamed at the top of her lungs. "Go away! Run! Get out of here!"

She heard Miriam's footsteps going rapidly toward the back of the hall. Dropping to all fours, Karen crawled behind the nearer sofa. There was no other sound, only

Miriam's footsteps. What had happened to Mrs. Grossmuller? Had she left? Was she standing in the rain scratching her head and wondering what the devil was going on? Was she lying bleeding on the steps?

Miriam fired again from the doorway. The bullet thudded into the sofa behind which Karen crouched. She realized she was still holding the poker. It wasn't the most effective of missiles, but it would have to serve. If she threw it spear-fashion and ran in the opposite direction. . . .

The pounding and calling broke out again, farther away now and muffled by closed doors. Another shot rang out. This time the bullet didn't come anywhere near Karen. She sank her teeth into her lower lip, fighting hysterical laughter. Good old Mrs. Grossmuller. A little thing like a bullet wouldn't stop her; she had gone around to the back door. And Miriam was losing her head, firing blindly in the direction of the knocking. Karen had lost track of how many shots she had fired. Not that it mattered. Now was the time to move, she could not delay any longer.

She rose to her knees, arm back, ready to throw. Then she heard something else that made her wonder if her brain had finally cracked. The racket from the back continued, but surely—surely that was the sound of a key in the front door. The lock stuck, as it always did.

There was only one person who had a key to the house.

Karen knew what was about to happen and she knew there was little she could do to prevent it. A scream or a cry for help would only bring Cheryl bursting in to her assistance. She pulled herself to her feet.

Miriam stood in the front doorway of the parlor. Her face was unrecognizable; every nerve twitched uncontrollably, every feature was drawn askew by distorted muscles. The gun in her hand swung in wild arcs, from the parlor to the front door to the back of the house, where Mrs. Grossmuller kept up her assault. The front door opened.

It was not Cheryl.

Mark said, "Hello—Mrs. Montgomery, isn't it? We met at a party, I believe."

Miriam shook her head. "I don't..."

"It's nice to see you again," Mark said conversationally. Rain darkened the shoulders of his raincoat and ran down his face. He didn't move.

Karen knew what he was trying to do. She knew it wasn't going to work. He had covered up his astonishment well, but whomever he had expected to find, it was not Miriam, and he could have no idea of her mental condition.

Miriam gave a small whimpering sound and steadied the gun. The trigger clicked on an empty chamber, and at the same instant Karen threw the poker. It struck Miriam across the shoulders and sent her staggering forward into Mark's raised fist.

He didn't even glance at her as she fell, but took two long steps and caught Karen in his arms.

"You hit her," Karen gasped. "You hit—"

"You're damned right I hit her. Are you hurt? Are you all right?"

There was no way she could answer, he was holding her so tightly she could hardly breathe, much less talk. But she dropped the poker and put her arms around him. That seemed to be the answer he wanted.

THE dress was never found. Cheryl had thrown it away, the trash had been picked up on schedule, and no one seemed interested in sifting through acres of garbage looking for its fragments.

"It doesn't matter," Tony said. "We have enough on her without resurrecting a decade-old crime, which could be a messy thing to prove after all this time. She'll never to go prison anyway."

"Why not?" Cheryl demanded. "Aren't two murders enough?"

"One. They think the Givens woman will make it."

It was later that evening and they were sitting in the parlor. Karen suspected the kitchen would not be her favorite room for a while; she would probably be compulsively scrubbing the floor at least once a day for days to come.

Cheryl, who had done the initial scrubbing, looked less distressed than angry. After finding that there was no such address as the one she had been given, she had driven straight back to Georgetown to find the street blocked by ambulances and police cars and a fire engine that had come by mistake. For several minutes thereafter she had required more attention from the medics than had Karen.

"Miriam'll end up in an institution," Tony went on. "Her husband can afford the best."

He appeared depressed for a man who had seen two outstanding cases closed, and who was supposed to be helping a friend celebrate her survival. In fact, it was a singularly quiet gathering for a celebration.

"She should have had help ten years ago," Karen said. "And he—her stepfather. It had been going on for five years when she . . . when she did it."

"It's a good defense," Tony began.

"Oh, no, it happened. I have no doubt it happened.

She wasn't trying to persuade me of anything, she was remembering—reliving it."

"It doesn't matter," Tony said again. "She's well around the bend how. Any halfway competent lawyer can get her off on the insanity plea. Her confession probably won't be admissible."

"She confessed?"

Tony's shoulders hunched as if he were repressing a shudder. Miriam's condition seemed to have affected him more than all the nauseating physical details he had seen over the course of his police career. "It wasn't so much a confession as a catharsis. They couldn't get her to shut up. If you could have seen her—bright and animated, per-fectly poised—asking politely for a glass of water and ex-plaining that her throat was dry from so much talking. . . . Jesus."

"It's ironic, isn't it?" Cheryl said after a moment. "All our romantic ideas about long-lost treasures, and after all it wasn't a designer gown or a missing will or Dolley's jewelry—just a cheap, bloodstained dress."

"The real irony is that Miriam and Shreve brought the disaster on themselves," Karen said. "If they had left well enough alone, we'd have thrown the dress away and no one would ever have known."

"The guilty flee where no man pursueth," Tony said sonorously.

"I've never fully appreciated how true that is," Karen agreed. "When I remember the conversations I had with the two of them, I realize that every statement was misinterpreted—on both sides. When Miriam protested the price I asked for the dresses, she was really expressing amazement that I asked so little. And when I said I hoped she would buy more things, she interpreted it as meaning that there would be more demands for money, not only from her, but from Shreve. It would have been a rather ingenious blackmail method, actually; the merchandise was there, and as I kept telling everyone, the price depended solely on what people were willing to pay."

"I still don't understand why she killed Rob," Cheryl said, gazing at Tony with limpid blue eyes.

For once her attentive look and her appeal to his superior knowledge didn't improve Tony's morale. He answered almost reluctantly. "She—uh—explained that too. The house had been searched several times, without success; she thought Karen might have taken the dress to work and concealed it somewhere on the premises. She bribed Rob to let her in. They had been intimate—that's how she put it, intimate once upon a time—and she knew he'd do anything for money.

"What really killed the poor dumb bastard was a combination of curiosity and greed. Miriam told him Karen had something that belonged to her—implied it had been stolen. That wasn't good enough for Rob; he kept asking what it was. We'll never know whether he figured it out. Miriam thought he had—but as Karen has good reason to know, guilt makes people believe a lot of things that are false. Rob may well have had an inkling of the truth. After all, he had just written up that old murder case and he knew a lot about it. He knew Miriam was the girl whose parents had been killed; he may have suspected she did it. He wouldn't have been the only one to suspect her. However much he knew, he knew too much for Miriam. She believed she was already being blackmailed and she was not about to let someone else join the club.

"After they finished at the shop, he followed her in his car to that hamburger joint. It was closed by then; he left his car, and got in hers. She wouldn't tell us how she lured him into the woods. She just giggled and looked coy. . . . God, it was awful. But he wouldn't have been afraid of her. He was proud of his body and his muscles, and she was—is—a small woman."

"Maybe she forced him to go with her," Cheryl suggested. "At gunpoint."

"She didn't have the gun—not MacDougal's, at any rate. Mrs. Givens was the one who stole it. Both of them were in the house at different times; neither really trusted the other's honesty or competence. It was Miriam the first time, when Karen was attacked; she got in through a window, as I suspected. Then Mrs. Givens came to see if she couldn't retrieve the clothes by normal means, and Karen's reaction convinced her that Karen was aware of what she had and was determined to get as much money as she could for it. She stole the new house keys and had duplicates made; Miriam returned the originals next day, so Karen never realized they had been borrowed. Miriam was responsible for all the violence. Shreve—Mrs. Givens—didn't want that kind of trouble, she only wanted to find the dress and also play on Karen's nerves. I think she was always afraid of what Miriam might do. She knew only too well what her friend was capable of."

"Then Miriam was the one who almost ran Karen down?" Cheryl asked.

Tony couldn't stand it any longer. "Don't ask me, ask him!" He turned on Mark, who had not spoken a word, and who sat slouched in his chair, his eyes fixed morosely on the tips of his shoes. "He's the mastermind! The hero! Go ahead, buddy, enlighten the ignorant. Brag a little. Don't mind me."

"What?" Mark glanced up.

"You saved the day," Tony said bitterly. "Solved the case, dashed to the rescue, arrived in the nick of time—

leaving the cops with egg all over their faces. Tell us how you did it. You're entitled to gloat."

Mark slumped lower and tried to push his chin into his chest. "Sure, rub it in. I don't blame you."

"Rub what in? You saved—"

"Saved nothing!" Mark yelled. "What saved Karen was that loony old lady! There's a gallant rescuer for you! If she hadn't gotten Miriam rattled and conned her into emptying the clip, I'd be dead. Me—not Karen. Karen was going for Miriam with a poker when I walked in the door. I was about as much use as—as that goddamn dog!"

Alexander, resting in his velvet-lined basket, lifted his head and growled. It was only a feeble echo of his old growl, for he was still full of dope and his ribs were confined by tape and plaster.

Tony stared at his sulking friend. Then his lips twitched. "Well, well. It never occurred to me ... Sorry, pal. I guess I don't mind looking like a jackass so long as I have you keeping me company."

Cheryl glanced at Karen, her eyebrows lifting. Men, she seemed to be saying. Men. I'll never understand them.

At any rate, the air was considerably clearer after that. Tony loosened his tie; Mark sat up straight and ran his hands through his hair.

"Since I'm exposing my lack of intelligence I might as well tell all," he said amiably. "I didn't even pick the right killer. I thought it was Shreve. That's why I asked her to go with the group this weekend. I had to go myself, I couldn't get out of it, so I figured at least I could keep her away from Karen."

"That was a noble, self-sacrificing gesture," said Karen.

Mark looked at her uneasily and decided not to pursue the point. "I knew a number of things you didn't know," he explained to Tony. "Mostly from Cheryl. She talks all the time, and I usually don't hear one word in five, but when she was talking about Karen I tended to pay closer attention. She told me all about old Mrs. Ferris being Shreve's grandmother, and Shreve trying to get the clothes back. It meant nothing to me at the time, but it stuck in the back of my mind while we were discussing what the burglar might have been looking for. But there were so many other possibilities—historic jewels, those expensive dresses.

"I had also read Rob's book. Your description of the way he was cut up stirred my memory again, but I didn't make the connection. The names were misleading rather than helpful; I knew Miriam only by her married name, and as I learned later, she had never assumed her stepfather's surname. So even Karen, who had known Miriam by her maiden name, wouldn't have connected her with the Ferguson case unless she had read the story."

"Which I didn't," Karen admitted. "I skimmed through most of the book, but the only stories I actually read were the nice harmless ones about Georgetown ghosts. There was no photograph of Miriam—"

"Rob wouldn't have used one," Tony said. "He was skirting the edge of libel on that story anyway, especially with the title—'Lizzie Borden or Jack the Ripper?' Lizzie being, as we all know, the proper daughter who was accused of murdering her father and stepmother. Actually, Rob got the idea from some of the reporters who followed the case at the time. The parallels were too close to miss. I missed them, though. All the times we've discussed the Borden case..."

"It's the classic of all classic crimes," Mark said thoughtfully. "Miss Elizabeth Borden was actually brought to trial for the murders of her father and stepmother. She got off; the townspeople simply couldn't believe a prim, proper lady would do such a vicious thing. But the clincher was the fact that the police never found a bloodstained dress. People are still arguing that one; a dress was burned—witnesses said there was no blood on it, but were they correct? Did she strip and commit the murders naked? Nobody knows. But the essence of that case was the bloody dress, just as it was in the Ferguson case. Miriam was suspected by the police—but there she was, in the same dress she had worn all day, and it didn't have a spot on it.

"After reading the story again and looking at the pictures I realized that Mrs. Ferris lived next door to the Ferguson house, and I began to wonder whether Shreve had had something to do with those killings. It simply never occurred to me that there was another woman involved. Again, the thing that misled me was the difference in the names.

"When I got back from Atlanta Tuesday morning—this morning, for God's sake—I can't believe it . . . I went straight to the office. I called Tony around lunchtime, but he wasn't in. I didn't reach him until early in the afternoon. I had no idea anything had happened. When he told me, I . . . Well, I won't attempt to describe my state of mind. I'd been wrong, dead wrong, that was all I could think. I started calling here. I guess I called every fifteen minutes. I had no idea where you had gone; if I had known, I'd have been even more scared than I was. Finally I couldn't stand it any longer, so I grabbed a cab and came on over. The first thing I saw was Karen's car, and then I felt better; I figured she'd just gotten home. But when I got to the door there was that—that old lady. She turned coolly to me and said, 'What an extraordinary thing! That was a bullet. Don't you think it is extremely bad manners to shoot at someone who is knocking at one's door? They needn't answer if they don't choose to see me just now.'"

His imitation of Mrs. Grossmuller made Karen laugh. "Wasn't she wonderful?"

"Wonderful," Mark agreed gloomily. "I said, 'Are you sure it was a shot you heard?' and she said, 'I assure you I could hardly be mistaken, young man; before I poisoned him in 1965 my late husband the Judge greatly enjoyed shooting things.'

"So," Mark went on, "we conferred—briefly—and she said she'd go to the back door and create a diversion. I—uh—I had keys. I'd asked the locksmith to make extras for me...."

He looked as if he expected a reprimand. Karen said tactfully, "Anyway, Mrs. Grossmuller was super. Cheryl, I wish you could have seen her face when Mark let her in and she saw poor Shreve lying on the floor, and all that blood. I thought for a minute she was going to make some remark about poison, and how much neater it was. . . . She just looked the situation over, nodded calmly, and said it looked as if we had things under control, and where was that nice little dog? She was the one who rushed Alexander to the vet. I must send her some flowers."

"I already did," Mark grunted.

"What kind? No, don't tell me—red roses?"

"What else?" Mark smiled faintly.

There was a brief silence. Then Cheryl said, "It's stopped raining. The sun is coming out."

"I'm starved," Karen said suddenly.

"What would you like?" Cheryl started up. "There's some salad—"

"I don't want anything healthy. I want ice cream. Lots of ice cream."

"Sounds good," Tony said, grinning. "What kind?"

Karen thought. "Pralines and cream. Or butter pecan."

"I'll see what's available." Tony got to his feet.

"Chocolate," Mark said absently.

"Cheryl?"

"Can I come with you?" Cheryl asked.

"Sure." Tony's grin expanded. "Let's go, babe."

As they left the room Karen called, "Pralines and cream *and* butter pecan."

"I thought you were on a diet," Mark said.

"Not anymore." Karen settled herself comfortably in her chair. "I'll never be a size 6 again, and I don't care. I like myself the way I am."

"Do you think I don't recognize a cue when I hear it?" Mark pulled her out of her chair and onto his lap. "Okay, I like you the way you are too."

After a long interval, during which she discovered what had been missing in Tony's kisses—only one thing, but it was the one that counted most—Mark said, "I guess we'd better get married. Ruth won't like my moving in unless we're properly engaged."

"Your concern for Ruth touches me, but I wouldn't want you to do anything rash."

"Look what happened the last time I forgot to ask you."

After another, longer interval, Karen murmured, "That wouldn't happen again."

"Oh? I was beginning to worry about Tony. Did he—"

"None of your business."

"Right. None of my business. Do you think he and Cheryl will make it?"

"I'm more hopeful than I was. I'm going to suggest that he refuse to rent to us unless she puts out."

"My dear girl, how vulgar," said Mark, imitating Mrs. Grossmuller. "So you're going ahead with the shop, are you?"

"Any objections?"

"God, no, I wouldn't dare object. Besides, I've always wanted a wife who has her own income."

"Mark."

"Mmmm?" said Mark, his lips against her ear.

"It was sweet of you to minimize what you did to spare Tony's feelings—"

"Sweet, hell. I was threatened with extreme bodily harm by my own sister if I didn't."

"—but I know what you did, and I think you're brave and noble and brilliant and wonderful. . . ."

This time it was the telephone that interrupted them. Karen went to answer it. Her exclamation of delight brought Mark to the door.

"Pat! Pat, darling, where are you? Still in Borneo? How is Ruth? Is Mrs. Mac all right? How are you? Oh, great. Yes, I'm fine. What have I been doing?" She glanced at Mark, and laughed softly. "Well, Pat, you aren't going to believe this. . . ."

BARBARA MICHAELS is the author of *Ammie, Come Home* and, most recently, *Be Buried in the Rain*. She was born and brought up in Illinois and received her Ph.D. in Egyptology from the University of Chicago. Ms. Michaels is a frequent book reviewer for the *Washington Post* and has served as a judge for the Edgar Awards, given by the Mystery Writers of America. She lives in Frederick, Maryland.